Sympathy Transformed and George Eliot's
Realistic Writing

同情美学与乔治·艾略特的现实主义书写

温晓梅 著

河南大学出版社
HENAN UNIVERSITY PRESS
·郑州·

图书在版编目(CIP)数据

同情美学与乔治·艾略特的现实主义书写/温晓梅著.--郑州:河南大学出版社,2023.10
ISBN 978-7-5649-5647-9

Ⅰ.①同… Ⅱ.①温… Ⅲ.①乔治·艾略特－文学研究 Ⅳ.①I561.065

中国国家版本馆 CIP 数据核字(2023)第 196460 号

同情美学与乔治·艾略特的现实主义书写
Tongqing Meixue Yu Qiaozhi·Ailüete De Xianshi Zhuyi Shuxie

责任编辑	马 博 时二凤
责任校对	王 珂
封面设计	马 龙

出版发行	河南大学出版社
	地址:郑州市郑东新区商务外环中华大厦2401号 邮编:450046
	电话:0371-86059701(营销部) 网址:hupress.henu.edu.cn
排 版	郑州市今日文教印制有限公司
印 刷	广东虎彩云印刷有限公司
版 次	2023年10月第1版
印 次	2023年10月第1次印刷
开 本	787 mm×1092 mm 1/16
印 张	18.75
字 数	363 千字
定 价	59.00 元

版权所有·侵权必究
本书如有印装质量问题,请与河南大学出版社营销部联系调换

前　言

乔治·艾略特是十九世纪英国卓越的现实主义大师，其现实主义美学宗旨之实现与激发读者的同情力密不可分。本书通过将作家对同情概念的认识放入人类思想史的发展进程中加以考察，试图阐明其通过强调同情的美学意涵与人文关怀力量以应对后者在构建认知与道德体验时所展现的相对性，同情由此成为人协调内外关系、重建内在秩序以及实现内在转化的重要心理机制。

自我与社会的关系问题是艾略特现实主义书写探讨的重要议题，体现其现实主义小说艺术的社会关注与精神表达。艺术能够激发人的审美天性，依靠同情力的延展以及想象力的创造性活动，帮助人挣脱自然法则的桎梏，并通过自我发现、自我控制以及自我认知展现精神层面的自主。由此，人不仅提升对外在世界的适应性，外在世界也将伴随个体精神层面的转变演化出更好的状态。于是，艾略特将情感作为认识对象，忠实揭示人性并展示人的心灵成长轨迹，试图借助艺术手段干预读者的感受力来探讨自我融入社会有机体的途径。在艾略特的艺术理想中，同情凭借情感的互通以及美学的想象过程，让个体处于关系的链接之下，从而超越自我的局限并通过他者视角解释自我、解读外在世界。通过强调自我的内在转化以实现对不可知他者的融入，同情在艰难的夹缝中实现了外在环境决定论与人自由意志的兼容。在信仰缺失与国家意识薄弱的维多利亚时代，同情成为难能可贵的解释自我、恢复内在秩序的手段，并借助个体自我认知的提升达成维护传统、增强共同体凝聚之目的。

基于此，本书首先将同情看作一个连续的历史现象，回顾与梳理其发展轨迹并为研究艾略特将同情与现实主义书写的联结提供理论背景。作为一个反复出现在人类思想史中的词汇，同情经由修辞学、道德哲学、经验主义美学以及浪漫主义诗学的发挥，被赋予了丰富的内容。而纵观其流变过程不难发现，同情的关键在于主体借助想象活动重建缺席者的境遇与意图，这种心理活动很大程度上取决于主体对他人心灵经验与身体感觉的感知。因此，艾略特在恪守艺术激发同情力的基础上对同情进行了修正性探索，并忠实地还原同情在运作过程中所表现出的多样性、差异性乃至对抗性等特点。

在她看来，同情是个体"参与"他人经验的必经路径，作为一种生命体验与解释情感的媒介，它让个体依凭自身身体经验的共通性与类比性，实现对他人情感的传递或思想的转化，但是却无法达成对他人经验的对等复制。正因如此，艾略特在描述同情运作时频繁使用"转化"（transform）及其变体（transformation 或 transformative），一方面表示同情的意涵在不同的语境中发生变化的历程；另一方面则展现自我以美学视角和人本关怀维度在心灵世界构建他人经验的过程，从而提升自我无法表达的、无法理解的心态。因此，相对于认知对他人，同情更易于提升自我认知。

无论是同情还是现实主义书写，都依赖于自我对他者以及外在世界的认知活动。认识的有限性既形成了现实主义书写的内在张力，也造成同情施展过程中不稳定的状态。因为同情对他者经验的转化与现实主义书写对读者心理的转化如出一辙，同情的不稳定性随即与艾略特现实主义书写中出现的非现实主义现象形成互动。于是，艾略特的现实主义小说一方面致力于展现英国外省乡村生活的田园诗意，另一方面也将哥特式恐怖、浪漫式热情以及史诗般瑰丽等元素杂糅于一处。这种艺术气质与智性思考的结合让艾略特在呈现艰难的现实之同时，也将神秘和不确定性渗透进读者的阅读体验，并引导其通过想象型认知和道德判断形成主体性以及主体意识。

在整个创作生涯中，艾略特在拥护和反思中将同情与现实主义书写进行实验性结合,这一过程表现得未必完美,但是艾略特对此过程的忠实再现,恰是其现实主义书写的开放性与包容性之所在。不仅如此,艾略特借助同情流露出对不可知他者的包容和尊重,更是其现实主义书写的伦理价值。在高度发展的现代社会,该艺术思想依然具有深刻的现实意义。

Preface

As a doyenne of realism in the Victorian age, George Eliot expects to arouse the reader's sympathy through her realistic writing. Putting Eliot's understanding of sympathy in the history of human thought, this study aims to clarify Eliot's efforts for emphasizing the aesthetic implication of sympathy and its humanistic value, so as to cope with the relativity or limit when man constructing moral and epistemological experiences via sympathy. Sympathy then becomes an important psychological mechanism for people to coordinate inward and outward relationships, reconstruct inner order and achieve internal transformation, so the willed individual's inner transformation may promote a better state of social transition.

The relationship between the self and society is an important topic explored in Eliot's novels, embodying the social concern and spiritual expression of her realist art. Along with the development of technology, the advancement of empirical science, the expansion of urbanization, and the decline of religious faith, a synergy is formed in the Victorian age and it gradually conveyed a message of determinism, which consequently and constantly compressed the space for man to fully display his individual will and subjective originality. Under this circumstance, art takes the responsibility to help man break loose from natural laws by stimulating his aesthetic nature which relies on the extension of sympathy and the creativity of imagination. Man thus achieves some spiritual autonomy through knowing himself. During this process, sympathy brings man under the link of relations by emotional intercommunications and urges man to accomplish inner transformation to achieve integration with the incomprehensible other. It struggles to achieve somewhat compatibility between external environmental determinism and human free will. Men then change from isolated individuals into relationship-beings coexisting with the others, or independent parts into interdependent parts of a larger whole. Apparently, the group living and social existence of every individual is bound to enhance the harmony of society and the cohesion of the community. When the national identity becomes weak and faith turns to be a myth, sympathy becomes a valuable means of interpreting the self and restoring the inner order.

  Based on the above consideration, the opening section of this book situates sympathy in the changing political and social contexts, delineating its evolutionary trajectory. As a key term reappearing in the history of human thought, sympathy is endowed with rich implications after being elaborated by the ancient rhetoricians, the moral philosophers, the empirical aestheticians, and the romantic poets. Sympathy thus becomes a half-divine and half-empirical potentiality relying on affective connections and the power of imagination. Throughout the long history of exploration, interests in sympathy are always bewildered by the epistemological questions whether there is a possibility to know the other or how to construct the mental activities of an absent person. Generally speaking, before Eliot, sympathy is basically regarded as an imaginative process leading to some kind of self-evident understanding or natural identification while this book argues in the first place that Eliot focuses her attention onto the way of knowing the self instead of knowing the other based on the fact that she makes a more reflective exploration of sympathy and a faithful record of the diversity, difference, and even contradiction when sympathy is operated.

Sympathy is a necessary path for the subject to participate in the other's experience. As a medium of interpreting or translating emotions, sympathy allows the subject to realize the transmission of other people's emotions or the transformation of ideas based on universality and analogy of life experience, but it is impossible for him to achieve a complete reciprocal copy of the other's mind. It is for this reason that this book perceives the fact that Eliot frequently uses "transform" and its variants "transformation" or "transformative" to describe the process of reconstructing the others' experiences in one's own mind, and the course of self-transformation to generate follow-up thoughts. As the finding of this research, such transformation is precisely an exaltation of those states of mind that cannot be articulated or even comprehended. This psychological process is to transform the primitive sensory experience into sympathy, the aesthetic pleasure of sympathy into self-knowledge, and self-knowledge into the dynamic reciprocity of social meliorism. This inner transformation is Eliot's unique contribution to explain the evolutionary causality from an aesthetical perspective, yet it demonstrates the infinite potentiality of human care to construct cognitive and moral experiences via sympathy. As a result, if realism is to be achieved, this psychological transforming process must be faithfully revealed.

In short, whether it is sympathy or realist writing, it depends on some cognition of the other and the outside world. The limit of knowing not only forms the internal tension of realist writing but also causes instability for extending sympathy among human beings, so George Eliot has to adopt more openness and tolerance to invite the elements of Gothic horror, romantic enthusiasm, and epic magnificence into her work. The sense of romance, mystery, and uncertainty will guide readers to form subjectivity through imaginative cognition and moral judgment, so as to demonstrate the infinite potential of art for the growth of the human mind. Naturally, as an inseparable part of Eliot's realism, these "non-realistic" phenomena also express clear and real appeals, implying the possibility of reality or the possible state of the ideal.

During this process, when the epistemological function of sympathy is limited and the moral mission is relative, the aesthetic identification will be introduced in for supplementation. This combination may exhibit itself imperfectly, but Eliot's faithful record of the difficulty of this process is precisely the unique charm of her realist writings. Moreover, sympathy makes it possible for Eliot to tolerate and respect the unknowable other, which is the very humanistic value of her realism. In light of this, once the concept of sympathy is deconstructed, Eliot's realistic writing will inevitably collapse. The belief that sympathy, as a social dynamic mechanism, introduces the society into a fluid mode through exchanging ideas and emotions will also become a mockery. Therefore, in today's highly developed modern society, it is still of historic and realistic significance to study George Eliot's effort of integrating the relationship of the humanistic foundation without sacrificing the aesthetic values of art by extending sympathies.

List of Abbreviations

AB *Adam Bede*

DD *Daniel Deronda*

MM *Middlemarch*

MF *The Mill on the Floss*

TLV *The Lifted Veil*

Such *The Impression of Theophrastus Such*

Letters *The George Eliot Letters*, 9 vols

Essays *Essays of George Eliot*

Selected Essays *George Eliot: Selected Essays, Poems, and Other Writings*

Essays Complete *The Essays of "George Eliot" Complete*

It was felt that English sympathy as a Rule was bound up with English Art…

(*The Art-Journal*, 1861.)

The text, whether of prophet or of poet, expands for whatever we can put into it, and even his bad grammar is sublime.

(George Eliot, *Middlemarch*, Book I: Chapter V, 1871-1872.)

No chemical process shows a more wonderful activity than the transforming influence of the thoughts we imagine to be going on in another.

(George Eliot, *Denial Derronda*, Book 5: Chapter 35, 1876.)

Table of Contents

Introduction ·· (1)

Chapter 1 Sympathy as a Continuous Historical Concept ········ (44)

    1.1 Sympathy as the Embryo "Pity" in Aristotelian Tragedy ·· (52)

    1.2 Sympathy as the "Secret Operation of Feeling" in the Age of Sensibility ································· (54)

    1.3 Sympathy as the "Sympathetic Imagination" in the Romantic Aesthetics ································ (68)

    1.4 Sympathy as the "Extension of Sympathies" in the Victorian Novel Theory ····························· (74)

Chapter 2 The Realism-cum-sympathy Aesthetics in *Adam Bede* (86)

    2.1 The Realism-cum-sympathy Aesthetic and an Enlarged Moral Awareness ·································· (88)

    2.2 *Adam Bede* and Adam's Inarticulate Suffering ············ (97)

    2.3 Sympathy Transformed and the Growth of Higher Feelings ································· (102)

    2.4 Realism and the Humbly Faithful Dutch Painting ······ (114)

Chapter 3 Sympathy and the Epistemological Relativism in *The Lifted Veil* ……… (125)

   3.1 *The Lifted Veil* and Latimer's Nightmare ……… (126)

   3.2 The Other People's Mind and the Epistemological Relativity ……… (132)

   3.3 Sympathy Transformed and the Growth of Mind ……… (147)

   3.4 Realism and the Cultural Schizophrenia ……… (153)

Chapter 4 Sympathy and the Sublime Enquiry in *The Mill on the Floss* and *Middlemarch* ……… (162)

   4.1 Maggie Tulliver's Anger and Dorothea Brooke's Terror ……… (166)

   4.2 The Divisive Social Body and the Sublime Enquiry ……… (174)

   4.3 Sympathy Transformed and the Emergence of the Sovereign Self ……… (183)

   4.4 Realism and the Panoramic View of the Organic Whole ……… (195)

Chapter 5 Sympathy and the Political Vision in *Daniel Deronda* ……… (204)

   5.1 *Daniel Deronda* and Daniel's "Sabine Warrior" ……… (208)

   5.2 Community Lost and Individual Socialized ……… (216)

   5.3 Sympathy Transformed and Restoration of the Communal Consensus ……… (227)

   5.4 Realism and the Myth-making ……… (240)

Conclusion ……… (251)

Bibliography ……… (260)

Introduction

1. Research Background

British scholar Stjepan Mestrovic in *Postemotional Society* (1996) addresses that modern people are gradually materialized and deprived of autonomy by the joint-force of mass culture, information technology and commodity economy. Under such social circumstances, men's emotional structure is accordingly changed into the "postemotional" one which is stimulated, replicated and mass-produced to meet the need for public entertainment. Emotions of this kind are artificial, rootless feelings and could be replaced or traded, orienting to emotions rather than thoughts thus cutting off the link between emotion and action, which consequently weakens man's ethical demand for truth, goodness and beauty, yet replacing it with a pale, mechanical "ethic of niceness" emphasizing the everyday-life joy and comfort. Men, therefore, start to pursue the corporal experience of pleasure and vision-based epistemological acquisition instead of the traditional aesthetic approaches empathizing feeling training and regulating emotions. However, the disappointing fact is that many literary classics could have been the ideal way for nurturing genuine feelings are reduced to the objects of consuming mechanism and the current artistic commitments, by contrast, devote to creating works based on elusive physical sense, which brings readers a spiritual illusion after a bodily carnival. All these factors intensify the tendency of moral panic and ethics anomie in the present social transition stage. Feeble emotions, the collapse of ethics and the aesthetic decline seem to entangle with each other, and the decadence of one party makes worse of another. Under such social context, a reflection on the functions of the classic literature for remodeling the natural, noble, genuine and irreplaceable feelings is of great significance. However, reading reality today is not optimistic.

American scholar Harold Bloom in the prelude to *The Western Canon* (Chinese version) declares that people now are stepping into the worst stage in man's reading history and have to witness the obvious decay of literate (2). He labels the present as a "Chaotic Age" and expected to wake up public awareness toward reading literature canons. In his book of *How to Read and Why*, Harold Bloom also stresses the reason for his emphasis of reading.

> The pleasures of reading indeed are selfish rather than social. You cannot directly improve anyone else's life by reading better or more deeply. I remain skeptical of the traditional social hope that care for others may be stimulated by the growth of individual imagination, and I am wary of any arguments whatsoever that connect the pleasures of solitary reading to the public good. (22)

To Harold Bloom, reading is urgent, but the realization of any social aim in reading is questionable; for reading only satisfies the private and solitude hours. His assertion makes sense in some aspects, yet also urges one dispute more obvious to be explored. Is reading only serves private and individual aim? Or can it accomplish some other higher goals? Surely the other side of literary criticism casts different shades of light. Louis Althusser, for instance, saw literature as an "Ideological State Apparatus" that "endlessly transforms (concrete) individuals into subjects and endows them with a quasi-real hallucinatory individuality" (Althusser 93), ① to regulate the state power through implementing man's ideological shaping. Such opinions could find support in many classical western critical theories: the ancient Roman critic and a leading lyric poet — Horace (December 8, 65 BC-November 27, 8 BC) in *Art of Poetry* has concluded the aim of the poet is "to instruct" and "to delight" (100). ② With these two values, Horace integrates the educational and aesthetic functions of artistic works in the wider social domain—for what the poet writes will give pleasure and moral education inspiring the reader's real life. Pseudo-Longinus's *On the Sublime* in the 1st century AD aims to advocate a rhetorical sublimity which stems out of the noble soul of orators or the poets and lifts the reader's imagination to the infinity or the ethic order, so they may transcend the limit of boundary and stress the aesthetical pleasure of literature. As heritage to such tradition, critics never stop to trace clues for realizing the social aim of literature, and being a substantial part of it, literary imagination constructed during the reading process is believed to meet this end and is thus always emphasized. For modern critics like Martha Nussbaum, see the literary imagination released in reading as "an essential ingredient of an ethical stance that asks us to concern ourselves with the good of other people whose lives are distant from our own" (*Poetic Justice: The Literary Imagination and Public Life* xvi), thus propel readers to pursue "from a stifling confinement into a

---

① "Ideological State Apparatus" is a term employed by French Marxist philosopher Louis Althusser, since ideology reflects the imaginative relationship between human beings and their own living conditions. Literature, as a product of the imagination, intervenes into the process with no doubt.

② In Greek, "Horace" is put as Quintus Horatius Flaccus.

space of human possibility" ("Exactly and Responsibly: A Defense of Ethical Criticism" 362). She viewed it as "an essential part of both the theory and the practice of citizenship" (*Poetic Justice: The Literary Imagination and Public Life* 52). What worth noting is that Martha Nussbaum's formulation relies strongly on her belief that the release of sympathy generated by literary imagination may work as a powerful catalyst in forming a political community. Such an advocate reminds us of the old topic which could date back to the Aristotelian ethical ideal: "Every skill and every inquiry, and similarly every action and rational choice, is thought to aim at some good." (Aristotle, *The Nicomachean Ethics* 3) So if we investigate the literature work in a public sphere instead of a private or the solitude one, all arduous work may agitate the social goodness which is exactly what literature brings to us. Literature, from the moment it was born, has an enchanting power over its readers, and that's why Plato drove poets out of his Republic, fearing the poetry may disintegrate the willpower and courage of the warrior in the polis. When critics fully realize this point and start to treat fairly the power of literature, it blossoms in different models and yielded high. Taking the 19th century for instance, England particularly, the cultural elites anchor their hope on literature, expecting it to integrate feelings, reconstruct aesthetical awareness and ethical order by nourishing the capability of sympathy in novel writing, so as to strengthen the social bond and promote the social community.

Among all these Victorian writers, George Eliot is no doubt the most outstanding one who stresses the realism-cum-sympathy aesthetics, hoping to accomplish the social and ethical functions of literature through promoting awareness of sympathy in realistic narrative.① Her manifesto as a fictional artist is to cultivate sympathy so as to arouse sentiments and train feelings and then make them the weapon to counter the savage trend of individualism, guiding the individual to find an appropriate balance between self-knowledge and self-restraint following an aesthetical quest. She strongly believes the novel is tool for an education of man's potential of sympathy—the ability to feel with and feel for other people or the ability to sensitize us to the emotions of others. It transcends the limits of our own experiences or perspectives and retains the totality of individuality by relating the individual to a larger whole. Such an endeavor is really inspiring for solving the present postemotion-related problems. Therefore a systematic investigation of Eliot's artistic advocates will illustrate how the literary text performs an ethical, aesthetic and even civic virtue in the public sphere by adjusting or regulating the individual's mental world in private.

2. George Eliot and Her "Sympathy"

George Eliot (1819-1880) is not an unfamiliar name to anyone who has interests in Victorian literature and culture. She established her fame for her irreplaceable contribution to the English fictions and the moral visions in them. As a learned intellectual, a diligent novel writer, and a literary critic with keen observation, George Eliot apparently stood out among many Victorian novelists. Her unique position as both literary theorist and contributor to new science of mind revealed a more complex

---

① George Eliot showed her literary ambition in her essay for the *Westminster Review*, "The Natural History of German Life" (1856). She famously insists on the significance of cultivating the sympathies in novel writing and bringing readers to a better understanding of their fellow-beings.

psychologized literary aesthetics; her tremendous effort of having deep philosophical reflection merged into novel writing won her respect and redeem from many modern critics; her writings delineated an imagined community from provincial England to the European Casino; her writing techniques presented both "pictures of a monotonous homely existence" and the quiet inner psychological world as well; and her thoughtful thinking toward humanity and fate of the whole mankind makes her stand out among her contemporaries. Literary masters like Henry James, Marcel Proust, Edith Wharton and Virginia Woolf all show their admiration to George Eliot for being influenced by her writing in one way or another (Plotz 76-90). Eliot's contemporary, Vida D. Scudder notices that:

> Never, surely, were books more wistful than those great novels, *Romola*, *Middlemarch*, *Daniel Deronda*. Their animus is wholly new: it is neither scorn nor laughter; it is sympathy. This **sympathy**,① more than any other quality, gives to the work of George Eliot a depth of thoughtfulness unsounded by the shallow criticism on life of her predecessors. (Scudder 185)

Charles Dickens also couldn't repress his feelings after reading *Adam Bede*:

> The whole country life that the story is set in, is so real, and so droll and genuine, and yet so selected and polished by art, that I cannot praise it enough to you. And that part of the book which follows Hetty's trial (and which I have observed to be not as widely understood as the rest), affected me far more than any other, and exalted my **sympathy** with the writer to its utmost height. ② (*Letters* Vol. 3 114-115)

---

① The bold is intentional.
② The bold is intentional.

The "sympathy" impressing Vida D. Scudder and generated in Dickens is an outstanding characteristic of Eliot's novels. F. R. Leavis in *The Great Tradition* (1948) praised Eliot to the pantheon of "the few really great" novelists, who "not only change the possibilities of the art" but are "significant in terms of the human awareness they promote; awareness of the possibilities of life" (Leavis 2). In George Eliot, Leavis saw the novelistic form as a matter of "responsibility toward a great human interest ... a responsibility involving, of its very nature, imaginative sympathy" (Leavis 29). The imaginative sympathy becomes the core intention of Eliot's artistic creation bring her reputation and the wide acceptance of her work as well. In order to explain George Eliot's stress on the notion of sympathy, a brief introduction of her biographical experience is necessary.

George Eliot is actually the pseudonym of Mary Ann or Marian Evans—the daughter of an estate manager at South Farm near Nuneaton, Warwickshire. Before starting her writing career, she has acquired five European languages and contributed to Victorian intellectual and cultural life as a translator, reviewer and editor. She translated David Friedrich Strauss's *The Life of Jesus* (1846), Ludwig Feuerbach's *The Essence of Christianity* (2008) and the *Ethics* by Spinoza (unfinished), and all these works exert a deep influence on her personal life and her literary creation. "From Feuerbach in particular, she [derives] an emphasis on forms of feeling and sympathy that had the potential for sociability" (Voskuil 239). She believes man's innate nature of feeling, and with "sensations man has in isolation; feelings only in community" (Feuerbach 283). Then writing with sympathy to promote a loving community becomes Eliot's artistic pursuit, for she believes sympathy is an essential access to feeling and feeling is comprehensible only by sympathy. Besides these facts, Eliot perhaps is especially distinctive among the novelists of her time for being a subeditor of *Westminster Review* —a Victorian journal known for its progressive articles and wide-ranging book reviews, which provided her chances to collide with the most brilliant and liberal spirits of her age. Her rich experience and extensive intercourse with the thoughts of her age qualify her with keen insight to view social and intellectual problems. Through constant combinations with all great writers and critics in the Victorian age, Eliot's mind is marked by "independence, a synthetic tendency, and broad sympathy" (Fleishman ix). She then devotes her understanding of life and art into making new forms of novels. Throughout her writing life, Eliot altogether produces seven sagas: *Adam Bede* (1859), *The Mill on the Floss* (1860) and *Silas Marner* (1861) are the first three which describe the daily life in rural England. *Romola* (1863) is a historical novel presenting the religious strife of Renaissance Italy, which is "considered by many of her contemporaries as her greatest work, [and] is undoubtedly the least read now" (Dolin 221). *Felix Holt the Radical* (1866) focuses on the British domestic political reform. While *Middlemarch* (1871-1872) adopts a kaleidoscopic view presenting the outlook of the Victorian society. It is marked as "the greatest Victorian novel" by George Levine (Levine 2) and becomes the best-selling of all Eliot's work. *Daniel Deronda* (1876) is the last novel situating in modern Britain yet projects the plots onto Jewish Zionism. Besides these, she also tries a variety of writing styles including some shorter texts like *Scenes of Clerical Life* (1856-1858), *The Lifted Veil* (1859) and "Brother Jacob" (1864); poem collections of *The Spanish Gypsy* (1868) and *The Legend of Jubal and Other Poems* (1874) are her brilliant contribution to the Victorian poetry; *The Impressions of Theophrastus Such* (1879) is not "a story" and fills itself with enormous cultural contemplation. These works cover a wide range of topics and involve philosophic, theological and scientific backgrounds, which formulates a coherent set of ideas about art and articulates the seldom voice of "high culture", promising to feed any appetite for anyone who likes the Victorian flavor.

In a society of progress with rapid changes, Eliot becomes more convinced that feeling is a comparatively more stable nature of man to serve as a binding agent to unite people. Influenced by romanticism, she agrees that art is born from the burst of human feeling, such affective nature reminds her that highly cultivated work of art will offer the directions to people who are sunk into the troubles of this kind or that, because "art is the nearest thing to life" (*Essays* 144). However, feelings are born of an introverted and selfish drive inside man, any practice purely stressing feeling of "pain and happiness" like what Benthamite does will lead to the expansion of self-interest. Under this condition, the most effective moral action is not to eliminate man's feelings, but to make them sublimated, or to sublimate "the egotistic impulses" (Newton 39). For Caroline Levine, selfishness needs to be "directed, not excluded, if realism is to be achieved" (4). Fully responding to the sublime aesthetic phenomenon, through the operation of sympathy, Eliot realizes man's freedom and evolutionary capacity will transcend the boundary of self and intuitively imagine another's state of mind, and such process will help men make a moral judgment and eventually make art accomplish its moral end. Moreover, Charles Darwin's *Descent of Man* (1871) and Thomas Henry Huxley's *Evolution and Ethics* (1893) all capture the fact that the innate sympathy secure man's survival in the long evolutionary process and it serves as the key to strengthen society and reinforce moral behavior for the realizations of the social self by suppressing one's own natural cravings to some degree. Man through an evolved psychological faculty could adapt to the natural environment and evolve into a moral development, which highlights George Eliot and her contemporaries.

"Sympathy" becomes a word reoccurring in Eliot's novels, essays and letters; someway, it implies all her artistic idealism and also becomes a key to solve Eliot's labyrinthine artistic advocates. Through operating sympathy, Eliot tends to integrate the relations of feeling, aesthetics and moral construction, so as to realize the pragmatic functions of novel writing. Her endeavor is different from those in the age of Enlightenment splitting the relation between emotion and reason, or those of aestheticism which separates the connection between art and morality.

Once a piece of artistic work, no matter whether it is a novel, a piece of poetry or work of a similar kind, is presented to readers and audiences, whether it can stimulate the aesthetic activities and moral judgments will determine the accomplishment of its social functions. The earliest efforts can be traced back to Aristotle's discussion on relations between "pity", "fear" and Catharsis (Katharsis) in tragedy. As a synonym of "pity", sympathy is a heating concept discussed in the aesthetical and moral philosophical domain. In addition, it also concerns with the literary criticism and overlaps with today's hermeneutics, psychoanalysis approaches. Terms like "empathy" or "inner imitation" are also closely associated with the concept of sympathy, or becoming its "variant". Thereby, systematic studies on Eliot's sympathy will be inspiring not only in comprehending Eliot's art of the novel, but be quite instructive in investigating the above-mentioned notions or methods as well. In short, by attending to how Eliot shapes her work through extending sympathy, we gain refreshed ideas of Eliot's realistic novels and obtain new insight into the affective conditions that sympathy may involve in the whole Victorian age at the same time.

3. Literature Review and Argument

As one of the most significant writers of prose fiction in the

Victorian age and one of the leading writers of the nineteenth-century realism, George Eliot has occupied large parts of critique and never escaped from the scope of academic vision, thus the achievement of the related researches has sprung up from day to day. No matter it is the biographic study, gender, Marxist, ethical or post-colonial criticism, it will find the soil in Eliot's artistic realm to sow its seeds and harvest the bunch of fruits. Generally speaking, the basic type of academic studies on George Eliot belongs to biographical researches. For instance, Gordon S. Haight collects Eliot's letters in seven volumes (1954-1955), then Haight represents the subsequent book of *George Eliot: A Biography* (1968), combining her letters with her fictional writing; Rosemarie Bodenheimer's *The Real Life of Mary Ann Evans: George Eliot, Her Letters and Fiction* (1996), reveals the relationship between Eliot's life and her writing; Eliot's remarks and life episodes are documented in *A Monument to the Memory of George Eliot: Edith J. Simcox's Autobiography of a Shirtmaker* (1998) by Constance M. Fulmer and Margaret E. Barfield; the similar supplementing works as *The Journals of George Eliot* (1998) is edited by Margaret Harris and Judith Johnstone; and *George Eliot: A Critic's Biography* (2006) from Barbara Hardy lists general history of criticism on Eliot's works. Besides the biographical research, the similar panoramic studies about George Eliot's life experience and her main artistic advocates can be found in some author companions like the *Oxford Reader's Companion to George Eliot* (2000) by John Rignall and the *Cambridge Companion to George Eliot* (2001) by George Levine. These are important resources offering "original essays by various critics on broad topics such as Eliot and religion, philosophy, science, politics, publishing and gender" (Nancy 110). The book of *A Companion to George Eliot* (2013) edited by Amanda Anderson and Harry E. Shaw tries "not only to bring together exciting new work on Eliot by important scholars working in the field, but also to give as full a sense as we can of the ways in which Eliot's work speaks to contemporary intellectual questions" (1-2). These studies altogether present the primary sources for researches on George Eliot and they are essential for the explanation of this book.

George Eliot is a marvelous woman writer in the Victorian Age, and naturally, feminist scholars will interpret Eliot's works through the perspective of feminism. Elaine Showalter in "The Greening of Sister George" (1980) addresses that "Eliot's unquestioned ascendancy as a fictional realist and moralist defines the boundaries of aspiration for the women forced into secondary status in relation to her" (Showalter 293). Sandra M. Gilbert and Susan Gubar in *The Madwoman in the Attic: The Women Writer and the Nineteenth-Century Literary Imagination* (1979) prove that George Eliot expresses a kind of anxiety for being a female writer (489), and these two works are the typical ones among the many. In her essay "Silly Novels by Lady Novelists", Eliot's way of treating woman authors always troubles the feminist critics who "may be inclined to read it as symptomatic of what has often been claimed is her reluctance to identify with feminist social and political aims" (22), and for most of the time, Eliot's attitude toward woman issues is believed to be conservative.

Another basic type of study concerns the novelist's artistic thoughts and their relations with Victorian social, political or natural science. There are countless studies in this category. Taking Gillian Beer's *Darwin's Plots: Evolutionary Narrative in Darwin, George Eliot and Nineteenth-Century Fiction* (2000) for example, this work serves as a distinctive intersexual analysis of Darwinian language in Eliot's novels; in addition, critics recent devote an interest in Eliot's discussion of cultural issues like class, race, or national identity, especially in her last novel *Daniel Deronda* and the essay collection—*Impressions of Theophrastus Such*.

Post-colonial critics find Eliot in *Daniel Deronda* and *Impressions of Theophrastus Such* shows sympathy for the imperialism. The post-colonialists like Said say that "for Disraeli's *Tancred* and Eliot's *Daniel Deronda*, the East is partly a habitat for native peoples (or immigrant European populations), but also partly incorporated under the sway of empire" (Said, *Culture and Imperialism* 63). Because Eliot has abundant knowledge in philosophy, artistic criticism, religion and even modern science in the Victorian age, her art could be seen as a kaleidoscope involving her understanding of these topics and its collision with that of other intellectuals. Since the related research on these topics are too many to list, the literate review below aims to narrow down its scope to the academic studies focusing on Eliot's interest in the notion of sympathy and its relations with her realist art.

In order to make the whole review concise and straightforward, this project basically classifies all sympathy-related academic contributions into the following categories: the first and foremost one includes the efforts of defining Eliot's sympathy and exploring its origins. The second group briefly covers the interdisciplinary analysis: the ethical perspective stresses sympathy with moral significance from altruism; the epistemological domain often reveals links between sympathy and knowledge; Formalist analysis focuses on the impact of the structure and format for readers to sprout a sense of sympathy, and text interpretation from the standpoint of cultural studies is also remarkable. The third category cannot be fixed by definite classification. Researches of this kind investigate Eliotean sympathy from a conceptual point of view or in a particular piece of work. Based on such classification, this project gives a general diachronic literature review of the available resources.

3.1 Interpretations of the Concept and Origins of Eliot's Notion of Sympathy

This kind of researches focuses on defining Eliot's concept of sympathy and tracing its origin in religion, in moral philosophy or in empirical science. Among all these achievements, Mary Ellen Doyle in *The Sympathetic Response*: *George Eliot's Fictional Rhetoric* (1981) has done some pioneering work to examine Eliot's understanding of sympathy. she points out that the Eliotean sympathy implies three qualities: "simple pity, a sense of mental or moral compatibility, and that deep intellectual and imaginative union which makes the reader thoroughly comprehend what it would be like to be a given character" (20). Thus, she focuses on the word "rhetoric" of Eliot's works and discusses how the author manipulates her language and forms, talking to her readers "to imagine and to feel the pains and the joys" of her characters. Elizabeth Deeds Ermarth's "George Eliot's Conception of Sympathy" (1985) offers a comparatively comprehensive analysis. With some psychological knowledge, she admits that sympathy to Eliot is the heart of the moral life and Eliot's sympathy "depends upon a division in the psyche, a split in consciousness that permits two conflicting views to exist simultaneously" (23). It is a hard psychic negotiation between the self and the other and the success of sympathy is to discover the difference. Her remark is unquestionably brilliant, yet she neglects another fact that Eliot also stresses on the spontaneous flow of feeling, neither does she attach much importance to the aesthetic implication of George Eliot's notion of sympathy. As what has been showed in *The Lifted Veil*, division in the psyche will bring about a split self, therefore ways for integrating the double consciousness are the very topic Eliot tries to explore. As a result, the imaginative nature of sympathy is stressed for it is the imaginative capacity that will harmonize the relationship between the self and the other. There have been lots of critical interests stressing on the imaginative sympathy recently; Forest Pyle, in his article "A Novel Sympathy: The Imagination of Community in George Eliot" (1993), defines sympathy as "the imaginative impulse that, transcending the egotism and renouncing the desires of self, promises to bridge the epistemological and ethical gap between self and world" (Pyle 6). Such an imaginative process also entails the projection of the self onto others for imagination is "a mental power making present what is absent through the production of images" (Pillow 349). Forest Pyle then concludes there must be an impossibility of Eliot's realism. In contrast, George Levine notices that "it is the imagination that compels us to sympathy and knowledge", then he affirms "for Eliot the imagination is both intrinsically selfish and essential to the aims of realism", because "it is neither good nor bad but simply inevitable that the imagination will project the desires and expectations of the self on the world" (Levine, Surprising Realism 66). Moira Gatens in "The Art and Philosophy of George Eliot" (2009) maintains an opinion that the sympathetic imagination grounds our disposition to feel sympathy for our fellow human beings. It is this disposition and potential for the refinement of our moral knowledge that Eliot sought to realize in her novels.

Moreover, a great deal of social psychologists and philosophers of virtue ethics believe novel reading serves as a stimulus to role-taking imagination and emotional responsiveness, thus to construct a sense of morality and epistemological experiences. Rae Greiner in his "Sympathy time: Adam Smith, George Eliot, and the Realist Novel" (2009) suggests that sympathy involves the positing of another person within a narrative: "sympathizing with the other isn't a matter of seeing and knowing", much less being in contact with other bodies, but "situating the other in an imaginative narrative temporality" (296). Rather than a "spontaneous eruption of emotion", then, successfully sympathizing requires seeing behavior "in the light in which the impartial spectator would view it" (297). Rae Greiner in *Sympathetic Realism in Nineteenth-Century British Fiction* (2012) also adds an inspiring understanding of sympathy by distinguishing sympathy as a form rather than a feeling, a theory of the transmission of feeling rather than a feeling itself. Greiner focuses less on the particular emotions we feel but the formal properties of how feelings transmit in the first place, which is particularly impressive. Howard Sklar in *The Art of Sympathy in Fiction: Forms of Ethical and Emotional Persuasion* (2013) sees sympathy as an important aspect of our emotional response to the fictional characters. And surely any definition needs to trace the root to justify its conclusion.

In this perspective, Comte, Feuerbach, Spinoza, Hume, Smith, and Schiller are the main figures discussed as intellectual resources inspiring Eliot's understanding of sympathy. David Hesse's book-length study *George Eliot and Auguste Comte: the Influence of Comtean Philosophy on the Novels of George Eliot* (1996) and Lesa Scholl's "George Eliot, Harriet Martineau and the Popularisation of Comte's *Positive Philosophy*" (2012) believe that Eliot's admiration of sympathy and altruism could be traced back to August Comte's idea of "religion of humanity", a secular religious system based on humanist principles; Miriam Henson's "George Eliot's *Middlemarch* as a Translation of Spinoza's *Ethics*" (2009), Moira Gatens in "Compelling Fictions: Spinoza and George Eliot on Imagination and Belief" (2012) and "'A Constant Unfolding of Far-Resonate Action': George Eliot's *Middlemarch*, Spinoza, and the Ethics of Power" by Zachary J. Hardy (2015) relate Eliot's notion of sympathy to Spinoza's ethics thoughts; Lynn Voskuil in "George Eliot among Her Contemporaries: A Life Apart" (2013) and Hazel Mackenzie in "A

Dialogue of Forms: The Display of Thinking in George Eliot's 'Poetry and Prose, From the Notebook of an Eccentric' and Impressions of Theophrastus Such" (2014) associate Eliot's advocates of Sympathy with Feuerbach's religious belief that man's sympathy and love is the manifestation of God's will and the expression of humanistic concern. For many scholars, *The Essence of Christianity* by Feuerbach provides what Elizabeth Deeds Ermarth calls "the psychic conditions for sympathy" (24). To Ermarth, as well as Suzy Anger and Moira Gatens, Eliot's notion of fellow feeling or sympathy responds greatly to Feuerbach's concern that sympathy requires an individual to recognize the difference between, in Feuerbach's terms, "I" and "thou" (Feuerbach, 128).① Ermarth proceeds to claim that "Feuerbach cherishes the 'qualitative, critical difference between men'" as a foundation for forging connections, and Eliot also theorizes how "any constructive action must be preceded by the recognition of difference". (25) This investigation is truly inspiring. Ellen Argyros in her "*Without Any Check of Proud Reserve*": *Sympathy and Its Limits in George Eliot's Novels* (1999) include Rousseau's influence on Eliot's forming her idea of sympathy. Deborah Guth with *George Eliot and Schiller: Intertextuality and Cross-cultural Discourse* (2016) treats Schiller's aesthetics of sympathy as the main source for Eliot to investigate sympathy in the aesthetic domain. Referring to Hume and Smith's influence on Eliot, Sally Shuttleworth in *George Eliot and Nineteenth-Century Science: The Make-Believe of a Beginning* (1984) carries out an in-depth discussion. Hence it can be seen that researchers have related Eliot's advocate of sympathy with many main figures who ever contribute to the enrichment of the implications of sympathy,

---

① See Ermarth, 25-26; Suzy Anger, *Victorian Interpretation* (Ithaca: Cornell Univ. Press, 2005), 116; and Moira Gatens, "The Art and Philosophy of George Eliot," *Philosophy and Literature* 33.1 (2009): 78.

although redeeming these works as the primary sources, this project offers a general evolutionary routine of the implications of sympathy, instead of associating Eliot's sympathetic writing with a particular source. Based on a retrospective survey, this subject locates the target issue of impossibility or possibility of knowing the other through sympathy that have confused many thinkers and therefore argues Eliot's initiation of stressing the possibility of figuring out the mental chaos of the self by transmitting, transfiguring other's emotional situations although those situations are kept unknowable or at least not fully knowable to us.

3.2　The Interdisciplinary Studies of the Eliotean Sympathy

Since the notion of sympathy embodies rich implications in social, philosophical, aesthetical domain and in the literary theories, the interdisciplinary interpretation of sympathy is also flourishing in studying Eliot's art. Namely, the moral, epistemological, cultural, and aesthetical sides of sympathy are covered as follows. Traditionally, critics treat Eliot's emphasis on sympathy as a way to shape man's moral outlook. These ethical studies tend to value sympathy as an effective way to destroy selfishness and builds altruistic or benevolent actions. Studies of this part recently explain the moral implications of sympathy by associating it with ethnic terms like "alterity" or "otherness". Barbara Hardy's *The Novels of George Eliot* (1959) views George Eliot as a moralist, and she especially emphasizes the themes of egoism and sympathy. She sees, above all, "the tragic education of the egoist" in growth towards redemptive sympathy (236). She keeps in view the line of interpretation that makes George Eliot a great creator of women characters. Hardy also emphasizes another line of criticism that leads to later developments, an appreciation of the narrative voice in the novels, the speaking style of the moral and philosophical commentator. In *George Eliot and Nineteenth-Century Science*

(1984), Sally Shuttleworth concerns herself with organic theory carried out from biology to social analysis. Shuttleworth raises the questions of whether Eliot conceives of organic social evolution as progress, and whether she sometimes expresses ambivalence towards the ethics of self-subordination, submitting the ego to the demands of the social organism by means of sympathy and duty. Like Shuttleworth, Suzanne Graver shows interests in the organic theory yet shifts attention more fully from its scientific application to its application to social theory. Forest Pyle in "A Novel Sympathy: The Imagination of Community in George Eliot" (1993) discusses the narrative conversion or "transferral" of the (mystifying) imagination, and Eliot's "aesthetic teaching" would eventually make "community" into existence. We never see in Eliot a fully coherent community governed by the principle of sympathy, by "wide fellow-feeling". Such remarks deserve further explanation. Michael Carlon (2010) in "'Famished Tigress': Sympathy and the Other in George Eliot's Fiction" suggests that sympathy subsume empathy as well as clairvoyance proceeds through several actions, such as presently fulfilling the other's needs and anticipating future ones; she fashions sympathy as a prerequisite for self-actualization. As one part of the ethical dimensions of research, some scholars relate the concept of sympathy with religious morality. Elisabeth Jay in *The Religion of the Heart: Anglican Evangelicalism and the Nineteenth-Century Novel* (1979), points out that George Eliot is "the one major novelist to portray Evangelicalism with detailed fidelity and imaginative sympathy" (209). Peter Hodgson in *The Mystery Beneath the Real: Theology in the Fiction of George Eliot* (2000) states that Eliot propagates a religion of humanity based on service and sympathy because service for her is included under sympathy, and it is not a unique or disconnected concept (8). For this reason, generic terms like "empathy" and "fellow-feeling" should not be seen as isolated terms in

Eliot's artistic ideal because they need other terms together to constitute the meaning of sympathy.

Although critics cherish an ideal to relate George Eliot's adoption with ethical concern, the other side of the criticism voices questions of whether the ethical function of sympathy could be accomplished. Elizabeth Deeds Ermath notes that Eliot's "particular view of sympathy… has little to do with selfless benevolence" (25); and Rosemarie Bodenheimer, Brigid Lowe, and Forest Pyle also treat the sympathetic process too complicated to handle.① T. H. Irwin in "Sympathy and the Basis of Morality" (2013) asks "whether sympathy, as opposed to general principles, is indeed the basis for morality in Eliot". He then distinguishes sympathy into three types, namely cognitive, affective, and practical. He points out that the most important type in Eliot is practical, insofar as it involves moral evaluation of particular situations. By Irwin's account, Eliot herself demonstrates that sympathy may not be enough; we may need general principles and the form of moral judgment associated with them. The fact is, the actual practice of sympathy, through sympathetic imagination, is an acquisition of the other's mind or feelings, it's such a complicated process even for Eliot herself. It welcomes principle while resisting it; it appeals for altruistic yet involves a self-projection; it seems more like self-control with self-actualization by negotiation. So, to Caroline Levine, "selfishness needs to be directed, not excluded, if realism is to be achieved". In "Surprising Realism" (2013) she agrees that we project our imaginings and desires onto the world. However, this projection can take radically different forms and

---

① See "George Eliot's Conception of Sympathy" by Elizabeth Deeds Ermath, *The Real Life of Mary Ann Evans*: *George Eliot, Her letters and Fiction* by Rosemarie Bodenheimer, "Eliot: Sympathy, or the Imagination of Community" in *The Ideology of Imagination*: *Subject and Society in the Discourse of Romanticism* by Forest Pyle, and *Victorian Fiction and the Insights of Sympathy* by Brigid Lowe.

sometimes can provide the force by imagining the situation of others. George Eliot always tries to move the minds of characters and readers beyond the limits of the self. Which relies much on the fact to what extent we know the other people? And the negotiation between the self and the other is decided by handling these issues in a balanced way. Otherwise, any altruistic action could be seen as self-sacrifice. So while some critics advocate Eliot's commitment to sympathy as a way to get over selfishness and to bind the individual to others; there are some who noted the complex side of realizing the moral end; John Kucich's *Repression in Victorian Fiction* (1987) describes how "the libidinal dynamics of Eliot's characters actually point to an asocial model of desire, grounded in repression, that subverts the most general of her fraternal prescriptions" (116). And Jeff Nunokawa's "Eros and Isolation: The Antisocial George Eliot" (2002) observes reading ability functions as an escape from other people. Despite the "gospel of unity to which the likes of Dickens and Eliot devote all the fluency at their command" (843), Nunokawa notes the novels also demonstrate a desire for "the withdrawal that protects us from the invasive gaze of others"—a withdrawal they identify with the pleasures of the experience of reading (842). In short, it seems to be much more cautious to attribute sympathy to the realization of a moral end.

Sympathy involves interactive migration through emotional transcendence; it involves knowing what others have known and feeling what others is feeling. So researchers naturally associate sympathy with the epistemological foundations. Martha Nussbaum in *Poetic Justice* (1997) claims that reading novels enables us to use our faculties of sympathy, and spectators being sympathetic will be better citizens with social justice. For it will involve understanding imaginatively and deeply what is going on both for perpetrators and for victims. Nussbaum carries out a valuable inquiry of sympathy-related research, but the obtainment of justice still remains a doubt because not all the novels dealing with victims of calamities. So a better way for us to appreciate the potential of sympathy still worth being discussed. George Levine in *The Cambridge Companion to George Eliot* (2001) relates sympathy with knowing, and asserts people's sympathy will be attracted by constructing suspense. Rae Greiner's "Sympathy Time: Adam Smith, George Eliot, and the Realist Novel" (2009) points out that Eliot's emphasis on sympathy distinguishes her aesthetics from the earlier modes: "it situates its discourse of representation not only by reference to feeling, as the aesthetic tradition more generally does, but also, in distinction from the aesthetic tradition, by reference to *a feeling for social others*" (294). For feeling for others will go through a complicated transforming process of inner struggles and justifications. Eliot elaborates such a process in a documental way. In quite a number of innovative studies, Rae Greiner's research is really distinctive in exploring the relations between sympathy and knowledge. With the help of Adam Smith's concept of "momentary", Rae notes that the occurrence of sympathy is neither eternal nor immediate. George Eliot's *The Lifted Veil* proves that Rae Greiner's views are quite persuasive. So it is obvious that there are a lot of issues to be resolved between sympathy and understanding. To George Eliot, although harboring a positive ideal, the limit of knowing the other people's mind confuses and entangles her throughout her whole writing career, which influences her very much and perhaps it is the very reason causing the making of *The Lifted Veil* in which the hero acquired a clairvoyance into other's mind yet suffered from a miserably moral life. Sympathy thus is nevertheless not an equivalent of absolute knowing but an imaginative stupidity. It strongly calls for an aesthetic force.

Extending Sympathy is an important theme in realism tradition, and then the discussion of ways to excite sympathy also shares popularity, which prompts many researchers' interests to investigate at the formalist or rhetorical level. Darrel Mansell in "George Eliot's Conception of 'Form'" (1965) writes an article systematically introducing George Eliot's conception of form. In his article, Darrel Mansell addresses that Eliot's novel "embraces a broad diversity of characters and events" to present a kind of "panoramic view" (651). On the basis of research of Eliot's essay—"Notes on Form of Art", the author asserts that George Eliot's "form" is a combination of the "outward appearance" and "inward relations", and the more relations there are, the higher form it is (653). Darrel also observes that Eliot compares the higher form to the "higher organism" which the author doesn't offer an elaborate exploration. In this sense, Suzanne Graver and her book of *George Eliot and Community: A Study in Social Theory and Fictional Form* (1984) can be a splendid work in discussing Eliot's concept of form by including the idea of community at the heart of studying George Eliot and finds that Eliot's protagonist often struggles to find or to survive the painful absence of a spiritual community. Her study then shows that George Eliot's unhappy acknowledgment of many reasons why people in the industrial age can't find a mutually supportive or identity-nurturing community. Graver proceeds to discuss the attractiveness to Eliot that the society is analogous to an organism, with different parts interdependent and functioning together for the sustenance of the whole, and Eliot then invents novel to both reflect and foster the organic unity of society through sympathetic aesthetics.

There also emerged more and more scholars attempting to demonstrate the ways in which sympathy can be produced by fictions, among which, George Eliot is included. For example, Wayne C. Booth makes an important departure and presented a "variety of techniques by which sympathy for characters may be cultivated" in *The Rhetoric of Fiction* (1983); Monika Fludernik in "Eliot and Narrative" (2013) proposes that Eliot's realism strongly rests upon the power of involving the readers. Eliot creates narrators who invite readers to share their perceptions and values, their mixture of judgment and sympathy. Such a narrative style will help readers improve their knowledge by evaluating the fictional world and the characters within it.

The combination of sympathy with cultural studies is an important attempt. In *Scenes of Sympathy*, Audrey Jaffe explores the dynamics of sympathetic identification in fiction by Victorian British writers. The official nineteenth-century ideology of sympathy was celebrated as a solution to the problems of class division, may have promoted it as a Utopian expansion of the narrow bounds of the liberal self. Rae Greiner's *Sympathetic Realism in Nineteenth-Century British Fiction* also focuses on form, which distinguishes Greiner's studies from other recent works on fellow-feeling in the nineteenth-century novel, including Suzanne Keen's study of *Empathy and the Novel*, which considers the responses provoked in readers by fiction; or Rachel Ablow's and Audrey Jaffe's analyses of affective extension in plot and theme; Greiner is interested less in how the reader responds to a novel's effects than in the means through which the novel elicits or thwarts a response in which it depicts the reach and limitations of its characters' sympathetic imaginations. Rachel Ablow in *The Marriage of Minds: Reading Sympathy in the Victorian Marriage Plot* (2007) sets out to give extra historical depth by relating sympathy to the marriage law, in particular, the doctrine of coverture, under which "the wife's legal identity was effectively absorbed into her husband's" (10). From the above discussion, we can conclude that these interdisciplinary interpretations are really highlighting and provide thorough understandings of Eliot's advocates of sympathy. But as a response to the turn in contemporary literary criticism, studies from a philosophical perspective seem to be more important than various methods or writing techniques. So Kyriaki Hadjiafxendi in "'George Eliot', the Literary Market-Place and Sympathy" (2007) challenges to associate Eliot's authorial formation as a promoter of sympathy and it is an "extension of solidarity played a formative role in her literary authorship". Kyriaki Hadjiafxendi associates Eliot's adoption of sympathy as a principle of aesthetic judgment with her perception of her authorial role as "women of true culture" (34). It is insightful to treat sympathy as a key to reveal the typical Victorian cultural issues like publishing, marital status or class conflicts. Since culture is an all-embracing term, culture-related topics including political justice, religion, education, etc., will also be discussed by other scholars. These researches are too many to be enumerated, so this project just lists a very small part of it, so as to save room for deeper exploration of the sympathy-related alchemic achievement.

The last but not the least is the aesthetical concerns in Eliot's sympathy-related researches. Actually, sympathy as an aesthetic construction in Eliot's novels has long been recognized. For example, Forest Pyle in his "A Novel Sympathy: The Imagination of Community in George Eliot" (1993) and Hina Nazar in "Philosophy in the Bedroom: Middlemarch and the Scandal of Sympathy" (2002) both point out that Eliot's emphasis on sympathy distinguishes itself from the aesthetic in earlier modes: "it situates its discourse of representation not only by reference to feeling, as the aesthetic tradition more generally does, but also, in distinction from the aesthetic tradition, by reference to a feeling for social others." (294) Marc Redfield, in "George Eliot's Telepathy Machine", says that the general association between sympathy and the aesthetic indicates a limitation of sympathy: "sympathy is always already an aesthetic experience, one that can only take place within the realm of fiction, mimesis, representation, and reproduction." (136) Some other scholars discuss sympathy from pure aesthetic perspective and therefore attach much attention on visual presentation or symbols in Eliot's work, such as Audrey Jaffe's *Scenes of Sympathy* (2002) or Thomas Albrecht's "Sympathy and Telepathy: The Problem of ethics in George Eliot's the Lifted Veil" (2006). A. H. Miller in his book *The Burdens of Perfection: On Ethics and Reading in Nineteenth-Century British Literature* (2006) and Rae Greiner's "Sympathy Time: Adam Smith, George Eliot, and the Realist Novel" (2009) both address sympathy as an aesthetical force for it involves man's imagination and feelings. Nowadays, there have been growing interests toward the significance of effect in the aesthetic discourse, which has harvested a large number of achievements in exploring Eliot's experiment and engagement with feelings in art. Without focusing on Eliot's representation of affective experience, scholars like Michael Bell and Forest Pyle have attempted to analyze Eliot's dealing with emotion by revealing its philosophical bearings. On the basis of the above achievements, this project typically involves the aesthetical notion of the sublimity into investigation. The realistic writing and the sympathetic imagination all confront with the conundrum that we can't absolutely know the other; this is a typical situation of the sublime aesthetics, under such situation, this project finds that Eliot investigates sympathy with the notion of the sublime, and sympathy with its innate imaginative drives, serves as a breakthrough for people to counter the mystery or the invariable force to accomplish a sense of self-transcendence or self-discovery. Such an internalization process involves an aesthetical judgment that is capable of uniting the self with the incomprehensible into a whole.

3.3 Other Researches

Since the notion of "sympathy" ever functions as a key term and activates the philosophical discussion, aesthetic exfoliation, and literary creation in the eighteenth century, critics' examination of sympathy is naturally focusing on the eighteenth century. ① Scholars like Brigid Lowe points out: "Sympathy, although it has been widely considered in relation to eighteenth-century fiction, has received very little attention in work on nineteenth-century texts." (Lowe 9) More and more scholars realize the potential of sympathy in the nineteenth literature has equal weight; they have studied sympathy as a commonness of the whole Victorian novels. Among their discussions, George Eliot's novel is included. Brigid Lowe in *Victorian Fiction and the Insights of Sympathy: An Alternative to the Hermeneutics of Suspicion* observes a politically subversive power of the Victorian novel in the teeth of a critical consensus—marked by "creeping solipsism and self-righteousness" (4). Brigid Lowe contends that contemporary theory falls prey to exactly the mechanistic and competitive ideology of liberal self-ownership that the "best Victorian novels" are determined to resist. What the novels have, and what the critic lacks, is sympathy. Rachel Ablow's *The Marriage of Minds: Reading Sympathy in the Victorian Marriage Plot* is an excellent discussion of the complications of sympathy in *The Mill on the Floss*. Ablow points out: sympathy "makes selfishness impossible", but it runs the risk of "making [the] other into merely an extension of the self". (71) As a result, George Eliot

---

① The achievement of investigation of sympathy is often associated with the eighteenth century, see Marshall, David. *The Surprising Effects of Sympathy: Marivaux, Diderot, Rousseau, and Mary Shelley*. Chicago: University of Chicago Press, 1988; Frazer, Michael L. *The Enlightenment of Sympathy: Justice and the Moral Sentiments in the Eighteenth Century and Today*. Oxford University Press, 2010; Lamb, Jonathan. *The Evolution of Sympathy in the Long Eighteenth Century*. Routledge, 2015.

strives in her presentation of sympathy to "eradicate selfishness while preserving self-consciousness" (71, 94). This seems to be a challenging task with no satisfying solutions.

It is well known that the process of sympathy is transcendental or metaphysical; some scholars endeavor to incarnate the sympathetic process with the operation of energy, finance economy or sonic vibration etc. Beryl Gray's *George Eliot and Music* (1989) and Delia Da Sousa Correain's *George Eliot, Music and Victorian Culture* (2003) both mention that Eliot adopts metaphors of musical vibration to describe the human sympathy that binds man to man. Hina Nazar in "Philosophy in the Bedroom: Middlemarch and the Scandal of Sympathy" (2002) offers a fine account of the drawing-room and the bedroom in Middlemarch as the "social space" in which Eliot can fully imagine the sympathy for "concrete others", realizing her reading of Feuerbach's philosophy of "essential humanity". Anna Kornbluhin with her article—"The Economic Problem of Sympathy: Parabasis, Interest, and Realist Form in Middlemarch" (2010) finds Eliot wants sympathy to be economically operative if articulating sympathy with the economic in addition to the aesthetic, Eliot therefore engages in a rapidly changing complex of values in which "economy" is more and more figuratively inflected. Thus sympathetic effect can be economically efficacious and it impugns sympathy as the paramount bourgeois bargain—feeling ethically aggrandized by the aesthetic sensation of common humanity, and therefore politically absolved of the responsibility to restructure the economic inequality that debilitates experiential commonality. Kirstie Blair in his "Contagious Sympathies: George Eliot and Rudolf Virchow" (2005) advocates that contagion acts as a form of sympathy, and people may infect each other in social interaction. Tapan Kumar Mukherjee's "Sympathetic Vibrations: Fictional Treatment of a Scientific Concept in the Novels of George Eliot

Compared and Contrasted with Analogous Treatment by Contemporary Victorian Novelist Charles Dickens" (2015) invites the scientific concepts of sympathetic vibrations, which "is a harmonic acoustically induced resonant phenomenon wherein a passive string or vibratory body responds to external vibrations", Eliot uses a harmonic likeness while making an artistic use of them. All these efforts function as an incarnating process of the operation of sympathy. They are of great help to check the sympathizing process more vividly and more straightforwardly. However, all these metaphors like energy, finance economy, sonic vibration or disease contagion bring much aesthetics implication than clarifying the mystery of imaginative sympathies.

Although critics listed above have illustrated how important the notion and operation of sympathy is to George Eliot, some other scholars also cast doubts into Eliot's approval of sympathy in artistic creation.

> In the past several decades in particular, many critics have sought to show how Eliot's most valued moral practice, sympathetic response to others, is complicated by factors such as egotism, power, or the difficulties attending communication. Much of this work is fundamentally skeptical of Eliotic sympathy and aims to show that despite Eliot's best intentions her novels, in part because of the reach of their psychological and sociological realism, cannot avoid registering skepticism too. (Anderson and Shaw 10)

The following part of this review is to scan some hostile attitudes or doubts toward sympathy for fairness.

One of the most influential remarks comes from Raymond Williams, and he argues that industrial novels have a contrary effect on their readers. "Sympathy was transformed, not into action, but into withdrawal" (*Culture and Society* 119). Suzanne Keen also observes sympathy often fails to bring about ideological thrust.

Victorian critics and readers were the first to question the accuracy of social fiction, recognizing its ideological thrust, and, as often as not, registering distance from the characters and situations not through an excess of sympathetic identification, but through an understandable distaste for social fiction's characteristic lecturing and sermonizing. (*Victorian Renovation of the Novel* 114)

For this reason, some recent critical accounts note that there is a limit to realize the ethical aim of sympathy. Lisbeth During's "The Concept of Dread: Sympathy and Ethics in *Daniel Deronda*" finds in the novel a genealogy of morals that begins in dread, and which is explicitly opposed to an ethics of sympathy. Ellen Argyros's "*Without Any Check of Proud Reserve*": *Sympathy and Its Limits in George Eliot's Novels* (1999) is very typical to call Eliot's doctrine of sympathy into question. Different from other appraisal and embracing voices, she investigates the limits of the sympathetic imagination in Eliot's novel. Ellen "hazards the possibility that some differences may be insuperable or may be transcended only at the sacrifice of legitimate desires and claims" (Bailin 325). The main limit for Allen is whether the sympathetic imagination can complete the idea of knowing others' inner feelings, because sometimes people can't even understand those of their own. Secondly, Ellen finds Eliot and the narrator spare different sympathy toward the different characters. For example, Maggie Tulliver in *Mill on the Floss* deserves more sympathy than Tom; Hetty in *Adam Bede* (1859) is depicted as miserable as somewhat she deserves it, yet Grandcourt in *Daniel Deronda* seems to stay away from the sympathetic imagination of readers. For the first case, we can say that Ellen blurs the boundary of the real and the fictional, for all artists present the universal scenery or the common physical experience but not the particular. A. S. Byatt ever addresses smartly that "reading lets us into someone else's privacy while we retain our own. It is in this sense that I can say that I know George Eliot better than I know my husband. I have shared her inner life" (qtd. in Irwin xxxiii). Sympathy only realizes the sublimation, replacement or migration of emotions, and let emotions lead to judgment and understanding when full knowledge of others is impossible. In other words, Eliot aims to manage the unspeakable suffering, the incomprehensible other and the infinite world with sympathy, and which is also the main issue argued in this book.

For the second limit listed by Allen Argyros, which means that some characters in the novel can't share the reader's sympathy to the same degree, that is because these characters themselves lake of rich feelings and sympathy to arouse the readers'. Moreover, sympathy is by no means of a "universal benevolence". Ellen also pointed out "the impossibility of transcending the boundary of self and entering into the consciousness of pain of another" (4). However, Argyros's patient explication of the "limit" in Eliot's conception of sympathy and its real practice yields "the occasional insight, neither adds much new material nor draws sufficiently on previous studies" (Bailin 325). For the larger web of "intersecting and conflicting discourses" on the limits of sympathy is the topic Eliot fully examined and problematized, and it cannot be a target for being attacked. In addition, some studies declare that *The Lifted Veil* and *Daniel Deronda* announced the realization of sympathy in the social or moral sphere may end up with illusion. Neil Hertz's *George Eliot's Pulse* (2003) and Leona Toker's *Towards the Ethics of Form in Fiction: Narratives of Cultural Remission* (2010) try to prove that *Deronda* stages a crisis of the sympathetic faculty. These inquiries prove that there still remains some dispute in understanding Eliot's advocate of sympathy extension in art. And that's why the importance of sympathy to George Eliot is revisited and reinvestigated in this project.

George Eliot's preference of art to generate sympathy is also questioned by J. H. Miller in his *Reading for Our Time*, "critics have made much of the high value Eliot gives to 'sympathy', etymologically 'feeling with', as the basis of morality" (53), and he also asserts that "[Eliot] did not, the evidence of her novels suggests, have much confidence that people (as opposed to telepathic narrators) have spontaneous insight into what another person is thinking or feeling" (10). Of course, "it is not new to see George Eliot's work as engaged in examining sympathy and its limits, or to see Eliot's conception of sympathy as complex" (Sperlinger 254). That's why proper ways should be found to understand the application of sympathy rightly, but not always accuse sympathy of its limit, or thereby attack the efficacy of Eliot's realistic writing. It is basically on this consideration that leads to the writing of this book.

Moreover, critics such as Rosemarie Bodenheimer, Brigid Lowe, and Forest Pyle (among others) have illustrated the contexts in which Eliot's application of sympathy may be understood recently. Lowe notes that the "starting point for sympathy is similarity"; the Oxford English Dictionary suggests that it involves seeking commonality or "fellow feeling" with the other (and particularly relates to suffering). Lowe also calls for a reading of nineteenth-century fiction a more complete sense of sympathy. Rosemarie Bodenheimer particularly points out: "Once she had deconstructed sympathy, the fictional form she had shaped was as obsolete for her as it would be for the young writers of the next generation." (*Real Life* 265) This means if the doctrine of sympathy is deconstructed, on which the kingdom of realism George Eliot builds will also collapse. In addition, Henry Nancy voices out a similar worry:

> The realism that was praised in the mid nineteenth century for extending sympathy to common, unheroic people was often

criticized at the end of the twentieth century for its essentially middle-class perspective. Such responses suggest that how we read George Eliot's writing has everything to do with our own historical context, but to appreciate her works properly, we need to know something about their contexts. (*The Cambridge Introduction to George Eliot* Viii)

So a release of internal tension of Eliot's advocates on sympathy requires restitution of larger cultural forces. In this book, an investigation of the rise of Victorian novel theory is particularly included, which aims to justify Eliot's advocate for extending sympathy as a common phenomenon in its specific historical setting, so this project locates the notion of sympathy in the wide theoretical background of the Victorian novels and its association with the prosperity of realist writing, so as to offer justifications for Eliot's high involvement into sympathy in her art. As has been mentioned in the beginning of this section, the present researches mainly concentrate on sympathy in the eighteenth century philosophy and literature, and the representative works include Michael L. Frazer's *The Enlightenment of Sympathy: Justice and the Moral Sentiments in the Eighteenth Century and Today* (2010) and *The Evolution of Sympathy in the Long Eighteenth Century* (2015) by Jonathan Lamb. As to sympathy in the nineteenth century, it witnesses a transitional point as Gillian Beer in *Darwin's Plots: Evolutionary Narrative in Darwin, George Eliot and Nineteenth-Century Fiction* has pointed out:

> By the 1850s the concept of sympathy, or of accord between inner and outer world, is formulated as the "pathetic fallacy" by Ruskin. This famous phrase is often stripped of the force with which it describes as a "fallacy" the attempt to centre the natural world upon man's sensibility. (45)

Despite this fact, Eliot still harbors faith toward the virtue of sympathy by refreshing the understanding of it in art, so as to enlarge man's sympathy to counter against the natural world, expecting it in turn to restore the inner order. Such an effort is really challenging and it is more worthy of respect.

Taking all these factors into consideration, this project intends to supplement the discussion of sympathy in the nineteenth century into an academic investigation of sympathy as a whole and continues historical concept, and launches a defense for Eliot's efforts to pursue the possibility to activate the potentiality of sympathy in realistic art. Eliot should not be attacked because of the "limit" of sympathy; instead, her glorification of the concept of sympathy and the reflection on the existing problems in its real practice carries the exploration of sympathy much further than other artists in her time. She is exactly aware of the relativity and limitation in sympathy-based epistemology and morality and tries to emphasize the aesthetic implication of sympathy and its humanistic value to cope with the emerging problems. Sympathy then becomes an important psychological mechanism for people to coordinate the inward and outward relationships, reconstruct inner order by stressing the internal transformation or conversation within, so the willed individual may promote a better state of social transition. Taking this point into the discussion, systematic studies on Eliotean sympathy in this book will not only enrich our comprehension of sympathy but also deepen our understanding of Eliot as a marvelous realistic novelist.

3.4 Related Studies in China

As a response to the continuous interest in Eliot from foreign academic studies, domestic researches have also yielded fruitful achievements. In brief, domestic researchers are inclined to interpret

Eliot's work from a wide range of critical approaches in literature: feminist, psychoanalysis, colonial criticism, poststructuralist and cultural studies are the usual methods with which a particular text analysis by Eliot will be interpreted. Moreover, the sudden emergence of interdisciplinary researches propel exploration of the relationship between Eliot's novel and science, painting, music, medicine, economics, and the research interests in other disciplines is also on its way. But compared with the foreign critics' attention paid on the Eliotean sympathy and its importance to Eliot's whole artistic ideal, the related domestic concern seems comparatively insufficient. Even so, there are some scholars who have accomplished marvelous jobs that inspire the writing of this book.

Briefly speaking, Gao Xiaoling in her articles of "Feeling is Knowledge" (2008) and "George Eliot's 'Sympathy' and Its Philosophical Origin" (2009) explain the origin of sympathy in George Eliot's novels and based on such understanding she proves that sympathy serves as essential way for knowledge through feeling transmission and imagination other's situations. She believes that sympathy "means common inner experience shared by the whole human community. It is not only a moral concept confined within the realm of literature, but a cognitive concept involving the profound influence of modern philosophers such as David Hume, Spinoza, and Feuerbach" (61). Yin Qiping in his article—"From the Self to the Not-self: The Road for the Cultivation of the Mind in *Daniel Deronda*" (2015) asserts that "sympathy is the inevitable course from the self to the not-self", and Eliot's concept of "sympathy" both belongs to the category of cognition, aesthetics and that of morality. He then proceeds to trace the origin of aesthetical cultivation of sympathy back to Schiller and demonstrates in *Daniel Deronda* that to "listen" is to sympathize, and the transformation of Gwendolen's worldview depends on the improvement of her "listening comprehension". These two scholars have observed that the doctrine of sympathy has emerged into the artistic writing of George Eliot and makes a valuable contribution in introducing Eliot's artistic claims of sympathy to Chinese researchers. Meanwhile, Jin Wen in her "Enlightenment Understandings of Sympathy" (2018) charts two notions of sympathy as emotional synchronization and emotional entanglementy manifested in the eighteenth century novels such as fiction by Fielding. Zhu Yu in her book "Wordsworth as a Listener" (2018) focuses on the notion of sympathy in the Romantic age and demonstrates that the ability of listening plays a vital role in imaginative sympathy in Romantic poet like William Wordsworth. All their works are of importance in instruction and inspiration for the study of this project. Based on these brilliant works, this study particularly investigated sympathy in the Victorian historical context by relating the function of sympathy for tuning the novel as a serious form of art. George Eliot's special innovation of realism-cum-sympathy aesthetic contributes to the nineteenth century affective aesthetics. Meanwhile, sympathy between minds is far from being ideal to realize the expected moral, epistemological or aesthetic end, or at least it is not easy. The moral and epistemological relativity when sympathy is working and George Eliot's way to cope with this issue from the aesthetical dimension with human care is what exactly this project is going to concern.

Altogether, there are four doctoral dissertations concerning with George Eliot:

Liao Changyin in his *"Paradoxical Narration—A Study of the Paradoxes in the Political Modernization in George Eliot's Three Later Novels"* (2006) explores the issue of paradoxes in the political modernization presented by Eliot in her three later novels; *Research on the Labyrinthine Texts in the Perspective of Narrative Theories* (2009) by Zhu Taoxiang studies the formal attributes of labyrinthine text in *Middlemarch* form the double perspective of comparative poetics and narratologies. Gao Xiaoling in her "Feeling is a Power" (2010) associates feeling with knowing; Wei Xiaohong in *The Art of Psychological Depiction in George Eliot's Major Novels* carries out a systematic study on Eliot's depiction of the character's psychology in the perspectives of the environment, the action and the discourse by means of the documental and textual analysis. *Historiographical Awareness and the Building of a National Community in George Eliot's Novels* (2016) by Zhao Jing investigates Eliot's efforts to build a multi-level English national community by history-rewriting, so as to reveal the relationship between the literary imagination and the community construction.

The above reviews indicate that there is still some room in studying Eliot's understanding of sympathy and its association with her realistic writing. Her artistic ideal of stimulating personal inspiration by sympathy extension for other's benefit or the communal good is especially of great significance. The current social background needs exploration to reactivate people's feelings for the aesthetic and ethical reconstruction on the basis of man's knowledge of his self. Therefore, this book mainly projects a strong interest in sympathy, expecting to present an archaeological research of the doctrine of it, in its relation to sublime aesthetics, moral philosophy and probably political consideration. In these contexts, sympathy to bring about cognitive experience of the self instead of the other, for the other's mind sometimes keeps unknown or at least not fully known to us. Sympathy in Eliot's efforts is not only the instinctive and spontaneous compassion for a sufferer, but also a conscious process of achieving emotional alignment by overcoming negative components of affective relationships such as alterity, apathy, and abjection. It accomplishes the evolutionary process of the individual by adjusting himself to coordinate with the outward forces. "In the mid-nineteenth century, Victorians looked enthusiastically toward the potential of a society in which the highly evolved cultivation of sympathetic feelings might take new forms." (Henry, *George Eliot and the British Empire* 41) To the Victorians and to George Eliot, sympathy embodies too much hope for social regulation and national renewal through mental adjustments. With her talents and intelligence, challenges the possibility of renovations of the transformation of both the society and the individual. Briefly, Eliot leads people to transcend subjectivity of the self to realize an extra-textual aesthetics and intra-text ethical construction by observing "the self" in relations. Through exposing the crucial role of emotional attachments through sympathy for the development of the self, she illustrates ways of how to interact and establish community with others, thus build a democratic world based on common feeling, collective action, and public responsibility.

4. Theme and Structure

With text analysis, this project finds that Eliot frequently uses the word "transform" and its variants "transformation" or "transformative" to describe the process when sympathy is working. Nancy Henry has noted that the proper appreciation of George Eliot's writings depends on the knowledge of their contexts (Henry, *The Cambridge Introduction to George Eliot* Viii). The word "transform" and "transformation" in the Victorian age are very popularly used to describe the rapid social change.① The word "transform" means the process of changing in form,

---

① Jürgen Osterhammel in *The Transformation of the World: A Global History of the Nineteenth Century* (2015) points out that the nineteenth century consists of constant transitions and transformations.

appearance, nature, or character; or a process of converting one substance into another. It is well-known people's minds need to make the corresponding mental conversion if they want to keep in accordance with the outside world. Sympathy is a vehicle to realize this aim by the transmission or translation of man's feelings and mentality. Since the way people integrate their feeling or emotions depends very much on their lexical grid provided by their own language (qtd. in Konstan 1), sympathy is by no means a uniformed notion, and the implication of it varies with the way people figuring out their emotional or mental states. In the first place, emotions are transformed into the object of knowledge. Secondly, Sympathy is a necessary path for the subject to participate in the other's experience. As a medium of interpreting or translating emotions, sympathy allows the subject to realize the transmission of other people's emotions or the transformation of ideas based on universality and analogy of life experience, but it is impossible for him to achieve a complete reciprocal copy of the other's mind. That is why the word "transform" is adopted to describe the process of reconstructing the experience of others in one's own mind, and the course of self-transformation to generate follow-up thoughts. The third layer of the word of "transform" embodies the possibility of exalting those states of mind that cannot be articulated, or even comprehended by integrating things that can never be fully grasped with the senses by interesting with them as a whole. It involves an aesthetic inquiry joined with the primacy of the social good. Therefore, this book focuses on the transformative force of sympathy to improve self-knowledge in different contexts and delineates relationships between the vicissitudes of sympathy and its influence on Eliot's realistic writing.

Based on such considerations, the opening section of this book situates sympathy in the changing political and social circumstances and demonstrates a trajectory of the evolutionary process. As a word that reappears in the history of human thought, sympathy is endowed with rich implications after being elaborated by the ancient rhetoricians, the moral philosophers, the empiricism aesthetics, and the romantics. Sympathy thus becomes a half-divine and half-empirical potentiality relying on the power of imagination. And it ranges from the rhetorical appeals to common sense to the accounts of aesthetic judgment; from the philosophical sources as a moral sentiment to its literary implication. However, throughout the long history of the exploration, interests in sympathy are always bewildered by the epistemological questions of the possibility to know the other, which brings about many skeptical voices in the real practice of sympathy as a binding force. By sketching the historical context of nineteenth-century Britain, this project also relates the function of sympathy for tuning novel as a serious form of art. George Eliot's special innovation of realism-cum-sympathy aesthetic contributes to the nineteenth century affective aesthetics. She, with her keen insight of humanity and the ardent love toward fellow-being, explores the possibility that sympathy could present in the Victorian Age. Generally speaking, before Eliot, sympathy is basically regarded as an imaginative process leads to some kind of self-evident understanding and natural identification, while Eliot undoubtedly focuses her attention of sympathy onto the way of knowing the self instead of knowing the other based on the fact that she makes a more reflective exploration of sympathy and a faithful record of the diversity, difference, and even contradiction when sympathy is operated. As a result, if realism is to be achieved, Eliot must faithfully reveal the difficulty in this psychological transforming process.

Through applying basic text analysis, the following parts will show that George Eliot's attitude towards sympathy is neither as always enthusiastic nor consistently doubtful, but a process of approval involving reflection. She mainly treats sympathy as an evolutionary spirituality capable of constant transformation to achieve some epistemological, aesthetical or political aim. In the early stages of her creative career, for the admiration of sympathy and the ethical vision thus established, Eliot in *Adam Bede* promulgates the aesthetic of realism-cum-sympathy, in which sympathy as a cognitive model transforming pain into sympathy, and sympathy into knowledge. This epistemological model relies upon the immediate sensation. Such a fact makes *Adam Bede* present the pastoral poetic scenery with the warmth of human care. Eliot's realism in this period shares characteristics of the Dutch painting which stresses the detailed presentation of the everyday themes and celebrates the ordinary people.

The third chapter serves as a vital turning point expressing Eliot's reflection on sympathy. In the novella of *The Lifted Veil*, Eliot expresses her doubt on the reliability of sensation and feeling for fostering epistemology and the sympathetic potentiality. The absolute or definite knowing of other people's mind will blur the boundary of the self and the other, and consequently damage man's power of sympathy. Or, in other words, sensation and feeling can't realize sympathy if it is self-directed. And the unknowability of the other will appeal for the intervention of sympathetic imagination in its aesthetic sense. Realistic writing in *The Lifted Veil* thus commits to presenting the "reality" on the one hand, yet demonstrating an outlook of "cultural schizophrenia" on the other, considering the fact that the outside world cannot be fully understood.

The fourth chapter contributes to reveal the process of self-development when man does not trace the roots to reveal the external reality and the ideal inner state. In the Victorian age, the unknown, the infinite and the inexhaustible belong to the "sublime" category. Under this circumstance, Sympathy serves as a breakthrough for people yearning for self-transcendence. In *The Mill on the Floss* and *Middlemarch*, Eliot examines the greatness of the spiritual power for the secular sublime in a relatively closed community. Sympathy, through raising feeling and sensation to a sublime level, transforms the individual into a self-transcendental process of self-discovery and self-renunciation, so as to explore the "realistic possibility" for social meliorism. That is why realistic writing in these works presents a panoramic view of organic provincial life. It serves as the faithful reproduction of the external and internal docking moments of self-shock, fear, and the subsequent regulation process.

Although the process is hard, sympathy works smoothly in an environment of a relatively enclosed sphere of the provincial life. The emotional transmission of human beings can be carried out and the promotion of knowledge is realized. But once it enters a broader political horizon, sympathy manifests itself as an attitude of neutrality and an action of paralysis. The fifth chapter centers on Eliot's last novel *Daniel Deronda*, in which Eliot turns her vision to a broader social and political realm to reflect on the political nature of sympathy. Sympathy, on the one hand, aims for an effort to transcend social hierarchy, and on the other has to legislate some political community to find the preference for itself. After balancing, sympathy to Eliot is by no means a universal benevolence, but evolves into a collective identity and communal consensus based on the core of the national and the cultural heritage. For the compliment of such aim, *Daniel Deronda* exhibits a combination of realism, epic narrative, and myth-making. By doing this, the artistic vision sets up an imaginative construction internalizing the ideals of the community in the art world and exerts influence onto the reader's mental experiences. The phenomenological revivification of such perceptual experiences constitutes the subtle mixture between the spirit and the reality, the community and the society, which leads individuals to focus on the transformative power of spiritual initiative to respond to social changes in a particular historical context.

In order to unfold the course of how sympathy becomes a psychological mechanism for people to coordinate inward and outward relationships, reconstruct inner order and achieve internal transformation, and particularly to investigate its profound role in making art the best tool to improve man's self-knowledge so as to promote a better state of social transition, an elaboration on the evolutionary trajectory of sympathy in the following chapter seems to be a necessary and fundamental work to this study.

Chapter 1
Sympathy as a Continuous Historical Concept

Today, when mentioned, the word of "sympathy" is always viewed as a feminine trait and has been attached with the color of being "feminized" or "sentimentalized", and that is why it would be so easily banished from men's realm of reason or judgment. The fact is that the word "sympathy" has nothing to do with gender prejudice initially; instead, it had been functioning as a key term activating the philosophical discussion, aesthetic exfoliation and literary creation theories in the eighteenth and the nineteenth century. It is crucial to moral sensibility and irreplaceable to the aesthetics of reception. It means a feeling of elementary humanity and a sentiment of forgiveness and generosity as well. So while consulting the dictionary for the meaning of "sympathy", it is no surprise that we may encounter various explanations. Among all explanations, an invariable ingredient concerning "feeling for the suffering" or "feeling with others" is always associated with it, which embodies the possibility of relating the self to the other and promises the potentiality of breeding prosocial behaviors. For instance, according to *the Oxford Advanced Learner's Dictionary*, sympathy means "the feeling of being sorry for somebody; showing that you understand and care about somebody's problems"; sympathy, in *The Random House Dictionary* (2nd ed.), simply means "harmony of or agreement in feeling" (agreement in any feeling), with an additional explanation as "sharing the feelings of another, esp. in sorrow or trouble". So it is not difficult to find more or less variations in explaining the meaning of sympathy in different dictionaries. Moreover, there are also divergences in accounting for its epistemological root. For instance, *Oxford English Dictionary* says that the implication of sympathy derives from the Greek term of "pathos"—Greek rhetoric indicating kind of appeal to emotions of the audience. It is one of the three modes of persuasion, alongside "ethos" and "logos".① In contrast, many other scholars also insist that the present implication of sympathy actually etymologically roots in the old Greek term—"eleos", which is now known as "pity"②— one of the two tragic pathos aroused by tragedy, together with *phobos* (fear). "That (etymologically pity) is now conventionally associated with it (sympathy), so that it came to mean something like feeling with, as well as feeling for, another" (Burgess 297). Obviously, there still remain varieties and divisions concerning the

---

① As to the etymological root of sympathy, another statement favors of the Greek concept of "sumpatheia", which means "to feel with", "having a fellow feeling", or co-affection. It is used by the Stoics to refer to commonly observed interactions between elements of the universe. See Laurand, Valéry. "Universal Sympathy: Union and Separation." *Revue De Métaphysique et de Morale*, 2005 (4): 517-535.

② Sophie Ratcliffe in *On Sympathy* points out that the cognate term with "sympathy" is "empathy", which coined from the German "Einfühlung", describing "the experience of relating to a work of art ... and has now come to "designate imaginative reconstruction of another person's experience"(8). She also mentions "pity" is another word closely relating to sympathy. Although pity now bears the color of "condescension and superiority to the sufferer"(8), it was firstly explored in-depth in Aristotle's *Poetics* as an experience of tragedy with emotional and cognitive response — a cumulative, integrated response to the realistic and mimetic representation for aesthetic pleasure. Such implication laid a foundation for further exploration of sympathy in art theory. Based on such consideration, this book is most inclined to agree with treating "pity" as the epistemological root of "sympathy". Other terms like "compassion" or "empathy" would be considered as synonyms and would be distinguished if necessary.

meaning of sympathy and its origin. To modern scholars like Martha Nussbaum, sympathy itself is "frequently used in British eighteenth-century texts to denote an emotional equivalent" to what some contemporary critics would term as "empathy" or "compassion" (Nussbaum, *Upheavals of Thought* 302). Nussbaum's words remind us another troubling situation about "sympathy" at present, for sympathy is always mingled with words like "pity", "empathy", and "compassion", and for most of the time they can even interchange with each other, yet the fact is that they actually bear different emphasis if we try to differentiate them. Although it seems natural when different dictionaries provide various answers to explain a word, people have to admit that the notion of sympathy has brought about much more confusion. It has gone through various changes along with the history of human thought, and each stage invests fresh understanding into it based on a particular historical context, which truly sets obstacles for the present exploration of the concept of sympathy.

When David Marshall in his *The Surprising Effects of Sympathy* attempts to define the notion of sympathy, he traces back to its origin and says: "Our sympathy-and the pleasure we seem to take in it - depend on the violence and suffering inflicted on those who appear as spectacles before us." (48) Then questions follow. Why do others' pains become the spectators' aesthetic pleasure concerning the notion of sympathy? And why sympathy always interweaves with the notion of pity, compassion or empathy, what's the difference between them, if there is any? When George Eliot equals the "extension of sympathy" to the essence of her realistic aesthetics, what's the consistency with those previous claims? Ratcliffe's confession may make some point:

> For a contemporary critic, as for Eliot, one of the main challenges when writing about the idea of sympathy is the

vagueness that surrounds the term itself. The confusion begins on the level of definition, with the difficulties of distinguishing "sympathy" from a number of cognate terms. (Ratcliffe 8)

So in order to resolve the puzzles and reveal Eliot's originality or contribution while reflecting the notion of sympathy in literary theory, an elaboration on the trajectory of transforming pity into sympathy seems necessary and fundamental.

When we retrospect into the history of human thought, there are rare concepts which people have infinite longing to figure it out but could never fully handle it, and it is no exaggeration to say that the notion of sympathy could be one of them. In order to present the issue fairly, we have to admit that critics' glorification of sympathy, as well as the bias towards it, celebrates the same long history. On the one hand, numerous philosophers and thinkers have been chanting its social, moral and aesthetical values: for instance, Jean-Jacques Rousseau believes in a natural susceptibility to feel sympathy for others. He considers "pitié", the French synonym of sympathy, as an original feeling in human nature and presents it as the origin of all natural virtues. He invents the political ideal with pity activated by our imagination to defend over vanity, cruelty, and inequalities of civil society; the moral philosophers, like David Hume and Adam Smith, announce sympathy to be the "glue" adhesive for social combination and would be beneficial for the improvement of the social ethics. On the other hand, sympathy has long been attacked for its effectiveness and validity of realizing such ends. The blame started as early as the Stoics' advocating to banish the emotion of pity, namely Lucius Annaeus Seneca, who acknowledged pity as an uncontrollable emotional situation and labeled it as a characteristic of a weak soul ready to be irrationally moved by appearances (Star 125). That is why taking pity or sympathizing with others unconditionally will bring nothing but increase one's own ignorance.

Such claims had been echoed by philosophers like Kant, Nietzsche or Sheller, etc. Kant argues that we don't need to treat pity as a duty for "if another person suffers and I let myself (through my imagination) also become infected by his pain, which I still cannot remedy, then two people suffer" (Kant 34). Nietzsche also thinks that pity is morally worthless: "Pity is a squandering of feeling, a parasite harmful to moral health ... Pity does not depend upon maxims but upon affects; it is pathological" (Nietzsche 199). From these assertions, it is not too hard to observe that people are afraid that they will be controlled by others or manipulated by them if concerned with pain or feeling sorry for others' suffering. That's why Kant then emphasizes the importance of antimony and Nietzsche stresses the notion of self-control. In order to soothe the tension and hospitality toward pity, when time comes the shift from the rational model to the one which leaves a place to feelings, David Hume simply considers pity to be a secondary affection which arises out of sympathy, a principle which explains how opinions, sentiments, and emotions can be transferred from one individual to another. He views pity as the communication or transferral of the suffering pain, or misery of the recipient of pity to the pitier via imagination, considering the fact of suspicion of sympathy, Adam Smith hence differentiates the pity from compassion to survive sympathy.

> Pity and compassion are words appropriated to signify our fellow-feeling with the sorrow of others. Sympathy, though its meaning was, perhaps, originally the same, may now, however, without much impropriety, be made use of to denote our fellow-feeling with any passion whatever. (Smith 10)

Since then, pity has been gradually stereotyped as the synonym of

Chapter 1 Sympathy as a Continuous Historical Concept

sympathy yet bearing a slight difference in meaning. ①

Of course, the divergence in understanding sympathy existed in the past but also occurs in modern times. For example, many modern scholars can't tell the difference and sometimes alternatively use "sympathy" and "empathy". The fact is that these two words bear sufficient difference likewise. In short, empathy (feeling with) is a modern variant of sympathy (feeling for), just as Suzanne Keen has put it:

> Empathy may precede and lead to sympathy, but as has been amply demonstrated, mature sympathy, pity, and compassion do not necessarily result from empathy, nor does empathy inevitably lead to helping. Each of these states, including a disposition to help, can be brought about by cognitive processes other than empathy. (22)

Their relations can be demonstrated in the following illustration:

Empathy:	Sympathy:
I feel what you feel.	I feel a supportive emotion about your feelings.
I feel your pain.	I feel pity for your pain. ②

That is to say, when mentioning empathy we refer to an emotion in its own right, we feel what we believe to be the emotions of others, and it simply means a mental "projection" onto aesthetic objects in modern thinking, including inanimate objects; in contrast, when sympathy is used, it probably involves a situation in which feelings for another person occur, compared with the spontaneous, responsive sharing of an

---

① According to Charles Horton Cooley in *Human Nature and The Social Order*, pity is not necessarily moral or good, yet it is sometimes mere "self-indulgence". Whether it is egoistic or altruistic depends on the fact involving "reference to another person".

② For this illustration, see *Empathy and the Novel* by Suzanne Keen (5).

appropriate feeling as empathy which operates "without any particular evaluation of that experience" (qtd. in Ratcliffe 8). This fact makes sympathy always potentially associate with a prosocial or altruistic action. To Charles Horton Cooley, sympathy, "the content of it, the matter understood, is chiefly thought and sentiment, in distinction from mere sensation or crude emotion" (138). As to thought and sentiment, which "are from the first parts or aspects of highly complex and imaginative personal ideas" (139). So sympathy carries far richer implication than empathy, and it involves a more complicated mental synthetic process than we have speculated. Any misuse or misunderstanding may result in the decline of its charm.

Generally speaking, sympathy has been invested with moral, epistemological and aesthetical implications during the long process of evolution, so it is not surprising to find that sympathy would be included in the argument of literary theory. There are lots of writers and poets, such as Samuel Richardson, Nathaniel Hawthorne, William Wordsworth, Marry Shelly, and even Dickens who either illustrated the danger of sympathizing with others, or endeavored to elaborate the necessity of sympathy in their artistic creation. While mentioning artists who combine sympathy with artistic creation in an aesthetic discourse, George Eliot "represents the culmination" (Redfield xi). Considering this fact, the following part of this project will offer a general representation of the trajectory of sympathy as a continuous historical concept, which is vital to reveal the evolutionary track of Eliot's understanding of the notion of sympathy, and it will explain that George Eliot's announcement that "the great debt we owe to the artist is the extension of our sympathy" was neither an abrupt decision, nor an original one, but rather an absorption, elaboration on and succession as a continuous historical concept based on the historical context of Victorian Age. So Eliot's efforts to treat sympathy as a psychology of imaginative self-assimilation to establish a psychological unity by drawing readers into deep emotional absorption by experiencing that of the characters depicted will also be revealed. Such a process is vital for readers to stay away from detached critical judgment, yet to generate a sense of identification instead. ① This training in art appreciation will help readers to conquer the divisive force laying between the self and the incomprehensible object so as to generate an assimilative pattern for cognition. In most of the previous thoughts, it is believed that sympathy will guarantee an undifferentiated conception of the psychology of mimetic experience between the self and the other, the reader and the character, which becomes previously the main issue that George Eliot wants to challenge in her writing project, she realizes that the imbalance in the cognitive function of sympathy and magnifies the aesthetical implication of it. The following part of this chapter intends to list the main contribution to expand the connotation of sympathy. Basically, "pity" in Aristotelian Rhetoric serves as the embryonic form of sympathetic imagination experiencing the poetic representation; in the age of sensibility, sympathy with human care becomes a mechanism for the secret operation of feelings which relates the parts of individual person into a whole; it's equal to "altruism" or "fellow feeling" in terms of imagination to moral philosophers; Under the hand of the empirical aesthetics and the romantics, sympathy offers a channel to sublimate the anti-social passion into an aesthetic principle so that the divisive self may be integrated. The romantics further explore the ethical dimension of the aesthetic implication of sympathy since the rationally organized laws and its commandments in art will fall upon readers as a moral education unless

---

① Identification here means a cognitive process of mastering the similarities and difference between the self and the other, the readers and the characters, but much more often, difference are the very thing to be identified, so as to help people to produce an ethical understanding of recognizing virtues and vices.

sympathy works. As a result, when sympathy emerges itself into the Victorian novel theory, the aesthetic power of sympathy needs to be fully explored, and the task of integrating the moral and the cognitive implication in the aesthetical one seems to be a problem Eliot, as well as other Victorians, needs to solve.

1.1 Sympathy as the Embryo "Pity" in Aristotelian Tragedy

Although the modern meaning of sympathy undergoes a gradual historical change, it always associates with the aesthetic pleasure through spectating others' suffering; such implication should date back to Aristotle's discussion of "pity" in tragedy. When pity is aroused, spectators sympathize with another's suffering and anticipate that they may suffer from a similar situation in the future. This implication is the fundamental connotation of sympathy. In *Rhetoric*, Aristotle defines pity as:

> A feeling of pain caused by the sight of some evil, destructive or painful, which befalls one who does not deserve it, and which we might expect to befall ourselves or some friend of ours, and moreover to befall us soon. In order to feel pity, we must obviously be capable of supposing that some evil may happen to us or some friend of ours, and moreover some such evil as is stated in our definition or is more or less of that kind. (Aristotle, *Rhetoric* 91)

This definition shows that pity is not a simple feeling; it concerns with identification of others' suffering and a social instinct of connecting the self to the other. But pity is not felt toward those who are too close and important to us. Under these conditions, pity will give way to full immersion in grief; similarly, nor would too much distance between people bring about pity. Pity to Aristotle seems to "involve a degree of sympathy or fellow feeling" yet allows "the sense of difference between oneself and the object of pity", so pity "can never lose at least a subliminal awareness of its spectatorial role", no matter "however engaged or absorbed an audience may become" (Halliwell 216). Pity functions as a catalyst between characters and spectators when Aristotle further discusses the tragedy in his *Poetics* (2011), and it involves a strong emotional absorption and a highly reflective attitude on the part of spectators. The spectators feel pity and terror for they feel strongly sorry for the noble man suffering the misery they do not deserve, and they also feel terrible at the thought such experience may fall upon themselves. With a delicate balance between the psychological involvement and proper distance, pity here serves as a vital experience to transfer the painful into a pleasurable experience. As to the reason for audiences to enjoy the artistic representation of events which may distress them in the real life, Aristotle attributes it to a medical term—"catharsis" which means "purification" or "purgation". It derives from the medical meaning of curing through removal and evacuation of harmful elements from man's body. Aristotle believed the enjoyment of tragedy would have the same therapeutic effect, for the viewing of the noble people's suffering and pain which they do not deserve may provoke the audiences' or the readers' pity and fear—the emotional outflow made the unwanted and painful emotions release, or the potentially disruptive emotions are purged, then the spectators find their souls refined or purified.

Modern scholars like Martha Nussbaum argued persuasively that the benefit of catharsis arises from the clarification of moral values through the self-reflective activity by the audience's emotional response to tragedy. She claims: "For Aristotle, pity and fear will be sources of illumination or clarification, as the agent, responding and attending to his or her responses, develops a richer self-understanding concerning the attachments and values that support the responses" (Nussbaum 388). Pity and fear, through the work of "katharsis", realize the moral education of tragedy. Moreover, Aristotle's stress on the emotional reaction to art also transforms the enjoyment of tragedy into an aesthetic activity. This pleasure lies in a safe distance from what is happening that makes an intellectual understanding of a given situation possible. "When we transpose what 'purgation' means in the context of physiology to the context of human beings witnessing not live events but artistic formulations of them, we arrive at the 'aesthetic' meaning of the term" (Schaper 133). So generally, in Aristotle's understanding of tragedy, through the operation of catharsis, man transcends the limits of their capacities; he obtains the recognition of humanity at its best, at its most precarious, at its most vulnerable, and yet as triumphant by us as agents. "Pity" in Aristotelian Rhetoric builds up the connections between aesthetic response and man's moral judgment, it could be seen as an embryo on which the suffering then becomes the beautiful, and it can be called an etymological sense of experiences occupying the spectators, which lays rich foundations for the later discussion of shaping ethical beliefs in moral philosophy, emotional transformation and imaginative construction in both empirical aesthetics or literary criticism in age of sensibility and later on.

1.2 Sympathy as the "Secret Operation of Feeling" in the Age of Sensibility

Northrop Frye in the 1950s introduced one of his most influential notions—the "age of sensibility", which simply refers to a broad description of literature after Pope and before Wordsworth. During this period, sympathy is so widely discussed as a social and aesthetical term. The whole eighteenth century is thus seen as a century of "feeling, sensibility and sympathy" (qtd. in Gaston 129). And a general retrospect of the development of sympathy in this time period cannot be ignored.

1.2.1 Sympathy as the "Secret Operation of Feeling"

The present discussion of sympathy is not unrelated to the prosperity of the seventeenth-century philosophical and aesthetical reflection and the mid-eighteenth century Britain moral philosophy.① According to suggestions from most historians and philosophers:

> Sympathy first became a key term in the seventeenth and eighteenth centuries as part of an attempt to counter Thomas Hobbes's vision of human nature as fundamentally selfish and of society as merely a way to limit otherwise-violent competition between individuals. (Ablow 1149)

The seventeenth-century English philosopher Thomas Hobbes, with his *Leviathan* (1651), saw man as a creature with "egoist psychology":

> Because the condition of man... is a condition of war of every one against every one, in which case every one is governed by his own reason, and there is nothing he can make use of that may not be a help unto him in preserving his life against his enemies, it followeth that in such a condition every man has a right to everything, even to one another's body. (Hobbes 91)

Hobbes's claim for man's selfishness consequently blazed the way for the rampancy of Epicureanism and utilitarianism, while thankfully the other side of the coin revealed a fact that more and more thinkers and

---

① See Gaston, Sean. "The Impossibility of Sympathy," *The Eighteenth Century* 51.1-2 (2010): 129-152.

philosophers disapproved of such advocates and started to turn to the factors of feelings like benevolence and affection for solution. These factors were treated as virtually innate human nature suitable for natural affinity and sociality. Among them, the notion of sympathy and the magical operation of it were especially emphasized. While mentioning the contributors who engaged in this exploration, Anthony Ashley Cooper—the Third Earl of Shaftesbury (1671-1713) is undoubtedly the most outstanding one.

Under the influence of the Cambridge Platonists — a group of theologians and philosophers at the University of Cambridge in the middle of the 17th century, who believed a syncretizing habit of mind and the coherent nature of society and universe, Shaftesbury got convinced that not only human nature is fundamentally good but also the natural world is vitally and magically connected. The society is an organic "system" in which man and the natural world celebrate a harmonious relation and the circulations and communication of feeling are also natural and congenial. A vital and magical world can't sustain without emotional connections. Shaftesbury's project is to let the "secret operation" of human sympathy relate the parts of the individual into a whole. So Shaftesbury, in the artistic sense, treated sympathy or "participation with others" as an organizing principle toward order, in which the internalization of self and the conversion within is strongly emphasized. This could not only improve the self-knowledge, but deepen our understanding of "human nature" as well. Moreover, Shaftesbury's understanding of sympathy also relates to his aesthetic thinking: participating with sympathy equals that we start a kind of "communication". Since sympathy makes the circulation of feeling possible, it will naturally realize the aim of moral and social coherence. What is notable is that Shaftesbury believes such an exchange of affection

Chapter 1 Sympathy as a Continuous Historical Concept

occurs not only between people in society but also between artist and audience:

> Of all other Beautys which Virtuosos pursue, Poets celebrate, Musicians sing, and Architects or Artists, of whatever kind, describe or form; the most delightful, the most engaging and pathetick, is that which is drawn from real Life, and from the Passions. Nothing affects the Heart like that which is purely from it-self, and of its own nature... This Lesson of Philosophy, even a Romance, a Poem, or a Play may teach us; whilst the fabulous Author leads us with such pleasure thro' the Labyrinth of the Affections, and interests us, whether we will or no, in the Passions of his Heroes and Heroines... Let Poets, or the Men of Harmony, deny, if they can, this Force of *Nature*, or withstand this *moral Magick*. They, for their parts, carry a double portion of this Charm about 'em. For in the first place, the very Passion which inspires 'em, is it-self *the Love of Numbers*, *Decency and Proportion*; and this too, not in a narrow sense, or after a *selfish* way, (for who of them composes for *him-self*?) but in a friendly social View; for the Pleasure and Good of others; even down to Posterity, and future Ages. And in the next place, tis evident in these Performers, that their chief Theme and Subject, that which raises the Genius the most, and by which they so effectually move others, is purely *Manners*, and the *moral Part*. ①(Shaftesbury I: 85)

Here Shaftesbury's worldview that the moral and the aesthetic are fully interpenetrated in art is revealed. Since art are created from real life and passions will influence readers or spectators to welcome the good and

---

① The capitalized and the italic are original.

the pleasurable, for Shaftesbury, the true poet is the moral artist "who can imitate the Creator, and is thus knowing in the inward Form and Structure of his Fellow-Creature"①(Shaftesbury I: 129). Morality and beauty are so closely connected because both depend on inward form. The true poet exhibits a kind of sympathizing force to combine parts together: "he forms a Whole, coherent and proportion'd in it-self, with due Subjection and Subordinacy of constituent Parts"②(Shaftesbury I: 129). It is significant that Shaftesbury grasps the point that sympathy could realize the psychological integrity. When the artistic work expresses in miniature a sympathetic "coherence" and "proportion" of the cosmos, the readers or the spectators experience it through mental activity also. Enjoying artistic work will unquestionably train the transcendental act of sympathy. Mimesis and affectivity are presented as the conditions for a powerful sympathy between artists and audiences; the author "interests us" and this "interest" leads inevitably to a kind of delight so that the sacrifice of internal control is amply compensated by the experience of aesthetic pleasure. As Shaftesbury observes later in his *Characteristicks*:

> When by mere Illusion, as in *a Tragedy*, the passions of this kind are skillfully excited in us; we prefer the Entertainment to any other of equal duration. We find by our-selves, that the moving our Passions in this mournful way, the engaging them in behalf of Merit and Worth, and the exerting whatever we have of social Affection, and human Sympathy, is of the highest Delight. (Shaftesbury II: 61-62)

Aesthetic appreciation absolutely brings the highest delight through sympathy; however, this doesn't mean that Shaftesbury fully approves

---

① The capitalized are original.
② The capitalized and the italic are original.

the effectiveness of the sympathetic operation. In fact, he casts doubt onto the circulation of passion. That is to say, sympathy serves to unite society yet to divide it also. For example, sympathy felt during the war will mislead people to be too emotional, and the principle of "reason" should be valued to weaken the misleading of emotions. By reason, people could "look into ourselves" and judge or measure passions. For the same consideration, Shaftesbury then invites "disinterestedness" into the aesthetical domain. Here, "disinterestedness" is an idea later claimed by Edmund Burke for redemption under a condition of the sublime, and Kant identifies it as the "sine qua non" (necessary condition) of aesthetic judgment, or the English psychologist Edward Bullough (1880-1934) applies it to the idea of "psychical distance" during the appreciation of art. It is a very crucial element for discussing sympathy, which would be investigated further in the following parts of this project.

Although Shaftesbury tries to make sympathy a practicable notion, he becomes aware of the fact feeling is unmanageable and the sympathetic relationship between self and other, the self and the society is far more complicated. For scholars today, "the power of sympathy threatens not only to blur the boundaries between self and others but, more dangerously still, to cast the self into oblivion" (Lobis 233). So Shaftesbury's justification of sympathy as a human state to serve the social and communicative end seems solely an approach for the sublimation of socialization. In general, sympathy connects men through universal feelings, it is a magic operation. Shaftesbury's project of involving sympathy into the moral and aesthetical thinking is a crucial contribution which would be taken up and absorbed in the work of his successors, and his neglecting or circumventing questions about the limits of human understanding when sympathy works also run through an entire line of the relevant thought.

1.2.2 Sympathy as the "Moral Sentiment"

It was not very long before Hume declares Shaftesbury's appeal to sympathy of parts as the "uniting principle of the universe" to be a "philosophical fiction"—a dumb theory which appeals for an explanation with a more sound and experimental investigation of human nature (Hume 951, 752). For moral philosophers, universal sympathy relies much on a social sympathy to sustain. The Scottish Enlightenment thinkers such as Francis Hutcheson, David Hume and Adam Smith see sympathy as evidence of a natural bond between people and introduce it into the social moral realm. They believe that men are connected through their feelings, and sympathy allows feelings to be shared. Under their hands, sympathy becomes the faculty of the mind by which a person can enter into the thoughts and feelings of another through the exercise of the imagination. With the capability of entering into or imagining other people's thoughts, sympathy serves to guarantee social stability grounded in similarity and interdependence. During this period, man's understanding toward sympathy no longer simply carries the meaning of "feeling sorry" or "pity for others' misfortune", yet was embodied with more cognitive, ethical and aesthetic implications. For instance, Samuel Johnson echoed with his contemporaries, in his *Dictionary of the English Language* (1755), he defined "to sympathize" as "to feel with another; to feel in consequence of what another feels; to feel mutually". In order to elaborate the trajectory of the notion sympathy in this time period, two classic texts—David Hume's *A Treatise of Human Nature* (1739) and Adam Smith's *Theory of Moral Sentiments* (1759) need to be consulted and backtracked. These two books could be the spokesmen in the 18th Century which cast the eyesight onto the mechanism of sympathy, wishing to keep a balance between man's claim of individualism and those of sociability combining with a close study of human nature.

Take Hume for a detailed explanation, unlike Thomas Hobbes, Hume believed that men are social creatures—"the creature of the universe, who has the most ardent desire of society, and is fitted for it by the most advantages. We can form no wish, which has not a reference to society" (Hume 559). He understood sympathy as the faculty that makes passions "pass with the greatest facility from one person to another, and produce correspondent movements in all human breasts" (Hume 906). For it contributes a lot to the formation of man's ideas, impressions and the generation of feelings. On the part of Hume, man cannot form ideas and impressions without concerning with others' feelings, and his pride and humility cannot be sustained either if there is no reinforcement of others' emotions. The lucky thing is man's feeling is transpersonal, and the mechanism of sympathy fulfills such transmission.

Hume introduced sympathy into the circle of social science and understood sympathy as a way to form a society of moral and sentimental relations. He referred sympathy to an emotional response stemming from the recognition of another's emotional state or condition: "Sympathy is not itself a sentiment or feeling. It is rather the mechanism by which we come to enter into the feelings of other people including their admiration and disapproval of ourselves." (Wright 204) Sympathy now allows us to enter into others' feelings, and it surely needs to invite the cognitive capability in man's epistemological domain—it will help a man know himself better and foster our sense toward others. Hume describes this procedure with the "mirror metaphor": "That the minds of men are mirrors to one another, not only because they reflect each other's emotions, but also because those rays of passions, sentiments and opinions may be often reverberated, and may decay away by insensible degrees." (Hume 562) Yet a problem also occurs during the conversion of another person's feelings and passions with that of one's own. For many modern critics: "Unfortunately, he (Hume) never returns to a key element of his original mechanism of sympathy, namely that the whole process begins with the force and vivacity of the idea of ourselves being transferred to those of the other person." (Wright 212) Jennifer Herdt points out that man's ability to partake in others' interests depend basically on our own self-esteem and the strength of our own egos: "our affections depend more upon ourselves" (46), unless we have a healthy and strong sense of self, otherwise we cannot have a full sense of the other person. However, the fact is that people's capability varies; such variability will definitely influence the validity of real sympathetic operation. So although Hume exhausts to preach his belief in sympathy and its social functions, he "seems not to have taken full advantage of it in explaining how we develop an extensive sympathy for others" (Wright 212), which makes his realm of moral construction a utopia, too good to approach. This may serve as some explanation for Hume's own despair after trumpeting his confidence in sympathy and social nature of man:

> I am first affrighted and confounded with that forelorn solitude, in which I am placed in my philosophy, and fancy myself some strange uncouth monster, who not being able to mingle and unite in society, has been expelled all human commerce, and left utterly abandoned and disconsolate. Fain would I run into the crowd for shelter and warmth; but cannot prevail with myself to mix with such deformity. I call upon others to join me, in order to make a company apart; but no one will hearken to me. Everyone keeps at a distance, and dreads that storm, which beats upon me from every side. (Hume 412-413)

It's hard for people to imagine that Hume devotes his life to calling for sympathy and sociability on the one hand while savoring the taste of a solitary and monster-like life on the other.

Therefore, Hume's advocating of sympathy as the "emotional contagion" to contemporary psychologists seems weak. Hume notices that sympathy is an operation of imagination: "Sympathy, as I have already observed, is nothing but the conversion of an idea into an impression by the force of imagination." (Hume 653) However, he makes no more exploration on the operation of it. In other words, "Hume seems relatively unconcerned with the question of how we really know what other people's feelings truly are, a problem Adam Smith makes central to his account of sympathy in *A Theory of Moral Sentiments*" (Pinch 30). Before awaiting a deeper exploration until Adam Smith, Hume's contribution to the observation of the aesthetical aspects of sympathy could be first discussed. Hume and most the aesthetic theorists in the eighteenth-century treat sympathy as a mechanism of sharing feelings not only between people but also between people and artistic works or representations. Although Hume admits that feelings obtained from artistic works are less solid, he and other aestheticians stress that feeling from the world of representation and feelings from the same objects in reality are equally illustrative. For Hume, the feelings of the passions caused by poetical fictions are "mere phantom". Notwithstanding the passion "feels less firm and solid" (Hume 202), Hume acknowledges that "a passion, which is disagreeable in real life, may afford the highest entertainment in a tragedy, or epic poem" (Hume 202). So in *Treatise's*, Hume moves from interpersonal sympathy naturally to an aesthetic one:

> A spectator of a tragedy passes through a long train of grief, terror, indignation, and other affections, which the poet represents in the persons he introduces. As many tragedies end happily, and no excellent one can be composed without some reverses of fortune, the spectator must sympathize with all these changes, and

receive the fictitious joy as well as every other passion. (Hume 568)

Hume believes passions raised by real life can be represented in aesthetical ways; the power in poetry or painting is owing to the power of imitation, through the operation of sympathy, man's aesthetic response can activate his awakening of social and moral awareness.

Hume's understanding of sympathy laid foundation for Adam Smith, who continues the exploration of sympathy by further bridging the distance between autonomous individuals. In *The Theory of Moral Sentiments* (1759), Adam Smith devotes the first chapter "Of Sympathy" to appeal for the master-sentiment countering with the innate selfishness of man. He gives insight into the weight of sympathy. For Smith, our moral sense is derived from being an attentive spectator of the actions of others, and then we form the judgments which we may apply to our own conduct. But the testing of the moral validity depends on "changing places in fancy" with the person we are judging: "We enter as it were into his body, and become in some measure the same person with him, and thence form some idea of his sensations, and even feel something which, though weaker in degree, is not altogether unlike them." (Smith 9) As a result, the morality of a society is thus created by series of actions of imagination in which each person is able to call up an "analogous emotion" in response to the feeling of another and is, therefore, able to check the conduct of others and that of his own.

Consequently, Adam Smith stresses the importance of the imagination to excite feelings and emotion transport. By "imagination" we place ourselves in others' situations and access to the sensory life of another, even things that he himself fails to do. This situation sounds remarkably like the transfer of roles in reading poetry or novels. For Smith, the act is not so much aesthetic as social: "This is the source of our fellow-feeling for the misery of others... It is by changing places in fancy with the sufferer, that we come either to conceive or to be affected by what he feels." (Smith 10) Sympathy extends the imaginative world of the poet, and critics associated sympathy with a dramatic extension of the self. The sympathetic imagination under Smith's hands seems to be suspended between self-regarding and other-regarding consideration (Halliwell 85-86). So Smith observes that sympathy involves a kind of judgment, and he also notices the tension arising from the synthetic practice: "We often derive sorrow from the sorrow of others is a matter of fact too obvious to require any instances to prove it"; and "we have no immediate experience of what other men feel, we can form no idea of the manner in which they are affected". (Smith 9) So Smith declares that the appropriate management is ensured by the "impartial spectator" — a detached monitor within the individual subject, which may help the subject to imagine the other from a proper perspective. And the proper performance of sympathy is similar with the manner that "we judge of the productions of all the arts which address themselves to the imagination" (Smith 26). All these facts show that sympathy to Smith "is not at all a purely instinctual reaction but manifests cognitive interpretation", since it "in its strongest forms depends on understanding, reason, and judgment of a situation, on knowing the causes of another's suffering". (Halliwell 86) Such cognitive interpretation of sympathy may be said as an enormous contribution in understanding the operation of sympathy, yet it also tends to set the stage potentially blocking to excite the moral feeling, so the moral purpose sympathy originally promises will be destroyed someway either, which will be a critical issue reflected in George Eliot's novella— *The Lifted Veil*, and the cognitive issue concerning with sympathy will be discussed in detail in the third chapter of this book.

In short, "sympathy" in moral philosophy can simply be seen as a faculty, a mechanism, and an irresistible relation of "correspondence" between individuals. Whether it is to Shaftesbury, Hume, or Smith, the treatment of sympathy always concerns with a belief in natural affection towards other person involving an epistemological activity. And such cognitive activities embody both identification and entire agreement. Sympathy then somewhat implies a self-evident phenomenon, which actually raises lots of questions such as: "how do we pass from recognizing another's feelings as belonging to them to experiencing them as our own? What exactly do we feel as a result?" (Ablow 298) These questions have troubled the philosophers. Thankfully, sympathy under those moral philosophers' hands turns to be epistemologically problematic but aesthetically secure, which revitalizes the situation of investigating sympathy in the aesthetical domain.

1.2.3 Sympathy as an "Empirical Aesthetical Experience"

It is just noticeable that Both Smith and Hume link sympathy to the organizational principles of the society. Smith believes our sympathy makes us good citizens, and Hume insists that our sympathy tempers our self-interest. Although trying hard, neither of them succeeds in reconciling the tension between the assumptions of fellow feelings and the possibility of knowing other people. On the one hand, the epistemological questions raised by moral sentimentalism shed some shadow on the real practice of sympathy, which brings about the divergence between knowledge acquisition and ethical inclination; On the other hand, the aesthetic response seems to hold prospect in the discussion of sympathy. Although there leave many practical or epistemological problems in a moral philosophical investigation, sympathy proves to be a dynamic word in the eighteenth-century realm of aesthetics. "The ability to be affected by or to enter into the feelings of others, is the concept of *par excellence* of the eighteenth century" (Ellis 18). Since men are creatures of feelings, and the realm of the aesthetic is defined by both emotional excess and subject autonomy, so it doesn't seem abrupt for sympathy to enter into the discussion of empirical aesthetics when the latter becomes dramatically flourishing.

The most outstanding aesthetician holding the optimistic advocate for imaginative sympathy is Edmund Burke, who presents a sympathetic model in his *Philosophical Enquiry into the Origin of Our Ideas of the Sublime and the Beautiful* (1757)(1901). Compared with Hume and Smith, Burke seems more optimistic about the efficiency of man's sympathetic imagination. He believes that it is by sympathy that "we enter into the concerns of others; that we are moved as they are moved, and are never suffered to be indifferent spectators of almost anything which men can and do suffer" (Burke 70). Such an advocate places oneself in the midst of other's life and revolves around the aesthetic responses to others' suffering or misfortune. For Burke, sympathy must be considered as a sort of substitution, by which "we are put into the place of another man, and affected in many respects as he is affected" (Burke 70); unlike Smith's impartial spectator, who sympathizes only as a dispassionate onlooker, Burke prefers detachedly speculating how we might feel in the same situation. Burke attributes a divine force to sympathy, we are involuntarily involved in others' misfortune. Or rather, we're willingly inclined to a scene of suffering driven by innate feelings of compassion.

Moreover, Burke sees sympathy as a channel for the sublime delight. In *Philosophical Enquiry into the Origin of Our Ideas of the Sublime and the Beautiful* (1757)(1901), Burke advocates "the sublime" to be an aesthetic category opposite to "the beautiful", which arise from the passion of pain and terror and a desire of self-reservation implanted by God as an instinct in our nature. It is the sublime and the desire for self-reservation that make people socialize, or in other words, to sublimate the anti-social passion into an aesthetic principle so the community that might have been threatened by terror may also be reconstituted by taste. This is why Burke claims that people may take delight in viewing the terrifying event of tragedy. It is God's way of drawing people together with sympathy. Obviously, he rejects the impenetrability of the sublime as a barrier to sympathy, but a channel instead. Although the notion of sublime varies a little after Kant and Sheller evolve it, it always means things or passions strong enough to exceed man's understanding, and it needs to invite man's imagination or intellectual sense to readjust to these occasions. Since pain is a source for the sublime, sympathy always plays a vital role to sublimate pain into aesthetic pleasure, whereby, sympathy to appreciate art and literature will train the mind to respond to the similar suffering in real life. It is a premise to the integrity of the individual and will relate the one to the many. Since the operation of sympathy means "entering into the concerns of others", it needs the sympathizer to remove some subjectivity, switching the perceptive of the self into that of the not-self with imaginative activities. The Romantics express much interest in this process when they join the relay race. They expect to achieve social ethics while pursuing the aesthetic response of sympathy through narrowing sympathy down to the imaginative activity which negotiates the relationship between the self and the other, the self and the not-self.

1.3　Sympathy as the "Sympathetic Imagination" in the Romantic Aesthetics

While the moral philosophers attribute theaesthetic implications to the notion of sympathy, the artists, especially the Romanticists also endeavored to constitute the ethical dimension of the aesthetic in their consideration of sympathy. Being a literary school emphasizing much on feeling and emotional communication between readers and poets, British Romanticism treats sympathy in art higher than any other literary trend. "The need for sympathy was nowhere more apparent than in the field of Romantic literary aesthetics" (Rudd 24). Take Shelley for example, in his *A Defence of Poetry*, Shelley claims that the creative imagination as a form of sympathy will bind the poet to his fellows, nature, and the social environment. Such binding will let him be enriched morally.

> Poetry acts in another and diviner manner. It awakens and enlarges the mind itself by rendering the receptacle of a thousand unapprehended combinations of thought. Poetry lifts the veil from the hidden beauty of the world... The great secret of morals is love; or a going out of our own nature, and an identification of ourselves with the beautiful which exists in thought, action, or person, not our own. A man, to be greatly good, must imagine intensely and comprehensively; he must put himself in the place of another and of many others; the pains and pleasures of his species must become his own. The great instrument of moral good is the imagination. (Shelley 39)

Shelley asserts that poetry and other forms of art may awaken the minds of readers, the rationally organized laws and its commandments in art will fall upon them as moral education. Through the power of such aesthetic discourse, sympathetic imaginations help one feel for another. In this sense, it turns into an instrumental tool for moral good.

> Sympathy also becomes that special power of the imagination which permits the self to escape its own confines, to identify with other people, to perceive things in a new way, and to develop an aesthetic appreciation of the world that coalesces both the

subjective self and the objective other. (Engell 143-144)

Romantic poets basically emerge themselves into nature and enjoy the unity with it. They must initiate a sympathetic imagination with their poetic talents to enter the feelings and experiences of the other. They believe only by doing so could they create the best poem. John Keats in his poem "On Seeing the Elgin Marbles" (1817) gives a vivid expression: "Of godlike hardship tells me I must die/Like a sick eagle looking at the sky". If the poet wants to see like an eagle, he must forget the existence of himself and think or do like an eagle. This presents a question—how could we know the view of an eagle or what does it think? That is why although Wordsworth in his Preface to the *Lyrical Ballads* even suggests creating community of feeling through sympathizing and ennobling of others experience, he in his poems like "Old Man Travelling" or "Simon Lee" also demonstrates the limits of sympathy; Even if trumpeting that "Poetry is the spontaneous overflow of powerful feelings", Wordsworth finds he knows "no book or system of moral philosophy written with sufficient power to melt into our affections" (103). It seems impossible "becoming the same person" as another.

As to Coleridge, he believed that "by a law of our Nature, he, who labours under a strong feeling, is impelled to seek sympathy; but a Poet's feelings are all strong" (*Poems* xiv). The poet's feeling may be too strong for the reading public and they may not be interested in the poet's individual feeling, nor could they share some common experience to the same extent, or even the similar one is hard to approach. Admit it or not, in romantic poems, there's unavoidable imbalance between the poet and the subject they want to present, the poet and the reader, and the ego and non-ego. While other poets either ignore the tension or choke by recognizing it, John Keats wrote to his brothers George & Thomas on Dec. 22nd 1817:

> It struck me what quality went to form a Man of Achievement, especially in literature, which Shakespeare possessed so enormously—I mean Negative Capability, that is when Man is capable of being in uncertainties, mysteries, doubts, without any irritable reaching after facts and reason. (Keats *Selected Letters* 41)

John Keats used "Negative Capability" to describe the process of formulating or clarifying knowledge by negating the ego. In other words, man needs to satisfy uncertainty, mystery, and doubt in the process of knowing, not eager to find the skinless truth. To put it in another way, the aesthetical power of sympathy should be highlighted. Keat's "Negative Capability", in the study of this book, carries more or less a similar color as George Eliot's understanding of sympathy, but the latter leads the whole exploration to a further and far-reaching depth. It's an obvious fact that the Romantic writing is concerned with the poet's self-involved stand by imputing too much personal feelings or experiences into their work, which makes their poetries present a narcissistic outlook and finally influences the effectiveness of evoking sympathy. So when Romantic poetry gives way to realistic novels, the mechanism of sympathy needs some variation.

From the above discussion, we can conclude that sympathy before the Victorian Age "is a ready aesthetic sensibility that has both empirical and intuitional sides"(Engell 143), involving an epistemological stance. It is a moral sentiment to thinkers such as Shaftesbury, Francis Hutcheson, David Hume, Adam Smith, etc., who made not reason but feeling the basis of moral perception, thus putting great stress upon the faculty of sympathy—an innate nature of man that makes moral understanding dependent upon feeling sharing and imagination. They expected it to counter Thomas Hobbes' advocating that human beings are naturally egoistic and are hostile towards each other. Sympathy at this time period arose from the necessity of sociability, yet the limits of human understanding was ignored or circumvented. This question was a central preoccupation in the eighteenth-century philosophical discussion of sympathy. That's why though the moral philosopher harbored an enthusiasm toward sympathy and struggled to find justification for it, they themselves were put into the tight spot. Meanwhile, their shifting the discussion to an aesthetical concern brought about a new perspective. This leaves room for the artists and aesthetics to secure their theories with a moral sense. Consequently, the adoption of the mechanism of sympathy theorized the aesthetic response and its moral relations together in the eighteenth and early nineteenth century.

Central to both aesthetic and social ethics, sympathy becomes a compelling subject for passions that may start understanding or communication. James Rodgers explains that the use of sympathy during this period can be concluded in the following three ways: sympathy serves as "an occult force, spurned by mechanistic science"; and it is "a useful physiological concept, revived by the mechanists and taken over by their opponents"; and it becomes "a social mechanism or sentiment important to moral philosophy". (Rodgers 134) The first usage refers to the magic operation of how two apparently different people seek each other out; the second one explains the nature of the relationship between various organs of the body, and the third concerns Smith's claims that sympathy works as the moral glue which binds a society of isolated individuals together. ① This shows that sympathy is vital to relate the individual to the society. Although the concept of sympathy enjoys enormous popularity, its core weakness of the possibility of actually knowing the other's mind binds its

---

① See Roberts, Nancy. *Schools of Sympathy: Gender and Identification through the Novel*. McGill-Queen's University Press, 1997. 134.

way all along. Even in the Romantic period, such doubt never vanish among the poets, nor will it disappear amidst the novelists. For instance, in Mary Shelly's *Frankenstein*, sympathy fails to serve as a binding force between people, and virtues end up with isolation or futility. The figure of monstrosity she describes repels rather than evokes sympathy; moreover, the monster himself cries for sympathy every time he approaches man, yet fails always. So when the Victorian Age came, sympathy, if there is a choice to survive, has to go through some changes. "While eighteenth-century philosophers were primarily concerned with sympathy as a kind of social adhesive, nineteenth-century writers often saw it as a potentially useful way to motivate acts of generosity and care." (Albow 1150) Their solution is to combine the notion of sympathy with novel theories and amplifies its aesthetic force.

  The nineteenth-century meaning of sympathy, while still retaining some of its previous connotations, took on a decidedly Romantic cast. Thus, while retaining its social sense as an agency which could transcend individuals' isolation and help bind them together, sympathy began to be seen as primarily ***an aesthetic force.*** [1] In other words, poetry and art, or more precisely the vision of the *poet* or *artist*, were considered to be the primary means of exerting and experiencing sympathy. Sympathy came to mean a projective identification, a method of achieving imaginary or artistic union. (Roberts 60)

  The projective identification needs man's epistemological power to differentiate the boundary between the self and the other.

---

[1] The italic and the bold are intentional. Walter Jackson Bate also recognized that sympathy as the imaginative projection is crucial to Romantic aesthetics; and sympathy in Victorian criticism, maybe in a humbler way, hesitated the very specific meaning. See W. J. Bate, "The Sympathetic Imagination in Eighteenth-Century English Criticism", *English Literary History*, xii (1945): 144-164.

To the Victorians, George Eliot included, the aesthetic power of sympathy needs to be fully explored to maintain the autonomy of the self and the integrity of the other, so as to achieve a harmonious accordance between the inner and the outside world. In a period of rapid development of science and machinery, the sympathetic process makes art the best tool to reconstruct the divisive self with the limitless potentiality of humane care.

1.4 Sympathy as the "Extension of Sympathies" in the Victorian Novel Theory

Sympathy and social feeling for fellow creatures described by Hume and Smith constitute core elements of the enlightenment moral philosophy and the subsequent English philosophy. This nearly automatic association of spontaneously shared feelings with socially beneficial action transmits to the Victorians, who were to develop the romantic idea of the sympathetic imagination into a device for personal and social renovation. It is known to us all that in the 1830s Britain witnessed the spectacle of poetry losing its glory. With the vivid characterization, rich plot and relatively flexible creative approaches, English novels born in the Renaissance became a mature form of literature, providing consolation for people struggling in the pre-industrial and industrial society. Novel reading thus enjoyed great popularity among the literate and the rising middle class, serving as the main occupation for "lighter hours".

Being confronted with the faith crisis and the subsequent moral decline, the Victorian society had to figure out some substitute to comfort man's soul, and the novel was expected to fulfill such a mission. The social or moral responsibility undertaken by religion now falls on literature. For instance, the Victorian icon Matthew Arnold suggests that literature takes the place of religion and philosophy to provide emotional support for people losing their confidence in faith. As a response, novel writing became a social wide phenomenon, and G. H. Lewes in **1847** in his article—"The Condition of Authors in England, Germany and France" even asserted: "Literature has become a profession, it is a means of subsistence, almost as certain as the bar or the church." (Lewes **285**) However, in the earlier stage and mid-nineteenth century, the cruel fact is that the novel was still seen as "amusement rather than an art" (Stang x). In order to justify the position of the novel, the first job for many Victorians, especially Victorian novelists like George Eliot and her life companion G.H. Lewes, George Meridith, Anthony Trollope and so on, is to "argue the case for fiction as a fully serious art form" (Eigner and Worth **3**). ①

1.4.1 Novel as an Art

As mentioned above, one of the significant orientations of the Victorian literature and art is to help people suffering from the faith crisis to preserve the tradition while exploring ways and means to establish a modern nation, so the elites emphasize much on the shaping force from cultural influence, hoping literature and art to deploy an irreplaceable power to nourish self-integration, or if it is possible, even unite the whole nation. Under such conditions, the intellectuals and novelists devote themselves into a serious discussion of ways that the novel, like poetry or drama, as a literary form of serious art, accomplishes its function of bridging the self and the outside world and adjust the

---

① The mature Victorian criticism of prose fiction is said to start in 1830s, 1832 to be exactly, which is the year of Walter Scott's death. Then it gradually "forged a coherent, if not a symptomatic aesthetic of realism". See Eigner, Edwin M., and George J. Worth, eds. *Victorian Criticism of the Novel*. Cambridge: Cambridge University Press, 1985.2.

relationship between them. "A genre which consciously divorced itself from philosophical interests and made virtues of its languid lack of aesthetic principles and its *ad hoc* mode of construction" (Eigner and Worth 2) could never fulfill the traditional functions of a leading art form.① So the critics tried to integrate the philosophical interest, aesthetic principle and the proper form into the making of the Victorian novel as a particular form of serious art.

Critics like G. H. Lewes firstly announce that the novel shares the principle of unity of actions or time with Drama. However, as a genre peculiar to itself, the novel is said to address the most enchanting and permanent kind of interest by Edward Bulwer-Lytton, and "it is gentle, vanquishing, and subdued" (Eigner and Worth 32). These intellectuals, therefore, inherit from the Romantic belief that the power of art is to excite noble feelings. Since novels serve people as a companion in the solitudary hours. "The novelist can appeal to those delicate and subtle emotions, which are easily awakened when we are alone" (Eigner and Worth 32), and they make novel an ideal tool for training and nourishing man's feelings or mind. By doing so, novel reading will help readers to promote or sustain the mind with imaginative intensity, emotional vigor and intelligence, which will restore the harmony of their faculty. Accordingly, the aesthetic effect of the novel could enter into details without meanness compared with other forms of art, which entrusts novel with an unrivaled power of describing nature, man, and feeling. That's why it "displays other and loftier beauties to the best advantage" (Eigner and Worth 23). And if the novelist "aims at loftier and permanent effect, he will remember that to execute grandly we must conceive nobly" (Eigner and Worth 26). With the detailed loftiness, the novel will stimulate readers' intense imagination, which leads them to organized

---

① The italic is original.

Chapter 1 Sympathy as a Continuous Historical Concept

inner harmony.

> He [novelist] will suffer the subject he selects to lie long in his mind, to be revolved, meditated, brooded over, until form the chaos breaks the light, and he sees distinctly the highest end for which his materials can be used, and the best process by which they can be reduced to harmony and order. (Eigner and Worth 27)

When the novelist projects his "materials" to the readers' mind, he also leads the readers to an anticipated harmony and order. This dramatic authority was seen as a "powerful instruments of virtues" to instruct the readers by example rather than percept (Stang 7). The Victorians treat this instrument as knowledge of man and their daily life. And this integrates novel with abundant philosophical thinking and profound knowledge, or in other words, the novel provides a significant epistemological way.

E. S. Dallas, a famous Victorian "man of letters" and an incisive critic addressed: "After all, the question of supreme interests in art, the question upon which depends our whole interests in art is, what are its relations to life." (Dallas 287) Compared with the mechanism or evolutionary determinism which was prospering under the name of scientific discovery in the Victorian Age, novel reveals nothing but the mystery of human life, for "the real subject matter of novels is the human mind, 'internal history'" (qtd. in Stang 36). Novelists and artists show readers the universal experiences with vivid examples, and unfold the mysteries of human nature, to wake up man's freedom in face of "scientific determinism and show man that he can control his own actions through knowledge" (Stang 36). In this sense, the novel reminds man of his power and his right as well. It fills the readers' minds with love of virtue and impels the soul to go after goodness. Nor are these all, novelists like George Meredith even has much higher ambition, he believes: "Close knowledge of our fellows, discernment of the laws of existence, these lead to great civilization." (qtd. in Stang 77) As a response to this appeal, the best novel of this period, is nothing but the work "directed towards his own and his reader's self-knowledge, and not amusement in the sense of escape from oneself" (Stang 34). For the realization of this aim, the Victorian novelists and intellectuals need to present the novel in its best form, to let the readers know the real and feel the true. And a true picture of life invites the discussion of an aesthetic theory of realism.

1.4.2 Art as Realism

The Victorian critics believed that the real art of this time period should present convincing pictures of life. Thus a humble and faithful representation of nature in art will appeal to "the observant and reasoning faculties" of the readers (qtd. in Stang 146). If the novel is aimed to represent life as it is, it needs to be like a biography, providing an account of life vividly and truly. That's why the novel is by no means a romance that involves man's pure imagination. Novel then is expected to be a mirror, reflecting things projecting onto its surface. and the truthfulness refers to the "objects in the exterior world mirrored exactly in the work of art" (Stang 160). To achieve this, it needs not only to delineate the external reality but present a vivid picture of man's emotional life. For the truth of visuality and truth of feeling are two reliable bases for realistic art. The fact is all realistic arts are not the mere copy of nature or of man's ordinary life. Art "lift it above imitation and raise it to its highest level. These are mind or thought, imagination, and emotion" (Thomas 5). Novelists thus "drew from life, having studied human nature, in all its varieties, as it is, and not through the distorting medium of their own fanciful conceptions" (qtd. in Stang 152). In short, realistic art somewhat presents an ideal outlook while it is basically realistic. "The highest art is the nearest approach to nature", so what realistic writings exactly provide is an approximately "realistic probability". (qtd. in Eigner and Worth 8)

Realism, as an aesthetic activity, then calls on representing the real yet permitting a distance from the real as well. "The truthfulness of the work of art is not measured by how successfully it eliminates point of view and subjectivity from the representational space, but rather depends on the mediating role played by empiricist subjectivity." (Garratt 74) The reality in realistic art then becomes an "experiential reality", as G. H. Lewes ever put it. Perhaps for this reason, the realist novels enable people to go through a wider range of experience than which their actual life permits. Novels afford chances we live in the lives of others and enable us "to pass by sympathy into other minds and other circumstances" (qtd. in Stang 66). Such an experimental process offers a new way of improving man's knowledge of himself. E. S. Dallas, in *The Gay Science*, one of the major works on critical theory in the Victorian period pointed out that no one "is better employed than he... who widens through fiction the range of our sympathies and teaches us not less to care for the narrow aims of small people than for the vast schemes of the great and mighty" (qtd. in Stang 66). It is through sympathy generated in novel appreciation that makes the private individual be "invested with a new importance" (qtd. in Stang 66). Under this mode of knowing, "knowledge of human nature is not to be obtained through observation, but through sympathy" (qtd. in Eigner and Worth 14). Sympathy then, the keyword to waken men constrained by selfish interests in the Victorian age, becomes "essential to the epistemology of realism" (Eigner and Worth 14). And the best novelist of this time period must associate the notion of sympathy with their works.

Except for the fact of presenting the true appearance of nature and society, realistic art strongly relies on the truth of feeling. For G. H. Lewes, "the joys and sorrows of affection, the incidents of domestic life aspirations and the fluctuations of emotional life, assume typical forms in the novel" (Lewes, "The Women Novelists" 49). So realism is also a realistic portrayal of true feelings. The vivid representation of this complex and inner texture always marks the finest nineteenth-century fiction. This belief results in a consensus among artists that art should embody enormous feelings and the feeling made art a fine tool to feed the individual situation.

Since the intensity of feeling marks the excellence of a Victorian novel, the mechanism to feel it must be stressed. Back in the romantic period, William Hazlitt (1778-1830) ever suggested the term "gusto"' to describe the intense feeling and awareness associated with a particular object or idea, which means feelings will be aroused through the power of imagination. When appreciating an artistic work, "the mind does more than examine an object, it embraces it until the last iota of pleasure and pain is wrung from the embrace and its associations" (Engell 204). What needs to be pointed out is that all emotions felt when experiencing the aesthetic contexts as genuine emotions, but all these feelings are a self-centered thing, and feeling alone cannot balance the sensual and intellectual faculties, nor could it be translated into thought or action. The moral aspect and function of the novel this time reset much upon the fact of regulating feelings and emotions. So in order to make feeling felt or to let the feeling be sublimated, there needs an organizing principle. Sympathy as a medium is thus highly inspired.

1.4.3 Realism as the Extension of Our Sympathies

When the Victorian age came, it is obvious that sympathy either acting as quality of novel writing or as a medium to connect the private

Chapter 1 Sympathy as a Continuous Historical Concept

and social spheres, has long been investigated and explored, which resulted in an established fact that the association with art and sympathy has been a natural and taking-for-granted thing:

> Throughout the nineteenth century writers, painters, and musicians allow themselves to be inhabited or haunted by their immediate predecessors and contemporaries; the notion of sympathy is not some vague formula, but amounts to the very *etat d'esprit* (state of mind) that presides over artistic creation as such. (Ellison 89)

So the notion of sympathy has been wildly emerged into the blood and thought of Victorian artists and contributed much to the process of making novel a form of art. This consequently made the concept of sympathy a widely discussed term in Victorian criticism.

Isobel Armstrong in his book *Victorian Scrutinie* lists some evaluative words about Victorian criticism to describe the literary quality: words used frequently include "human", "sympathy", "the sympathies" (often linked with "human"), "the affections" or "feelings", so on and so forth. These words seemingly have nothing to do with artistic qualities (6). Besides that, Isobel Armstrong also notes:

> Flagrantly moral and even more flagrantly uninformative. Much less easy to grasp is the use of the word "sympathy", or "the sympathies", another almost imperceptible word in the Victorian critical vocabulary, yet one of the most powerfully evaluative words that could be used. (8)

This means even though the quality of "sympathy" has emerged into the blood of Victorian literature criticisms; admittedly it is also an intangible and obscure word for scholars and critics to grasp. So in order to restore the intact appearance of sympathy in the Victorian Age, figuring out the traits of the characteristic operation of sympathy might be a preferable choice.

The Victorian novelists generally enabled the readers "to pass by sympathy into other minds and other circumstance", so art could affect moral construction and make people "wiser and large-hearted," and the relationship between art and morality as Shelly has ever claimed could be achieved someway (Stang 66). The combination of the doctrine of sympathy and Victorian novel theories made fiction then as "a profoundly enriching exercise in making us *know* emotionally and imaginatively the things we *already know*. The central and commonplace experiences and truisms of life are to be reanimated into central truths" (Armstrong 25). In short, sympathy in the Victorian age now is more like a social agent which firmly involved with social and moral requests. It is known that Britain went through one of the most important periods of modernization in her history ever in the mid-nineteenth century, and it brings industrialization and urbanization into the country at a speed never before possible, which dragged the whole country into the mud of noise and turmoil. The famous psychologist James Sully believes that noise would become a perilous threat to the civilized mind. In his essay "Civilization and Noise" (1879), he points out that the noise produced by London's working-class would impair the sensibilities of the educated classes, and then Sully calls for attention to the nourishment of man's mental world. In "George Eliot's Art" (1881), Sully particularly suggests that Eliot, as a novelist, carries exceptional powers of sympathy and provides a "transparent medium" which asserts influence onto the reader's mind.

The mind provides sensibility to feel others, which is vital to any harmonious society. "The novelist can appeal to those delicate and subtle emotions, which are easily awakened when we are alone, but which are torpid and unfelt in the electric contagion of popular sympathies."

(Eigner and Worth 32) In this way, the Victorian novel became a didactic tool by cultivating noble feelings instead of direct moralizing by stimulating the psychological and physiological responses of readers. That is to say, fiction requires some manipulative power, and this force is deeply rooted in the impact on people's feelings. Consequently, the mechanism of sympathy is once again widely embraced and highly valued. Novelists, using their wit to project themselves into different feelings and situations, "is always associated with this more liberal view of sympathy—not so much because it established the autonomy" of their arts, but as because "it granted a more flexible notion of the far-reaching humanizing power of art". (Armstrong 59)

As discussed in the previous section, Novel provides an ideal way to offer self-knowledge for people and help restore their belief in life; for George Meredith, "science cannot help man in this job of knowing himself; all it can show is his relation to other animals ... mechanistic physics and Darwinian biology, [are to] deny man's humanity and freedom" (qtd. in Stang 35). So the duty of the novelist is to reaffirm human freedom and work on revealing "close knowledge of our fellow, discernment of the laws of existence, these lead to great civilization... the novel, exposing and illustrating the natural history of man, may help us to such sustaining roadside gifts" (Meredith 398). If man, by reading the novel, acquires intelligence and self-knowledge which may serve as an evolutionary force, he will shake off the rule of "the survival of the fittest", and he will transcend physical limit and enjoy spiritual freedom. He can control his present and direct his future. And all these realizations of such aims depends on the novelist's ability to extend our sympathies.

Based on the discussion of sympathy as a continuous historical concept, it is not difficult to see that sympathy can be a half intuitive and half empirical conception occupying the most significant part of man's moral and aesthetic pursuit. The moral connotation is too didactic, and pure aesthetics is metaphysical, for these two are always entangled with the epistemological problems, that is to say, the realization of sympathy in moral and aesthetical aim relies on the degree we know the nature and the other person. If the previous thinkers choose to ignore or circumvent the fact, the Victorians can't escape from it for it has emerged profoundly into the novel theories. In Victorian criticism, sympathy serves as a ready aesthetic sensibility that has both empirical and intuitional sides. Since it has been attached with much aesthetic sense for the imaginative act of identification with feelings between writers and readers, if the Victorians expect to step into the shoes and make the realistic novel an art for epistemological acquirement and dedication through the extension of sympathy; it needs to handle sympathy with a proper connotation:

> The wide use of sympathy while discussing novel writing indicates the nature of the moral basis of Victorian theories of art. The morality of Victorian criticism depended much on the way in which the notion of sympathy could be interpreted and operates. The morality of Victorian criticism depended almost exclusively on the way in which the notion of sympathy could be interpreted and it is through subtly changing, diverse and even conflicting interpretations of the word. (Armstrong 25)

Although many critics and novelists in the Victorian Age have noticed or discussed the notion of sympathy, it is George Eliot who realizes a combination of both theory of sympathy and the artistic practice. George Eliot devotes an affirmation, hesitation and reflection to the exploration of sympathy based on absorbing the previous ideas. She grasps the subtle changes, and the "diverse and even conflicting interpretations" of it (Armstrong 11), yet treats it as a social agent or an organizing force without any swaying. She expects to bring society into a dynamic and mobile mode in which thoughts and feelings could be exchanged and communicated. Sympathy as both an end and a method, under the hand of George Eliot, launches a survey for ways to integrate the potentiality of cognition, aesthetics and ethics. She thereby "represents a culmination of a discourse of sympathy" in the artistic domain (Redfield xi). Generally speaking, after the long line of evolution, "sympathy requires seeing other people as we see ourselves, sharing and understanding their situations, and changing places with them in our own imagination" (Graver 264), and it needs identification of others' situation and involves an agreement with it. However, it is not very long before Eliot detects the variation of man's intelligence and understanding. The maze of relationships among "the aesthetic of realism, the theory of perception, the consequences of an embodiment for the problem of knowledge, and the tension in relativism between situatedness and the aspiration for transcendence" seems too tough to handle (Garratt 38). Combining the special context of the Victorian era, George Eliot cherishes the affective aspect of literature and the aesthetical implication of sympathy, regarding sympathy as a power with constant evolution transferring through the fields of epistemology, aesthetics and moral philosophy by sublimating feelings and sensation. George Eliot saw sympathy primarily as an evolutionary spirituality, persuading the self to accept the difference or the unknowability of the other, or satisfying the self with deliberate moral stupidity, so as to enable the self to obtain a secular or spiritual self-discovery and transcendence from the mundane travails or the earthly desire. Sympathy then became a notable ethical resource pertaining to conscious will and self-control while facing the sublime unknown or feeling the sublime smallness as an atomistic individual in the wide social body. With the operation of sympathy, the anti-social passion is sublimated into an aesthetic principle so that the self will be restored into autonomy for achieving harmonious integrity with the society, and the society will recover as an organic body with numerous regulated individual mentalities.

Chapter 2
The Realism-cum-sympathy Aesthetics in *Adam Bede*

The previous chapter has outlined the general history of the notion of sympathy and its connection with the birth of Victorian novel theory. The Victorians are thus known to have paid much emphasis on the realistic writing and attached great importance to sympathy. Among all Victorian novelists who show interest to include sympathy into their realistic arts, George Eliot seems to be the most outstanding one for having investigated both sympathy and realism and the possible ways to integrate them into a unified whole. That is why she has accomplished a "culmination" for the exploration of sympathy (Redfield xi).

When the term of realism is referred to in art at present, it is expected to be the journalistic techniques to make the literature something close to real life with facts or general stereotypes of human nature, and what worth noting that George Eliot is the first person to define this term. [1]"Although [Eliot] has often been faulted for excessive moralizing

---

[1] According to Caroline Levine, Eliot in 1856 reviewed the work of John Ruskin and defined the prominent word of "realism" although *Oxford English Dictionary* names John Ruskin as the first English writer to use the term. See Levine, Caroline. "Surprising Realism." *A Companion to George Eliot* Eds. Amanda Anderson and Harry E. Shaw. Chichester: John Wiley & Sons, 2013. 75.

and improbable plots, she is rarely excluded from studies of the realistic novel, looming large in critical assessments of realism from her own time to ours" (Levine, "Surprising Realism" 63). In this sense, "grasping the specificity of Eliot's realism, then, might get us to something like the heart of Victorian realism" (Levine, "Surprising Realism" 63), or the heart of sympathy since "the notion of sympathy has become the very '*etat d' esprit* (state of mind)" in Eliot's arts (Ellison 89). She not only initiates the term of realism but also enriches the implication of it by presenting the realism-cum-sympathy aesthetic, which provides a fresh understanding of the 19th century affective aesthetics in which the external forces and consciousness reacted with each other to present an ideal aesthetic form. ① Such combination is perfectly manifested in Eliot's *Adam Bede*.

Realism begins as a literary movement both in response to and as a departure from the idealism in the Romantic period. It is characterized by recreating reality as it is. Moreover, it places emphasis on describing the material and physical details of life, as opposed to the natural world characterized by the Romantic poets. Many Realistic novelists divert their attention away from the softer aspects of Romanticism like intense sentimentalism because they believe that those characteristics will misrepresent the harsh realities of real life. They then start to pay attention to the ordinary people in the ordinary situation and present them faithfully. "Realism achieves critical mass in 1856, the year George Eliot turns to write fiction" (Duncan, "Realism" 835). George Eliot is perhaps

---

① Kerry McSweeney in *George Eliot: A Literary Life* (1996) proposed the notion of the realism-cum-sympathy aesthetic (49, 60), considering the fact that the fundamental principles of art and of morality are the same and that "in making clear to ourselves what is best and noblest in art, we are making clear to ourselves what is best and noblest in morals" to Eliot (50). It embodies Eliot's original artistic ideal for realizing her moral education through aesthetical edification in realistic art.

one of the most special ones among all Victorian writers for having written for the London periodicals from 1851 to 1858. She writes reviews especially for the *Westminster Review* from 1855 to 1857, during this time, her constant contacts with the excellent writers, intellectuals and the aesthetician of her time constantly and continuously reinforce her understanding of realism in art. Moreover, she becomes aware of the fact that the didactic lectures or moral mission and the aesthetical edification of the realistic art are to be realized by enlarging and stimulating the reader's sympathy. Then the creed of extending sympathy as a novelist's duty is testified and reaffirmed in Eliot's life-long writing career.

2.1 The Realism-cum-sympathy Aesthetic and an Enlarged Moral Awareness

In order to investigate George Eliot's understanding of sympathy and its integration with her realistic writing, we'd better examine her essay "The Natural History of German Life" (1856) and her review of John Ruskin's third volume of *Modern Painter* (1856). These works embody Eliot's original ideal as a novelist. Since then, "art has the moral and social function of extending our sympathies is one that informs her fiction" (Rignall 284), and she combines sympathy with her realistic aesthetics in novel writing for some moral purpose by thinking for others and devoting to the communal good.

2.1.1 Sympathy and the Moral Purpose of Art

George Eliot's essay "The Natural History of German Life" appeared in *Westminster Review*, in July 1856. It has long been considered one of the most important essays from Eliot for it "sets out the aesthetic principles and organic understanding of social life that were later to inform her fiction" (Rignall 284). The main theme of the essay is a review of two works by the German social historian Wilhelm Heinrich von Riehl, *Die Burgerliche Gesellschaft* (1851) and *Land und Leute* (1853). These are the first two parts of his book—*Naturgeschichte des Volks*, a pioneering "natural history" of German society. As an admirer of Riehl and his work, George Eliot makes up her mind and decides to make it more widely known in Britain, not only for its intrinsic merits but also "as a model for some future or actual student of our own [British] people" (*Essays* 147), and it also comes to become a model for Eliot to follow in her future writing career.

George Eliot then reviews Riehl's work in "The Natural History of German Life" by noting the difficulty in finding an accurate portrayal of the working class in fiction or in non-fiction for the previous artistic work has misrepresented them as "political and social theories" (*Essays* 142). In paintings, ploughmen, shepherds, and villagers are all "idyllic". Artists portray rural, working men and women not as they are, but as they think what they ought to be, so Eliot praises Riehl's works (both non-fiction) for providing a "natural history" of the German people, and in particular the real appearance of the German peasantry and their living state. As opposed to writers "of wide views and narrow observation" (*Essays* 142) who merely spread prejudice, Eliot calls on writers to contribute to the social reform through vivid description of the common people in their ordinary lives:

> If any man of sufficient moral and intellectual breadth, whose observations would not be vitiated by a foregone conclusion, or by a professional point of view, would devote himself to studying the natural history of our social classes, especially of the small shopkeepers, artisans, and peasantry... and if, after all this study, he would give us the result of his observations in a book well-

nourished with specific facts, his work would be a valuable aid to the social and political reformer. (*Essays* 147)

Through revealing things or people as what they are, the novelist may attract the reader's "sympathies" and let them be extended to the actual plight of the poor. The novelist furthers their moral development towards a state of caring for others. That is why "art is the nearest thing to life; it is a mode of amplifying experience and extending our contact with our fellow-men beyond the bounds of our personal lot" (*Essays* 145). In this sense, art in all its forms becomes a moral one. George Eliot defines the function of art and duty of the artist as shown below:

> The greatest benefit we owe to the artist... is the extension of our sympathies. Appeals founded on generalisations and statistics require a sympathy ready-made, a moral sentiment already in activity; but a picture of human life such as a great artist can give, surprises even the trivial and the selfish into that attention to what is apart from themselves, which may be called the raw material of moral sentiment. (*Essays* 144-145)

Sympathy provides moral sentiments, and then art attracts these sentiments through revealing common people's real state, taking along with a social and moral responsibility, so as to destroy people's self-absorption and attach their feelings to other creatures.

Sympathy and sympathetic imagination make such a process possible. In the moral and intellectual sphere, man has the power to "live for a higher object than his own happiness, the good for others" (Stang 41). That is why Eliot claims that "if art does not enlarge men's sympathies, it does nothing morally" (*Letters* III: 111). Art fulfills its moral and social functions by extending sympathy, and sympathy realizes the communications of people's feelings or passions represented in art for they can be felt and imagined.

> The only effect I ardently long to produce by my writings, is that those who read them should be better able to imagine and to feel the pains and the joys of those who differ from themselves in everything but the broad fact of being struggling erring human creatures. (*Letters* III: 111)

The process of feeling and imagining constitutes the core of the sympathizing process. As Rae Greiner has stressed that "sympathetic realism" is more like a "formal operation" than the affective content, through which the imagination composes a shared continuum of feeling and cognition amid the unknowable minds of others (*Sympathetic Realism* 18-19). Since art aims at extending our sympathies, paintings or novels mispresenting their subjects will direct the spectators' or the readers' sympathy to a false way. The idealized representation of the working classes is especially evil because it prevents true sympathy towards those who have extremely hard lives. So Eliot's aim is "to make matter and form an inseparable truthfulness" (*Letters* V: 374). She points out that Dickens's ability to capture the world's externals with "the delicate accuracy of a sun picture" (*Essay* 146) is impressive. She suggests, however, that Dickens does not accurately represent their "psychological character—their conceptions of life, and their emotions" (*Essay* 145). For Eliot, both the external and internal traits should be rendered with the same significance. As she expresses it in the early part of her career, "truthfulness" in literature or art involves not just physical replication, but also a copy of human existence and shared emotions. In the review of "The Natural History of German Life", and as in much of her future work, she would try to represent accurately both the external and the internal lives of the ordinary people. She regards this type of art as "realism", a word adopted by Eliot three months earlier while reviewing the third volume of John Ruskin's *Modern Painters*.

2.1.2 Realism and the "Aesthetic Teaching"

In April 1856, George Eliot reviewed the third volume of John Ruskin's *Modern Painters* and maintained that Ruskin's achievement as a critic lying in the fact that he places emphasis on the truth of nature:

> The truth of infinite value that he teaches is realism—the doctrine that all truth and beauty are to be attained by a humble and faithful study of nature and not by substituting vague forms, bred by imagination on the mists of feeling, in place of definite, substantial reality. (*Select Essays* 368)

Realism as a style of art is to make "a humble and faithful study of nature" and a truthful representation of it. When some Victorians insist that realism "refers to objects in the exterior world mirrored exactly in the work of art, is an inherent element in the nineteenth-century novel" (Stang 160), Eliot further responds in reviewing "The Natural History of German Life" to include the representation of the inner world of ordinary people in artistic representation. However, the inner world is hard to handle, and "a humble and faithful study of nature" is thus not enough to present the complexed reality. The mirrored reflection of life is also limited for "[t]he mirror is doubtless defective; the outlines will sometimes be disturbed, the reflection faint or confused; but I [Eliot] feel as much bound to tell you as precisely as I can what that reflection is, as if I were in the witness-box narrating my experience on oath" (*AB* 5). Since it is hard to reveal the exact truth, the realistic can only swear to tell the truth like a legal witness. This metaphor expresses the very hardness in revealing truth, both internal and external, in all realistic arts.

So the truth represented is nothing but what has been reflected into the novelist's mind, and there must be some distortion "when it [truth] is transformed—one should almost say translated, rather—into art" (Stang 160). Eliot admits that it is the duty of the novelist to keep this distortion down to a necessary minimum. In other words, although Eliot aims to reveal the true reality of mind and nature, she also keeps alert that it is hard to achieve. As Dolin claims that:

> The central problem for Eliot's realism, therefore—that it calls upon the authority of objective physical evidence, but cannot do so from any truly objective standpoint—is solved in essentially moral terms: truthfulness, once we accept that it cannot be fully achieved, is an even more urgent ethical responsibility. (Dolin 81)

That's why Eliot claims that art is "the nearest thing to life" rather than art is life. She then believes that art is "a mode of amplifying experience and extending our contact with our fellow-men beyond the bounds of our personal lot" (*Essays* 145). However, the literary realism with distortion is not the worst thing, for it leaves room for the aesthetic teaching as Eliot always expects.

Eliot emphasizes that fiction should present a true picture of real life. And it needs to be "the application of ideas to life" and provides "flash conviction on the world by means of aroused sympathy" (qtd. in Stang 166). Fiction for Eliot offers something that none of the dominant forms of Victorian thought like philosophy, theology, anthropology, sociology, political economy or even history could provide: ideas that were "thoroughly incarnate, as if they had revealed themselves... first in the flesh and not in the spirit" (*Letters* IV: 300). However, "in imaginative literature, temperament and sensibility are at least as important as ideas" (Mcsweeney 34), the art of this kind will help people transcend reality. A great imagination never falsifies reality but it is "at once the most precise and homely in [its] reproduction of actual objects, and the most soaringly at large in [its] imaginative combinations" (*Such* **195**). Eliot then anticipates fusing realism with the aesthetic teaching, teaching concerning "rousing the nobler emotions, which make mankind desire the social right" (*Letters* VII: 44). Such teaching cannot be reduced to formulation, for Eliot believes "aesthetic teaching is the highest of all teaching because it deals with life in its highest complexity. But if it ceases to be purely aesthetic—if it lapses anywhere from the picture to the diagram—it becomes the most offensive of all teaching" (*Letters* IV: 300). Now it's clear to Eliot that the very essence of art then rests upon its power in aesthetic teaching.

Although the Romantic sentimentalism should be banished out of realistic writing, ways to reveal the depictive truth should stay. "At the heart of Eliot's literary realism lies this quest for what we might call depictive truth. The quest is partly of Romantic lineage" (Henberg 24). As Eliot has reaffirmed this understanding in "The Natural History of German Life":

> The thing for mankind to know is, not what are the motives the moralist thinks ought to act on the laborer or the artisan, but what are the motives and influences which do act upon him. We want to be taught to feel, not for the heroic artisan or the sentimental peasant, but for the peasant in all his coarse apathy, and the artisan in all his suspicious selfishness. (*Essay* **145**)

Art reveals the apathy and selfishness of the common people like peasant or artisan, and the readers may understand those person's feelings and situations to deepen understanding and enlarge life experience of their own. Taking *Adam Bede* for instance, The narrator similarly finds a moral necessity to find a place for the common experiences of common people in the realm of art, adding that:

> It is so needful that we should remember their existence, else we may happen to leave them quite out of our religion and philosophy, and frame lofty theories which only fit a world of extremes... let us always have men ready to give the loving pains of a life to the faithful representing of commonplace things. (*AB* **198**)

Eliot then insists upon the same standard of realistic depiction for art as what she has been influenced by Riehl's social science. Her realism, thus, launches a survey of the human race "under the animist's knife" (qtd. in Eigner and Worth 3). To Eliot and most Victorians, it is the artist's responsibility to accurately interpret and represent reality. As the artist attempts to do this, he simultaneously depicts the anxieties, desires, and factors causing such emotional states as well. For example, the topic of nature is still focused upon, but realistic literature acknowledges the fact that the human mind is a separate entity from nature. Therefore, realistic literature aims to answer the question of how the mind can possibly know or understand nature accurately, and naturally, the complexed society becomes an important part of this nature, so is the other people's mind. This fact makes realistic writing an ideal tool for representing both the internal world and the external one and capturing particularly the crucial moment when these two collapse with each other.

Basically, that man obtains knowledge through experiences has been publicized since John Locke. The personal experience is severely limited but it serves as the first mode of learning and requires continuous amplifications. As a means of extending our experience, we are endowed with the capability of sympathizing with others. Through sympathy, we get a similar experience with the others and amplify our own cognition, and such cognitive activities are particularly stressed in art for art is an ideal way to enlarge our life experiences. In Eliot's advocates of realism, there is an inseparable relationship between realism, sympathy, and athletics, Kerry McSweeney in *George Eliot*: *A Literary Life* simply adopts the expression of the realism-cum-sympathy aesthetic to demonstrate the integration of the three.

> What is distinctive about Marian's employment of the criterion of realism is the way in which it is linked to questions of sympathy and fellow-feeling. The linkage is even closer in her first two fictional works, both of which contain extended passages of narratorial commentary promulgating the aesthetic of realism cum sympathy. (McSweeney 45)

Which means that the fundamental principles of Eliot's art and her understanding of morality are united to celebrate the same importance, when "in making clear to ourselves what is best and noblest in art, we are making clear to ourselves what is best and noblest in morals" (McSweeney 50). In short, the aesthetic of realism-cum-sympathy embodies Eliot's originate artistic ideal for realizing the moral mission of art through aesthetical edification, and the realistic feature of art depends very much on the vivid description of such process. So the following section will study how the aesthetic of realism-cum-sympathy is manifested in *Adam Bede*—a work in which "fairly a typical of the kind of interest and feeling the novel roused in the Victorians—a warm, generalized, largely in discriminate sympathy for all the characters" (Doyle 23). In this novel, the realization of the moral function and the aesthetical edification of realistic art is resting upon "lesson" of sympathy by figuring out the self's unspeakable and inarticulate suffering and that of the other.

2.2 *Adam Bede* and Adam's Inarticulate Suffering

2.2.1 *Adam Bede* as a Story in the Farmhouse

Adam Bede (1859) is the first full-length novel by George Eliot after finishing *Scenes of Clerical Life*—a collection of three novellas published in 1856. *Adam Bede* is not serialized in Blackwood's magazines but is published directly in three volumes, and it turns out to be a runaway success. The novel sets the social circumstance in a fictional village of Hayslope, and the story focuses on several local families and their interwoven lives. By that time Eliot has established her fame as an editor, essayist, and reviewer, but though, as she later reflected, "it had always been a vague dream of mine that some time or other I might write a novel", she feared she was "deficient in dramatic power". (qtd. in Collins 48) However, the huge success of *Adam Bede* and its attractive dramatic arrangements like seduction, infanticide or love romance prove Eliot that she has no need to worry for writing. "Although some reservations were expressed, the general response to *Adam Bede* was overwhelmingly laudatory" (Rignall 2). And to E. S. Dallas, *Adam Bede* is "a first-rate novel" (qtd. in Rignall 3). The critics praise highly the novel partly because "the farmhouse, not the country house, is at the center of *Adam Bede*, Eliot's first full-length novel, and this alone was a momentous departure in English fiction" (Parrinder 272). George Eliot, with her keen observation, presents a true life experience of common people like peasants, carpenters, etc. As what has been promised in the essay of "The Natural History of German Life", Eliot not only gives a vivid description of the external world around the farmhouse but also provides a detailed delineation of the inner activities of the characters.

In *Adam Bede*, Dinah Morris is a Methodist preacher who arrives in Hayslope to provide her service to the villagers. Mr. and Mrs. Poyser are her uncle and aunt with whom she has been living; Seth Bede and Adam Bede are brothers and work as carpenters. Seth loves Dinah, but she rejects his marriage proposal. Seth's brother, Adam Bede is a foreman at the carpentry shop which is owned by Jonathan Burge. Adam Bede is an honest, laborious, gentle and respected carpenter so Jonathan Burge wants him to marry his daughter, Mary. But Adam loves too much Hetty Sorrell, who is Mr. Poyser's niece and living with the Poysers, helping with the family chores. Unluckily, Hetty Sorrell is attracted by another handsome young man—Captain Arthur Donnithorne, a son of a landed local gentry.

Captain Donnithorne flirts secretly with Hetty after meeting her at the Poysers for the first time. They see each other in the woods many times and even develop a sexual relationship. Captain Donnithorne leaves Hayslope to rejoin his regiment and Hetty has to accept the marriage proposal from Adam. By the time Captain Donnithorne leaves, Hetty is pregnant, but neither of them knows it. The approaching date for marrying Adam and the unexpected pregnancy arrest Hetty in panic and she decides to meet Arthur, but she doesn't find him because the latter has already gone to Ireland. After giving birth to a child, Hetty leaves it in the forest to death and finally, she is arrested for infanticide. When Dinah visits Hetty in the prison, Hetty confesses that she hadn't killed the child intentionally and is eventually sentenced to be "transported". Finally, Adam realizes that he is in love with Dinah. He then proposes and the two get married. Captain Donnithorne at last returns back to Hayslope. He and Adam come to a reconciliation and stay to be friends despite of an unhappy past experience. At the last moment, the village of Hayslope recovers its regular serenity and harmony.

The whole story offers a vivid picture of the patrol realism of both nature and people living in it. The marvelous fact is that "while *Adam Bede* has its share of intense dramatic events, it also challenges the efficacy of these extraordinary moments as a means to connect with people and create sympathy" (Griffith 9). It is these dramatic moments at which sympathy leads the characters to know the world in the aesthetic of realism.

2.2.2 Hetty's "Limited Range of Music" and Adam's "New Awe and New Pain"

In *Adam Bede*, Hetty Sorrel is depicted as a "poor wandering lamb" (*AB* 75). She is beautiful; she is innocent; yet she is unimaginative, and most importantly, she is unsympathetic. Eliot compares man's soul to "those cunningly fashioned instruments" (*AB* 107). And Hetty's soul is always the one which has "only a very limited range of music, and will not vibrate in the least under a touch that fills others with tremulous rapture or quivering agony" (*AB* 107). In the village of Hayslope, Hetty cares about nothing and her connection with the world relies on two facts: her involvement with Arthur Donnithorne and her beautiful attraction to other villagers. But neither could afford her reliable way of knowing the human world. For the first fact leads her to meet Arthur secretly in the wood of beeches and limes, and the second fact makes her satisfied with her beauty and it reinforces her sense of ego-centricity.

> In a mind where no strong sympathies are at work, where there is no supreme sense of right to which the agitated nature can cling and steady itself to quiet endurance, one of the first results of sorrow is a desperate vague clutching after any deed that will change the actual condition. Poor Hetty's vision of consequences, at no time more than a narrow fantastic calculation of her own

probable pleasures and pains, was now quite shut out by reckless irritation under present suffering, and she was ready for one of those convulsive, motiveless actions by which wretched men and women leap from a temporary sorrow into life long misery. (AB 378)

Because there is no sympathy at work in Hetty's mind, her soul cannot reach out for other people and neither will hers be read by the others. She only calculates her own pleasure or pains a little, which makes her indulge in the fantasy for herself. She covers the facts of fornicating with Donnithorne and getting to be pregnant. Because of her habitual emotionless and self-closed way of life, her secret keeps undetected by the others. When she is sent to prison for infanticide, she still prefers to keep in silence.

Sympathy is to understand other people's minds and situations and translate them into one's own mind. In this situation, man needs to render in words to express the experience of the other and that of his own. When man "seem [s] emotionally impoverished, insufficiently responsive to the integrity of human feeling, which ultimately can be respected only by silence"(Adams 228), in this silent moment, man struggles to suspect his immediate sensory experiences and claims authority to his feelings. If man fails this process, it will lead to the failure of his sympathy. So the "moral development is charted in a struggle to find a more adequate vehicle for his more complex emotions" (Adams 230).

The moment Adam gets to know the unfortunate suffering of Hetty, he feels irritated. But he can't do anything. His pain and worry for Hetty intertwines and troubles him for the whole night. His thought of the suffering of Hetty in light of his own suffering, and there comes an epiphany on the morning of Hetty's trial:

Deep unspeakable suffering may well be called a baptism, a

regeneration, the initiation into a new state. The yearning memories, the bitter regret, the agonized sympathy, the struggling appeals to the Invisible Right—all the intense emotions which had filled the days and nights of the past week, and were compressing themselves again like an eager crowd into the hours of this single morning, made Adam look back on all the previous years as if they had been a dim sleepy existence, and he had only now awaked to full consciousness. It seemed to him as if he had always before thought it a light thing that men should suffer, as if all that he had himself endured and called sorrow before was only a moment's stroke that had never left a bruise. Doubtless a great anguish may do the work of years, and we may come out from that baptism of fire with a soul full of new awe and new pity. (AB 476)

In this episode, Adam's "deep unspeakable suffering" arrives at a new capacity for pity. Here, being newly "awakened to full consciousness" means being aware of the suffering of others and having a new-found ability to feel sympathy. "Adequate knowledge involves a movement away from the passions such as pity, but Eliot speaks, not of losing pity, but acquiring a newly deep feeling of pity" (Zenzinger 429). The case of Adam shows the process of "moving from a passion induced moral blindness to profound knowledge", "from a self-imposed separation from others to the recognition that true freedom requires other people" is worth studying, and that "individual suffering must be placed in the context of universal suffering". (Zenzinger 428) The newly born pity and awe help Adam make an "active resolution" that he wants to "go into court" and "stand by her". Sympathy, in this case, realizes both the transformation of feeling and the emergent of an action.

The contrast between Adam and Hetty shows that there is a close relationship between feeling and sympathy. Sympathy and the growth of higher feelings mean a new knowledge of both the other and the self. Compared with Hetty indulging in her own mental world and her habitual silence, Adam chooses to figure out ways to express his suffering and experiences a process of "rectification of his harsh character by suffering and learning to sympathize with the suffering of the others, even those who caused his pain" (Doyle 23). After passing into "an exaltation of precisely those states of mind that cannot be articulated, or even comprehended"(Adams 235), Adam finally finds new feelings and evolves his feelings into sympathy. Much importantly, Adam obtains a new understanding of other's world and that of his own.

2.3　Sympathy Transformed and the Growth of Higher Feelings

James Louis claims that "the Victorians felt driven by a moral imperative to understand their world" (Louis 30). That is what Eliot does want to accomplish in her writing. Then how man can obtain such knowledge becomes a problem for Eliot to investigate.

2.3.1　Sympathy and Feeling

"Sympathy and feeling are crucial, in George Eliot's view, not only for moral judgment, but also for knowledge in general" (Anger 82). K.M. Newton lays out that Eliot is convinced that feeling "is a means of knowledge" (Newton 52) under the influence of the Romantics. In order to fully reveal the fact that feeling and sympathy can provide man knowledge, Feuerbach's religion of humanity needs to be invited into this discussion. Sympathy is defined as "the one poor word which includes all our best insight and our best love" in *Adam Bede* (*AB* 546). This definition makes people couldn't help relating Eliot's sympathy with the Feuerbach's humanism, "for Feuerbach argues that benevolence, sympathy, and love—qualities Christianity attributes to God—are innate qualities natural to humans" (Griffin, "George Eliot's Feuerbach" 491). For many scholars, *The Essence of Christianity* particularly provides what Elizabeth Deeds Ermarth calls "the psychic conditions for sympathy" (Ermarth: 24).① Ermarth explains that "Feuerbach cherishes the 'qualitative, critical difference between men'" as a foundation for forging connections, and Eliot also theorizes how "any constructive action must be preceded by the recognition of difference" (Ermarth 25). And differences will offer the epistemological dimension for sympathy. If "any knowledge depends on the recognition of other minds" then "sympathy is essential to the ability to know anything at all". (Anger 116) The productive interplay of "sense" and "feeling" through sympathy realizes knowing.

> Feeling is sympathy; feeling arises only in the love of man to man. Sensations man has in isolation; feelings only in community. Only in sympathy does sensation rise into feeling. Feeling is aesthetic, human sensation; only what is human, is the object of feeling. In feeling man is related to his fellow man as to himself; he is alive to the sorrows, the joys of another as his own. Thus only by communication does man rise above merely egoistic sensation into feeling;—participated sensation is feeling. He who has no need of participating has no feeling. (Feuerbach 353-354)

The feelings turn to be introverted, and in sensations, man is

---

① Elizabeth Deeds Ermarth, Suzy Anger and Moira Gatens agree that Eliot's notion of fellow feeling responds to Feuerbach's suggestion that sympathy requires an individual to recognize the difference between, in Feuerbach's terms, "I" and "thou". See Ermarth, 25-26; Suzy Anger, *Victorian Interpretation*: 116; and Moira Gatens, "The Art and Philosophy of George Eliot," *Philosophy and Literature* 33.1(2009):78.

isolated, but the feelings are social. Sympathy with feelings will extend outward from the "egoistic sensation", and in feeling man can be related to his fellows and his fellows to him, thus man is alive to other peoples in feeling sharing.

For feeling is the innate power of God, so is sympathy. As what has been promised in the essay "The Natural History of German Life", all ideas originate in the "spirit", and it should be incarnated. Eliot then provides lots of sensory experiences to incarnate the formation of ideas through interchanging of feeling and sympathy. To Eliot, her "admiration for Feuerbach has sometimes been taken as evidence of her belief that certain knowledge is inaccessible, that all truth claims are illusory" (Anger 83). Although some knowledge is inaccessible, "certain knowledge is indeed possible through the senses" (Anger 83). As early as in *Scenes of Clerical Life*, Eliot expresses her belief in finding knowledge through sense.

> Ideas are often poor ghosts; our sun-filled eyes cannot discern them; they pass athwart us in thin vapour, and cannot make themselves felt. But sometimes they are made flesh; they breathe upon us with warm breath, they touch us with soft responsive hands, they look at us with sad sincere eyes, and speak to us in appealing tones; they are clothed in a living human soul, with all its conflicts, its faith, and its love. Then their presence is a power. (*SCL* 263)

Ideals can't be felt, neither can it be sympathized, but the incarnate sense can be felt and it will lead man to knowledge. The human sense like "breathing" "touching" and "speaking" will help our understanding of "warm breath" "soft responsive hands" "appealing tones". Without the aid of such "flesh" signals, the ideas will be hard to understand. At the same time, these ideas become dynamic once they are materialized, stemming from their freshly sensational state. Even beyond their anthropomorphic humanity, these fleshly ideas have "power" in their newly acquired "presence". In particular, they possess the power to be not merely sensory but involving sympathetic, humane care. With their "appealing tones" or "responsive hands", the incarnated ideas express an ever-reciprocated fellow feeling. Such incarnation of sense can also be seen in *Adam Bede*, in which there are people "whose faces I know whose hands I touch for whom I have to make way with kindly courtesy" (*AB* 199). It is through numerous senses that lead man to obtain knowledge with sympathy.

In *Adam Bede*, when Adam first appears in the story, the readers hear his voice singing a hymn, and from his high voice, his figure is guessed: "such a voice could only come from a broad chest, and the broad chest belonged to a large-boned muscular man nearly six feet high, with a back so flat and a head so well poised that when he drew himself up to take a more distant survey of his work." (*AB* 6) While Seth Bede is presented to the readers, the readers "see" him: "Seth's broad shoulders have a slight stoop; his eyes are grey; his eyebrows have less prominence and more repose than his brother's; and his glance, instead of being keen, is confiding and benignant". (*AB* 6) Moreover, the readers can "see that his hair is not thick and straight, like Adam's, but thin and wavy, allowing you to discern the exact contour of a coronal arch that predominates very decidedly over the brow" (*AB* 6). The character of these two brothers is presented to the readers by fully arousing their sensory cognition. Since the sense is the most direct medium for man to obtain knowledge, once the sense is convinced, man will be reaffirmed that he knows, and such knowledge is an essential way for people to generate sympathy.

Sense brings man direct knowledge, so is feeling. In *Adam Bede*,

Hetty lacks rich feelings, and she only indulges herself into a narrow fantastic calculation of her own pleasures and pains, and that is why she can't obtain knowledge through sympathy. However, when she is prisoned and is convicted to be guilty, she is so feared and trembled. And such feeling of fear becomes a medium and pushes her to communicate with Adam, and it is the first time Hetty gets to know Adam:

> When the sad eyes met—when Hetty and Adam looked at each other—she felt the change in him too, and it seemed to strike her with fresh fear. It was the first time she had seen any being whose face seemed to reflect the change in herself: Adam was a new image of the dreadful past and the dreadful present. (AB 514)

With the feeling of fear, Hetty looks at Adam, and the sad eye contact connects the two people. Adam's sad eyes remind her of her sad life experience. The dreadful past and the dreadful present hang over Hetty, and this becomes a new knowledge to her. She realizes Adam's pain she has brought to him and in his pain, she knows more about herself. Such knowledge is not a formulation of feeling equals feeling, but a feeling leads to the growth of higher feelings.

2.3.2 Sympathy Transformed and the Growth of Higher Feelings

In *Adam Bede*, Adam is described as a person of "strong conscience and the strong sense, the blended susceptibility and self-command" (AB 199), which makes him ready to feel what others are feeling or sense what others are sensing. His spiritual evolution by operating sympathy and feeling can be traced in his meeting with Arthur after Hetty is sentenced to be "transported".

Adam holds strong rage toward Arthur, for it's Arthur's fault to seduce Hetty and plunge her life into an abyss of chaos. His heart is broken the moment he thinks of Hetty's suffering. "Deep unspeakable suffering may well be called a baptism, regeneration, the initiation into a new state" (*AB* 476). He needs urgently to figure out his unspeakable, inarticulate suffering. This process is a transformative process of changing pain into sympathy.

> Let us rather be thankful that our sorrow lives in us as an indestructible force, only changing its form, as forces do, and passing from pain into sympathy—the one poor word which includes all our best insight and our best love. Not that this **transformation** of pain into sympathy had completely taken place in Adam yet. ①
> (*AB* 546)

The word "transformation" means the process of changing in form, appearance, nature, or character; or a process of converting one substance into another. To Eliot, the painful feeling cannot be destroyed, for it is an immediate primitive experience we receive from the outside world. However, it can be changed into other new forms of feeling like joy or pleasure through the working of sympathy.

When Adam realizes his pain of losing Hetty he goes to the Grove by Donnithorne Chase where he meets Hetty to propose. And it is also the same place where Arthur and Hetty make their secret meetings. In this special place that Adam unexpectedly meets with Arthur who is also troubled by the uneasiness for Hetty's suffering. Facing with Arthur, Adam is so obsessed with "sudden rage" and he is ready to knock him down. "These thoughts about Arthur, like all thoughts that are charged with strong feeling, were continually recurring" (*AB* 520). Different from the vigorous militant of "florid, careless, light of speech" in Adam's memory, Arthur displays all the "signs of suffering", and "Adam

---

① The word of "transformation" in bold here is intentional.

knew what suffering was—he could not lay a cruel finger on a bruised man" (*AB* 521). Adam restrains his rage and keeps the temporary calmness. When Arthur offers to invite the Poysers to stay in Hayslope and announces his decision to join the army, Adam couldn't repress his anger: "When people's feelings have got a deadly wound, they can't be cured with favours." (*AB* 523) Knowing that Adam has misread him, Arthur is also irritated, but this irritation is "subdued by the same influence that had subdued Adam's when they first confronted each other—by the marks of suffering in a long familiar face" (*AB* 524). The two man's rage toward each other is buffered when they realize that both of them are suffering from pain and both of them are irritated at the same time.

As to Adam, his feeling of pain helps him understand the suffering of Arthur who claims that "you would suffer more if you'd been in fault" (*AB* 525). Adam admits, "I've known what it is in my life to repent and feel it's too late. I felt I'd been too harsh to my father when he was gone from me—I feel it now, when I think of him. I've no right to be hard towards them as have done wrong and repent" (*AB* 525). It is the knowing of Arthur's pain and suffering that Adam overcomes an "inward resistance" toward Arthur. When the moment comes that Adam gets to know Arthur's regret and remorse for what he has done to Hetty, especially when Adam realizes that Arthur will "never know comfort any more" (*AB* 526), Arthur's intense pain and unspeakable suffering is clarified. Arthur confesses that "[he] couldn't get a full pardon—that [he] couldn't save her from that wretched fate of being transported" (*AB* 526). Neither will Adam, both of two young men are troubled by the same thing and are facing the same pain and torture. "[F]or the first time feeling his [Adam] own pain merged in sympathy for Arthur" (*AB* 527). Once sympathy is achieved, Adam eliminates his rage and recovers the trust in Arthur. This reconciliation episode shows that Adam evolves his temper into a universal love for his fellows. He then decides to make the world a bit better place for people to enjoy it. And sympathy, or at least through the operation of sympathy, Eliot makes Adam improve the knowledge of himself and his connection with people in the community.

It is not difficult to see that feeling realizes sympathy, and sympathy increases man's knowledge. "Adam is speaking about an increase of power, but this increase in power comes, not from a replacement of inadequate ideas with adequate ideas, but from the love of one human being for another" (Zenzinger 432).

> The growth of higher feeling within us is like the growth of faculty, bringing with it a sense of added strength. We can no more wish to return to a narrower sympathy than a painter or a musician can wish to return to his cruder manner, or a philosopher to his less complete formula. (AB 593)

Feelings are a growing faculty of man, together with a quick operation of sense. Feeling and sense bring man basic knowledge toward life, and this knowledge urges man to articulate the unbearable state of mind and suspect the immediate sensory experience so as to generate love or tolerance to other human beings. When at last Adam realizes that he has been attracted by Dinah—the devoted and devout Methodist preacher, the latter is afraid that her personal love may distract her piety and contribution to God. Adam replied:

> For it seems to me it's the same with love and happiness as with sorrow—the more we know of it the better we can feel what other people's lives are or might be, and so we shall only be more tender to 'em, and wishful to help 'em. The more knowledge a man has, the better he'll do's work; and feeling's a sort

o'knowledge. (AB 571)

Feeling others' pain will reinforce man's understanding of that pain and that man. To Adam, so is to feel the love. The more man feels love, the more man knows of love. Love, both divine and secular, is not contradicted with each other when it serves as a means toward knowledge. Till now, on Adam, a trajectory that it is sense and feeling that leads him to knowledge, knowledge for sympathy, and sympathy for love is clearly exhibited. But on the other main figure Dinah Morris, George Eliot also leaves space for "sympathetic divination" in which imagination becomes a critical element to operate sympathy.

2.3.3 Imagination and "Sympathetic Divination"

Since there are "certain knowledge is indeed possible through the senses" (Anger 83), this kind of knowledge should be inferred through imaginative power, as Feuerbach asserts:

> I extend the horizon of my senses by the imagination; I form to myself a confused conception of the whole of things: and this conception, which exalts me above the limited stand-point of the senses, and therefore affects me agreeably, I posit as a divine reality. I feel the fact that my knowledge is tied to a local stand-point, to sensational experience, as a limitation; what I feel as a limitation I do away with in my imagination, which furnishes free space for the play of my feelings. This negativing of limits by the imagination is the positing of omniscience. (Feuerbach 275)

Sensory experience to knowledge is somewhat limited. Then the expansive imagination will be invited to fill the "free space". The imagination as the catalyst that transforms a "limited" perspective into one that is "limitless". Eliot then expands this idea into her art to fully stimulate the imaginative potentiality and allows it to build up a sustained and symbiotic relationship with the sensory experience. Eliot parallels feeling and imagining as two faculties equally vital to her project of evoking sympathy. The aim of her writing is to help the readers "to imagine and to feel the pains and the joys of those who differ from themselves in everything but the broad fact of being struggling erring human creatures" (*Letters* III: 111).

Dinah Morris manages an ideal imaginative mode that has been cherished by Eliot. "She closed her eyes, that she might feel more intensely the presence of a Love and Sympathy deeper and more tender than was breathed from the earth and sky" (*AB* 173-174).① In solitude, She is "simply to close her eyes and to feel herself enclosed by the Divine Presence; then gradually her fears, her yearning anxieties for others, melted away like ice-crystals in a warm ocean" (*AB* 174). Dinah's imagination, that is, negotiates the fine line between allowing her sympathy to generate its own boundlessness and keeping this boundlessness under control. It is magnified by a singular sensory self to contact with the world outside. "She saw too clearly the absence of any warm, self-devoting love in Hetty's nature to regard the coldness of her behaviour towards Adam as any indication that he was not the man she would like to have for a husband" (*AB* 174).

In her solitude moment of imagination, she seemingly sees Hetty's coldness towards Adam and her unwillingness to marry Adam. This doesn't excite "Dinah's dislike" toward Hetty, however, she generates a sense of "deeper pity" instead. Such pity "had gathered a painful intensity; her imagination had created a thorny thicket of sin and sorrow, in which she saw the poor thing struggling torn and bleeding, looking with tears for rescue and finding none" (*AB* 174). In Dinah's

---

① The capitalized is original.

imagination, she sees Hetty's helplessness for being trapped in pain and sorrow, such emotional intensity urges her to feel Hetty's trouble, and this imaginative process reinforce her sympathy. "Dinah's imagination and sympathy acted and reacted habitually, each heightening the other" (*AB* 175). As a result, the omniscience of imagination shifts the sensory feeling with others into sympathy. With a combination of secular feelings and a divine force of imagination, Dinah got a keen knowledge of other people. For modern critics, "intellect and imagination are not separate faculties; that the highest knowledge is felt knowledge" (Dolin 88). Dinah knows clearly Hetty's nature but she simply sympathizes with her with love and tolerance. With the "sympathetic divination", Dinah can know others' inner world insightfully. After she returns back from prison, she meets with Adam:

> Dinah, with her sympathetic divination, knew quite well that Adam was longing to hear if Hetty had said anything about their trouble; she was too rigorously truthful for benevolent invention, but she had contrived to say something in which Hetty was tacitly included. (*AB* 130)

Dinah's keen feelings enable her extra sensory awareness of Adam's desire to know Hetty's information, but the true fact about Hetty may hurt Adam. With sympathy, she grammatically modifies her word and contrives not to mention Hetty's staff. On Dinah, sympathy with a divine imagination makes her even wiser and kind. This is the knowledge of man's self. For it is the intrinsic nature of man's imagination to connect knowledge with morality by somewhat reasoning and it is likely to reconcile the tension of the subjective and the objective. Like Dinah, she knows Hetty's vanity very well but she chooses to pity her weakness, in other words, she knows but not to disclose, and behind such epistemological activity reveals the infinite power of human care and the

Chapter 2 The Realism-cum-sympathy Aesthetics in *Adam Bede*

divine love.

From the above explanation, we've got to know that sympathy serves as a medium for man to understand their unspeakable mentality or emotional state. During such a process, sense, feeling, and imagination entwine with each other to realize some epistemological mission. When man pursues knowing he expects "a necessary condition for full knowledge" and "a sympathetic disposition will allow one to escape subjective bias, to see from other viewpoints, and so attain a sort of impartiality" (Anger 86). Adam's sympathetic process experiences a process in which he transforms his pain into sympathy, and sympathy for the universal love; and his pain is transformed into higher feelings. "The growth of higher feeling within us is like the growth of faculty, bringing with it a sense of added strength" (*AB* 593). This strength will invest our knowledge with moral implications.

Eliot's tremendous efforts to present the lives of villagers in Hayslope, the charm of every person is so irresistible that makes *Adam Bede* redeemed as "'a first-rate novel' whose author takes rank at once among the masters of the art" (qtd. in Rignall 2). Eliot extends her interest to "the faithful representing of commonplace things" (*AB* 199). Her conception of the essential goodness of human nature links the high moral vocation of the artist to evoke sympathy and fellow feelings. The common people with daily travails are all invited into the work. Their happiness, their sorrows and their efforts to get rid of painful experiences are also vividly revealed. To present those themes truly, she associates her effort with the artistic technique of the Dutch painting. The following section of this book intends to disclose how the technique of the Dutch painting makes the final shape of Eliot's realistic writing in *Adam Bede*, and how the Dutch painting styled realism may help extend man's sympathy.

2.4 Realism and the Humbly Faithful Dutch Painting

Adam Bede is an early example of the realism for which Eliot becomes celebrated and it offers the first systematic defense of her aesthetic of realism based on her understanding of sympathy. In *Adam Bede*, Eliot sets out her commitment to realism as a literary genre—to give a "faithful account" of things as they are, a commitment she will continue to develop during her whole writing career. She turns to early modern Dutch painting to justify her choice, so as to illustrate the quotidian life of the non-elite, and thereby provocatively extended philosophical and literary approaches to representation. In addition, "Eliot's celebration of the mundane reveals the sublimity of everyday experience" (Gould 404). In order to reveal how Eliot's principle of realism is highlighted by the technique of Dutch painting, we might as well, first of all, investigate what the notion of Dutch painting is.

2.4.1 Dutch Painting and the Detailed Realistic Style

In art, "Dutch Realism" is a rather loose term referring to the style of Dutch Baroque art that blossomed in the Netherlands after the final phase of the Eighty Years' War for Dutch independence (1568-1648). The representative artists include the humanistic canvases of Rembrandt, the ethereal genre painting of Jan Vermeer, and the precise still lives of Willem Kalf. In their arts, they offer a description of what Dutch life is like and contain an equal measure of reality and artifice. As to the birth of this kind of art, it can be treated as a realistic form of the Protestant art contrast to the Catholic Counter-Reformation Art — for it avoids the monumental themes or idealized splendor of High Baroque painting, and focuses instead on everyday themes portrayed in convincing detail. Unlike the grand, dramatic style of "high art" favored by Rome, Dutch realistic art is characterized by a more modest, down-to-earth approach. To put it simply, Dutch artists focus their attention on the ordinary Dutch people, Dutch houses and rural scenery to meet with the taste of the growing Dutch middle class (mostly merchants and traders) and reveal their livelihood or everyday life. The product is generally referred to as the "Dutch school" or "the Dutch painting" (Yeazell 2).

The Dutch painting enjoys popularity in the Nineteenth-century England and is especially welcomed by the novelist and the art critics. Leslie Stephen claims that the novelist needs the "Dutch painting of extraordinary minuteness" and George Henry Lewes seems to contend that Austen's "sympathy with ordinary life" is in the Flemish analogy (qtd. in Yeazell 2). To the critics, the novel also needs to present "scenes of common and domestic life" (Yeazell 22). Since Dutch artists offers an equal measure of reality and artifice, "Dutch painting as only a faithful imitation of mundane reality, devoid of any moral or spiritual meaning, was to see partially at best" (Yeazell 22). And to most nineteenth-century novelists as well as their critics, the everyday life should be redeemed. And above all, the charm of Dutch painting does lie in its potentiality to provoke man's power of sympathy:

> The Dutch school of art will ever be the most popular ... because it appeals to the popular sources of sympathy and wonder. Everybody has sympathy for the concerns of every-day existence— for the elegant repose of the lady at her toilet—for the joyous revelry of peasant life. Everyone has wonder for the excellence addressed to the eye. (qtd. in Yeazell 22)

In Chapter 17 of *Adam Bede*, Eliot stops unfolding her story a little and discusses the influence from Dutch painting on her writing by admitting "a source of delicious sympathy" in a type of painting that "lofty-minded people despise" should be valued in her realistic art.

2.4.2 Realism and the Dutch Painting in *Adam Bede*

Art is the subject defined by George Eliot in her 1856 essay "The Natural History of German Life": "[a]rt is the nearest thing to life; it is a mode of amplifying experience and extending our contact with our fellow-men beyond the bounds of our personal lot." (*Essays* 145) Art provides opportunities for people to contact people fellow-men and to extend their sympathies. she expresses this principle in the early stage of her writing career, 'truthfulness' in literature or art involves not just physical replication, but acknowledging ordinariness, rather than exceptionalism, at the level of human existence and shared emotions. In *Adam Bede*, these principles are clearly manifested:

> It is for this rare, precious quality of truthfulness that I delight in many Dutch paintings, which lofty-minded people despise. I find a source of delicious sympathy in these faithful pictures of a monotonous homely existence, which has been the fate of so many more among my fellow-mortals than a life of pomp or of absolute indigence, of tragic suffering or of world-stirring actions. (*AB* 196)

Eliot's admiration of Dutch painting is reinforced by the narrator of the novel. The narrator finds a source of delicious sympathy in these faithful pictures of everyday existence. To both the narrator and George Eliot, the depiction of common people under daily circumstances means too much.

[I turn] to an old woman bending over her flower-pot,① or eating her solitary dinner,② while the noonday light, softened perhaps by a screen of leaves, falls on her mob-cap, and just touches the rim of her spinning-wheel, and her stone jug, and all those cheap common things which are the precious necessaries of life to her—or I turn to that village wedding,③ kept between four brown walls, where an awkward bridegroom opens the dance with a high-shouldered, broad-faced bride, while elderly and middle-aged friends look on, with very irregular noses and lips, and probably with quart-pots in their hands, but with an expression of unmistakable contentment and goodwill. (*AB* 196-197)

In order to demonstrate the peculiar characters of Dutch paintings which impress Eliot so much, several pictures mentioned above are to be illustrated as follows:

Figure 2-1. Gerrit Dou: "Old Woman at the Window, Watering her Flowers" (1660-1665). Kunsthistorisches Museum, Vienna.

---

① This probably refers to the painting of "Old Woman at the Window, Watering her Flowers" (1660-1665) by Gerrit Dou.
② This probably refers to the painting of "Women Eating in an Interior" (1632-1637) by Gerrit Dou.
③ This probably refers to the painting of "The Wedding Dance" (1566) by Pieter Bruegel.

Figure 2-2. Pieter Bruegel: "The Wedding Dance" (1566). The Detroit Institute of Art, City of Detroit.

According to George Eliot, the ordinary people depicted in these Dutch paintings are not beautiful, but they are of "the other beauty", and "which lies in no secret of proportion, but in the secret of deep human sympathy" (*AB* 196-197). It is these arts that remind the viewers that there is a world of ordinary people sharing the "contentment and goodwill" of all human beings. Their simple way of life and their genuine humanity are of the same value to art presentation. So it is not difficult to conclude that two factors make Eliot fall in love with Dutch paintings: the faithful representing of the commonplace of the things and the power of provoking sympathy. The following section aims to find how these two facts are realized in *Adam Bede*.

Since art is the nearest thing to life and life is full of diversities and complicities, art should represent such diversities and complicities truly. Another most common fact is that life is made up of those people who share the similarity with us like "those old women scraping carrots with their work-worn hands, those heavy clowns taking holiday in a dingy pot-house, those rounded backs and stupid weather-beaten faces that have bent over the spade and done the rough work of the world" (*AB* 198). And they cannot be banished from "the region of Art"; on the contrary, "it is so needful we should remember their existence" (*AB* 198), which thus becomes the very essence of art.

> Therefore, let Art always remind us of them; therefore let us always have men ready to give the loving pains of a life to the faithful representing of commonplace things—men who see beauty in these commonplace things, and delight in showing how kindly the light of heaven falls on them. (*AB* 199)

Such representation of the ordinary people and their lives is what Eliot called in several essays "the working-day business of the world" of high art. She holds the opinion that the unexceptional lives of unexceptional people deserve attention, "not the comic, grotesque, or picturesque treatment they were usually accorded in traditional hierarchies of art" (Dolin 82). That mistreatment will direct men's sympathy in the wrong direction. "At its worst, Victorian culture waskitsch culture, a triumph of middle-class intellectual mediocrity" (Dolin 82). This kitsch culture comes from "lofty-minded people" and the idealistic friend. In their eyes, Dutch paintings present vulgar details. "What good is there in taking all these pains to give an exact likeness of old women and clowns? What a low phase of life! What clumsy, ugly people" (*AB* 196)! For George Eliot, the scheme of her writing is to correct this prejudice. And that is why *Adam Bede* is full of similarities from Dutch painting. And this comparison is particularly obvious in the opening section of the whole story:

> The Green lay at the extremity of the village, and from it the road branched off in two directions, one leading farther up the hill by the church, and the other winding gently down towards the valley. On the side of the Green that led towards the church, the

broken line of thatched cottages was continued nearly to the churchyard gate; but on the opposite northwestern side, there was nothing to obstruct the view of gently swelling meadow, and wooded valley, and dark masses of distant hill. That rich undulating district of Loamshire to which Hayslope belonged lies close to a grim outskirt of Stonyshire… (*AB* 19)

The scenery while approaching Hayslope is so fresh with a valley, cottage, and meadow, reminding us of the beautiful Dutch landscape paintings with the contrasting light and shade like a photo. The similarity is so obvious if the following two pictures are invited into comparison with Eliot's description of natural scenery in Hayslope.

Figure 2-3. Meindert Hobbema: "A Woody Landscape with a Cottage" (1665). National Gallery, London.

Figure 2-4. Meindert Hobbema: "Entrance to a Village" (1665). Metropolitan Museum of Art, New York.

By observing the above paintings, it will not be difficult to find that Eliot is influenced by the Dutch painting to reveal a detailed delineation of the village life. Moreover, she also gives a vivid description of ordinary people in the village who seem to stands beside the reader:

> Your true rustic turns his back on his interlocutor, throwing a question over his shoulder as if he meant to run away from the answer, and walking a step or two farther off when the interest of the dialogue culminates. So the group in the vicinity of the blacksmith's door was by no means a close one, and formed no screen in front of Chad Cranage, the blacksmith himself, who stood with his black brawny arms folded, leaning against the doorpost, and occasionally sending forth a bellowing laugh at his own jokes, giving them a marked preference over the sarcasms of Wiry Ben, who had renounced the pleasures of the Holly Bush for the sake of seeing life under a new form. (*AB* 19)

The villagers are hustling with the burdensome works and one is next to the other. These "clumsy" or more or less "ugly" people seem to be isolated from each other yet related to each other at the same time. The pictures are so fleshly and dynamic that it will be easy to touch the viewers. Of course, it is not just "a need for picture, in other words, that drew the beginning novelist [Eiot] to the model of the Dutch" (Yeazell 117). Sympathy and feeling embodies in these pictures is the very thing that George Eliot cares. The impulse of Eliot's art is to "dissolve the satire in demands for sympathy" is worthy of a particular examination (qtd. in Yeazell 117).

The character of "truthfulness" in literature or art involves not just physical replication, but appeals for ordinariness, rather than exceptionalism, at the level of human existence and their shared emotions. "Human feeling is like the mighty rivers that bless the earth: it does not wait for beauty—it flows with resistless force and brings beauty with it" (*AB* 198). With the technique of Dutch painting, Eliot aims to evoke the sincere feeling of the fellow being as a binding force for human beings. "It is our habit to say that while the lower nature can never understand the higher, the higher nature commands a complete view of the lower. But I think the higher nature has to learn this comprehension, as we learn the art of vision..." (*AB* 177) This is the reason why, in *Adam Bede*, Eliot praises Dutch genre paintings so much. Their faithful representation of a monotonous homely existence demands that art should always remind people of "the other beauty". To find the beauty on these people man will generate human feeling toward them, and emotional feeling working with imagination becomes the basic mode to generate sympathetic understanding. In reviewing Ruskin's *Modern Painters*, Eliot insists that the fundamental principles of art and of morality are the same and "in making clear to ourselves what is best and noblest in art, we [readers] are making clear to ourselves what is best and noblest in morals" (*Selected Essays* 368). It is in Dutch painting that man finds beauty, and it is in Eliot's novel man finds sympathy, consequently, in art, men find moral inspiration.

To sum up, George Eliot strives to depict a mundane reality in which our sympathetic understanding of the ordinary people is illustrated in *Adam Bede*—her first long novel. She describes it as "a country story—full of the breath of cows and the scent of hay" (*Letters* Ⅱ: 387) in which the principle of realism is best manifested as a kind of faithful representation of commonplace things. The aim of such an unsentimentally realistic and unidealized artistic representation of common people is expected to extend our sympathies, and sympathy realizes epistemological expansion and moral consciousness.

During this process, every man is always confronted with intense emotional suffering beyond words, sympathy then serves as a vehicle for him to figure out his complicated emotional state by transforming pain into sympathy. It is a procedure of exaltation of the states of mind which can't be articulated or comprehended. In *Adam Bede*, Eliot holds an ideal of realism-cum-sympathy aesthetic in which sense and feeling lead people to know himself or speculating other's situations, and this knowledge urges him to sympathize. The growth of the mind is realized by the growth of higher feelings of love and tolerance. *Adam Bede* then seemingly demonstrates an ideal routine in which sympathy brings knowledge and knowledge invites moral awareness. However, the complex conception of feelings, the instability of mind and the difficulty of revealing them in art make sympathy far from being an ideal notion. Eliot soon discovers that responsiveness or feeling for others may be overwhelming and hard to handle.

>[Eliot] altered the nature of her plea for sympathy with ordinary people as she had expressed it in *Scenes* and *Adam Bede*. Her new cautiousness and skepticism about sympathy—even her

warning about its dangers, as seen in the preternaturally knowing Latimer in *The Lifted Veil*—accompanied the less accessible, more experimental, textual and aestheticized prose of her late novels. (Henry, *The Life of George Eliot: A Critical Biography* 124)

So the following chapter aims to make a survey on Eliot's unusual novella—*The Lifted Veil*, in which the epistemological mode that the direct sensory contact through sympathy may promise a reliable pathway to knowledge or a safeguard for morality remains to be discussed and reflected if it is not to be subverted.

Chapter 3
Sympathy and the Epistemological Relativism in *The Lifted Veil*

George Eliot's artistic ideal is to present a truthful picture of the ordinary people in the common circumstances, and that is what she has accomplished in her first two pieces of work: *Scenes of Clerical Life* (1856-1858) and *Adam Bede* (1859). In these two works, the pastoral realism under her craft is so marvelous that it wins her fame and reputation. With the success of these two works, Eliot's ideal that sympathy may fulfill the duty of directing man's egoism and private feeling to a larger wholeness of community and society is tested and verified. Sympathy—"the one poor word which includes all our best insight and our best love" (*AB* 546), succeeds in passing from pain into sympathy by imaging or entering into the mind of others based on the similar experience of one's own. To Adam in *Adam Bede*, as well as to George Eliot, the world is knowable and understandable through sympathy. Other's pain will be perceived in analogy to our own miseries, and our pain will change its form "passing from pain into sympathy" (*AB* 546). However, such ideal is shattered along with the publication of Eliot's novella—*The Lifted Veil*, in which "the optimistic and sympathetic impulses of her early works were encroached upon by extreme and bitter doubts" (Mahawatte 28). George Eliot increasingly finds that full identification of other's situations doesn't mean entire agreement with it, and the absolute knowledge of the other will unexpectedly damage man's power of sympathy; for any knowledge obtained without the safeguard of sympathy and human love will not lead to true understanding. She then introduces the issue of epistemological relativism into her sympathy-related consideration. And such consideration convinces Eliot that sympathy does not equal full knowledge, instead, the successful operation of sympathy relies heavily upon a somewhat epistemological "stupidity" or "ignorance". It concerns with comprehending the difference between the self and the other or admitting the unknowability of the others. That is why *The Lifted Veil*, "one of the most widely read and discussed works" among Eliot's entire work corpus (Small xi), serves as a crucial turning point at which Eliot reflects on the implication of the notion of sympathy. To Eliot, absolute knowing provides no difference between the self and the other, no space for imagination and no possibility of mental transformation for any individual, yet these elements are the very fundamental conditions for the effective operation of sympathy.

3.1 *The Lifted Veil* and Latimer's Nightmare

The Lifted Veil (1859) was written when Eliot thought her "head was too stupid for more important work" (*Letters* Ⅲ: 60), and it was originally published in Blackwood's *Edinburgh Magazine* (July 1859). Eliot's publisher Blackwood considered the story to be inferior to *Adam Bede*. For this reason, he persuaded Eliot to publish the story anonymously. It is such a special work by George Eliot that many readers felt at loss the moment they read it. While being asked by G. H. Lewes for the impression on *The Lifted Veil*, Edith Simcox confessed: "I was put out by things that I didn't quite know what to do with, it was a shame to give such things a moral." (Fulmer and Barfield 28)① However, G. H. Lewes finds it "striking and original" (Fulmer and Barfield 28). So, it would be necessary to give a general illustration of the striking and peculiar quality of this piece of work in advance.

3.1.1 *The Lifted Veil* as "an Outlier"

The story is devoted to its eccentric description of the controversial theories of mind like phrenology or animal magnetism, and physical medicine as blood transfusion or reanimation experiment. Totally different from the previous works *Scenes of Clerical Life* (1856-1858) and *Adam Bede* (1859) which focus on a simple, quiet and realistic part of the pastoral life, *The Lifted Veil* provides a delicate delineation into the inner world of people. To modern critics, it "springs from a visionary foreboding of our modern spiritual moribundity" (Pinion 122), and illustrates an artistic kingdom of "mystery and imagination" (Flint 95). As to the design of plots, it intertwines with the sin of murder and incest, the horror of death and resurrection, the mystery of prophecy and clairvoyance, which is by no means consistent with Eliot's attempt to reproduce the "faithful pictures of a monotonous homely existence" like Dutch paintings (*AB* 197), let alone character of realistic writing in its traditional sense. To her contemporaries and the following researchers, *The Lifted Veil* is such "an outlier in Eliot's works" (Kenneday 370). In 1873, Eliot's publisher Blackwood realized that *The Lifted Veil* had gained an unexceptionally increased admiration and therefore proposed to include

---

① Edith Jemima Simcox (1844-1901) is a British writer, trade union activist, early feminist and shirt-maker. She has been good friends with George Eliot and her soul mate—G. H. Lewes. In her unpublished Autobiography of a Shirt-Maker, she records her precious days staying with them.

this work in a collection of tales published by Blackwood. However, Eliot declined this suggestion:

> I think it will not be judicious to reprint it at present. I care for the idea which it embodies and which justifies its painfulness ... But it will be well to put the story in harness with some other productions of mine, and not send it forth in its dismal loneliness. There are many things in it which I would willingly say over again, and I shall never put them in any other form. (*Letters* V: 380)

Such an assertion reveals Eliot's cherishing this small piece of work and the urgency to discuss it by relating it with her vast artistic project as a whole. To George Eliot, "the value of realist representation lies in its power to prompt two responses: sympathy and knowledge" (Levine, "Surprising Realism" 63), and *The Lifted Veil* shuttles back and forth between these two ends, trying to figure out the predicament confusing both the protagonist Latimer and Eliot as a writer: whether the epistemological function that sympathy needs will enlarge man's sympathetic ability as the cognition promises, which seems to be a troublesome topic worthy of scrutiny.

The Lifted Veil tells of a horrible story that departs sharply from the usual realistic writing esteemed by British fiction tradition. It is "celebrated as the nearest Victorian successor to the more famous horror-story about scientific experimentation with death and life" like Mary Shelley's *Frankenstein* (1818) (Small xi). And it also begins with the most striking opening among all her other works:

> The time of my end approaches. I have lately been subject to attacks of angina pectoris; and in the ordinary course of things, my physician tells me, I may fairly hope that my life will not be protracted many months... If it were to be otherwise—if I were to

live on to the age most men desire and provide for—I should for once have known whether the miseries of delusive expectation can outweigh the miseries of true provision. (*TLV* 3)

This opening builds a dismal mood for the whole story, and the protagonist—Latimer in this story not only suffers from the pain of angina pectoris but also the misery of a bitter mentality, for he foresees his death:

For I foresee when I shall die, and everything that will happen in my last moments. Just a month from this day, on September 20, 1850, I shall be sitting in this chair, in this study, at ten o'clock at night, longing to die, weary of incessant insight and foresight, without delusions and without hope. (*TLV* 3)

Through the first-person male perspective, Latimer foresees the date of his death. It is so queer and unlike the realistic fiction for which Eliot is best known. However, such an opening successfully captures the readers' curiosity and guides them to a cognitive journey of mysterious experience to figure out: how and why? Along with Latimer's flashback and recollection, the aesthetic distance between the reader and the novella is gradually shortened, and the veil of the novel is also slowly lifted.

3. 1. 2   To Know or Not to Know: Latimer's Epistemological Predicament

Latimer, the narrator and the protagonist of this novella, is a sensitive intellectual with a weak bodily physique. His loneliness and arrogance make him always like a weirdo in the eyes of others. As the title— *The Lifted Veil* indicates: "To lift the veil is to peep at the forbidden, to access taboo knowledge." (Flint 456) Latimer is invested with the power to see into the future and read the thoughts of others after a serious illness. This "cursed" gift helps him to lift the veil covering people's face and get into their inner world; however, the following experience is surprisingly unpleasant:

> The rational talk, the graceful attentions, the wittily-turned phrases, and the kindly deeds, which used to make the web of their characters, were seen as if thrust asunder by a microscopic vision, that showed all the intermediate frivolities, all the suppressed egoism, all the struggling chaos of puerilities, meanness, vague capricious memories, and indolent make-shift thoughts, from which human words and deeds emerge like leaflets covering a fermenting heap. (*TLV* 14)

The ability to read others' minds does nothing good to Latimer's life. On the contrary, he feels bored for his absolute knowledge of other's evil and hypocrisy under the mask of friendliness and goodwill. Luckily, the arrival of Bertha Grant, the fiancé of Latimer's brother, intrudes into Latimer's oppressing and depressing life. She is the only one who escapes from Latimer's foresight and insight. In Latimer's omniscient world, Bertha is the "oasis of mystery in the dreary desert of knowledge" (*TLV* 18), saving him from the endless boring insights of the outside world. She seems to be covered with a veil, being detached from Latimer yet displaying an irresistible charm like a Siren.① While longing to know Bartha, the anxiety caused by the yearning for uncertainty satisfies Latimer with the pleasure of common cognitive activities. Although such fact sounds like an unintelligible self-torture, it brings hope and expectation into Latimer's life, and a handful of his mellifluous moments lies in the fact that he keeps ignorance of Bartha and all her inner world.

---

① In Greek mythology, the Sirens are dangerous creatures, who lured nearby sailors with their enchanting and irresistible singing voices to shipwreck on their island.

Chapter 3 Sympathy and the Epistemological Relativism in *The Lifted Veil*

When he foresees that Bertha will become his wife, he suffers from a trauma since Bertha is "no longer a fascinating secret, but a measured fact" (*TLV* 21). So when the two finally got married after the accidental death of Latimer's brother, their marriage is entangled with indifference, disdain, alienation and even hatred, which turns their marital life into a disaster. The dramatic moment comes when the newly hired maid was seriously ill. At the maid's deathbed, Bertha's unusual uneasiness again triggers Latimer's curiosity. "[W]hen the last hour had been breathed out, and we all felt that the dark veil had completely fallen. What secret was there between Bertha and this woman" (*TLV* 41)? Now, a new veil once again plagued Latimer's cognitive activities. His clairvoyance into everything seems useless once again. Eventually, the visit of Charles Meunier—Latimer's childhood playmate brings a dramatic reversal into the story for he gives a blood transfusion experiment to the dying maid. A brief resurrection of the maid clarifies Latimer's doubt and reveals Bertha's attempt to poison her husband. The veil covering Bertha's face is finally lifted and a horrible story emerging from man's spiritual world is revealed.

It is not difficult to see that Latimer's epistemological activity is prevented by the image of a veil, but such prevention does not stop his pursuit of the unknown, the thirst for truth and the desire to control the other; to the opposite, it excites them. As a response to the gothic metaphor of the veil image, Eliot stresses a sense of illusion and terror with which the protagonist is confronted. In addition, the defilade property of the veil seems week under the penetration of man's clairvoyance, insight, and mind—reading. Unlike the unexpected ending in traditional Gothic novels, Bertha's plot to poison Latimer in the story's climax is hinted when he foresees his wife's hatred on him. In other words, the veil does not seem to reveal any facts that are not known or at least not predictable. In this sense, to lift the veil is to invite disappointment instead of fear or shock, and that is why lifting the veil is not an easy thing. Latimer seems to be trapped into an epistemological predicament that his longing to know is always frustrated by what he will get to know, so he prefers to remain ignorant of others or of the future.

It has been discussed for many times that sympathy is the power of sharing other people's mind and their circumstances to moral philosophers like Hume, Adam Smith, and Ludwig Feuerbach from the perspective of humanism and materialism also elucidates the epistemological dimension of his notion of sympathy: "any knowledge depends on the recognition of other minds", then "sympathy is essential to the ability to know anything at all" (Feuerbach 126). The fact is that Latimer's knowledge of others does not improve his sympathy or fellow-feeling toward others, but strengthen his isolation and detachment with them. To know or not to know, that's a question. It seems to George Eliot that knowing what others think turns out to be a kind of torture. Then how to deal with the relationship between "sympathy and knowledge": the very two responses that realist representation aims to prompt, becomes an issue waiting for further exploration.

3.2 The Other People's Mind and the Epistemological Relativity

Generally speaking, *The Lifted Veil* deals with Latimer's problem in life for suffering from his powers of clairvoyance. In the 19th Century, some people believed that they may possess what we now refer to as "psychic" powers, which enables them to see into the future or the past, or read the minds of other people, as what has happened to Latimer. In the novella, these gifted powers do not bring Latimer any spiritual good, or do any good to improve his intimacy with others. He is dominated by a divisive power from his "double consciousness" and can't keep a balance between the other's thoughts and that of his own. When the daily thoughts of those around him are revealed to him, he faces a world of pettiness and the consequent boredom finally drags his life into the mud of repulsion. In this way, Eliot offers an enquiry into the relationship between sympathy and knowledge and addresses the idea of epistemological relativity when sympathy is working. As a result, the epistemological limitation in knowing reinforces the aesthetic concern of sympathetic imagination.

3.2.1 The Empirical Science and the Realm beyond Man's Knowledge

In the mid-Victorian age, the decline of religion has become an indisputable fact, which leaves the believers who have long sought an explanation from the religious beliefs fall into unprecedented confusion. At this time, science, after being developed in-depth in the industrial revolution, gradually became a new force to explain the world. Even Eliot herself has to admit:

> The supremely important fact of the period was the gradual reduction of all phenomena within the sphere of established law, which carries as a consequence the rejection of the miraculous [and] has its determining current in the development of physical science. (Eliot, *Essays Complete* 271)

Whether it is Darwin's theory of evolution, Charles Lyell's principle of uniformity, or John Tyndall's discovery in physics, its popularity pushes the empirical science to new heights in which cognitive model based on calculation, experimentation, and rational thinking became a fashion. People were convinced that there are connections between things and they believed that man's spiritual behavior must also be determined by some material factors, then the so-called pseudosciences like phrenology, mesmerism and physiological interaction were introduced into the explanation of man's spiritual world in the name of science. The admiration of empirical science gradually conveyed a message of determinism that constantly compressed the space in which men fully display their wills and subjective originalities. However, whether all activities in the name of science will unveil the mysteries of human life seems troublesome to many Victorian thinkers. They prefer to keep a reserved attitude on this issue. To the modern scholars, the uncontrollable zeal for explaining becomes the very barrier in the path of man's pursuing knowledge:

> Man's indefatigable zeal in designing explanations of phenomena which would place him at the centre of reference was seen, indeed, by some of the most creative scientists of the period as the major stumbling block to the advance of knowledge. (Beer 15)

The Victorian's admiration for science and their thirst for knowledge are vividly reflected in *The Lifted Veil*.

Latimer declares: "I thirsted for the unknown." (*TLV* 3) His father thinks that all modern scientific education would be helpful. He even asks the phrenologist to find the "defects" of his son's brainpower, and then to tailor a set of educational programs for him. "Private tutors, natural history, science, and the modern languages, were the appliances by which the defects of my organization were to be remedied" (*TLV* 6). But it seems that all these efforts are completely unproductive, for Latimer shows little interest in the spoon-feeding education of machines, zoology or botany in the name of science. He confesses:

> I was very stupid about machines, so I was to be greatly occupied with them; I had no memory for classification, so it was particularly necessary that I should study systematic zoology and botany; I was hungry for human deeds and humane motions, so I was to be plentifully crammed with the mechanical powers, the elementary bodies, and the phenomena of electricity and magnetism. (*TLV* 6)

Latimer shows little interest in modern scientific knowledge but he longs to know human behaviors and human motions; and the Victorians regard the emotional communication between people may work as the current or magnetic operation mode, therefore Latimer's tutors teach him knowledge of the similar kind to highlight the way in which man's feeling and emotion flow. However, such an analogy of knowledge infusion does not have much effect on Latimer's understanding of other people's emotional world. In his mind, physical science to explain why the water flows downhill is not important, but the sound and scene when water is dropping or running seems fascinating. The beautiful things are beautiful and any mechanical analysis may damage its beauty. That's why the imaginative works from Plutarch, Shakespeare, and Don Quixote exhibit its irresistible charm to Latimer:

> I was glad of the running water; I could watch it and listen to it gurgling among the pebbles, and bathing the bright green water-plants, by the hour together. I did not want to know why it ran; I had perfect confidence that there were good reasons for what was so very beautiful. (*TLV* 7)

The sad fact is that Latimer's simple and universal feeling toward life was gradually wiped out, after being baptized by the so-called scientific training, and the illness turned Latimer's sensitivity into a pathological delusion, causing mental torture and the pain in his future life. So the efforts of using a "scientific" mechanism to unveil the mysteries of interpersonal life and human consciousness seem to play the opposite role.

In *Middlemarch*, the young doctor Lydgate regards doctoring and medical treatment as the best profession in the world for it may exhibit the perfect combination of the imagination and the ambitions.

> Whereas Fever had obscure conditions, and gave him that delightful labor of the imagination which is not mere arbitrariness, but the exercise of disciplined power—combining and constructing with the clearest eye for probabilities and the fullest obedience to knowledge. (*MM* 105)

He then tries to reveal any tiny activities that can't be obtained even by the microscopes, hoping to illuminate the connection between the living organisms.

> Lydgate regarded as rather vulgar and vinous compared with the imagination that reveals subtle actions inaccessible by any sort of lens, but tracked in that outer darkness through long pathways of necessary sequence by the inward light which is the last refinement of Energy, capable of bathing even the ethereal atoms in its ideally illuminated space. (*MM* 105)

Lydgate's well-trained imagination in science only reveals the "inextricable web of affinities" in evolution. It will find out orders of the natural sequence but can do nothing to figure out the complexities of love and marriage. Lydgate then has to admit that there are problems in life that could not be solved by a scientific method, but his solution is to follow the lead of his sensuous instinct. Since "each lived in a world of which the other knew nothing" (*MM* 106) when sensuous instinct becomes the only explanation of his understanding toward life, Lydgate has nothing to do but lets sensation be the drive of all actions. For instance, his marriage with the selfish Rosemond Vincy is based on her irresistible sex appeal and he turns a blind eye to the latter's expanded material desire; and their failed marriage eventually ends up both his professional career and his original intention in scientific research.

In the case of Latimer as well as that of Lydgate, the mechanical science itself will deny man's freedom and humanity, and even any psychological analysis of man's inner world relying on science would convince man to be a particular compound and encourage him to behave that way. "Science cannot help man in this job of knowing himself; all it can show is his relation to the other animals" (Stang 35). Luckily, "as the scientific outlook became less humanistic, less congenial to concerns with human agency and morality; and as novelists sought to recover the romantic faith in imagination that had lapsed through the mid-Victorian years" (Kucrick 227). To George Eliot, stimulating the reader's imagination of sympathy and recovering their humanistic or romantic side will help them counter the constraints of the established rules. Once again, the aesthetic power of art is particularly stressed by Eliot.

Lydgate's endeavor in science to reveal the connection of things and Latimer's clairvoyance are two extreme ways in man's pursuit of knowledge. But both of them end up with unhappiness or isolated life. Their failure reinforces the idea that there are things that may go beyond the reach of man's power of knowing. That is why Latimer requests to stop absolutely knowing others and return to normal life. That is also the reason why Eliot in *Middlemarch* welcomes satisfaction with the state of "stupidity" (*MM* 135). Terry Eagleton addresses:

> Total omniscience keels over inexorably into solipsism. In a curious sense, if you knew everything you would know nothing, because subjectivity would inflate to such immense proportions that

it would overwhelm and cancel its object, leaving nothing outside itself to know. (Eagleton 52)

In this fictional story, Latimer's prevision makes him see too accurately and objectively. His excessive knowledge almost entirely dissolves the primary differential boundary marking the self and the other. He gets to lift the veil which screens off the unknowable. However, the presence of Bertha Grant reminds Latimer that there is a world where epistemological relativity lies. Resistant to Latimer's mind-reading, Bertha embodies "the blessed possibility of mystery, and doubt, and expectation" (*TLV* 31). Although Bertha is neither physically attractive nor temperamentally easy-going, she stands for an important sense as an epistemological difference to Latimer for we are defined by what we are not. She is the difference, and meanwhile, she is the unknown for Latimer's epistemological activities. She, with this unique charm, reminds him of the meaning of life and the content of knowing. Here, ignorance is not bliss but makes a happy human life possible. By stressing Latimer's fascination with Bertha, Eliot fully "underscores the necessity of grasping the relativistic conditions that produce knowledge and regulate knowability" (Garratt 182).

The idea of the relativity of knowledge in which "unknowability and doubt are its essential features" is particularly important for us to discuss the concept of sympathy (Garratt 185). For man has no power of accessing the experience of all other human beings, he does not always know directly what was going on in other people's mental states. This refreshes the way we understand the operation of sympathy if it is understood as the capability of "entering" into the thoughts and feelings of the other, as what has been claimed by Hume or Adam Smith. However, under the craft of Eliot, entering into others' minds via imagination can't get full knowledge of the other's inner world. "Each man has the full and perfect knowledge of his own consciousness; but no living being can penetrate the consciousness of another" (qtd. in Garratt 183). Although the absolute reality is unknowable, "we can possess positive knowledge of its unknowability" (Garratt 237). For Eliot, the proper way is to stress the imaginative space of the aesthetics of sympathy. The imagining process of sympathy as an anesthetic force will negotiate between the known and the unknowable, and ease the tension between the desire to know and the impossibility of knowing. George Eliot herself admits that "intelligence so rarely shows itself in speech without metaphor,— that we can so seldom declare what a thing is, except by saying it is something else" (*MF* 168). So the following section will focus on the comparatively concrete image of "veil" recurring throughout the whole novella, the peculiar implication of veil will highlight our understanding of the relationship between sympathy and knowledge.

3.2.2 The Implication of "Veil" and the Imagination Space of Sympathy

The image of the veil is originally introduced as a mask for Muslim women to cover their faces, and it gradually extends its meaning to a symbol signifying the barrier blocking man's visionary or perception. Since the veil image is always associated with the sense of a mysterious other, its unique color of mystery and ambiguity fully stimulates the imagination and inspiration of the poets and the novelists. In the romantic poetic tradition, the veil image becomes an important motif of "expectation" or "revelation", and the task of Romantic art is to uncover the veil of life and present truth to readers and audiences. To Percy Bysshe Shelly, "poetry lifts the veil from the hidden beauty of the world" (Shelley 39). It is an extension of human intelligence, but if the revealed truth is not in accordance with the expectation, a huge aesthetic tension will be presented. That is why Shelly, in "Lift Not the Painted Veil Which Those Who Live", suggests people not to lift the veil of life, for what people finally get is nothing but an illusion. The veil image under the craft of Nathaniel Hawthorne in *The Minister's Black Veil* (1863) bears all the speculation of man in which love and suspicion, justice and evil, truth and absurdity intertwine with each other, leaving a huge suspense to trigger the reader's imagination. In these two cases, the veil image indicates a conflict between the known and the unknown, implying a contrast between the expectation and the revelation. So the image of a veil is frequently adopted in the Gothic tradition to increase the suspenseful and mysterious atmosphere. Sandra M. Gilbert and Susan Gubar addresses that there is "a long Gothic tradition which embraces the veil as a necessary concealer of Grotesque revelations of sin and guilt, past crimes and future suffering" (Gilbert and Gubar 469). As an outstanding master of art, Eliot blends the Romantic poetic implication and Gothic epistemological pattern of the veil image to serve her realistic writings. In the veil image lies a buffering time and space for Eliot to propose an inquiry into the excess of releasing the epistemological anxiety in the Victorian age: that is, how would a human know the absolute other rather than turn it into a part of habitual self-extension? Or how could man maintain the self while projecting desire onto the other? One of the most important ways is to invite the intervention of the aesthetics of sympathy. Its unique imagination space can suppress the original and emotional impulses of lifting the "veil", or break the deadlock when confronted with the huge gap between expectation and the revelation, so as to interpret emotions and regain self-governing.

Sympathy is said to be the bedrock of Eliot's realist art. She even regards the "extension of our sympathies" as the artist's responsibility (*Essays* 144). And the practice of sympathy will realize the ethical purposes and aesthetical value of arts. In *Adam Bede*, sympathy is defined as "the one poor word which includes all our best insight and our best love" (*AB* 546). Sympathy was a poor world for it implies the most abstract mental representation and the most potential human capability. It is essential for ordinary people of instinct and fellow feelings to form the human association. As is mentioned in the first chapter, sympathy is not the same with its modern synonyms like "compassion" or "pity", nor can it be simply equivalent to "feeling". It is more precisely a "form"—a form to realize identification through feeling what others are feeling or knowing what others have known. The mode of identification is based on an entire agreement or kind of self-evident understanding. However, in Latimer's case, he knows too much and his intelligence cuts off his association with other people. For the Empirical aesthetician, namely Edmund Burke, he claimed: "It is by this principle (sympathy) chiefly that poetry, painting, and other affecting arts, transfuse their passions from one breast to another. Sympathy for Burke is a close contact between two minds. And it will achieve the transformation and replacement of the emotions expressed by the artist into the mind of the appreciators, and the latter thus forget their own fear or sublimate them into an aesthetic pleasure. In Burke's time, "a growing reliance on feeling as a means of insight, allied to the current belief that the best poet was the one with the widest experience, led to the development of sympathetic imagination as an aesthetic idea" (Burke & Boulton, Introduction xxxix). Adam Smith echoes with Burke and gives great prominence to the notion of "imagination". With this imagination, sympathy accomplishes the process of self-transcendence.

Sympathy with imagination becomes a key element in linking the self and the other and exhibits the potentiality for establishing altruistic and prosocial behavior. When Hume sees sympathy as a vision-oriented instinctive reaction, or when Smith believes that sympathy is an imaginary process of putting the self into others' circumstances, sympathy becomes a mechanism realizing an idealized identification. Sympathy during this time period becomes a half intuitive and half empirical conception which relies largely on the autonomous flow of feeling. By revealing Latimer's horror and boredom, George Eliot points out that the realization of identification relying on the autonomous flow of feeling is too ideal, and there are underlying dangers of invading the other and obliterating the self. Therefore, Eliot's understanding of sympathy starts to pay attention to the imaginative potentiality in aesthetic matter, in which the end of epistemological node is to accept the other's "difference" and generate a tolerance of human care. Sympathy to her is "not so much of understanding, but one based on our sense of shared incomprehensibility, of shared otherness" (Stfanie 103). To ensure the validity of sympathy, it requires:

> A certain detachment, the suspension of the desire to project the self onto the other. But sympathy and knowledge both demand attachment too; they depend on the desire to come close to another, to recognize the inevitably social ingredients of selfhood, and to envisage an otherness outside oneself. That is, the task of knowing and feeling for others yields impulses both toward and against the self, both desire and denial, both sociability and isolation, both lively fantasies of possibility and the recognition of unyielding otherness. (Levine, "Surprising Realism" 63)

Caroline Levine then reaffirms: "it is the imagination that plays back and forth between self and other, always selfish—projecting from the self—and yet acting as precisely the faculty that allows that self to develop a relation to the other". (Levine, "Surprising Realism" 63) In short, the process of imagination plays a vital role in operating sympathy. Eliot herself admits that the main theme of her writing is to have her readers produce better capability "to imagine and feel the pains and the joys of those who differ from themselves in everything but the broad fact of being struggling erring human creatures" (*Letters* III: 111). Imagining and feeling "the pains and the joys of those who differ from themselves" then becomes the main tune for Eliot's realistic writing and the key to understand Eliot's understanding of sympathy. This process includes an outward activity oriented to the other and the introverted imagination to the self. "Powerful imagination is not false outward vision, but intense inward representation and the creative energy constantly fed by susceptibility to the veriest minutiae of experience, which it reproduces and constructs in fresh and fresh wholes" (*Such* 110). So sympathy with imagination will also be a creative representation of other's inner world. Relying on the imaginative process, people project their own desires on the other and realize the self-reflection by grasping the difference of the other or accepting the contrast between the expectation and the reality, thus integrating the relationship between the self and the other. It includes two important steps: differentiation between the self and the other and the reconciliation between the self and the self. Therefore, sympathy is by no means an equivalent of "knowing"; it is more of knowing what we can't understand.

 These qualities are what exactly Latimer in *The Lifted Veil* lacks: endless insight and foresight make him already aware of the inner activities of others. He cannot display his power of imagination, which makes him ignore the difference of others or the relationship between him and the other. All these facts, in turn, prevent the growth of the sympathy in him, for "imagination and sympathy acted and reacted habitually, each heightening the other" (*AB* 175). Dorothea Brooke in *Middlemarch* undoubtedly builds up a perfect model in handling this toughness. She questions directly the value and significance of Casaubon's work when she sees her pedantic husband immersed in chaotic, disorderly research all day. Dorothea's interrogation "gave loud emphatic iteration to those muffled suggestions of consciousness which it was possible to explain as mere fancy, the illusion of exaggerated sensitiveness" (*MM* 128). Casaubon knows his work is meaningless. Being sensitive and unimaginative, Casaubon can't handle the direct interrogation from his wife, which seems to lift the veil in his world of consciousness and sparks his fear and anger. In contrast, Dorothea gives different responses. Once she understands that her husband has devoted his life to worthless research, she generates a deep sympathy for him for the first time:

> It had been easier to her to imagine how she would devote herself to Mr Casaubon, and become wise and strong in his strength and wisdom, than to conceive with that distinctness which is no longer reflection but feeling... that he had an equivalent centre of self, whence the lights and shadows must always fall with a certain difference. (*MM* 135)

The process of capturing the other's "difference" starts from the attention to others outside ourselves, and stops with a separation to the idealized state of self-speculation, which is vital for the realization of sympathy. The practices of sympathy basically, involve a process of identification. Or, in other words, to sympathize with the other, one must identify with the difference between the self and the other. Without such differences, the practice of sympathy seems impossible. That's why full knowledge of the other tends to weaken sympathy instead of strengthening it, for that makes it impossible to realize self-transcendence. In the light of this, Latimer's clairvoyance is thus "cursed", and Eliot in *Middlemarch* asserts that most people live in "stupidity", because a keen insight into the lives of ordinary people is like hearing the sound of growing grass or the heartbeat of a squirrel. "We should die of that roar which lies on the other side of silence" (*MM* 124). Compared with Casaubon's "different self", the "green grass growth" or the "squirrel heartbeat" seems more difficult to know, but imaginative construction urges man to produce certain irrelevance instead of "lifting the veil" with inquiry or generate the desire to control. Man, therefore, is saved from the trouble to "die of that roar" (*MM* 151).

The imaginary process of sympathy involves feelings and thoughts of the other and interlaces with that of one's own. However, Latimer can't handle his consciousness and that of his own; he just let them run as a "double consciousness" working simultaneously. Failing in generating sympathy, he can't construct integration between the self and the other or reserve proper boundary between the two sides. Usually, it will stimulate man's negative feelings like pains and shocks when finding the difference of the other. In this sense, the veil in front of Latimer symbolizes an imaginative space in the aesthetics of sympathy. It does not melt the self and the other, nor will it lead to the disappearance of the self but form a connection. In the aesthetic domain, the senses see two isolated objects, but the imagination will find the connection between the two objects. "Where sense observes two isolated objects, imagination discloses two related objects" (Lewes 63). It is impossible to ignore the fact that imagination is by nature a self-directed behavior, but in the aesthetic activities of literature works, imagination makes it possible to allow the self to return to the maintained relationships, so the self becomes a spectator observing some wholeness including himself and transcends the narrowness of himself as well, which is conducive to the transformation of the isolated individual into a social one. Take Larimer for example, the revered sympathy by chance helps him build up two delightful life experiences.

Being a teenager, Latimer is sensitive and unrealistic. His character makes him disagreeable to his family members and alien to other children at his age, which makes it hard for him to form a close human relationship. Another youngster, Charles Munnier, poor and ugly, is also crowded out by the social circles. So it doesn't matter what kind of personality the two young men have, "the dreamy" and "the practical" are related to each other by a common "sympathetic resentment", which reinforces a community of feeling. They finally accomplishes a few happy times in each other's life. The second case is the moment after the death of Latimer's brother. Latimer understands the grief and isolation of his father's bereavement, which enables him to establish a rare father-and-son kinship.

> I felt a movement of deep pity towards him, which was the beginning of a new affection — an affection that grew and strengthened in spite of the strange bitterness with which he regarded me in the first month or two after my brother's death. If it had not been for the softening influence of my compassion for him—the first deep compassion I had ever felt. (*TLV* 28-29)

These two facts show that sympathy, imagination, and the flow of emotions allow Latimer to accept the differences of others which consequently stop the further extension of his "one-sided" knowledge. He then develops an intimacy toward other people. Once he truly enters the circle of human life, his accurate foresight and boring insight will disappear, which fully shows that the imagination becomes the key to interpret the interpersonal life. To Eliot, the imagination space in the aesthetics of sympathy allows the self to accept others' differences and realize the negotiation between the self and the other, and the self and the self. Such a procedure accomplishes a crucial process that G. H. Lewes describes it as "to know all is to forgive all" (Fulmer and Barfield 28), for sympathy also embodies a combination of "all our best insight and our best love" (*AB* 546).① Arts provide people with a rare opportunity to participate in aesthetic activities, in which man's imagination is fully stimulated. Artistic activity like novel-reading thus connects the self with things other than the self, so as to train readers to enhance the ability of feeling what others feel, knowing what others have known, and accomplishing what others have accomplished, so as to step out of the limit of the self and generate a habit of relating the self with a larger wholeness. Such training in art will definitely improve man's performance in real life experiences. Based on such consideration, George Eliot then devotes her realistic writing to fully provoking sympathy and knowledge—two principal responses from her realistic novels (Levine, "Surprising Realism" 63), expecting to explore the value of the realistic writing in its full sense. Sympathy concerns higher than the simple epistemological issue, and it means no longer the full knowledge of the other, but involvement of aesthetical concern with imagination.

3.3 Sympathy Transformed and the Growth of Mind

Sympathy basically is seen as a power entering into others' minds and gets to know the circumstance in others' consciousness, which is also the main epistemological implication that the concept of sympathy embodies. In the novella of *The Lifted Veil*, with the disastrous life experience of Latimer, George Eliot warns us that epistemological premise and the

---

① George Eliot had been influenced by the Higher Biblical Criticism which stresses love and sympathy to be the divine power of God. And Tolerance becomes a required feature of sympathy to show human care and generosity, which is essential for man to reach an accommodation between the self and the other, and a negotiation between the self and the self.

sympathetic potentiality fostered by mere sensation and feeling is unreliable. For it will urge man to satisfy their needs for the absolute or definite knowing of others and consequently damage sympathy. Or, in other words, sensation and feeling can't realize sympathy if it is self-directed. So the intervention of sympathetic imagination in the aesthetic sense is welcomed if the unknowability of the other is taken into consideration. Rae Greiner, in "Sympathy Time: Adam Smith, George Eliot, and the Realist Novel" (2009) observed that sympathy can be seen as an exercise of the imagination or a "speculation". Since we do not have immediate access to other people's feelings, sympathy bridges that gap through speculations about another's possible condition (297). This speculating process aims to reason the possibility of the unknown but not the absoluteness.

The limit of knowing means that the prerequisite for sympathy is not to know fully. As what Latimer has experienced, his ability to see into the future and other people's minds does not encourage his sympathy but destroys it. Latimer has "never been encouraged to trust much in the sympathy of my fellow-men", and his world is full of nothing but "darkness—no pain—nothing but darkness" (*TLV* 4). Seeing through everything causes losing faith in everything. Latimer is deafened by recognizing the triviality and frivolity of others, and his penetrating mind destroys his hope for life. The same sentiment is echoed in *Middlemarch*: "if we had a keen vision and feeling of all ordinary human life, it would be like hearing the grass grow and the squirrel's heartbeat, and we should die of that roar which lies on the other side of silence." (*MM* 135) Since man may die of the roar lying on the other side of silence if his inner world is crammed by insight or ill speculations, the direct fellow-feeling unchecked becomes increasingly commendable. In this sense, George Eliot in *The Lifted Veil* responds to the "Negative Capability" advocated by John Keats, the ability "when Man is capable of being in uncertainties, mysteries, doubts, without any irritable reaching after facts and reason" (Keats, *Selected Letters* 41). So referring to epistemological level, Eliot engages into a reflection that knowing "too much" would thus be excruciating and unlikely to invoke sympathy.

The world of epistemology is made up of two parts: "the unknowable" and "the knowable". As two sides of the dichotomy, the knowable is likely to emerge out of the unknowable, and vice versa. In the mid-Victorian age, when Darwin proposed the theory of evolution, "the empiricism shifted the psychological paradigm so that it moved beyond romanticism's charge of environmental determinism" and "Victorian empiricism toward embracing the self—the knowing subject—in terms of change and difference" (Grrantt 34). But the self is still the king of the body. Then "the mind is a thing of indefinite growth, adaptation, acquisition" (qtd. in Grrantt 34). In this way, man's acquisition of knowledge is also like an evolutionary development, emphasizing interdependence, transformation and instability. During this process, it is the change and adaptation that became the determinants forming man's subjectivity. John Locke has addressed that knowledge can be obtained through experiences. "Experience, from the empiricist point of view, provides the foundation of knowledge but also reciprocally modifies the contours of the knowing subject by being assimilated into its emergent identity" (Grrantt 33). Sympathy this time serves as a way of people to experience things outside the self, it stresses the difference and uncertainty and invites change and adaptation, so as to accomplish the improvement of knowledge. Comte's Positivism stresses that knowledge should be obtained by sense experience. And Feuerbach's "Religion of Humanity" explains that love and sympathy may lead people to true understanding. And sympathy undoubtedly takes the three sides together and realizes a combination of empirical sense experience with human care. Sympathy enables man to fully approach what has happened in the other's mind, and also leaves a space for people to evolve into higher acquisition in knowing.

Latimer's clairvoyance is like the omniscience of realistic writing. If it expresses all, it will exhibit none. Sympathy and knowledge, the two main responses that realistic writing ever promised to provoke will also be denied and dissipated. Since Latimer has told people what had happened in his life, he himself can't help questioning the readers: "Are you unable to give me your sympathy, you who react this? Are you unable to imagine this double consciousness at work within me, flowing on like two parallel streams which never mingle their waters and blend into a common hue?" (*TLV* 21) Definitely, Latimer feels anxious for attract reader's sympathy, but his consciousness and that of the readers' flows like a parallel streams for there is nothing to mingle with: his clairvoyance makes him know all but "the feeling of difference or otherness arises the judgment of not this", moreover, "which in turn evolves the distinction of self and the other. These two aspects are abstractions; in feeling they emerge simultaneously as correlations" (Lewes, *Problems of Life and Mind* 219). In short, the unknowability makes it possible for people to know and the sympathetic involvement will help a man make a generous component of evaluation and judgement. And art, the product of man's feeling and imagination, embodies the infinite power to provoke sympathy and to improve knowledge.

As has been discussed in the above sections, what makes *The Lifted Veil* different is its apparently devastating annihilation of human sympathy. The reason to explain this phenomenon is that absolute knowledge of the other allows no space for a man to discover the difference. There is no hope in the story and there will be no possibility of transformation in reality. So we have to admit that there are things beyond our reach. The limit of knowledge or the epistemological relativity invites sympathy as an imaging power further pushing forward man's epistemological activities. And it is art that can fully stimulate or train man's power of imaginative sympathy, for art concerns with man of life, and life is like nature, full of the mysterious and the infinite.

Eliot regards art forms, novels particularly, as the best tools for interpreting human life and revealing human nature. She believes that:

> Science has no sex: the mere knowing and reasoning faculties, if they act correctly, must go through the same process, and arrive at the same result. But in art and literature, which imply the action of the entire being, in which every fibre of the nature is engaged, in which every peculiar modification of the individual makes itself felt... (*Essay* 31)

It is for this reason that art is the nearest thing to life. Art provides people with a territory to imagine and to verify ideals or experiment emotions and ultimately helps man transform ideas into life itself, so art will improve man's self-knowledge to know himself and his life as well. As Eliot has addressed in *The Lifted Veil*:

> Conceive the condition of the human if all propositions whatsoever were self-evident except one, which was to become self-evident at the close of a Summer's day, but in the meantime might be the subject of question, of hypothesis, of debate. Art and philosophy, literature and science, would fasten like bees on that one proposition which had the honey of probability in it, and be the more eager because their enjoyment would end with sunset. (*TLV* 29)

Art is the best tool to explore all possibilities of life if the relativity of knowledge is acknowledged. Compared with cognitive ways to lift the veil of skinless facts like calculation or verification, art embodies the only chance to cherish the value of the probabilities and enjoy savoring the honey in it. In the process of the rapid advancement of Victorian technology and science, "possibility" rather than absolute knowledge should be the driving force for pursuing knowledge. So while reviewing Robert Mackey's *The Progress of the Intellect* Eliot ends her comment with the following words:

> A remnant of the mythical lurks in the very sanctuary of science. Forms or theories ever fall short of nature, though they are ever tending to reach a position above nature, and may often be found to include more than the maker of them at the time knew. To certain extent they are reliable and complete; as a system of knowledge they are reliable and complete; as a system of knowledge they are but intermediate and preparatory. As matter is the soul's necessary instruments, so ignorance, more or less mixed up with all its expressions and forms, may be said to be as it were the eyelid through which it gradually opens itself to the truth, admitting no more than it can for the time support, and, as through a veil, learning to support its lustre. (*Selected Essays* 284)

In her view, form and theory are never as complicated as nature, "veil" symbolizes an imaginative territory both for science and literature, nature and society. It is a space that welcomes the intertwined work of both imagination and sympathy. So through the eccentric story of *The Lifted Veil*, Eliot has continually tried to emphasize the issue that there's some mystery that can't be reached by the intuitive subjectivity or the absolute rationality with the empirical science. It is an imaginary space that expects the intervention of the aesthetics of sympathy.

> Science may have the power to strip the world of all delusions—to see all things just as they are—but if there is nothing left for the imagination to do, then we are consigned to a hell of certainties. "The Lifted Veil" makes a claim for the supreme value of uncertainty and ignorance in human existence; and a claim for the vital significance of art and literature as the supreme expression of the groping after truth. (Dolin 213)

In short, the limit of knowledge is the very fact man is facing in the epistemological realm. Under such conditions, the infinite power of art will come to supplement man's intellectual insufficiency. It does not aim to reveal facts; on the contrary, it intends to explore the proximities. This cognitive model will alleviate the cognitive anxiety of the infinite advancement of human intelligence in the scientific and mechanical age. Eliot then with her interest in science turns her sight onto a man in organic relationships, expecting to record the psychological activity of man evolving forms of primitive behaviors, and documenting the complexity and instability when man's inner world collides with the outside one. In this way, art demonstrates the adaptive response when men are directed toward outside situations. In this sense, Eliot's realistic writing is devoted to recording faithfully the shocking moment, most importantly, to record man's inner impression or activities when the shock falls upon him, so as to appeals to the subsequent process of self-regulation and self-control.

3.4 Realism and the Cultural Schizophrenia

As the doyenne of realism, realistic writing is the main approach of George Eliot's artistic creation. The premise of realism is to present things as they are based on the knowledge of both the self and things other than the self, so as to present a truthful picture of the reality. However, the epistemological relativity convinces Eliot that things outside the self are not fully manageable. So Eliot's realistic art promises to present the truth and reality on the one hand, yet it embodies a strong sense of incomprehensibility on the other. As a result, Eliot presents a striking outlook of cultural schizophrenia in *The Lifted Veil*:

> The creative tension within mid-Victorian literature comes from a cultural schizophrenia. If it was modern, materialist, factual, concerned with "things as they are", it was also in many ways Romantic, fascinated with the " savage " Gothic, melodramatic, idealistic. (James 2)

This trait makes researches on the novels in this time period diversified and complicated, and many novels that seem to be different from the realist tradition needs to be re-emphasized, re-explored and re-evaluated. *The Lifted Veil* is undoubtedly one of the most typical examples containing all the traits mentioned in the above assertion. Features like the factual, the romantic, the gothic and even the idealistic all weave together into the making of this novella.

The Lifted Veil interrogates the boundaries between the scientific knowledge and the supernatural, between the rational and the irrational. In this story, Latimer is both the narrator and the central protagonist. He is haunted by a "cursed" ability to read the minds of others. He can even foresee the fate that awaits him. The whole story is filled with unnatural forces such as foresight, insight, and mind-reading, or full of abnormal plots like blood transfusion, phonology or resurrection, etc. Besides, the idyllic and convivial joy of a community depicted in *Adam Bede* is displaced by the stifling suffering in *The Lifted Veil*, which ultimately leads to a consolatory and restrained form of life experience. As a representative of the realist writers, Eliot herself confesses that *The Lifted*

Veil embodies ideas "which justifies its painfulness", and there are many things she "would willingly say over again, and I shall never put them in any other form" (*Letters* V: 380). Since realism has been the bedrock for Eliot's artistic creation, the main task in this section tries to relate *The Lifted Veil* as an inseparable part of Eliot's whole project of realistic works and discloses Eliot's realistic concern behind the coat of "cultural schizophrenia".

As early as the Romantic age, man is convinced that powerful emotions can enhance insight and foreknowledge, but once the inner emotions are out of control, they will lead to disastrous consequences. Latimer isolates himself from the social circle. Moreover, his sensitiveness and paranoid make him gradually create a kind of self-protective insulation which prevents him from achieving normal communication of emotions with others, which in turn makes him generate the self-obsessive subjective speculation instead. This is a symptom of a typical paranoia in the eyes of modern scholars and an exaggerated reproduction of one-side knowledge in G. H. Lewes's words (Fulmer and Barfield 28). Man will suffer from the shock and terror to lift this veil. "No wonder, when there is this contrast between the outward and the inward, that painful collisions come of it" (*MF* 283). Latimer couldn't handle this painful moment thus he imagines a horrible story. Sally Shuttleworth even regards Latimer's encounter as an unreliable narrative. Latimer's inexplicable fear of others and his own painful experience stems from the rejection of self-divestment (Shuttleworth 201). Logan Pater describes Latimer as a "nervous narrator" in fiction (Logan 29), for *The Lifted Veil* reflects "on the ways in which relativism becomes incorporated at a narrative level, specifically as a problem of language and event, narrating and knowing" (Garratt 186). That is to say, Latimer's narrative emerges out of self-speculation behind the veil of consciousness, and the veil image becomes a barrier that obstructs Latimer to properly handle the recognition of the other human's consciousness, so the reliability of his narrative also needs to be questioned. In *Adam Bede*, when the village girl Hetty realizes that Arthur Donnithorne has some good impression on her and meditates she may one day marry the son of a gentry:

> But for the last few weeks a new influence had come over Hetty—vague, atmospheric, shaping itself into no self-confessed hopes or prospects, but producing a pleasant narcotic effect, making her tread the ground and go about her work in a sort of dream, unconscious of weight or effort, and showing her all things through a soft, liquid ***veil*** , as if she were living not in this solid world of brick and stone, but in a beatified world. (AB 117)[1]

The veil image isolates Hetty from communicating with other people; she indulges in a fantastic meditation and refuses the good willed reminder from her family members. The resulted self-interest and narrow understanding eventually lead her to savor the bitterness of life. Compared with Hetty's self-indulgence and self-meditation behind the veil, Latimer has experienced the sense of horror and shock by lifting the veil. He then displays the power of mind-reading or clairvoyance to interpret his understanding of life and reality. His understanding of life and reality is nothing but a kind of self-speculation. So both cases of Latimer and Hetty warn us that how to deal with the moment of lifting the veil becomes a tough question. In this sense, the clairvoyance, speculation, foresight and insight under the veil image disused in this novel are the "technology to investigate what kinds of knowledge matter" instead of the subject of the novella (Matus 127).

---

[1] The bold and the italic is intentional.

As has been discussed in the above sections, the unnatural forces such as the foresight, insight, mind-reading, and clairvoyance described in *The Lifted Veil* are incompatible with the realist principles Eliot ever promises in *Adam Bede*. What is revealed in this novella are somewhat obscure ideas even to the modern critics:

> If there is a difficulty for the modern critic in establishing the boundaries between the fantastic and the realistic, or between the different generic forms and transformations of the fantastic in Victorian fiction, that is because the fantastic is itself a liminal and transgressive mode, concerned with and moving between borderlands and boundaries: the boundaries of the conscious and the unconscious; the rational and the irrational; the "civilized" and the "primitive"; the religious and secular; the material and the numinous; the natural and supernatural; the self and the not-self. The fantastic is an interrogator of established categories: not least those of sexuality, gender, and social class. (Pykett 194)

So it is the complex of reality causes a variety and flexibility of realistic writing, and realism has to demonstrate tolerance and openness for taking in some abnormal and supernatural phenomena, making them a supplement to "all that is not said, all that is unsayable, through realistic forms" (Pykett 194). In this sense, the "cultural schizophrenia" is also one exhibition of realistic writing but not its contraction. It is a faithful record of the cultural schizophrenia staged in man's consciousness. Not is just this all, although these unnatural forces seem to be eccentric to the modem critics; most of them are popular or widely recognized phenomena in the field of psychology or sociology in the Victorian age. Eliot shows a deep interest in phenomena like phrenology—a theory that one's character and ability could be determined by the shape and size of his head,① or mesmerism②,— the precursor to modern practices of hypnotism; or clairvoyance③ — knowledge beyond that of everyday thought and perceptions. But Eliot has no idea about the consequence of these "scientific" experiments; she then makes an enquiry into these issues in her fictional world. So the novella of *The Lifted Veil* is more like Eliot's other piece of work, addressing a similar realistic appeal. Eliot "uses material from her interest in Victorian science to build her imaginative constructions of moral experience" (Kennedy **388**).

Although realism serves as the main theme of George Eliot's artistic creation, sometimes, she has to admit that she is quite overwhelmed by the idea of a gap between the human mind and the rest of the world. It is her responsibility to accurately interpret and represent reality on the one hand; and admits that the world outside the self is beyond reach. In an artistic way, Eliot truthfully records the toughness and the difficulties, and she simultaneously depicts the anxieties, desires, and doubts troubling the Victorians, or the hard moment that the mind collides with the outside world, so realism certainly encompasses these unique ideas to fully depict a true picture of man's inner world. A combination of the strengths of realism, romanticism and even the gothic is undisputedly ideal to fully explore the possibility of mental reality. As a result, *The Lifted Veil* may exhibit the quality of "cultural schizophrenia", yet it is the inner diffraction when the inner and outer visions collide or oscillate with each other. There is an imbalance between "the recording the visible details of a crowded material world, and giving a sense of the complex interior lives

---

① Phrenology has been debunked in the 20th century as a pseudo-science.
② Mesmerism is a bit of medical quackery developed in the 18th century by the German physician Franz Anton Mesmer (1734-1815).
③ Clairvoyance experiments share the popularity in the Victorian age, and the Scottish physician and chemist William Gregory (1803-1858) is a reprehensive researcher.

of perceiving experiential subjects" (Flint 37). All these reinforce our understanding of realism as what George Levine has summarizes, "uncertainty [is] an intrinsic part of nineteenth-century realism" (qtd. in Flint 37). In George Eliot's works, "even the most solidly incarnate realism requires a destabilizing remnant of something else—call it lyricism or romance or fable or some 'poor ghost' of an idea—to awaken the full potential of the human imagination" (Stfanie 103). Therefore, the feature of "cultural schizophrenia" is the inseparable supplement to Eliot's realistic writing.

To conclude, George Eliot presents a sense of "cultural schizophrenia" in *The Lifted Veil* by blending the Romantic poetic implication and Gothic epistemological pattern of the veil image. With constructing a mist of cognition dancing between aesthetics and cognition, she addresses inquiries into the futility of absolute or definite knowing and admits the unknowability of the other, so as to appeal to the intervention of imagination in the aesthetics of sympathy. During the process of sympathetic imagination, man gets a precious chance to train his sensory experience by self-governing and self-control, so as to distinguish the difference between the self and the other and accomplish the self-reconciliation complying with the aesthetic request. Moreover, it forms relations and links to integrate the self-other relationship and thus impels the transition of man from an individual agency to a social one. Compared with revealing the "skinless fact", this epistemological model exhibits the "possibility" of change based on imagination, which is more conducive to the formation of interpersonal relationships and the construction of social communities. Such an effort will not only alleviate the cognitive anxiety of the Victorian era but also allow Eliot once again to reaffirm the irreplaceable position of art and literature in the process of human exploration of truth. As an important and innovative realist novelist in the Victorian age, Eliot makes an experimental combination of horror and mystery with realism, making the mysterious and the uncertain permeate the reader's reading experience so as to guide them to gradually form an individual subjectivity through the transformation of imaginative cognition to moral judgment, which "takes her [Eliot] far from the humble realism of *Scenes of Clerical Life* or *Adam Bede*" (Menke 629). This will surely broaden the aesthetic field and writing space of realism and increase the flexibility of realism.

Although Eliot defines "realism" as "the doctrine that all truth and beauty are to be attained by a humble and faithful study of nature, and not by substituting vague forms, bred by imagination on the mists of feeling, in place of definite, substantial reality" (*Essay* 180), it is always hard to achieve. The reason always lies in the fact that to what degree sympathy helps man to know. Sympathy is by no means the absolute knowledge of the other. In *The Lifted Veil*, Latimer's too much knowledge reveals a reality in a horrified sense. Too much knowledge and too little sympathy dragged Latimer into a mental disorder. At this moment, a "dizzy sense of unreality" in Latimer's mind and a "cultural schizophrenia" under Eliot's craft both remind us that the reliable pathway to knowledge by direct sensory contact with the world should be re-examined, if not to be subverted. And Latimer's example underscores that sympathy can't be realized if the sensation and feeling are too self-directed. Knowing driven by pure feeling and sensation will easily blur the boundary between the self and the other and leaves no space for the other. That's why Latimer is trapped into the epistemological predicament "to know" or "not to know". In addition, the paralleled "double-consciousness" also brings a divisive power to separate Latimer from his connection with others. While Latimer is suffering from the absolute knowledge of the others, Maggie Truliver in *The Mill on the Floss* seems to be "more congruous with the mystery" (*MF* 329), and Dorothea Brooke in *Middlemarch* would like to remain satisfied with "the moral stupidity" (*MM* 135). With the full display of sympathetic imagination in the artistic sense, an organizing principle toward inner order is particularly valued, in which the internalization of self and the transformation within is strongly emphasized by Eliot. In *The Mill on the Floss* and *Middlemarch*, sympathy provides absolutes or universals to help a man take in an incomprehensible part and unite it as a whole. Both works reveal the potentiality of man's self-organizing process when facing the unknown or things beyond one's reach. Eliot advocates organizing the self into harmony with the unknowable or things that can never be fully grasped by senses, which is also what a moral choice implies. Sympathy as a mechanism no longer enters into the consciousness of others with an omniscient perspective but serves as a transformative agency to train feeling and imagination under the aesthetic request by integrating the self with the incomprehensible other so as to regulate man's mental world and transcend the daily triviality or frivolity for the spiritual truth or the communal good.

Chapter 4
Sympathy and the Sublime Enquiry in *The Mill on the Floss* and *Middlemarch*

In the third chapter, the issue of epistemological relativism has been discussed, with which Eliot is aware of the fact that things may maintain some incomprehensible state, and other people's mind also keeps unknowable or at least not fully knowable to us. As a result, the cognitive premise that sympathy promises won't stand long before facing the real practical dilemma. Like "Latimer" in *The Lifted Veil*, he may generate the feeling of rejection and antipathy towards others once he fully grasps others' inner world. His double consciousness — the consciousness of others and that of his own cannot be integrated with each other, which results in a divisive force to split him apart. So it is urgent for George Eliot to figure out the coping way to reorganize or reconstruct man's inner order by representing and understanding sympathy in other ways. To Eliot, sympathy, the operation of displacing other's feeling and situation into one's own is by no means the absolute knowing and total identification of others' feeling and situation in the cognitive sense, although sympathy will definitely invite some epistemological production, and it seems to be securer to investigate the conception of sympathy as an aesthetical phantom. In other words, if it is impossible for people to absolutely know the other's mind, it is possible for man to reconstruct the other's mind and sensory experience aesthetically through imaginations. The epistemological blank thus would be filled by the aesthetical transcendence. Since man's epistemological accomplishments should be obtained via the aesthetical approaches, the aesthetical implication of sympathy should be amplified and cherished.

The fact is that imagination and feeling are all the introversive, then how could these introversive abilities help man reach outside himself? This seems to be crucial to a question that any successful operation of sympathy needs to answer. More than this, to what extent can this sympathetic imagination approach to the perception of others' situations? How far or in which way will the sympathetic imagination carry on man's cognitive activities? Since the other's mind is full of the unknowable or part-knowable consciousness, how could man recognize the absolute otherness and accept it without turning it into his self-projection? This situation raises more questions than solutions. It's known that the empirical athletics or the romantics solve this problem through working sympathy as a half-divine and half-empirical capability. However, the mysterious operation of sympathy seems unconvincing to Victorians who have got used to the empirical reasoning and calculating skills, which means that Eliot needs to figure out new ways to interpret sympathy. In the Victorian age, and as always since the birth of aesthetics, the unknown, the infinite and the inexhaustible part in man's epistemological domain have been classified into the "sublime" category in the aesthetical domain. It involves an aesthetic judgment that "to be able to even think the infinite as a whole indicates a mental power that surpasses any standard of sense" (Kant, *Critique of Judgement* 11). In this situation, sympathy with its innate imaginative drive serves as a breakthrough for people to counter the mystery or the invariable force to accomplish a sense of self-transcendence through self-annihilation or self-discovery. This internalization process involves an aesthetical judgment by uniting the self with the incomprehensible into a whole. Since "every moral choice requires the consideration of a whole that can never be quite grasped with the senses", the aesthetical activity then is attached with the color of moral (Hancock 6). Then it is moral to guide man's emotional output and imaginative drives toward the others' benefit or the communal good.

When Forest Pyle defines sympathy, he points out that sympathy is "the imaginative impulse that, transcending the egotism and renouncing the desires of self, promises to bridge the epistemological and ethical gap between self and world" (Pyle, "A Novel Sympathy" 6). Such imaginative process also entails the projection of the self onto others for imagination is "a mental power making present what is absent through the production of images" (Pillow 349), as a result, it will be no surprise for the subject to involve into more or less subjective speculation while imagining and sympathizing. Based on this fact, Forest Pyle concludes that there must be an impossibility of Eliot's realism; while George Levine notices that "it is the imagination that compels us to sympathy and knowledge", then he affirms "the imagination is both intrinsically selfish and essential to the aims of realism" for Eliot, because "it is neither good nor bad but simply inevitable that the imagination will project the desires and expectations of the self on the world" (Levine, "Surprising Realism" 66). As has been investigated in the third chapter, Latimer's Gothic story for suffering from half self-speculation and half reality constructed in mind proves that Eliot has noticed that the imaginative projection on the other does exist. How these imaginative activities make sympathy successfully works and how sympathetic imagination in realistic work compels readers for knowledge turn to be the key issue for Eliot to discuss. And this chapter aims to investigate the concept of sympathy by relating closely to the notion of the sublime to demonstrate the fact that Eliot does involve a concern to guide imagination out of its introverted tendency by associating sympathy with man's aspiration for the sublime enquiry.

In *The Mill on the Floss* and *Middlemarch*, sympathy guided by the sublime leads man to relate himself to a large whole for expanding the mind. The inner power of feeling, reasoning and will power accomplish either a secular or a spiritual self-transcendence through self-annihilation or self-discovery. The introverted imagination, therefore, orients to an extraverted action. Such spiritual aspiration is an ongoing process that aims to negotiate the relationship between the self and the outside world when the two collide with each other. The primitive feelings, mostly negative, like terror, repulsion, pain and hatred generated while man facing the incomprehensible or the sublime will serve as a positive force for harmonizing the individual soul, for they could be transformed into sympathy and sympathy into expressing oneself by thinking for the others' benefit or communal good (Hardy 16; Haight 463-464).① It is a self-organizing process for maintaining harmony or keep accordance "between inner and outer world" (Beer 45). In Eliot's realistic writing, sympathy realizes the knowledge communication associated with moral sentiment and emotional intuition. In art, man attains the height of virtuous pleasure by (at least momentarily) restoring the harmony of reason, passion, and the senses, such training is the very essence of Eliot's understanding of aesthetical education of art. Both in *The Mill on the Floss* and in *Middlemarch*, Eliot not only aims to represent the authentic human nature in her art but also reveals the imbalanced, irregular nature for this

---

① For feelings like pain, terror and hatred are labeled as primitive emotions see Barbara Hardy's *Forms of Feeling in Victorian Fiction* (1985); and for Eliot is influenced and inspired by the Ancient Greek play writer like Sophocles' way of delineating the primitive emotions, see Gordon S. Haight's *George Eliot: A Biography* (1968).

representation process, so as to lead man step out of epistemological confusion or the messy emotional negation toward an inner order. Consequently, Eliot sets her character in numerous relations and presents a panoramic view of the organic whole including man and the wonderful incomprehensibility, and such sublime state will urge man to generate sympathy and individual sensibility for other people or for the common good if he wants to obtain knowledge of himself.

4.1　Maggie Tulliver's Anger and Dorothea Brooke's Terror

4.1.1　*The Mill on the Floss* and Maggie Tulliver's Anger

First published in 1860, *The Mill on the Floss* is George Eliot's second full-length novel. It is always believed to be her semi-autobiography. The story takes place in the fictional English village of St. Ogg's and focuses chiefly on the experience of the Tulliver family. It records the story of Maggie and her elder brother Tom from their childhood into young adulthood. Maggie, under the portrayal of George Eliot, is a beautiful creature with a truthfully and compellingly working mind. She is passionate, impetuous and ready to be cherished by her father and loved by her mother, however, the former has his sadness and troubles in running a mill, and the latter is always worrying about Maggie's hoydenish nature and bedraggled appearance. Maggie's brother Tom is several years older and he is in many ways to her opposite: stolid, self-righteous, and disinterested in human feelings or disciplinary learning. He never responds Maggie with enough love and equal feeling as the latter shows to him, which always makes Maggie frustrated and helpless. Family troubles cause Maggie to be sensitive and emotional. She finds nothing exciting but immerses herself into a "dream world", but such a dream world cannot give her satisfaction (*MF* 345). Instead, "She want[s] some key that would enable her to understand, and in understanding, to endure, the heavy weight that had fallen on her young heart" (*MF* 345). Most importantly, she needs to find a way to explain and to reduce her rebelling sentiment:

> She rebelled against her lot, she fainted under its loneliness, and fits even of anger and hatred toward her father and mother, who were so unlike what she would have them to be; toward Tom, who checked her, and met her thought or feeling always by some thwarting difference,— would flow out over her affections and conscience like a lava stream, and frighten her with a sense that it was not difficult for her to become a demon. (*MF* 346)

She can't handle her "anger and hatred" toward her parents, nor could she repel her strong feeling toward her brother or people around her. The whole world is more like a mystery to her. So in order to laid upon "the burthen" of large wants and endure "this wide, hopeless yearning for that something, whatever it was, that was greatest and best on this earth", she needs to acquire "knowledge of the irreversible laws within and without her" (*MF* 347). She then goes to "Latin, geometry, and the forms of the syllogism" which may promote the masculine wisdom like his brother, yet finds them remote from "the living world" (*MF* 347). Her encountering with *Thomas a Kempis* gives her the explanations that she has been longing for[①], which urges her to stop immersing herself in her personal pleasures. "Resign thyself, and thou

---

① *Thomas a Kempis* here means a work from Thomas a Kempis, a German-Dutch canon regular of the late medieval period. His most famous writing was a devotional classic called *The Imitation of Christ*—one of the most popular and best known Christian books on devotion.

shalt enjoy much inward peace" (*MF* **349**). Although the advice from *Thomas a Kempis* is to ask Maggie to renounce herself, this advice helps her see "the secret of life" (*MF* **349**).

> Here, then, was a secret of life that would enable her to renounce all other secrets; here was a **sublime height** to be reached without the help of outward things; here was insight, and strength, and conquest, to be won by means entirely within her own soul. ①(*MF* **349**)

It is the first time that Maggie knows that she can use her power, strength, and conquest to "win within her own soul". She won't be troubled by the outside world, nor will she indulge herself in the dream world any longer. It is also for the first time "she saw the possibility of shifting the position from which she looked at the gratification of her own desires" (*MF* **349**). The self-renunciation helps Maggie saw the possibility of shifting the point of view, which not only gets the flash conviction of life for "it flashed through her like the suddenly apprehended solution of a problem", but also "looking at her own life as an insignificant part of a divinely guided whole" (*MF* **349**). The ability to see the thing from other points of view is one of the most important qualities of sympathy, as what has been reinforced in *Daniel Deronda* that sympathy is "an activity of imagination on behalf of others" (*DD* **215**). Through seeing things from the other point of view, Maggie relates her lonely part to the divine wholeness. Her spiritual progress highlights a complicated relationship through sympathy by approaching to the sublime height. Similar to Maggie Tulliver's experiences, Dorothea Brooke in *Middlemarch* is preoccupied with another unpleasant intellectual bewilderment.

---

① The bold are intentional.

4.1.2 *Middlemarch* and Dorothea Brooke's Terror

Middlemarch, A Study of Provincial Life (1871-1872) sets its story in the fictitious Midland town of "Middlemarch" during 1829-1832. "Middlemarch" refers to the central English provincial counties and "march" or "marchland" in English means a border between counties. It is in this provincial background that involves such a complicated image of a society in which the political, agricultural, aristocratic, plebeian, religious and even the scientific are all included. It is a microcosm, local but also universal, containing body and mind knowledge, individual and communal life, birth and death episodes, tragedy and comedy plots, and even Britain and Europe transitions. It situates a work of realism encompassing the historical events like the 1832 Reform Act, the beginnings of the railways, and the death of King George IV, etc. It incorporates contemporary medicine or medical treatment and examines the reactionary views of a settled community facing unwelcomed social change. That is why in *Middlemarch*, the characters are thrown into a vast social body and their fates are more likely to be determined by the natural laws. The outside world seems more oppressing than ever to impacting onto man's mental and psychological world.

In the town of "Middlemarch", Dorothea Brooke, young and beautiful, passionate yet orphaned, desires to make something of her life different and is longing for "a certain spiritual grandeur" like Saint Theresa (*MM* 3).① "Her mind was theoretic and yearned by its nature after some lofty conception of the world" (*MM* 6). She then tries to look after the poor and dedicates herself unselfishly to a community, which influences her decision to marry an elderly and pedantic

---

① Saint Teresa of Avila (1515-1582), Spanish saint and mystic, founder and reformer of religious communities.

clergyman, Mr. Casaubon, who has spent his time constructing an unfinished academic writing—"Key to All Mythologies" (*MM* 40). Dorothea is always looking for chances to restore the sense of duty through intellectual assistance to her husband's work, but the latter refuses her favor which leaves Dorothea in frustration. Such an impression is particularly intensified during their honeymoon to Rome:

> A girl who had lately become a wife, and from the enthusiastic acceptance of untried duty found herself plunged in tumultuous preoccupation with her personal lot. The weight of unintelligible Rome might lie easily on bright nymphs to whom it formed a background for the brilliant picnic of Anglo-foreign society; but Dorothea had no such defence against deep impressions. Ruins and basilicas, palaces and colossi, set in the midst of a sordid present, where all that was living and warm-blooded seemed sunk in the deep degeneracy of a superstition divorced from reverence. (*MM* 124)

Dorothea's wedding journey to Rome serves as a typical example of how the outside world impacts the inner one. Rome as "the spiritual centre and interpreter of the world", brings "quickening power of a knowledge which breathes a growing soul into all historic shapes, and traces out the suppressed transitions which unite all contrasts" (*MM* 123-124). However, it seems overwhelmed and part-terrified to Dorothea by viewing the vast presence of ancient and modern art. The flood of feeling finds nowhere to flow.

Dorothea does not even know what to deal with such experiences. She is not only troubled by the intellectual bewilderment in Rome but also frustrated by finding the fact that she is reduced to be a victim of her marriage. The more she sees through it, the sadder she becomes. Although "the inward amazement" is too early to fully "recognize or at least admit the change, still more for her to have readjusted that devotedness which was so necessary a part of her mental life that she was almost sure sooner or later to recover it" (*MM* 124-125). In this sense, the outside world lashes Dorothea's inner one and drags her into the emotional abyss:

> With all the depths of her emotion roused to tumultuous activity, and with life made a new problem by new elements, she had been becoming more and more aware, with a certain terror, that her mind was continually sliding into inward fits of anger and repulsion, or else into forlorn weariness. How far the judicious Hooker or any other hero of erudition would have been the same at Mr. Casaubon's time of life, she had no means of knowing, so that he could not have the advantage of comparison; but her husband's way of commenting on the strangely impressive objects around them had begun to affect her with a sort of mental shiver. (*MM* 126)

The failure in marriage brings Dorothea shock and terror—similar feelings caused by the sublime experience.

As having been discussed in the previous section, the sublime interpreted by Pseudo-Longinus, Kant and Burke involve an awe-inspiring experience by encountering an object or an entity that greatly exceeds man's understanding. It results in emotional shock and ambivalence and an eventual understanding of the profound difference between the subject and the object. The sublime that describes the experience of external nature thus becomes inverted; Dorothea, instead of facing great physical height or mass, suffers from the experience the totality of immersion in the interior and she is "plunged in tumultuous preoccupation" (*MM* 124). Since her longing for the noble and the grandeur is frustrated by the everyday trivial, which tears her into parts and she needs urgently to find unity for her divided self. Both Maggie

Tulliver and Dorothea Brooke are imaginative, sensitive, harboring goodwill toward the rest of the world. However, their strong passion leads their imagination either to some dream world as Maggie or some impracticable devotion to others as Dorothea, however, the insensitive response of ignorance from the others always brings them a strong sense of loss, and that is why Maggie is always feel angered and Dorothea terrified. Their emotional cracks need to be integrated with some spiritual elevation and intellectual invigoration, to help them transcend the mundane.

In *The Mill on the Floss*, Maggie finds a "sublime height" reached with her power and strength. She can form insight, strength, and conquest to "win within her own soul" (*MF* 349). This spiritual inspiration comes from her reading of a book from *Thomas a Kempis* which suggests her stop being confined by the gratification of her own desire. It is known that Eliot expects her realist writing to evoke the readers' sympathy, feelings, and imaginations to sense other's needs and desires. For reading is properly an estimable tool to take man outside his own world and it is by this process art deploy the manipulating power over readers. Matthew Arnold ever used the "provincial spirit" to describe the phenomenon that feeling excessively as a reader was a sign of narrowness. In his Oxford lecture of 1864 published as "The Literary Influence of the Academies", he spoke of readers with "weeps hysterical tears, and its disapprobation foams at the mouth" and believed that readers contacting with broader horizons of thought and art, will never be inclined to such effusion. Maggie Tulliver then under the guidance of both sympathy and the sublime has burning private needs and inner admiration unified in a large circumstance.

Maggie was still panting for happiness, and was in ecstasy because she had found the key to it. She knew nothing of doctrines and systems—of mysticism or quietism; but this voice out of the far-off middle ages was the direct communication of a human soul's belief and experience, and came to Maggie as an unquestioned message. (*MF* 349-350)

When Maggie is oppressed by the outside forces from family troubles, the consequent compelling emotions overwhelm her, then her encountering with *The Imitation of Christ* wakes up her inner force, so she comes to know that there is a world-man's inner world can approach a "sublime height" without "the help of outward things". Walter Pater ever issued what amounts to a challenge to the modern artist:

> What modern art has to do in the service of culture is so to rearrange the details of modern life, so to reflect it, that it may satisfy the spirit. And what does the spirit need in the face of modern life? The sense of freedom. That naive, rough sense of freedom, which supposes man's will to be limited, if at all, only by a will stronger than his, he can never have again. (Pater 180)

To Pater as well as to Eliot, it is art this time that reminds man of his power and insight. A stronger strength will urge him to exceed the force working on him and transcend the limit of himself by obtaining a sense of freedom.

Eliot ever claims that all ideas of life embodied in art must be grouped "in the needful relations, so that the presentation will lay hold on the emotions as human experience" and it will bring "'flash' conviction on the world by means of aroused sympathy" (qtd. in Stang 156). The suggestion for *Thomas a Kempis* that "if he should attain to all knowledge, he is yet far off", and he needs to "go wholly out of himself" (*MF* 349). Such a "flash" conviction of life through sympathy echoes with the significant aesthetic operation of the sublime.① Taking this fact into consideration, the following section will highlight how sympathy serves as a breakthrough toward the sublime and how sublime guide the sympathetic imagination for an extroversive action, or as what Maggie has done to approach to "a sublime height" by exciting the power within, and the internal transformation successfully accomplish the process of self-transcendence.

4.2　The Divisive Social Body and the Sublime Enquiry

4.2.1　A Sublime Literature and an Elevation of the Mind

The contemporary reflection on the sublime today frequently refers to a noble and morally positive implication. It actually is a complicated and proliferous concept and has many dimensions of meaning. It is a technical term widely used by philosophers, aestheticians and literary theorists.② Generally speaking, it is aesthetic and ethical, philosophical and psychological, political and as well as rhetorical. Traditionally, the burst of interest in the sublime gives credit to the wide discussion in aesthetical discourse of the long Eighteenth Century. And sublimity becomes an aesthetical category and is basically understood as a quality and

---

① Charles Martindale's plea in *Latin Poetry and the Judgement of Taste* (2005) for an "aesthetic turn" in Classical studies highlights the enthusiasm for aesthetic value in Eliot's works.

② The discussion of the sublime is generally based on the source of Pseudo-Longinus's *On the Sublime* (1st century AD), Edmund Burke's *A Philosophical Enquiry into the Origin of Our Ideas of the Sublime and Beautiful* (1757) (1901), Immanuel Kant's *The Critique of Judgement* (1790), John Hipple Jr.'s *The Beautiful, the Sublime and the Picturesque in Eighteenth Century British Aesthetic Theory* (1957), Samuel Monk's *The Sublime: A Study of Critical Theories in XVIII-Century England* (1960), Carol Bernstein's The Celebration of Scandal: Toward the Sublime in Victorian Urban Fiction (1991), Tom Furniss's Edmund Burke's Aesthetic Ideology (1993), *etc*.

consequence of "greatness" or "the magnitude" in nature, especially the earth's splendors such as storms, volcanoes, waterfalls, and mountain vista. The discovery of and attraction to the sublimity of such phenomena will arouse fear and terror in the spectators. This is a result of the human mind's inability to comprehend such grand, infinite and limitless objects or concepts. Such quality constitutes a substantial source for earlier sensibility literature. To some extent, when the quality of the sublime is mentioned; the Gothic literary style is always brought into people's minds for the Gothic always brings about terror and awe in the readers, so is the tragic art for it also evokes painful effect.

What worth noting is the birth of the sublime has nothing to do with terrible or supernatural sense. On the contrary, it means an elevation and ecstasy of the mind affected by a great piece of art. Traditionally, the burst of interest in the sublime gives credit to Pseudo-Longinus (1st century AD). ① This Roman rhetorician sets the main paradigms of discussing the concept of sublimity and prompts the succeeding exploration. In contrast to the descriptions of the experience of the sublime under the craft of the aestheticians and philosophers, Pseudo-Longinus examines the sublime in the formulation of great rhetoric in literary discourse, particularly the rhetorical devices to construct the sublime style in poetry and oratory. Longinus defines sublimity (hypsos) in literature as "the echo of greatness of spirit", which means the moral and imaginative power of the writer may create a great piece of work (Longinus 162). Thus, for the first time greatness in literature is ascribed

---

① Pseudo-Longinus (1st century AD) is a name sometimes assigned to the author of *On the Sublime* (Peri Hypsous), one of the great seminal works of literary criticism. The earliest surviving manuscript, from the 10th century, first printed in 1554, ascribes it to Dionysius Longinus. Later it is noticed that the index to the manuscript of "Dionysius or Longinus". The problem of authorship embroiles scholars for centuries and finally is solved by a name of Pseudo-Longinus.

to qualities innate in the writer, Longinus critically condemns certain artificial literary works as examples of bad styles of writing, in contrast, those works stemming from genuine emotions and grand imaginations are good ones. He ultimately promotes an "elevation of style" in artistic creation(Roberts 8). To present the sublime style of writing, the first and most important source is "the power of forming great conceptions" (Brody 9). The concept of the sublime then generally refers to a style of writing that elevates itself "above the ordinary" (Brody 18). In addition, Longinus lists out five sources to construct sublimity in art: "great thoughts, strong emotions, certain figures of thought and speech, noble diction, and dignified word arrangement." (Longinus 150) The effects of the sublime then orient to the loss of rationality, an alienation leading to identification with the creative process of the artist and a deep emotion mixed in pleasure and exaltation. Namely, "the sublime leads the listeners not to persuasion, but to ecstasy" (Longinus 143). And the writer's goal is not so much to express empty feelings but to arouse emotions and imaginations in his audience. As a result, the sublime artistic work brings the audience a sense of ecstasy. With Pseudo-Longinus's contribution, qualities like enthusiasm, ecstasy, imagination, and pathos are all invited to characterize the notion of sublimity. Longinus's stress on the readers' reception and experiences of artist work establishes the foundation for the following elaboration of this concept. Edmund Burke (1729-1797) and Immanuel Kant (1724-1804) then especially investigate the concept of sublimity in the aesthetic domain. The sublime then means the absolutely large things with the greatness of dimension which brings painful or threatening experiences, it always brings in strong, intense feelings that the human mind could feel.

Whatever is fitted in any sort to excite the ideas of pain and danger, that is to say, whatever is in any sort terrible, or is conversant about terrible objects, or operates in a manner analogous to terror, is a source of the sublime; that is, it is productive of the strongest emotion which the mind is capable of feeling. (Burke 20)

Under the craft of Burke, the sublime is associated with things that may bring about pain, terror and danger, and artistic work of tragedy particularly evokes such feelings. However, tragedy appreciation may bring the spectators aesthetical delight. Such delight cannot be realized without the operation of sympathy.

For sympathy must be considered as a sort of substitution, by which we are put into the place of another man, and affected in many respects as he is affected; so that this. Passion may either partake of the nature of those which regard self-preservation, and turning upon pain may be a source of the sublime or it may turn upon ideas of pleasure. (Burke 26)

Sympathy realizes a substitution by putting one into another man's position. With a sense of self-preservation, pain and terror could be transformed into the ideas of pleasure. Sympathy in this sublime aesthetic domain becomes an important mechanism for transforming feelings like pain and terror into aesthetical pleasure and prosocial activities. Both art and the real events unfold before man's eyes will elicit real feelings. That is why training in art appreciation will improve man's behaviors in reality. So sympathy and the sublime stress very much on a self-transparent experience, helping man know his life and the world outside him. In *The Mill on the Floss*, Maggie Tulliver's encountering with *Thomas a Kempis* brings hope to Maggie for the book advises Maggie that "know that the love of thyself doth hurt thee more than anything in the world... If thou seekest this or that and wouldst be here or there to enjoy thy own will and pleasure, thou shalt never be quiet nor free from care" (*MM* 347-348). Since Maggie finds *Thomas a Kempis* for the latter gives her explanations of the "the secret of life", she makes her mind to imitate the unselfish practice in *Thomas a Kempis*, expecting to approach to the sublime hight that any great literature may promise. This fact urges her to fully display the inner power to win the outside world which is full of mysteries. In this sense, *Thomas a Kempis* is a sublime work and it gives a model for Maggie to aspire. She enjoys the "ecstasy" and "the suddenly apprehended solution of a problem" provided by the book, then she starts "looking at her own life as an insignificant part of a divinely guided whole" (*MF* 349). Since Maggie wants to observe things as parts in a larger whole, or in relations, she has to investigate others and herself in unification. The preferred way is to integrate herself with the others by "resigning" oneself, or renunciation. As sympathy cannot be limited to an ego-centered activity, Maggie's positing herself in relations will make it possible for her to generate sympathy.

Of course, the concept of the sublime, like the concept of sympathy, also undergoes an evolutionary process; the sublime height in the literature to evoke man's imaginations and feelings in *The Mill on the Floss* is replaced by a sublime smallness confronted with a huge social body beyond man's capability of understanding in *Middlemarch*.

4.2.2 A Sublime Social body and a Split Self

Dorothea Brook in *Middlemarch* is always long for some "lofty conception of the world", and she is "enamoured of intensity and greatness, and rash in embracing whatever seemed to her to have those aspects" (*MM* 6). She expects to make martyrdom for accomplishing those glorious goals. Someway, this mentality influences her decision to marry the old and pedant Edward Casaubon who is seemingly "engaged on

Chapter 4 Sympathy and the Sublime Enquiry in
The Mill on the Floss and Middlemarch

a great work concerning religious history" (*MM* 6). For the inward source in Casaubon for constructing the world "as it used to be, in spite of ruin and confusing changes" impressed Dorothea at the moment when she thought of she may participate in such glorious work, "with a view to the highest purposes of truth"— what a work to be in" (*MM* 12). Then her long suppression under "the indefiniteness" may be evolved into enthusiasm by discovering the end of life (*MM* 18). It will offer a "room for her energy" (*MM* 28). However, the real unhappy marriage tears Dorothea apart because of Casaubon's nature of selfishness, self-conceit and self-closing. The "large yet definite duties" Dorothea expects is minimized into a profession of hostess in Casaubon's house. She is suffered from another tape of inward uneasiness when confronted with the unmanageable world and the incomprehensible other. In *Middlemarch*, the sublime "registered in terms of social consequence rather than aestheticism" (Rectenwald 170). This means, a growing social body is to come and make a man a smaller and smaller part in it, and this fact will work as a divisive force splitting the man's self apart.

Kant in his *Third Critique* elaborates his understanding of the sublime as an aesthetic experience appealing for a reason while confronting the overwhelming excess either of greatness or power. In addition, "the sublime is introduced in *the Critique of Judgment* as a state of mind elicited by the representation of boundlessness or the infinite" (Makkreel 303). The characteristic feature of the sublime, or the "movement of the mind", "is referred by the imagination either to the faculty of cognition or to the faculty of desire" (Makkreel 303). Kant emphasizes the limitation of imagination when confronted with ideas of reason. The experience of the sublime is a result of a subjective one encountering something which is absolutely great or menacing. The sublime allows us to correlate miscellaneous phenomena and perceive them in a new light.

For some modern scholars,

> The judgment of the sublime involves a polar relation between 1) aesthetic pretension, which is absolute in lying at the basis of all comparison or reflective judgment, and 2) the limit of aesthetic comprehension, which is the absolutely great beyond all comparison. Thus, the imagination contains a simultaneous reference to an absolute measure and the immeasurable. (Makkreel 304-305)

In other words, imagination plays a key role in understanding the sublime: "the imagination has been assigned the dual function of apprehension and comprehension." (Makkreel 305) This imagination to Kant works in relation to the reason for reason strives to comprehend the infinite. The sublime enquiry thus "shows a faculty of mind surpassing every standard of sense" (qtd. in Makkreel 307). In approaching the sublime, the imagination, although it cannot encompass the infinite, surpasses the standard of sense and strives for a kind of completeness and integrity with the infinite. Man then becomes a part of the whole consisting of both him and the incomprehensible. In this way, the sublimity makes it possible the transcendence from the infinity. It is with such interiority and transcendent process that the openness of non-intellectual or non-ideal assimilates the outside into the inner and invests man with moral authority. That's why the virtue of the sublime is connected to the freedom of man and associates itself with aesthetic feelings. Kant's theory of empirical interest has affinities with the social nature of aesthetic experience in the empiricist theories, such as Hume's appeal to the operations of sympathy and imagination in aesthetic responses to art and nature. It is the expansion of imagination in relation to the aesthetic ideas that help man draw out a more productive mode, a level at which the sublime is also coming into play.

No matter it is the sublime in Pseudo-Longinus's rhetoric or in Burke's and Kant's aesthetics, it invites a response of strong emotions and imaginations. The intense, mixed emotions and expansion of imagination are particularly stressed while facing the sublime. The sublime, like other forms of aesthetic value, is dependent upon both perceptual qualities of objects as well as the response they cause in the subject. The most visceral part of the sublime reaction, a feeling of being overwhelmed by size or power, is linked to the ways in which an object strikes the senses and imagination. And the work of imagination is expanded and invigorated as it tries to cope with the infinite greatness or the incompressible other. This mental activity brings along with it feelings of anxiety and astonishment. And sympathy plays an important part in transforming those sensory experiences into uplifted pleasures. Artistic works also have the capacity to elicit mixed emotional responses associated with the sublime—anxiety, fear, delight, and terror, etc. The aesthetic enquiry into the sublime involves a conquering over those feelings when a man is being intensely struck by them. Profoundly, perhaps the best way we get in the arts to the metaphysical force of the sublime is to be trained to display our capacity for some kind of insight about the world or the human condition.

In addition, sympathy shares a similar implication with the notion of sublimity. For when the sublime is investigated, sympathy is always being tested or verified. Richard Payne Knight in his *An Analytical Inquiry into the Principles of Taste* (1805) keenly observed the relationship between the sublime and sympathy. He goes back to Longinus who had emphasized the elevation and the ecstasy of the mind to find evidence. All sympathies excited and appropriate expressions of energetic passion belong to the sublime since they "tend to expand and elevate the mind; and fill it with those enthusiastic raptures, which Longinus justly states to be true feelings of sublimity" (Knight 331). This view leads Knight to claim that the pathetic is always sublime for this term evidently denotes an energetic expression of passion. All sublime feelings, "whether they are excited by sympathy with external objects, or arise from the internal operations of the mind"(Knight 361), will exalt and expand the mind. Thus, in grasping the infinity, the mind exercises the power "of multiplying itself without end; and, in so doing, it expands and exalts itself, by which means its feelings and sentiments become sublime" (Knight 361). This principle of expanding or exalting the mind becomes the source of the sublimity no matter it is facing a vast object in nature or appreciating the vast social body, or even enjoying a piece of great work in art.

Since there is an affinity between the sublime and the notion of sympathy, sympathy always serves as a way for a man to approach the sublime, and sublime in turn guides man's sympathy out of the ego-centered tendency. In short, sympathy under the guide of sublime helps man accomplish a self-transcendence from the ego-centered tendency to open-minded mentality, viewing things as parts of a larger whole of relations. And man urges his power of imagination to negotiate the relationship between him and the rest of the world. Highlighted by this view, the following section will include *The Mill on the Floss* and *Middlemarch* into discussion, arguing how sympathy, relating closely to the notion of the sublime, realizes a critical inner transformation from an aesthetic vision into a moral extension, and guiding man's inside imagination to reach outside himself. Sympathy either associates with an automatic mimetic behavior of self-renunciation or with reflective and cognitive human endowment.

4.3　Sympathy Transformed and the Emergence of the Sovereign Self

4.3.1　Sympathy Transformed and a Self-renunciation

We've discussed much that the spiritual process of sympathy shares an affinity with the sublime for both welcome an exaltation or expansion of the mind by properly directing the intense feeling and imagination toward a larger whole. Echoing with the sublime implication and under its guide, sympathy in *The Mill on the Floss* functions in two critical ways, it helps man view himself as a part of relations and it elevates the immediate sense, which consequently results in a fact of "passionate moral idealism" (Guth 9).

Inspired by *Thomas a Kempis* which persuades her to renounce her personal joy and sadness, Maggie gets to know that there is a world "higher than mere personal enjoyment" and that is "the sacredness of life" (*MF* 556). She is enthralled and she finds that the remote voice of the narrator sympathetically captures her error. Her problems have been given answers from the ancient world. She decides to imitate what *Thomas a Kempis* has suggested: to renounce the self and cares about others' pains and suffering while being trapped by the emotional demands of a needy self.

Maggie encounters with Philip Wakem—son of the lawyer who has been beaten by Maggie's father after failing a trail. Philip is a talented, sensitive but physically deformed young man who offers to understand Maggie. They share mutual attraction but only keep their meetings secretly, for neither of their families would approve. Maggie has grown into a true beauty, and Philip's deformity is viewed as unfortunate. Then

Maggie has a deep emotional connection to Stephen Guest, the handsome and civilized gentleman who is also the fiancé of Maggie's cousin—Lucy. Stephen is so irresistible to Maggie and Maggie gradually finds she falls in love with Stephen. But Stephen is to marry Lucy and Philip is still waiting for Maggie. When fate brings Maggie and Stephen onto one boat and it flows away from St. Ogg, Stephen asks Maggie to marry him and leave to start a new life. Maggie then "sunk into this struggle with a temptation" (*MF* 556).

> Without the requisite participation or resistance, the sensation of sublimity will not arise at all, and, once it has, the feeling of sympathy and union will dissipate if the attention of the spectator is divided, as an excess of fear will draw him away from consciousness of and submission to the immeasurable power. (Costelloe 183)

Any sublime process will invite a participating and a resisting process, but the work of sympathy as a uniting force will prevent the spectator to be completed detached, divided and help him not to submit to the immeasurable power, retaining the harmony inside the self and building some connections with the others.

Under the irresistible temptation from Stephen, Maggie "sets out by maiming the faith and sympathy that were the best organs of her soul. And then, if pain were so hard to her, what was it to others"(*MF* 556)? Thinking of Lucy and Philip and the pains they will suffer, Maggie transcends the limits of herself, and connecting her with her family, friends and the past: "to remain where all the ties of your life have been formed,— is a true prompting" (*MF* 598). Finally, all spiritual activities wake her sense of duty and urge her to renounce her personal love and joy.

Life stretched before her as one act of penitence; and all she

Chapter 4 Sympathy and the Sublime Enquiry in The Mill on the Floss and Middlemarch

craved, as she dwelt on her future lot, was something to guarantee her from more falling; her own weakness haunted her like a vision of hideous possibilities, that made no peace conceivable except such as lay in the sense of a sure refuge. (*MF* 596)

In this sense, Maggie's devotion to duty and her following "the divine voice within [her]" lead her to leave Stephan and come back to St. Ogg. This decision is an active exercise of her moral consciousness rooted within sympathy and within her ability to perceive herself in relation to Lucy Dean and Phillip Wakem. Maggie thus retains her integrity by preventing her from falling. It is sympathy and the sublime keep her from being blind to other people's suffering; she displays full potentiality of man's will and spiritual admiration thus exhibits the power of self-control and self-organizing with sympathetic imagination.

The above assertion proves that the most visceral part of the sublime reaction, a feeling of being overwhelmed by size or power, is linked to the ways in which an object strikes the senses and imagination. Maggie's spiritual development also reflects that the sublime will polish "the instinctual sense" and elevate it into a "higher level of self-determination" to "harmonize warring inner needs" (Guth 80). When Maggie begins to reflect her affection toward Stephen, she says: "[i]f I had been better, nobler, those claims would have been so strongly present with me... if I had not been weak, selfish, and hard, — able to think of their pain without a pain to myself that would have destroyed all temptation" (*MF* 577). She then lets the nobler spiritual aspiration suppress the weak and selfish instinct and refuses Stephen's love, for she cannot take a good for herself "that has been wrung out of their [Lucy and Philip] misery" (*MF* 608). In short, although it is hard to struggle and negotiate with the self and the other, Maggie's "longings after perfect goodness" shows an ideal and passionate moral outlook.

Rather than liquidating the self in a stream of unleashed emotions to establish a bond between self and other, Eliotic sympathy instead requires making the more radical yet controlled affective leap from the perceived solidity of the particular individual and her circumstances to the more gaslike and diffusive generality of imagining the self through others. (Spillman 371)

It is an undeniable fact that sympathy intertwining with the sublime helps Maggie exhibits autonomy and freedom based on aesthetic imagination and inner vision (*MF* 578). Such change not only reshapes the individual's inner world but also imposes the transformative power onto other people's minds.

The aesthetic ideas of the sublime in the Victorian Age involves "anything which being itself great makes us great by the sympathy we have with it is sublime" (qtd. in Costelloe 234). It is always associated with "something extraordinary and of great power" to produce a "superiority and inward glorying":

> It appears to me, that we may often trace the source of this "inward glorying" to the greatness of the object itself or to the ideas excited & associated with it, as the idea of Deity with vastness of Eternity, which superiority we transfer to ourselves in the same manner as we are acted on by sympathy. (Gruber and Barrett 387-388)

The sublimity in Darwin's words "has a crucial subjective dynamic which may be unwittingly 'transferred' between object and subject" (Bradley 215). Such transferal carries a similar color with the working of sympathy. So when Philip Wakem, the abandoned pitiful creature, knows the struggle of Maggie and her sacrifice for his sake, he begins to recognize he has been a selfish relationship with a selfless Maggie:

Chapter 4 Sympathy and the Sublime Enquiry in
The Mill on the Floss and *Middlemarch*

> The new life I have found in caring for your joy and sorrow more than for what is directly my own, has **transformed** the spirit of rebellious murmuring into that willing endurance which is the birth of strong sympathy. I think nothing but such complete and intense love could have initiated me into that enlarged life which grows and grows by appropriating the life of others; for before, I was always dragged back from it by ever-present painful self-consciousness. I even think sometimes that this gift of transferred life which has come to me in loving you, may be a new power to me. ①(*MF* 608-609)

The birth of strong sympathy entrusts Philip new life for caring for others, and such transferred life helps him steps into an enlarged horizon. To Maggie and to Philip, sympathy as a way to approach the sublime constitutes the growth of the mind, and it involves the capacity to undergo and to understand emotional experiences by elevating the instinctive impulse into a higher level. Maggie Tulliver, who yearns for some unlearned secret of existence, with the passionately yet naively spiritual power approaches the sublime with sympathy, although the whole story ends up with tragedy, Maggie at least convinces people that man has a will to retain integrity and defense his freedom. He has the choice to admire the good and the noble.

Since Maggie Tulliver's story ends up with tragedy, which arouses a problem that as Alexander Bain (1818-1903) in his *The Emotions and the Will* (1859) underlines that the intellectual component of sympathy, associates it not with automatic mimetic behavior but also with reflective and cognitive human endowment. "It cannot be too much reflected on that sympathy is an intellectual endowment, and flourishes only under a

---

① The bold is intentional.

certain development of intelligence" (qtd. in Burdett 328). "Sympathy thus toggled uncomfortably back and forth between instinctual body and 'advanced' cognitive consciousness" (Burdett 328). In *Middlemarch*, the tension or imbalance between the instinctual body and the cognitive consciousness is intensely represented, and during this time, Dorothea Brooke has to face with more blocks than Maggie, and the former's admiration for higher spiritual life is replaced by worshiping the secular sublime. Her way to transcend from the mundane to the ethereal spiritual truth involves the intellectual growth of Self-discovery.

4.3.2 Sympathy Transformed and a Self-discovery

The nineteenth-century witnessed a booming of the secularization for "the age of Darwin, the age of steam, and the age of the first self-identified secularists" (Laporte 287). As one important manifestation, "romanticism was seen as a kind of aesthetic secularization or aestheticism as secularization, while a 'crisis of faith' narrative predominated in understandings of the Victorian period" (Rectenwald 2). In *Nineteenth-Century British Secularism* (2016), Michael Rectenwald defines the meaning of "the secular" as the "the non-religious" signifying the "the worldly aspects of 'this life'" (Rectenwald 4).

> That is, it gestured toward the concerns of existence on earth as opposed to eternity or another world, and to the activities for maintaining and living an earthly life as opposed to the aspirations of religious life or spiritual improvement. (Rectenwald 4)

When the notion of the secular is introduced, it means the happiness of this life and the earthly life. However, the post-secular does "signify a skepticism or antagonism toward secularism in recognition of the persistence or 'resurgence' of religion" and it "recognizes the persistence of religion and marks an acknowledgment of a religious and secular pluralism" (Rectenwald 6), and soon afterward considering the ethical resources and community-building efficacy based on religious belief.

That is why George Eliot is regarded as "a post-secularist" for she "acknowledged religion's ongoing viability, it's potential to contribute to individual, cultural, and national identity and the general weal" (Rectenwald 168). It is known that Eliot declared the "Holy War" of her lost Christian faith from the faith of Evangelicalism when she was young. ①She believes the power of sympathy instead of the dogmas of Christianity by the influence from free-thinkers like Ludwig Feuerbach (1804-1872), Auguste Comte (1798-1857), or Herbert Spencer (1820-1903). Although Eliot is labeled as a "godless writer" (Carroll 453) with a secular outlook, she never stops her exploration of the significance of religion in her art:

> Eliot often figured religion as a tissue that extended throughout and within the organic social body, a kind of living integument providing cohesion and shape, sustaining it in health and order. Religion could offer metanarratives that afforded meaning and coherence, ordering the experience of the subject, while enlarging the sympathies and recommending the dedication of individuals to broad social objectives. (Rectenwald 168)

As a result, George Eliot perhaps turns out to be "the key figure here as she sought with great success to make sympathy the bedrock of the realist novel's moral and formal work in secularising social contexts" (Burdett 320). In her artistic thoughts, sympathy seems to be more durable than doctrine, and she values "religious sentiment over theology, emotional truth over intellectual certitude, morality and generosity over

---

① George Eliot refused to go to church when she was still Mary Ann Evans after being influenced by the higher criticism that incorporated the literal and historical criticism into the investigation of the biblical writing.

'correct' doctrines," (Rectenwald 168), but she confesses that she "[has] not returned to dogmatic Christianity". Instead, she sees in relations "the highest expression of the religious sentiment that has found its place in the history of mankind, and I have the profoundest interest in the inward life of sincere Christians in all ages" (*Letters* III: 231). To restore the religious sentiment and the inward life of Christian tradition in its secular sense thus becomes the critical part of Eliot's involvement of reevaluating the significance of religion.

Simon During suggests that "Eliot's fictions mount an ambitious attempt at spiritual and intellectual invigoration and elevation" (During 428). Under her portrayal, Eliot reveals a community of an interactive whole which accommodates the infinite variety of beings and existences. And every being is so closely connected to every existence that Eliot observes the very possible way of the fusion of these disparities. As what has been investigated in the previous chapter, things may maintain some incomprehensible state, and other people's mind also keeps unknowable or at least not fully knowable to us. If a man wants to integrate the incomprehensible or the infinite he needs to exhibit a mental power beyond any standard sense. The consideration of a whole that can never be quite grasped with senses is also any moral choice requires (Hancock 6). That is no surprise that Eliot's fiction shows a strong ambition of spiritual and intellectual elevations.

It is well known that the notion of the sublime is a necessary quality for approaching religious experience:

> There is indeed an elementary religion, a certain religiosity, implied in the perception and enjoyment of the Sublime. The soul, awakened to a sense of the boundlessness of the universe, of its own essential littleness and inferiority, combines an aspiration after fuller knowledge with a devotional self-prostration in the presence

of that power, principle, or person, out of which we and all that we see, has proceeded. (Newman 14)

In the Victorian age, the experience of the sublime is not only fixed onto the religious sphere, John Ruskin sorts out all things that "elevates the mind is sublime", moreover, the "elevation of mind is produced by the contemplation of greatness of any kind, but chiefly, of course, by the greatness of noble things. Sublimity is, therefore, only another word for the effect of greatness upon the feelings" (qtd. in Costelloe 233). It is an "attribute of any object by which it expands or raises the feelings, so as to prevent them from dwelling on subjects little or momentary" (qtd. in Costelloe 234). In Ruskin's aesthetics, beauty arises from imitating nature while sublimity is the expression of human power over things beyond memetic. He particularly emphasizes "anything which being itself great makes us great by the sympathy we have with it is sublime" (qtd. in Costelloe 234). So it is through sympathizing the great things marks our own greatness, and this process of enquiry into sublime makes sympathy bears similarity with the sublime while surpassing the limit to measure the world. Since sublime is a totalizing aesthetics, so will be sympathy. This belief supports most of the Victorian aestheticians and artists and Eliot is no wonder one of them.

In *Middlemarch*, sympathy under the guide of the sublime offers while aesthetic means to cope with man's inability. Sympathy precisely serves as a vehicle for both a secular and religious sentiment and helps the individual to accept the other as a different equivalent with the self and realizes the transmission and replacement of common feelings. Thinking and feeling exactly as the others result in empathy, not sympathy (Greiner, *Sympathetic Realism* 159), so Eliot works to maintain a balance between the self and the other. In *Middlemarch*, when Dorothea finds her ideal husband is pedant, selfish and grim, she believes that "it had been easier to her to imagine how she would devote herself to Mr Casaubon" and appreciates his strength and wisdom, for "he had an equivalent centre of self, whence the lights and shadows must always fall with a certain difference" (*MM* 135). Dorothea's acceptance of Casaubon as a different entity that helps her producing a strong sympathy with Casaubon. She begins to tolerate his defect and faces with her failed marriage. Most importantly, she restores her belief in "reaching forward of the whole consciousness towards the fullest truth, the least partial good", for "there was clearly something better than anger and despondency" (*MM* 130). Dorothea reinterprets her feelings of anger and despondency caused by Casaubon in "the fullest truth", and treat Casaubon as her object to attempt to find unity inside herself. During this process:

> The other, for Eliot has "an equivalent center of self", and although everyone is perhaps given to see the self as sovereign, the sublime must reach for something more in order to offer the hope of a unified basis for instituting moral law. It must promise intersubjectivity, a consensus of two minds. (Hancock 6)

That is why sympathy is so stressed by Eliot, for it is sympathy that makes it possible to connect two minds. Moreover, as a post-secularist, Eliot starts to stress the power of sympathy in cultivating the man's character and personality, most importantly, man's elevation of the mind. While faced with the absolute unknowable social body, any person can recover the sovereignty of the self by "have our consciousness rapturously transformed into the vividness of a thought, the ardour of a passion, the energy of an action" (*MM* 177). He then begins to "reject the personal egoism and narrow ambition and embraces his (generally minor) role as a contributing participant in the grand project of social amelioration and the slow, gradual development of a general human character"; consequently, "the transcendental object of religious belief

Chapter 4 Sympathy and the Sublime Enquiry in *The Mill on the Floss* and *Middlemarch*

becomes the sublimity of secular causality stretching to eternity" (Rectenwald 170).

Realizing that there is a higher truth than personal anger and despondency, Dorothea finds "all her strength [is] scattered in fits of agitation, of struggle, of despondency, and then again in visions of more complete renunciation, transforming all hard conditions into duty" (*MM* 127). She reorganizes her mood and devotes herself to help his husband with his arduous work, expecting to find answers for all mythologies. When the latter died, she intends to finance a hospital for the town; she tries to comfort when she gets to know Tertius Lydgate is also suffering from a failed marriage. She tells Lydgate: "I would take any pains to clear you. I have very little to do. There is nothing better that I can do in the world." (*MM* 471) This radiant sympathy causes Lydgate to give himself up "for the first time in his life, to the exquisite sense of leaning entirely on a generous sympathy, without any check of proud reserve" (*MM* 471). Dorothea's transformational sympathy causes Lydgate to forget his ego and as well as his pride for a moment follows the guide of Dorothea's feeling. Even Rosamond Vincy is "taken hold of by an emotion stronger than her own" influenced by Dorothea's radiant sympathy. During the transformative process,

> If we had lost our own chief good, other people's good would remain, and that is worth trying for. Some can be happy. I seemed to see that more clearly than ever, when I was the most wretched. I can hardly think how I could have borne the trouble, if that feeling had not come to me to make strength. (*MM* 498)

Sympathy now is an unreplaceable mechanism for the interpersonal transfer of virtuous good and communal feelings. With sympathy, one's loss of good may be the other's regain of good.

Although Dorothea's path for spiritual aspiration has been hindered by numerous forces, she, at last, finds her feeling to the man she loves and harvest a happy marriage. In this way, "[t]he presence of a noble nature, generous in its wishes, ardent in its charity, changes the lights for us: we begin to see things again in their larger, quieter masses, and to believe that we too can be seen and judged in the wholeness of our character" (*MM* 470). Therefore, under the craft of Eliot, although the determining acts of man's life are not ideally beautiful, they provoke man's power and inner strength to elevate them out of the trivial mundane.

> They were the mixed result of young and noble impulse struggling amidst the conditions of an imperfect social state, in which great feelings will often take the aspect of error, and great faith the aspect of illusion. For there is no creature whose inward being is so strong that it is not greatly determined by what lies outside it... for the growing good of the world is partly dependent on unhistoric acts. (*MM* 514-515)

Sympathy now allows man's consciousness to enter into the secular realities, observing the self in a wide range of diverse outside world. It depends on the recognition of how hard it is to deny and renounce oneself in face of the powerful and the infinite. Under such circumstances, sympathy evolves into a spiritual aspiration for the good of others or the truth for oneself, which turns into strength for people to counter with the hard reality in return. During this process, sympathy serves either as a religious sentiment or a secularized evolutionary account to explain man's mental development of why and how we feel for others for the realization of self-discovery, thus, fiction writing expands possibilities of human life.

In *The Mill on the Floss* and as well as in *Middlemarch*, in order to present fully pictures of man's spiritual process and their struggle with the ego-centered tendency, George Eliot prefers to adopt a detailed depiction of character's thought and their reaction to a particular situation. The novel is thus considered as a panoramic presentation of life in the English countryside in which the story development is often interrupted by attempts to loop in political, economic affairs, etc. All are held together by one of the most complicated and brilliantly worked metaphors like "a web", or "a tissue", so as to disclose the visible or invisible connecting links between humans being and the outside world. In this way, Eliot put the self into connections so she could entangle the mysterious relationship between the inside world and the outside one. More importantly, Eliot tries to trace the gradual action of ordinary causes rather than exceptional, seeing the world of her novel as a microcosm in which all the parts related to the whole. This becomes a trademark of her realistic writing in *The Mill on the Floss* and *Middlemarch*.

4.4 Realism and the Panoramic View of the Organic Whole

Barbara Hardy in her *Forms of Feeling in Victorian Fiction* (1985) points out that "the forms and languages which represent affective experience" tend to break with the principle of mimesis in Victorian fictions, and "the narrative medium in all major Victorian novelists is reflexive, constantly diverting attention from verisimilitude to analysis" (13). In order not to fall into the trap of sentimentalism, the Victorian novelists have to include both scientific influence and the aesthetical presentation of man's affective life. In George Eliot's works particularly, "emotional experience precedes scientific and artistic taxonomy. Though scientist and the artist provide forms and languages which influence and direct our feelings by affecting our ways of thinking about feelings"

(Hardy 15). And the emotional experiences and bodily sensation can be translated for their "transcendent nature" into other forms of knowledge (*MM* 241). As having been discussed in the above sections, the realization of this transcendence seems impossible without a vehicle of sympathy. Sympathy relating the work of the enquiry into the sublime will translate the emotions of others and convert them into the internal experience, so the individual may accomplish integration with the larger whole of the social body or the incomprehensible other.

Since the sublime refers to the infinite and the abstract notion, and sympathy working with the sublime can help man see the relations and connections, so as to obtain a self-transcendence for self-discovery, which urges to Eliot put her characters into a vast social contest and observe man's mental activities in relations. To Eliot, the world is an associated organic wholeness, so she pays much attention to the relationships between the novel events. The best art form is thus often the organic whole of the relationship formation. This makes Eliot's novels show the intrinsic relationships like a panoramic style and blooms itself a plant. In her article "Form and Art" (1886), she expressed that the form of art strongly relies on inner relations. And the highest form of art is "the most varied group of relations bound together in a wholeness which again has the most varied relations with all other phenomena" (qtd. in Mansell 68). In other words, the highest form of art is the highest organism in which "there is a consensus or constant interchange of effects among its parts" (qtd. in Mansell 70). As a result, In *Middlemarch*, Eliot suggests that the universe is "tempting range of relevance" (*MM* 91), and thus offers description and analysis of the influences and interactions that make up a social life in "a panoramic view" (Eliot, *Letters* V 241). The high diversity and complicity of characters and events touch the reader affectively through "the extension of our sympathies", or "amplifying experience and extending our contact with our fellow-men beyond the bounds of our personal lot" (Eliot, *Essays* 144-145). For the potentiality of novel to invoke sympathy is founded on its attention to the lives of individuals within the "social medium" and society in *The Mill on the Floss* is described as "a divinely guided whole" in which one's "life as an insignificant part" in it (*MF* 349); or in *Middlemarch*, the society is described as a "certain primary webs or tissues, out of which the various organs are compacted (*MM* 95). In these two works and *Middlemarch* especially, Eliot further explains the limitations of human beings' thought as well as action. Part of the struggle involves characters' recognition that they are interdependent social beings in a network, and should be responsible for their effects on other beings; they have to learn that they have a position, a place in the system of things. Although such fact sounds negative for people who have been struggling for freedom, it has a positive effect: for people may recognize the limitations and can accept their immanence, which include a fact of a bodily temporality which only occupies space and time for some time in the world, and a mental potentiality which cannot know everything. Consciously assuming this position, people can choose the way to act better. One may well desire a "rapturous consciousness of life beyond self" (*MM*, "Prelude" xiii), but the possibilities of transcending—the body, the self or "domestic reality"— are severely limited, and most characters will come to know it with pain and difficulty. As a result, realism in these two novels then reveals a magic panoramic view to help man know himself and understand society.

"Knowledge, for Eliot, meant seeing relationships" (Gindele 258). For the recognition of the theory of relations, the idea of organic interdependence is to be investigated. To Eliot, society is an organic wholeness. The notion of "organic society" appears in Marx's conclusion to the preface of *Capital* (1867): "Within the ruling-classes themselves, the foreboding is emerging that the present society is no solid crystal, but an organism capable of change, and constantly engaged in a process of change." (Marx 93) In England, "the society is more alike of as sublime organism was ambiguous enough to demand sustained interpretative effort" (Payne 8). In such a society, the smallest change occurs in history may make the nature of the present moment radically different. The connection of the past, the present, and the future is closed related. Similarly, the social body is also an organic structure in which the social vitality depends much on the mutual relation of men through the transmission and transgression of feeling.

Eliot believed along with G. H. Lewes that the most highly evolved human being is always guided by feelings for other human beings. In her search for a moral framework as a replacement for religion, Eliot regards the individual as a coherent being connected to others or the outside world, and the coherency is realized with sympathy and moral sensitivity, then knowledge, feeling, and action may integrate into one entity or respond with each other. In Dorothea's case, "the coherent social faith and order" that Dorothea needs urgently is to "perform the function of knowledge for the ardently willing soul" (*MM* 664). To get this coherence was to develop the largest "vision of relations" and the fullest connection to other beings by transforming existing relationships. Then as an important part of Eliot's realistic writing, she faithfully recording the complexity any individual may face while transforming the outside connections into inner growth.

For instance, Tertius Lydgate—the tragic hero of *Middlemarch*, wants to make scientific discoveries as well as devoted to the general good of being a good doctor. He is always plotting to introduce new medical treatments and medical systems to the town of "Middlemarch". He has no interest in personal relationships of the provincial society, yet he devotes himself into the scientific researches to find "primary webs or tissues" (*MM* 95), which will contribute to the advancement of medical science and as well as the well-being of individual human beings. Nevertheless, Lydgate lives a divided life in which the intellectual and the emotional being existing in separate spheres: "The reveries from which it was difficult to detach himself were ideal constructions of something other than Rosamond's virtues, and the primitive tissue was still his fair unknown." (*MM* 172) His determination to professional devotion was gradually worn out by an unhappy marriage with Rosamond for her erosive obstinacy. Lydgate, with "the hampering threadlike pressure of small social conditions, and their frustrating complexity" (*MM* 115) finds himself always be oppressed by the reiterative force of "social lot".

> The web itself is made of spontaneous beliefs and indefinable joys, yearnings of one life towards another, visions of completeness, indefinite trust. And Lydgate fell to spinning that web from his inward self with wonderful rapidity, in spite of experience supposed to be finished off with the drama of Laure—in spite too of medicine and biology; for the inspection of macerated muscle or of eyes presented in a dish. (*MM* 216)

Lydgate is in a society of web-like connections but he neglects the complex interdependencies between the inward and outward life which comprise the social medium in all its fluidity. "With the imagination that reveals subtle actions inaccessible by any sort of lens" (*MM* 105), he believes he can approach the full knowledge of both science and life. However, all his ambition ends up in vain after his marriage to the selfish Rosemond Vincy loving material life always, and the latter drags him into serious financial crisis. Lydgate's failure demonstrates the causation between the outside force and the inner loss of control. His intelligence acquired through observing things under lens does him little favor to understand the meaning of life, for life is beyond scientific observation. The latter only reveal the cause and effect relation, like two ends of the line but making him separating from other social parts.

If Lydgate sets up an example of failure, Will Ladislaw then manifests the organicist aesthetic in a proper way. "Human nature resides with the organic, communal life of the people; yet one becomes fully human by quitting that life, struggling into individuation, into historical and ethical identity" (Duncan, "George Eliot and the Science of the Human" 476). Will appreciate the poet who has "a soul in which knowledge passes instantaneously into feeling, and feeling flashes back as a new organ of knowledge" (*MM* 143). The transmission of feeling seems to him "as if he were beholding in a magic panorama a future where he himself was sliding into that pleasureless yielding to the small solicitations of circumstance" (*MM* 483). The "magic panorama" will help Will enjoys the semi-detachment and forecasts his future based on present circumstances. Then he knows of his capacity and doesn't behave passively, on the contrary, he acts out in a more self-reflexive way instead. Since Knowledge someway means relations, Will's insight acquired via his connection with a larger wholeness provides him a more reliable way for knowing. Philip Wakem finds an "enlarged life which grows and grows by appropriating the life of others" (*MFL* 608), and this inner growth makes him understand Maggie's self-renunciation of Stephan's love and suggests the latter not throw her into self-reproach.

As having been discussed before, the high details and complexities of characters and events celebrated in *The Mill on the Floss* and *Middlemarch* are strongly related to Eliot's understanding of artistic form. To Eliot, "the relation of multiplex interdependent parts to a whole which is itself in the most varied & therefore the fullest relation to the other wholes" (Eliot, *Selected Essays* 232). To some extent, form means how things are related to its environments, and form then mainly concerns with the "inward" relationship. "Eliot thinks the more relations there are, the higher the form" (Mansell 652). When George Eliot discusses artistic form in organic terms in her "Notes on Form in Art", she claims that "highest form" is the "highest organism" in which the story needs to grow and unfold by itself (Eliot, *Selected Essays* 232). Since the complex relations are bound together in wholeness, there will remain a harmony if every part constantly interchanges effects with each other, and all these facts make a perfect art the best tool to explore the real possibilities in life.

George Levine ever remarked George Eliot as a realist "almost obsessed with sympathy's possibilities" (Levine, "Review" 83). It is her understanding of artistic form and the organic society, and most importantly, her unification of the two sides in artistic creation presenting numerous diversities and complexities makes man observe things and him in relations. Such enquiry provides a better tool for man to grasp the undergoing actions in the dynamic subtle world and expresses them into bodily sensation and, ultimately, human action. Since it is difficult to describe the internal feelings and internal effective communications in realist writing, a descriptive representation of the external, visible world is always preferred. In other words, their internal feelings are always arising from the experience of their physiological nerve tissue. When Will Ladislaw is aware of his passion for Dorothea Brooke, his nerves respond to his feelings:

> He started up as from an electric shock, and felt a tingling at his finger ends. Any one observing him would have seen a change in his complexion, in the adjustment of his facial muscles, in the vividness of his glance, which might have made them imagine that every molecule in his body had passed the message of a magic

touch. (*MM* 241)

This sensory experience brings an epistemological activity and such a process is manifested through the activity of nerve tissues responding to the external environment. For Eliot, the nervous system is a reactive and lively factor to reveal man's affections and mental activities.

But most of the time, man is confronted with situations that "we don't quite know what it is and cannot do what we would", and as Dorothea clarifies that man longs for "what is perfectly good", "even we are part of the divine power" (*MM* 244). "She yearn[s] towards the perfect Right, that it might make a throne within her, and rule her errant will" (*MM* 486). The recovery of the sovereign of her mind provides an opportunity to carries out the self-organizing process under the guide of other's profit or the communal good. This means to deploy sympathetic potentiality and observing the self and the other as a whole and related entity. In this way, Eliot makes man observe himself in relations. His struggle and resistance with the self-orienting mentality reaffirms the difficult process of integrating "the effort of knowing and the ethic of loving" (Levine, *Realism, Ethics and Secularism* 27). As a result, "[t]he art with which [Eliot] struggled, often so painfully, was the place where the ideas and feelings could be most strenuously imagined, tested, and transformed from theory into life (Levine, *Realism, Ethics and Secularism* 27).

To conclude, sympathy serves as a breakthrough for people yearning for self-transcendence and freedom when facing the infinite or the obscure. In *The Mill on the Floss* and *Middlemarch*, Eliot examines the greatness of the spiritual power to worship the sublime in a relatively closed community. During this time, Sympathy, through raising feeling and sensation with the enquiry into the sublime, obtain the knowledge of a man's self by the process of self-annihilation or self-discovery, so as to explore the "realistic possibility" for social meliorism. Under such circumstances; sympathy serving either as a religious sentiment or a secularized evolutionary account to explain man's mental development compatible with the external environment, demonstrates a spiritual aspiration for the good of others or the truth for oneself, which turns into strength for people to counter with the hard realities. That is why realistic writing in these works presents a panoramic view of organic provincial life. It offers a faithful reproduction of the external and internal docking moments full of man's shock, fear, and terror. Therefore, the subsequent regulation process to adjust the inner world with the outside one becomes an unseparated part of Eliot's realist fictional writing. As a result, Eliot harbors an enthusiasm toward a romance as well as an intense interest in the evolutionary routine of human psychology so as to reveal a full view of human life.

In *The Mill on the Floss*, all characters are confused by the ever-changing social environment, although Maggie tries to test the glamour of will power and spiritual aspiration, her life ends up with tragedy, so on Dorothea and Will in *Middlemarch*, Eliot leaves more space for natural tendency to fashion or express themselves, which leads to much more positives attitude toward the intrinsic aesthetic value of both art and sympathy. In short, since sympathy shares an affinity with the sublime for both welcome an exaltation or expansion of the mind by properly directing the intense feeling and imagination toward a larger whole. Sympathy, relating closely to the notion of the sublime, realizes a critical inner transformation from an aesthetic vision into a moral extension, guiding man's inside imagination to reach outside himself.

Chapter 5
Sympathy and the Political Vision in *Daniel Deronda*

Daniel Deronda is the final novel written by George Eliot, and it was first published in February 1876. At that time, Eliot had been dedicating to the writing career for almost tens of years; her understanding of life seems to be much more profound than ever. She then integrates her profound thinking of society and humanity into the making of *Daniel Deronda* and presents it as a work "touching the limit of Victorian fiction" (Hardy, "Introduction" 8). Moreover, *Daniel Deronda* "represents the culmination, and the most complex instance, of her (Eliot's) sustained interest in the sympathetic and determinative power" (Capuano 179). In this novel, sympathy is no longer a medium to animate the "faithful pictures of a monotonous homely existence" in *Adam Bede* (196), nor does it serve as a source for realizing "incalculably diffusive" effect in *Middlemarch* (515). On the contrary, the "direct promptings of the sympathetic feelings" that Eliot has ever advocated in her previous works are replaced by a "paralyzing" force of depowering "indignation against wrong and that selectness of fellowship" in *Daniel Deronda* (*DD* 443). It displays a seeming discontinuity with Eliot's other artistic works. The word "seemingly" is adopted because the following part of this chapter will prove that Deronda's "diffusive" sympathy is also an inseparable and supplementary part of Eliot's full understanding of sympathy, for the cure of impartiality caused by too much diffusive sympathy offers Eliot an opportunity to reconsider the political vision sympathy may embody.

Daniel Deronda is the only story set in the contemporary social background in George Eliot's day. The work's mixture of social satire and moral searching, along with its sympathetic rendering of Jewish proto-Zionist ideas, has made this work one of the most renowned fictions in the Victorian age. Consequently, it doesn't seem to be a delightful work for many of Eliot's contemporaries. Henry James, for instance, regards it as unusual for it transmits "messages from mysterious regions" (qtd. in Carroll 363); even to the modern critics, it is "pervaded by ghosts and 'spirits', by forecasting, foresight and 'second sight'" and deviates "entirely from the codes of domestic realism" (Royle, *Telepathy and Literature* 92). We've got to know that Eliot treats sympathy as the foundation to realize the ethical and aesthetic value of her realistic writing. Yet in the novel of *Daniel Deronda*, sympathy becomes both "automatic" and "occult",① associating "with paralysis and with processes of transmission and transmutation" (Burdett 329). Sympathy once again becomes "one of the great psychological mysteries" describes by G. H. Lewes (*Letters*, V 376). The last chapter of this book aims to explain the abnormity of sympathy in *Daniel Deronda*. With the development of the story, Deronda's "diffusive" and "paralyzing" sympathy is gradually healed and adjusted by finding his birth identity or his nationality, although it is a Jew. Deronda's "impartial sympathy" shifting into "sympathy practical" makes one thing clear: sympathy as a form of universal love needs to be explained and revised with a national intimacy

---

① Roger Luckhurst claimed sympathy in *Daniel Deronda* as "strange occult economies" (43).

of preference. Our understanding via sympathy, moreover, must join with our collective activities in the ceaseless transformation of the conditions in which we carry on our lives since everyone is nothing but a constituent of the human-environmental whole.

We've talked much about Eliot's efforts to fully display the potentiality of the transformed and evolved sympathy for the betterment of both the individual mentality and social regulation. Sympathy works well in the comparatively enclosed provincial life in which there is some remnant of sense of community exciting mutual understanding or feeling transmission. However, Britain was to step into a modern society at the end of the 19th century, and that is the exact background in which Eliot depicts *Daniel Deronda*. During this period, British people welcomed in a high development of industrialization, a rise of the empire and rampant colonial expansion. The subsequent social circumstance of flexibility and mobility becomes an inevitable choice for everyone to live in, which brings about many consequences and two of them is too prominent to be neglected: the first one is that it forces men to separate themselves from the natural and traditional homely life centering on the cooking fires and dinner tables; the second one is that it pushes Britain and British people into a wider political environment. More broadly, the former will invite a decline of sense of community in which sympathy or fellow feeling may hold people together as "members of a whole" (Tönnies 32-33); and the latter marks an end for sympathy to be a universal benevolence, but legislates itself in a particular political community to generate a preference. These facts encourage George Eliot to testify the efficacy of the political implication of sympathy and explore the political vision of sympathy embodies. For "the future was, for us, contingent and open to will and imagination's shaping powers" (During 434). Sympathy this time transforms between people as a form of "consensus", based on the

Chapter 5 Sympathy and the Political Vision in *Daniel Deronda*

common understanding of sensory universal life experience of bodily sensations and feelings, and evolves into the public will to assist in reconstructing the national community. As a result, her account of the actual workings of sympathy within the consciousness reveals a slight shift.

> [Eliot] had come to believe that the usual accounts of conduct, motivation, will, and aspiration needed to be enlarged and complicated; if they were not, man would increasingly acquiesce in the vision of himself as a being whose actions were determined by the operation of vast impersonal forces beyond his control. (Preyer 34)

In the wide range of political environment, the practice of sympathy, if it is expected to offer the possibility for people to obtain self-knowledge and national identification, has to be connected with a more enlarged and more complicated mission, so man can exhibit the power to triumph over vaster impersonal forces. Under such circumstances, "she turned to the wisdom literature of the mystics and visionaries, emphasizing the way in which a receptivity to elective affinities and visions ... is related to the possibility of discovering a personal destiny and a socially useful vocation" (Preyer 34). So the realist art of Eliot has to undermine, question, transgress and contribute to social and political change (Aouadi 6). It is precisely because of this reason that Eliot's realism draws on the creative features of epic narration and myth-making, so as to explore the potentiality of sympathy in generating a healthy political vision in which shared sensibility may highlight the sense of national identity, and national identity may promote the reconstruction of national community: sympathy exhibit a power of transformative magic for communal "consensus" to relate the individual to his national community. So Eliot's consistent interest that the visionary account of personal inspiration may lead to possible national renewal is once again emphasized.

5.1 *Daniel Deronda* and Daniel's "Sabine Warrior"

5.1.1 *Daniel Deronda* and the Two Plots

Daniel Deronda is the only novel set in Eliot's own time period—the late 19th century, and it highly involves in more unusual contemporary themes compared with her other works: a cosmopolitan European society is to come; the position of Jews needs to be considered, and British people show extraordinary enthusiasm toward overseas affairs and their likely prospects. In this story, the eponymous hero Daniel Deronda is depicted as an idealistic young aristocrat who comes to aid the middle-classed woman Gwendolen Harleth to step out of selfishness and self-centeredness and proceed towards compassion and love in the above social contexts.

Daniel Deronda is attracted by a pretty lady named Gwendolen Harleth playing roulette at a hotel casino in Leubronn, Germany. The two characters' life experience then interacts with each other, serving as a mainline connecting the whole story. They are mutually attracted but the emotional attachment is not strong enough for a marriage. Gwendolen Harleth feels dread about everything, and Daniel Deronda finds himself emotionally inactive with too much sympathy. Finally, the beautiful, stubborn, and selfish Gwendolen Harleth marries the rich, cruel aristocrat Henleigh Mallinger Grandcourt for being reluctant to become a governess after a family financial crisis. The latter already has several children and a mistress, Lydia Glasher. Gwendolen's marriage is doomed to be a failure for it is filled with cheating and abnormal intentions. After Grandcourt's accidental death, Daniel Deronda encourages Gwendolen Harleth to find a larger world outside herself and return back to family duty or normal social life with an "infused action of another soul" (*DD* 953).

Meanwhile, another storyline about Daniel Deronda is also ongoing. Deronda is adopted and raised up by a wealthy gentleman—Sir Hugo Mallinger. Both Deronda himself and the people around him speculate that he is Sir Hugo's illegitimate son, although no one is certain about this. During the process of proving his birth information, Deronda accidentally rescues a young Jewish woman, Mirah Lapidoth. While helping Mirah to find her brother, he also gets the chance of approaching the Jewish culture and is strongly impressed. Deronda meets with a consumptive visionary Mordecai who passionately harbors the will for the restoration of the Jewish nation and reconstruction of the Promised Land. Realizing his falling into serious ill, Mordecai wants Daniel to become his intellectual heir and continue his dream. After Daniel Deronda's Jewish identity is confirmed, Daniel chooses to marry Mirah and the newly married couple set off their way for "the East" to dedicate to Zionism.

The story reveals both Daniel's and Gwendolen's mental journey searching for the realization of self-value and self-knowledge. Two plots of Gwendolen's realistic story in Britain and Daniel's epic chapter of Zionism intersect and overlap with each other. Such an arrangement forms a unique artistic charm of the novel. Yet to this fact, the critics have expressed mixed reviews. George Saintsbury agrees with many contemporary critics that *Daniel Deronda* carries both these virtues and faults to the extreme: the portrayal of Gwendolen and Grandcourt is almost unanimously praised as an "overwhelming success" (Saintsbury 253), while Deronda's Jewish half is made to express rather abstract ideas. Henry James also notes that "Gwendolen Harleth" is a masterpiece, for she is known, felt, and presented, psychologically, altogether in a grand manner. Beside her and her husband there is a consummate picture of English brutality refined and distilled (for Grandcourt is before all things brutal), but "Deronda, Mordecai, and Mirah are hardly more than shadows" (James 422). The prominent critic F. R. Leavis in *The Great Tradition* suggests that the Jewish sections of *Daniel Deronda* are its weakest, and it would be improved by removing the Jewish storyline, leaving Gwendolen Harleth's story to stand on its own (137). In a letter to Harriet Beecher Stowe in 1876, George Eliot makes a defense for herself:

> As to the Jewish element in *Deronda* ... precisely because I felt that the usual attitude of Christians towards Jews is—I hardly know whether to say more impious or more stupid when viewed in the light of their professed principles, I therefore felt urged to treat Jews with such sympathy and understanding as my nature and knowledge could attain to. (Carroll, *George Eliot: The Critical Heritage* 405)

So Eliot means to launch a survey against the "narrowness and bigotry" of the English people, for "stupidity, which is still the average mark of our culture" (Carroll, *George Eliot: The Critical Heritage* 405). For many critics, her calling for sympathy and understanding of the Jew become the evidence of Eliot's admiration of Jewish culture and approval of Zionism, but such dominant explanation is being increasingly questioned. Some scholars express Eliot's sympathy cannot be limited to the Eastern races. "Eliot. Not only was she strongly pro-Jewish, notably in *Daniel Deronda* (1876), but she was also sympathetic to other groups subject to much prejudice, such as the Gypsies, as is evident in her verse drama *The Spanish Gypsy* (1868), and the Irish" (Newton, "George Eliot and Racism" 654); Some Jewish scholars believe *Daniel Deronda* "focused not on the 'Zionist' elements of the book", but "on its conclusions regarding the preservation of the religious tradition of the Jewish people and the spiritual values that had accompanied its history of suffering" (Werses 15). In other words, it is the spiritual values harbored in the Jewish people to preserve their tradition, religion and nationality worthy of admiration but not the Jews as a race. So considering the fact that the novel also gives a fair depiction of other dim Jewish figures like Cohen and Lopidoth, researcher Gerlinde Röder-Bolton asserts that "the novel is not asking for sympathy and compassion for the Jews, but it poses a more radical challenge. Deronda can find no political purpose in England" (Röder-Bolton 205-206). Somewhere outside England becomes an ideal place for Daniel to seek his political meaning and social significance. In this aspect, the most famous criticism comes from Edward Said. He, from his post-colonial perspective, interprets Deronda's returning back to Judaism and Zionism as Eliot's approval of the colonial policy from the British Empire—incorporating the East into the Western Map (Said, *The Question of Palestine* 65). Moreover, he also accuses Eliot of perpetuating in the novel a myth of empty land: "on one important issue there was complete agreement between the Gentile and Jewish versions of Zionism: their view of the Holy Land as essentially empty of inhabitants." (Said 66) Said's "condemnation, which transforms Eliot into a Zionist and an imperialist, has played a key part in subsequent criticism" (Nancy, *George Eliot and the British Empire* 13). Although Said's remark is prevalent but it is not impressive enough, otherwise Nancy Henry in her whole book of *George Eliot and the British Empire* will not say that "criticism of *Deronda* that searches for an ideology to condemn has narrowed the notion of context to a morally blameworthy imperialism, distorting our understanding of the text's mimetic and moral subtleties" (113). Namely, Eliot seems to present colonialism or imperialism as a morally controversial issue to the public. So to the interests of this research, Deronda's departure from England to find his social meaning and political purpose needs to be reexamined from other perspectives.

If the research is not limited to the topic of opposition and contradiction between the English and the Jew, but simply concentrating the human care and moral consideration on Eliot's writing as always, or, if it were possible, to rouse the imagination of her English readers "to a vision of human claims in those races of their fellow-men who most differ from them in customs and beliefs" (Carroll, *George Eliot: the Critical Heritage* 405). Things may be completely refreshed. For some critics, the creative imagination with which George Eliot "succeeded in bringing before us, in all its inward, compelling power, and in all its fiery, action-craving impetuosity" is especially worthy of study (qtd. in Röder-Bolton 209). Such inward, compelling power is what sympathy has always be stressed and promised, and then an investigation on the issue of sympathy will still be a safe touchstone for further explanation. In the following part, this project will combine the historical background in the late Victorian age, focus on the reasons causing Deronda to lose his political significance in England, and provide a sufficient basis to explain Deronda's returning back to the Jewish nation through blood relationship after receiving formal British aristocratic education, so as to demonstrate a particular political vision transformed and evolved from sympathy.

5.1.2 Daniel's "Sabine Warriors" and the Paralyzed Sympathy

Like Dorothea in *Middlemarch*, Deronda is described as a young man full of sympathy, but his diffusive sympathy can't arouse elevated feeling or passionate actions in him. He is increasingly troubled with physical paralysis and mental inactivity instead.

His early-wakened sensibility and reflectiveness had developed into a many-sided sympathy, which threatened to hinder any persistent course of action: as soon as he took up any antagonism, though only in thought, he seemed to himself like the Sabine warriors in the memorable story—with nothing to meet his spear but flesh of his flesh, and objects that he loved. (*DD* **442**)

Eliot describes Deronda as a "Sabine Warrior". The Sabines are the members of an ancient Italic tribe inhabiting the mountainous country in the east of the Tiber River neighboring Roman. In Roman mythology, the founding generation of Roman people lacked women to give births to enough offspring for the city-state in the early days, so they abducted a large number of Sabin women, and which turned to be an insult for the Sabines, who then decided to fight for their dignity. A three-year-long war followed afterward. Confronted with the great loss of their fathers and their husbands, those Sabine women can't stay calm and go to the battlefields, attempting to mediate both sides for peace. And this episode has been captured by many artists and has reproduced it in various ways. Among these artistic creations, "The Intervention of the Sabine Women" from the French painter Jacques-Louis David becomes one of the most marvelous pieces for it captures the exact heart-broken moment of the Sabine women intervening to stop the bloodshed. In this picture, one Sabine woman named Hersilia is throwing herself between her husband— the king of Rome, and her father—the king of the Sabines. Under their feet are lying the hybrid born babies. For Hersilia as well as for other Sabine women, it is hard to decide which side they should support for they have their old fathers on one side and their new husbands on the other. They are totally trapped in a neutral position for either side will offer her excuses to defend for the opposite. The stiffed and paralyzed gesture of the Sabine woman is tremendously impressive. And her paradoxical mental state involving hesitation, suppression and as well as the passionate longing to help is like what has happened to the hero of this story Daniel Deronda who is stuck by the very dilemma caused by too much diffusive sympathy.

Figure 5-1. Jacques-Louis David: *The Intervention of the Sabine Women*, 1799. Louvre Museum, Paris.

In the novel, Deronda's sympathy firstly appears as "an activity of imagination on behalf of others" (DD 215). This implication stems from the moral philosophers' definition of sympathy like David Hume and Adam Smith, which has been discussed in depth in the first chapter of this project, that is to say, we use the power of imagination to fulfill the replacement of other people's emotions or ideas into our own. This is also a process by which we reproduce or reconstruct the emotions or situations in others' minds and internalize them into our own experiences; thereby we demonstrate the will of self-control and generate moral consciousness. The key to this process is that we get rid of self-centered inclination. We feel the pain or happiness of others with the universal principle of intuitive feelings, and then make altruistic judgments from a spectator's perspective based on our understanding of others. Smith in his *The Theory of Moral Sentiment* (1759) simply used the "impartial spectator" to materialize this concept, demanding people self-abnegation and self-interpretation while sympathizing with others. So people obtain self-interpretations from the perspective of the other, and the consequent altruistic judgement is thus endowed with color of moral implication. Sympathy and the concept of "impartial spectator" were so highly regarded in the 19th century that they even became the guiding principle for university education to cultivate the character of a true British gentleman. Deronda has accepted this formal education and has been trained as a compassionate young gentleman. However, the sympathy in him does not help him with improving self-knowledge, but instead causes him to fall into a dilemma of moral predicament, emotional suppression and action paralysis.

Although he is rich in sympathy, the meditating medium to convincing people "in scrupulously trying to see as others saw, in thinking of vice not in the simple abstract but as part of complex individual histories" (Davis 279), Deronda needs more concrete historical backgrounds to know more himself. Unfortunately, he is left to be "the Sabine warrior" and has "nothing to meet his spear but flesh of his flesh", without knowing what to do next. Namely, too much sympathy castrates his power of action; George Eliot, also like those classically female mediators, advising that sympathy to "see as others saw" is very much problematic. Edith Simcox said that George Eliot's own "instinct to make allowance for the other side" accounted for what "may easily have been personal sympathy in her descriptions of Deronda's difficulty about the choice of a career" (Simcox 796). So, through Daniel Deronda's dilemma, George Eliot exhibits clearly the subtle threat to direct force and action from many-sided sympathy. Then Deronda needs to step out of "the mazes of impartial sympathy" (*DD* 922). To solve such a problem, the factors causing Deronda's dilemma should be investigated.

Bernadette Waterman Ward in "Zion's Mimetic Angel: George

Eliot's *Daniel Deronda*" said Deronda "is especially weak in so far as he is [a] Jew and a Zionist" (105). However, when Deronda's birth mother asked whether Deronda make himself a Jew, or turning himself into a Jew like his grandfather who strictly adheres to Jewish traditions and beliefs, Deronda reaffirmed: "That is impossible. The effect of my education can never be done away with. The Christian sympathies in which my mind was reared can never die out of me."(*DD* 816) This sympathy connects with "the impulse of my feeling—to identify myself, as far as possible, with my hereditary people" (*DD* 816-817). Sympathy offers a tool of connects the feeling of others and the fellow feeling of the hereditary people and transforms itself into a "consensus" or communal understanding sustaining the community, so as to offer a collective mission for preference to Daniel Deronda. It is a spiritually evolutionary process of an individual within a wider political domain to discover one's social identification and conform oneself to a particular national community. By revealing the possible fulfilling approaches, "national identity and reverence for one's culture (with tolerance and openness to others) seemed the most satisfying, redeeming values that Eliot could offer her own culture" (Henry, *A life of George Eliot* 214). By accomplishing such aim, sympathy embodies a political vision to integrate the relationship between self-actualization and social reconstruction. In order to map Deronda's psychic evolutionary process, it might as well trace back to the Victorian historical background and reflect its newly emerging problems.

5.2 Community Lost and Individual Socialized

5.2.1 The Rise of an Empire and a Lack of Social Cohesion

As having been mentioned in the above section, *Daniel Deronda* sets its historical background in the late Victorian age. This time period also witnessed two outstanding social characteristics: the first one is that the British society experienced the rise of the empire; the second one is that the British people observed a corruption of the previous moral system maintained by faith and a collapse of the social order derived from the hierarchy. If the "coherent social faith and order which could perform the function of knowledge for the ardently willing soul" has long faded away in *Middlemarch* (*MM* 3), things may become worse in *Daniel Deronda*, for the spread of imperial thought and the laissez-faire of individualism further intensify the social division, which leads to the infinite enlargement of the individual's self-ego or national arrogance. Under this social circumstance, the work of men's selfishness becomes signs of the continuing brutishness of English society. "Furthermore it is a dull society. It has no life because of the English tendency towards conformity" (Stang 38). This monotonous cultural atmosphere is absolutely unattractive, and society is thus filled with ruthless criticism, which results in a lack of potentiality for social progress. For most British people, everybody seems to be trapped in some personal trivials. Mallinger Grandcourt is "the presumptive heir to the baronetcy" of Sir Hugo (*DD* 108), cold and lazy, is seemingly rich yet deeply debt-ridden; Gwendolen's family from the middle class is facing with bankruptcy for the failure in overseas investment; Sir Hugo is much wealthier yet has long been troubled by the fact that there is no male heir to inherit his property. For Gwendolen as well as other British people, persons around are as stale books: "too familiar to be interesting." (*DD* 523) It is the casino or health resorts center that provides people with a few spiritual excitement or fresh feelings. The sick world "is all confusion" to Gwendolen and continually erodes her ability to express emotions and love (*DD* 550), all these facts bring endless anxiety and sorrow to people. Gwendolen's sense of "dread" and oppressiveness has become the universal feeling of all characters in the novel. Along with the development of imperialism and the colonial expansion of the empire, people shift their eyesight to overseas activities, hoping to alleviate the domestic crisis by which they are trapped.

As has mentioned above, the rise of the empire is one of the most obvious historic symbols of British society at the end nineteenth century. The subsequent expansion of colonial power has brought unprecedented glory to the British public. Benjamin Disraeli—the British Prime Minister announced that "the east is a career" (qtd. in Said, *Orientalism* xiii). John Ruskin encouraged "the more adventurous and ambitious" young English gentlemen to find "new seats of authority, and centers of thought, in uncultivated and unconquered lands" (514). Such mentality characterized by material acquisition and subjugation of others continues to ferment at people's psychological level and develops into the desire to dominate and to conquer, so they can give full play to the absolute freedom.

In the novel, the middle classes represented by Gwendolen want to fully exercise their freedom, she "seemed to be getting a sort of empire over her own life" (*DD* 355). She ever dreams of "go[ing] to the North Pole, or ride steeple-chases, or go to be a queen in the East like Lady Hester Stanhope" (*DD* 82);① Grandcourt from the aristocratic class finds delight of life "in mastering reluctance" (*DD* 387). "He had the courage and confidence that belong to domination, and he was at that moment feeling perfectly satisfied that he held his wife with bit and bridle" (*DD* 840). So when these two get married, Gwendolen naturally becomes a

---

① Lady Hester Stanhope (1776-1839) is a famous British traveler. She gave up the life of the British aristocracy and traveled to the Middle East alone. She fit into the local people's life and won their respect and became very famous both at home and abroad.

victim in "her husband's empire of fear", their marriage then turns out to be a game of suppression and resistance (*DD* 516). Moreover, when the two collided with other ethnic groups, the mentality of supremacy and superiority makes them enjoy the privilege of being the center of civilization, however, their pride and their arrogance demonstrate a full sense of English insularity.

> This handsome, fair-skinned English couple, manifesting the usual eccentricity of their nation, both of them proud, pale, and calm, without a smile on their faces, moving like creatures who were fulfilling a supernatural destiny—it was a thing to go out and see, a thing to paint. The husband's chest, back, and arms, showed very well in his close-fitting dress, and the wife was declared to be a statue. (*DD* 841)

In the eyes of other ethnic groups, this pair of couple fully demonstrated the indifference, conservativeness and arrogance of the British people. But it is difficult for them to perceive their own limitations since they just emerge into their own world. In the end, Grandcourt is buried into the Mediterranean by accident; and Gwendolen realizes that "our gain is another's loss" (*DD* 408). She then feels helpless and chose to listen to Daniel's exhortation for life.

It is easy to see that the rise of the British Empire had been accompanied by a decline of social coherence, which brings about a gradual alienation of human interpersonal relationships. Being dread becomes the dominating feeling among the British public. That is why to restore the intrinsic nature of human beings is so urgent. Among all human relations, the community is the very explanation to describe a natural, organic way of human grouping life.

The rise of the concept of "community" is closely related to the destructing consequence on a traditional natural home unit from the industrialization movement. In the advancement of the industrial civilization, along with the development of the social division of labor and the intensification of interest distribution, man separates themselves from the family's daily life centering on the cooking fire and the dinner table, which pushes the interpersonal relationship to alienation and isolation. The nostalgia for the good old days prompts people to reflect on ways back to group life. German sociologist Ferdinand Tönnies (1855-1936) then divides human group life into two paradigms: the community (Gemeinschaft) and the society (Gesellschaft) according to the dichotomy.

The "community" is a natural and organicunification of human group life. In contrast to the unnatural, mechanical, and individual-based unity of "society", the community seems to be more real and durable. Within the community, universal emotions, shared spiritual aspirations, and consensus identity become the bonds that establish connections among people, which give members the natural and self-evident understanding. The realization of this common understanding that can be achieved without pursuit allows members to maintain a fundamental unity. Therefore, community relations are the essential relationship between human beings. It contains the nostalgic feelings advocated by Raymond Williams to inspire man's beautiful imaginations (Williams, *Keywords: A Vocabulary of Culture and Society* 76); it is also the future vision that Zigmund Bowman pays attention to, so as to create a sense of warmth (Bowman 3). But generally speaking, "community stands for the kind of world which is not, regrettably, available to us—but which we would dearly wish to inhabit and which we hope to repossess" (Bowman 3). In other words, the community is a perfect unity of human will, and its generation has a certain sense of constructiveness, that is, the gap between social reality and the community is shortened by the freedom of imagination. According to Zygmunt Bauman, the greater distance between the community and society is, the more active man's imagination will be, and the more attractive the imagined community seems to become (Bowman 3-4). When the human will is turned into reality through the conception of the community, the social perfection process will be also achieved. And that's why the most important attribute of community is its cultural practice, which is intended to change the world with the transformed spirituality. Except for being a reference to society, the value of the community also lies in its irreplaceable function for the individual. Compared with struggling in the barbaric or isolated state, group life in community undoubtedly will provide the individual with an unprecedented sense of stability and security. But this does not mean that there an eternal harmony between the individual and the community will be maintained. For once the individual wants to truly integrate himself into the community, he must sacrifice certain freedom. That is because, in the limited space, the expansion of an individual's ego will inevitably impair the interests of the community as a large whole. As to the unknown situation to balance the restoration of community and the self-realization of the individual, it becomes the territory that literature and art strive to explore.

As has been discussed in the beginning part of this chapter, the decline of the sense of community becomes an obvious problem in late-Victorian Britain. In a highly developed society stepping into the modern world, a sharp rise of individualism turns the individual into an atomic unit only caring about its own benefits. The limitless exaggeration of ego and the self-centered mentality spreading in the late Victorian society brings about the inactivity of both individuals and the nation. Tönnies Ferdinand explicitly addresses that "there is no individualism in history and civilisation, except of the kind that flows from Gemeinschaft (community) and remains conditioned by it, or else of the kind that gives rise to and sustains Gesellschaft (society)" (Tönnies 13). This means that any individual needs to return to society or the community to seek support. However, compared with the instability and complexity of society, the community will provide a sense of stability and safety for the individual. As the first contributor to the idea of community, Tönnies Ferdinand believes that community, as well as its derivative forms, is rooted in the family model. Any individual who separates himself from family ties will become an orphan.

5.2.2 An Orphan Complex and a Neutralized Sympathy

Patricia Pulham claims that the nineteenth-century "realist perspective materialized in various forms: the historical novel, the social problem novel and the community novel. At the heart of all three forms is the question of self and society" (Pulham 446). The relationship of integrating the self into society is also a nuclear thought of Eliot's novel writing. Adam Bede, Maggie Truliver, and Dorothea Brooke, etc., none of these characters in George Eliot's novels are not committed themselves to the exploration for improving self-knowledge, so as to construct a loving community through self-cultivation, and Daniel Deronda is by no means an exception.

As a young boy, Daniel Deronda is passionate about life and he looks forward to a lofty career serving higher aim: "I would rather be a greater leader, like Pericles or Washington." (*DD* 210) His imagination develops accompanying by the speculation about his future. He feels that "noblemen have been known to run away from elaborate ease and the option of idleness, that they might bind themselves for small pay to hardhanded labor" (*DD* 205). However, the secret of his own birth is always an obstacle for him to approach higher admiration. He is adopted by Sir

Hugo, and the latter is said to be his birth father but no one is certain. He never stops his effort to inquire, and "these new thoughts seemed like falling flakes of fire to his imagination" (*DD* 202). The habitual speculation of his birth brings a disastrous impact on him when he thinks about he may be a fruit of any shameful misconduct.

> The impetuous advent of new images took possession of him with the force of fact for the first time told, and left him no immediate power for the reflection that he might be trembling at a fiction of his own. The terrible sense of collision between a strong rush of feeling and the dread of its betrayal, found relief at length in big slow tears. (*DD* 202-203)

Even if he is an illegitimate child of Sir Hugo, things are also disappointing. For he will not only be labeled as the "son of an English gentleman" (*DD* 788), but his life will also be linked to some scandals. All his talents only make him "a wonderful toy" rather than a great leader. If his parents are not Sir Hugo and his wife, they can also be some evil or immoral person, and then things may be even worse. It is precisely because of this fact that Daniel is so much curious about his birth information but he prefers to maintain ignorant. However, the puzzle about his birth secret is too strong to be dispatched and it results in an increasingly and incredibly conservative disposition in his nature. What is even worse, it causes "a tension of resolve in certain directions" in everyday life. When sympathy, "an activity of imagination on behalf of others", is displayed, it "did not show itself effusively, but was continually seen in acts of considerateness that struck his companions as moral eccentricity (*DD* 215-216). Such rarity in a subdued fervor of sympathy makes him dissociate from any group or community. As we get an unavoidable consequence, "his plenteous, flexible sympathy had ended by falling into one current with that reflective analysis which tends to neutralize sympathy" (*DD* 442).

To Eliot, "that indignation against wrong and that selectness of fellowship which is the conditions of moral force" (*DD* 443), and such moral force will lead man to make a moral judgement and put into further actions. To George Eliot and her soul mate G. H. Lewes, the moral force is nothing but an "aptitude to be affected by actions in their moral bearings", and this aptitude in all individuals "varies not according to their intellect but according to their native tendencies" and is "transmitted from forefathers" (qtd. in Henry, George Eliot and Empire). In *Daniel Deronda*, Eliot echoes with this proposition.

> At five years old, mortals are not prepared to be citizens of the world, to be stimulated by abstract nouns, to soar above preference into impartiality; and that prejudice in favor of milk with which we blindly begin, is a type of the way body and soul must get nourished at least for a time. (*DD* 20)

Since Deronda is an orphan losing all his biological information, his moral choice becomes impossible. His sympathy is "too reflective and diffusive", which cannot help him make a judgement but "paralyze in him" instead (*DD* 443). Since Daniel Deronda has neither the feeling of indignation nor the power of group cohesion, the only choice is to maintain a social neutral position. Under this circumstance, Daniel expects an "external incident" or "inward light" to "urge him into a definite line of action, and compress his wandering energy" (*DD* 443). He hopes to be "an organic part of social life, instead of roaming in it like a yearning disembodied spirit, stirred with a vague social passion, but without fixed local habitation to render fellowship real" (*DD* 443). Being a part of the organic society and feeling the pulse of it will activate his passionate enthusiasm to devote to society. He is not a wanderer anymore, but a person "in" society instead of staying out of it, which may offer justifications for Daniel Deronda's lofty admiration for the outside world. Yet his diffusive sympathy and analytic nature shatter his dream, hindering his sympathy and limits his actions. Sir Hugo kindly reminds Deronda: "it is good to be unselfish and generous; but don't carry that too far. It will not do to give yourself to be melted down for the benefit of the tallow trade; you must know where to find yourself." (*DD* 223) Sir Hugo's suggestion makes the very point, for Deronda's sympathy is to imagine on behalf of others, such habitual activities of explaining oneself from other points of view now lead Deronda nowhere to know himself. In the Victorian age, "culture" and "society" are "two interlocked concepts central to Victorian self-understanding" (Dolin 227). In other words, even if to explain oneself from the other's point may provide changes to know the present, one's past should be defined by the national life or his heritage people.

The fact is that both the notion of culture and the notion of society concern with "a complicated inheritance" (qtd. in Dolin 112). And the acquisition of such inheritance is unapproachable if there is no support from a family or a nation. The sad fact is that both family traits and the national community are denied in Deronda's life. It is acknowledged that Daniel Deronda and Gwendolen Harleth are both in a disturbing social environment, and their families are not truly complete either. Gwendolen lost her father in her childhood and she has to live with an "unpleasant" stepfather; Daniel is an adopted child by Sir Hugo. Grandcourt's only family attribute is the nephew of Sir Hugo to inherit the latter's property, so Sir Hugo has to buy the Grandcourt's right of inheritance to keep a house for his wife and his daughters. The main young characters like Daniel, Gwendolen and Grandcourt can be all regarded as the "orphans" of the society,① and it is impossible for them to inherit the significant cultural heritage through the rich and true blood relationship.

> This question of inheritance was a crucial one for the Victorians, for whom industrial modernity was both a liberation and an estrangement from the pre-modern past. The simultaneous autonomy and vulnerability of the modern subject is constantly rehearsed in the Victorian social novel. Orphans, most famously, appear in Victorian novels in proportions far in excess of their actual demographic incidence because they represented to the Victorians something of their own freedoms and fears—to create themselves out of nothing, unencumbered by a family identity that would tie them to the past, but ever anxious to find and reclaim their rightful place in a broken genealogy. But in other social narratives, too, the Victorians tried to imagine meaningful courses of action to deal with the traumatic newness of modern industrial existence. (Dolin **115**)

That is why Gwendolen always feels dreadful; Grandcourt is cruel and Daniel finds he cannot anchor his sympathy with particular preference. Their freedom and their fear are interwoven all the time for being an orphan in both a family and a society. "Just as community collapses, identity is invented" (Young **164**). When family attributes are weakened, national identity will emerge as a substitute for family affiliation and continues to provide some stability to the individuals. So when Gwendolen and Grandcourt choose to exert their freedom yet suffer from setbacks, Daniel embarks on self-discipline and begins a journey of

---

① Laura Peters explains the definition of orphans as children who lose their parents or one parent.

self-discovery and self-recognition in the communal environment of both family and nation. It is in this sense that Daniel Deronda should be regarded as Gwendolen's "double", exploring the solution to alleviate Gwendolen's anxiety and fear. As usual, Eliot responds to the outside crisis by articulating an ethical and aesthetical vision of inner development. Although we are defined by what we believe we are not, our self-knowledge and moral sense should be cultivated by a close connection with our "hereditary people" (*DD* 816). In other words, our past has to be explained by our family relationship and national belongings. It is for this reason that returning back to a particular community of family or nation seems obligatory.

5.3 Sympathy Transformed and Restoration of the Communal Consensus

5.3.1 Communal Consensus and Community "Felt"

As mentioned above, Daniel Deronda has been troubled by his "many-sided sympathy" which will "nullify all differences" that the successful operation of sympathy needs (*DD* 444). The subsequent habitual repression leaves him trapped into a dilemma of weak power in mobility and morality. His road of self-salvation lies in the fact of finding his family attribute and nation identity, so as to generate a preference for sympathy. However, that is the very thing Daniel Deronda can't find in England. He accidentally rescues a girl Mirah—a Jew who is looking for her long-separated brother. And the latter is passionate about her Jewish identity, although the Jews have suffered from prejudice and description in the European scope. She holds loyalty to her family and her faith although her father has treated her badly and she has long been separated from her mother and her brother, which infects Daniel who has been confused by the secret of his birth, and he volunteers to find Mirah's brother for her.

During this process, Daniel Deronda gets in touch with the Jewish people, Jewish culture and particularly a Jew Ziost-Mordecai. Deronda is shocked by Mordecai's strong faith in the restoration of a country for his people.

> The more exquisite quality of Deronda's nature—that keenly perceptive sympathetic emotiveness which ran along with his speculative tendency—was never more thoroughly tested. He felt nothing that could be called belief in the validity of Mordecai's impressions concerning him or in the probability of any greatly effective issue: what he felt was a profound sensibility to a cry from the depths of another and accompanying that, the summons to be receptive instead of superciliously prejudging. (DD 605)

Facing with Mordecai's strong belief in restoring the Jewish as a nation, Deronda's speculative tendency doesn't work. He respects what has been expressed by Mordecai. "Receptiveness is a rare and massive power, like fortitude" (DD 605). Such receptiveness is realized with the power of feeling. "I feel with you—I feel strongly with you" (DD 610). Facing with Mordecai's faith in nation and Mirah's zeal for family, Deronda is convinced that "community was felt before it was called good" (DD 651). According to Tönnies, any community explaining the natural and organic relationship of man is based on consensus. ① That is why "in a true community there is no motivation towards reflection, criticism or experimentation" (Bauman, 12). The mutual understanding will provide a state of sameness and naturalness to every member of it.

Sympathy is generally based on the perception of the other's situation. Mordecai's longing for the restoration of a Jewish nation activates the exact desire in Daniel for restoring a family or national traits. So Daniel does not discriminate against Mordecai's Zionism, nor does he judge, but he accepts the infection of Mordecai's emotions instead, which weakens the intelligence of his reflective nature. For Deronda, what he feels is Mordecai's faith in Jewish nation, and "every Jew" possesses common attributes passed down by "ancestors who have transmitted to them" a particular "physical and mental type" (*Such* 127). Deronda is brought up in England where he gets no idea of what a nation is and what a family is like, and Mordecai sets a model and refreshes his understanding of these ideas. Moreover, he feels the feeling of Modecai based not only on the universal feeling of human beings but also on a communal understanding of the same nation. "Such understanding becomes more likely, the greater the similarity of background and experience, or the more people's natural dispositions, characters, and ways of thinking resemble or complement each other" (Tönnies 33). Relying on emotional affection and blood ties, Daniel finally convicted his identity as a Jew.

---

① Tönnies uses the word "*das Verständnis*" which means "understanding, sympathy or insight" and Jose Harris translates the word as "consensus" or "mutual understanding" (Tönnies 32). However, Zygmunt Bauman particularly stresses that the world should be understood as "understanding shared by all its members" for "consensus is but an agreement reached by essentially differently minded people, a product of hard negotiation and compromise" (Bauman 10). So although the concept of consensus is adopted, this project inclines to accept it as a term referring to the social conformity with feeling or mutual understanding based on shared feelings in particular communal unit.

So after learning about his Jewish identity, Daniel is not shocked and frustrated. Instead, he is full of enthusiasm, yearning to be a Jewish man and a part of a suffering nation. "It was as if he had found an added soul in finding his ancestry", and "his judgment no longer wandering in the mazes of impartial sympathy, but choosing, with that partiality which is man's best strength, the closer fellowship that makes sympathy practical" (*DD* 922). Deronda's judgment no longer lingers in the maze due to the neutral sympathy, and the intimate fellowship makes sympathy more real as well. Sympathy now is more like a "mechanism by which we come to enter into the feelings of other people including their admiration and disapproval of ourselves. Sympathy allows us to feel what others feel" (Wright 204). With sympathy, man's emotions can be transferred and replaced, thus achieving social integration and cohesion. But sympathy points to a certain moral implication. Many-sided sympathy can only form a neutral dilemma, which requires a certain ethical standard to guide preference.

As a young man who received British orthodox aristocratic education, Daniel Deronda is carefully educated as a typical "English gentleman" by his adoptive father, Sir Hugo (*DD* 922). He is expected to find a decent career in the military or university. So his decision to return to the Jewish race through the relationship of blood relatives makes him like a shadow, hollow and inhumane.① However, when sympathy is working, it involves a critical point that for whom our feeling goes, and it involves a basic moral judgement varying according to one's native tendencies, which means that the heredity of the blood relationship gives people a strong moral awareness. "Without the 'sweet habit of the blood'

---

① For more exploration of the negative criticism on Daniel Deronda, see James, Henry. "Daniel Deronda: A Conversation." *George Eliot: The Critical Heritage*. Ed. David Carroll. London: Routledge & Kegan Paul, 1971. 417-433. & Leavis, F. R. *The Great Tradition*. London: Penguin, 1962. 137.

imposed by accident of birth and acquired before there is choice or knowledge, all subsequent knowledge may suffer from a fatal and mysterious defect" (Robbins 404). The enlargement of our moral feelings bases on the blood connection with our past. Deronda constantly searches for his birth information precisely because he needs to find a solution to his paralysis in action rooting in his moral paralysis. Although Daniel's returning to the Jewish race seems weak to define a character, it serves as a natural stability and unalterable biological genetic information to locate man's moral sense. This makes sympathy not only a fellow-feeling but also "a representation, a cultural image" (Jaffe 6). Sympathy thus becomes a cultural construction norm aiming for an effort to transcend social hierarchy on the one hand, and on the other hand, it has to legislate itself in some political community to find the preference for itself.

As a result, Deronda finds his own social role and steps out of the confusion and aimless wandering among the Jews. The integration into the national community also gives Daniel an emotional preference and a direction of action, and he finds the social and political goals which are absent in British society. Since "an individual man, to be harmoniously great, must belong to a nation", the formation of his characteristics cannot leave the support of the national community (*Such* 147). In view of this, Eliot has to reflect on the relationship between the individual and the national community and the relationship between the self and "a large whole".

> Only a nation, a society that she saw as based on filial sentiment, perceived national kinship, and common historical traditions ... could provide a realistic foundation for communal solidarity. These ties would make it possible for an individual to transcend selfish egoism and to feel a deep sympathetic concern, first toward his kin and men toward the extended family of the

nation. (Semmel 6)

So Eliot makes Deronda return back to the familial and national community that he belongs to, although it is a Jewish one. Sympathy then, with its unique aesthetic judgment and self-cultivation process, is conducive to generate emotional bonds for improving social cohesion and reducing differentiation. It will surely provide intelligence for clarifying community consciousness and broaden common understanding of the community based on interoperability and similarity of life experiences, thus transforming the individual of society into the self of community. So the community becomes the form of individual autonomy as a spiritual vision from the opposite side of individual choice of freedom. Surely, this will be helpful for the individual to devote to the restoration of a nation—an imagined community.

5.3.2 Sympathy Enlarged and Community "Imagined"

During the traveling days in Europe, advanced transportation and convenient capital operation made Elliot sense the arrival of a cosmopolitan Europe. This gave her a more intuitive and profound understanding of the changes in social classes and the turmoil in social structures. Most importantly, this offers her more opportunities to reflect on the domestic problems in England. Besides the fact of observing the disintegration of the social structure and dissolution of the traditional value systems, Eliot also seems to be more aware of the importance of Britain as a nation. "Better by half go to by-places in our own lovely country, and drive in carts over breezy lovely hills than go moiling on railways to see places not comparable for beauty with what one leaves behind" (qtd. in Mackenzie 1). The importance of a notion doesn't mean national arrogance, for the latter will intensifies the cultural crisis. Then Eliot's knowledge of the Jewish people and their faith in history and culture impress her a lot, and they sets a model for national revival. Eliot thus begins to reflect the relationship between the individual and the nation. To relate self to "the larger whole" becomes the focus of Eliot's realistic writing. This will decide the matter whether the individual can realize his self-value and how the national confidence is restored. Carlyle once called on activating the integration of spiritual power, organic community, and personal responsibility in man. For Eliot, the good cultivation of the individual through the extension of sympathy to the mutual understanding of the national community is always a preferred way.

Benedict Anderson's *Imagined Communities: Reflections on the Origin and Spread of Nationalism* (1983) points out that nation is an imagined and creative notion, for a nation is not a material entity like a country or a state. "It is an invisible and (at least partly) theoretical construction which elicits powerful emotional and imaginative identifications" (Parrinder 14). Eliot recognizes the transformative potentiality in literature and art and hopes that the transformation of man's sensibility may trigger social change through the sympathy inspired by art, more pacifically. She aims to find ways for integrating the individual into the restoration of national community.

Eliot confessed that "no chemical process shows a more wonderful activity than the transforming influence of the thoughts we imagine to be going on in another" (*DD* 514). For Gwendolen, her dissent or disapproval with others seems to be an uneasy process for "all the old nature shaken to its depths, its hopes spoiled, its pleasures perturbed, but still showing wholeness and strength in the will to reassert itself" (*DD* 514). Her deadly enemies of being dreadful and her disappointment could only be transformed (*DD* 794). After suffering from the unhappy marriage, she stretches her hand to Daniel for help. The latter's keen sympathy grasps "a passionate need" and "that heart might feel larger demands on him than he would be able to fulfill" (*DD* 947). Although Daniel understands Gwendolen's disappointing marital life and feels her pain and despair, he realizes that he is not the one to fill the blank of Gwendolen's unhappy marriage, and "a tragic transformation toward a wavering result" emerges, "in which he felt with apprehensiveness that his own action was still bound up", so in this miraculous process of inner transformation, Mirah's dear voice of melody reminds his true feeling toward Mirah, Daniel finally gets to know the duty of understanding others can't be the determent to decide his love life. In addition, he suggests Gwendolen to transform her pain by going back to family duty toward her mother and her young sisters for "other duties will spring from it" (*DD* 947). In a dutiful life or enlarged life, the ceaseless want of motive makes life dreary, but once men begin to act with that penitential, "loving purpose you have in your mind, there will be unexpected satisfactions—there will be newly opening needs—continually coming to carry you on from day to day. You will find your life growing like a plant" (*DD* 952). Sympathy serves as both an end and a process for mental transformation in one's individual life. The enlarged life purpose makes it possible for the inward conversion and the outward action, so is the national life because the enlarged combinational life depends on "the more glorious will be the energy that transformed it" (*DD* 647).

Under the influence of Mila and Mordechai, Daniel reinforces his resolution to participate in the great calling of national rejuvenation. Because of the imaginative and creative feature, the idea of the nation is comparatively easy to approach via the working of sympathy. In addition, the meaning of a nation to an individual always means the collective belonging and it will directly affect the individual's self-knowledge. The idea of nation is neither an inherent concept nor a groundless one. Its birth needs the traditions, myths, beliefs or identities that existed before. Taking the case of Daniel Deronda into the discussion, his education and the influence of Christianity are two ties connecting his new identity with Jewish people. The "Christian sympathy" has always been the essence of Daniel's nature.

When Daniel's mother asks her son whether he would become a Jew like his grandfather since Daniel has got to know his identity, the latter acknowledges: "That is impossible. The effect of my education can never be done away with. The Christian sympathies in which my mind was reared can never die out of me."(*DD* 816) At this time, sympathy as a cultural heritage helps Daniel achieve his national identity while also adhering to his British one. This makes a crucial point for our further exploration. "Eliot the idea of sympathy became increasingly identified with a sharing of the inheritance of the past, and more specifically with the sharing of one's national past with others belonging to the national community" (Semmel 13). It is well known that Christianity is derived from the wisdom of Judaism. The two are closely related to each other. And Daniel with Christian sympathy to return back to the Jewish, to Ragussis Machael, is likely to set out a journey of conversion, which means to spread the Christian faith among the Jews, which has been a long tradition of the English Christianity society (262-265). As an agnostic, such conversion still remains powerful. Its essence lies in the change of mental poise which has been fitly named conversion, "that to many among us neither heaven nor earth has any revelation till some personality touches theirs with a peculiar influence, subduing them into receptiveness" (*DD* 523). Sympathy is like this kind of conversion and accomplishes a process of spiritual change. "Victorians looked enthusiastically toward the potential of a society in which the highly evolved cultivation of sympathetic feelings might take new forms"

(Nancy, *George Eliot and the British Empire* 41). And in *Daniel Deronda*, this sympathy evolved into a strong faith in the national community.

It is obvious that the blood relationship gives the genetic code to Daniel of moral inheritance, then the nation as a collective wisdom provides Daniel's abundant cultural nourishment. The combination of the two provides the social condition for the improvement of self-knowledge. After establishing his own national identity, Daniel devotes himself to the revival of his nation. For any individual must belong to a nation:

> An individual man, to be harmoniously great, must belong to a nation ... if not in actual existence yet existing in the past, in memory, as departed, invisible, beloved ideal, once a reality, and perhaps to be restored. A common humanity is not yet enough to feed the rich blood of various activity which makes a complete man. The time is not come for cosmopolitanism to be highly virtuous, any more than for communism to suffice for social energy. (*The Impressions of Theophrastus Such* 197)

Eliot claims her understanding of the nation and its significance to the individual in *The Impressions of Theophrastus Such* (1879), her final work mainly expressing cultural criticism. A common humanity is not yet enough for a person to grow into a complete man, and a strong backbone of the nation is needed to connect the individual with his past and his future. In other words, there is no uniformed nature transcended national boundaries and culture, or at least, it is not the time.

For this reason, the revival of the nation is still an urgent problem to be solved. For Daniel, he finds different perspectives from Mirah and Mordechai, and from the Jews who remain sticking to pure spiritual life, while the English society is suffering from the oppressing fact that Christianity has been a myth, and social ritual has become meaningless. He is touched, affected and impressed. All these push him to restore his

Chapter 5　Sympathy and the Political Vision in *Daniel Deronda*　　237

faith in nation, not a nation of hollow and dread, but a nation with rich spiritual aspiration and strong feeling.

> Perhaps most difficult of all for her [Eliot] readers to accept is the way that Judaism is constructed as a healthy organicist alternative to the deadness of English society. For centuries the Jews had suffered persecutions and restrictions and yet, they had maintained their spiritual life. This self-conscious construct is held up as an ideal and a means to revitalize English society. (Röder-Bolton 209)

Although the word "alternative" seems strong, to Eliot, the Jews' spiritual aspiration is what was lacked by the English. With the Jews character like Mordecai, Eliot at least calls on the British nation to change its arrogant attitude, steps out of narrow self-enclosure, and adopts the posture of tolerance to absorb the advantages of other nations.

> The idea that I am possessed with is that of restoring a political existence to my people, making them a nation again, giving them a national center, such as the English has, though they too are scattered over the face of the globe. That is a task which presents itself to me as a duty; I am resolved to begin it, however feebly. I am resolved to devote my life to it. At the least, I may awaken a movement in other minds, such as has been awakened in my own. (*DD* 996)

Deronda's confidence in national identity starts with his sympathy for Mordecai's political vision. His sympathy helps him acquire an awakening in his mind—the connection and growing attitude toward national identification. It is also the very part of Eliot's appeal to call on the English people participating in a national renovation. If Jews who are in diaspora need a nation, so will the Great Britain people scattering around in its colonial expansion.

In the real expansion of the empire, the British people meet with people of other races and other nations. This binary opposition between the self and the other has deepened the British people's reflection on their national issues. This is also an important reason why Eliot introduces the story of the Jewish nation into her novel. Jewish people have been scattered around the world because of oppression and discrimination, and English has also penetrated into the corners of the world because of the expansion of its imperial power. The alienation from the national center will inevitably lead to different levels of division and divergence. To both sides, the gradual disappearance of the nation and the subsequent decline of culture or history are not a good thing.

> A human life, I think, should be well rooted in some spot of a native land, where it may get the love of tender kinship for the face of the earth, for the labors men go forth to, for the sounds and accents that haunt it, for whatever will give that early home a familiar unmistakable difference amidst the future widening of knowledge. (*DD* 20)

The way in which the Jewish people treat their history and the inheritance of tradition undoubtedly brings Eliot hope. And the Jewish faith and enthusiasm for the nation is what the British public lack by rejecting the past and tradition in the name of reason. Under such circumstances, sympathizing with the Jewish faith in a nation is in some way believing that the English nation could also be restored and rejuvenated. In short, Eliot regards "the importance of the nation and national feelings, and its utility in energizing sympathy with a larger community" (*Such* 147). By doing this, Eliot expects to connect the self with a larger whole. The accordance of the inner self with the outside world will not only offer the individual growth of mind but also contribute to the final shape of community awareness.

Any individual cannot separate himself from a particular nation, and vice versa.

> The life of a people grows, it is knit together and yet expanded, in joy and sorrow, in thought and action; it absorbs the thought of other nations into its own forms, and gives back the thought as new wealth to the world; it is a power and an organ in the great body of the nations. (*DD* 641)

The life of a people grows by uniting different individuals' joys and sorrows, by absorbing the thoughts of other nations, and then it emits new vitality. "The soul of a people, whereby they know themselves to be one, may seem to be dying for want of common action" (*DD* 641). The work of sympathy is a necessary tool for the formation of such common action. Based on this consideration, Eliot adopts a technique which she is good at—novel writing—as an intervention tool, to call for the recovery of national consciousness and reshaping the British tradition, so as to achieve a national rejuvenation in its true meaning.

From the above discussion, we can know that the Jewish people set a model for preserving a coherent culture and aspiring to national unity. The coherent national culture will satisfy what Daniel conceives as "the imaginative need of some farreaching relation" (*DD* 923). It is in this way that the self and the society thus connect and interact with each other. What needs to be discussed is, as has been mentioned in the opening section. Eliot turns to "the wisdom literature of the mystics and visionaries, emphasizing the way in which a receptivity to elective affinities and visions" (Preyer 34). She includes these factors into the romantic and epic narrative, which invites questions and criticism for its consistency with the principle of realism.

5.4 Realism and the Myth-making

As one of the most intellectual and talented novelists in the Victorian age, Eliot was more self-conscious about the aesthetic and moral dimensions of fiction. Since the aesthetic power of sympathy is more and more amplified, realism invented under Eliot's craft also responds accordingly. On the one hand, she advocates that realism should provide a faithful account of reality. On the other hand, she also tests the limits of that realism to the utmost degrees and welcomes unparalleled openness into her last piece of work. With Eliot deepening her understanding of society, humanity and as well as sympathy, "her work became more dense and allusive, less popular, and less autobiographical all at the same time as it moved in the direction of aestheticism and Modernism" (Henry, *The Life of George Eliot* 12). In *Daniel Deronda*, Eliot tries another experiment that "how mysticism may reshape the concept of personal identity—a trope that occurs fairly frequently within Victorian fiction" (Willburn 271). And all these factors makes *Daniel Deronda* featured as both a realist and an epic (Willburn 271), and the epic romanticism and the strong mysticism is often questioned whether it marks the end of realism in Eliot's realism writing (Tucker 35). The final part of this project will be devoted to proving how Eliot incorporates these unrealistic elements to invoke a dialogic discourse with others to foster a sense of community. As has been emphasized many times in the previous chapters, all these "unrealistic" elements are the unseparated parts of some kind of realistic appeal, which illustrates the extraordinary openness of realism. Let us illustrate this point with two typical examples depicted in *Daniel Deronda*: the mysterious working of Mordecai's vision and the mysteries operation of Daniel's sympathy.

5.4.1　Mordecai's Vision and Deronda's Sympathy

In *Daniel Deronda*, one of the most abnormal episodes in conflict with the realist tradition is Eliot's depiction of Mordecai's connection with Deronda through the transmigration of souls. Mordecai is described as a visionary, and he foretells Deronda's Jewish identity with a vision growing from a "second sight":

> "Second-sight" is a flag over disputed ground. But it is matter of knowledge that there are persons whose yearnings, conceptions—nay, traveled conclusions—continually take the form of images which have a foreshadowing power; the deed they would do starts up before them in complete shape, making a coercive type; the event they hunger for or dread rises into vision with a seed-like growth, feeding itself fast on unnumbered impressions. They are not always the less capable of the argumentative process, nor less sane than the commonplace calculators of the market; sometimes it may be that their natures have manifold openings, like the hundred-gated Thebes, where there may naturally be a greater and more miscellaneous inrush than through a narrow beadle-watched portal. No doubt there are abject specimens of the visionary, as there is a minim mammal which you might imprison in the finger of your glove. (*DD* 575)

With this second sight, he looks for a new body to replace his consumptive dying body. The moment he sees Daniel Deronda, he knows Daniel is the man. "Mordecai knew that the nameless stranger was to come and redeem his ring" (*DD* 586). Mordecai seems to foresee everything that will happen in his life. He knows he is dying, which makes it so urgent to find a soul to continue his ideal of Zionism. With his vision, or his "imagination", he constructs another man who seems to be something ampler, and the latter is to "help out the insufficient first—who would be a blooming human life, ready to incorporate all that was worthiest in an existence whose visible, palpable part was burning itself fast away" (*DD* 578). By doing so, the man under his vison or his second sight will be "the more beautiful, the stronger, the more executive self" (*DD* 578). He will be an ideal candidate for accomplishing his unfinished profession. And as Under Mordecai's expectation, Daniel Deronda appears to inherit Mordecai's Zionist ideal. Eliot expresses this process as Daniel breathing in Mordecai's soul. Mordecai's vision ultimately transforms into Daniel's soul as a "seed-like growth, feeding itself fast on unnumbered impressions" (*DD* 575). Particularly, Mordecai becomes spiritually incorporated into Daniel's physical body and mind when the former kisses Daniel on the lips in order to transmigrate his soul into Daniel's body at his dying bed. The reincarnation or rebirth notion reveals a strong color of mysticism and makes the novel be in incongruity with Eliot's realist writing of faithfully representing the reality she ever premises in her previous work.

In fact, the transmission, transmutation, and transmigration of souls and ideas between Mordecai and Deronda share a solid religious origin. Opposite to "philosophies and religious systems rests on eye-witness and facts", Judaism believes "the existence of God is more firmly proved by the revelation on Sinai than by the arguments of reason" (Irwin 170). So Adam obtains truth via intuition, and he is then endowed with some prophetic nature for he is the son of God.[①] The Jewish people follow their command of religious duty with cherishing highly the prophetic function of the heart and the divine blessings of nature. To Mordecai, Jews treat "heart the core of affection which binds a race and its families

---

[①] In Judaism, Adam is the legendary human ancestor and the first man created by God. The word "Adam" means "man" in Hebrew culture, referring to all human beings.

in dutiful love" (*DD* 646). So Mordecai believes there will be naturally someone to continue his work, a companion soul of better fortune or more strength. When he sees Deronda, he knows Deronda will be the very guy to pass on his soul:

> In the doctrine of the Cabbala,①souls are born again and again in new bodies till they are perfected and purified, and a soul liberated from a worn-out body may join the fellow-soul that needs it, that they may be perfected together, and their earthly work accomplished... though it were only in parable. When my long-wandering soul is liberated from this weary body, it will join yours, and its work will be perfected. (*DD* 658)

It's obvious that Mordecai believes Deronda to be his spiritual heir for being influenced by the Hebrew Mysticism with which man's soul can be transmitted and perfected. He is convinced of this fact because he finds Deronda not losing his heart, and Deronda has the ability to feel others' feelings. "Community was felt before it was called good" (DD 651). So Deronda feels Mordecai's enthusiasm toward the Jewish nation and Jewish people means he is one of them. This is no longer superstition but "the living fountains of enlarging belief. What is growth, completion, development? You began with that question, I apply it to the history of our people" (DD 651). It is the historical heritage units the two together. Then Eliot's project as a novelist is to "fit the theory or fable of Kabbalistic doctrine into the practical, naturalistic world of her narrative" (Irwin 172). Of course, such combination seems to be unnatural to

---

① Cabbala or Kabbalah is known as a set of mysticism in Hebrew philosophy. It provides a means of approaching God directly. While believing all creation is an emanation from the Deity and the soul exists from eternity. It is of great significance for people who are seeking to connect themselves with something that transcends the world when the secular existence seems to be more and more disappointing.

modern readers with analytic minds and without the basic background knowledge of Cabbala. However, it is a somewhat real presentation of the Jewish religious belief. We should admit that George Eliot has done all in her full strength to "show the philosophical concept of souls and their transmigration as a product of human need, and consequently a real part of the larger life of humanity" (Irwin 173). In short, the most abnormal non-reality episode in *Daniel Deronda* actually embodies too much realistic aspiration. Besides that, the secret work of sympathy plays an important role for Deronda to follow Mordecai's command, so it might as well for us to investigate another main non-real part in *Daniel Deronda*, exploring the real intensions of social need.

As has been discussed in the above sections, sympathy in Deronda's life is "too reflective and diffusive" and it drags him into the danger of paralyzing his power of action and puts him onto the neutralizing position based on which he cannot tell the right from the wrong. His impartial sympathy is healed by embracing Mordecai's zeal toward his nation and his faith in Zionism through intuitive sympathy. The moment when he knows he is a Jew, "it was as if he had found an added soul in finding his ancestry" (*DD* 765). It is well known that the task of widening sympathies is the core value of Eliot's realism as what we have been stressed numerously in the previous chapters. Daniel's sympathetic relationship to Mordecai "depends on a very different mechanism of affinity", for his sympathy is realized on "transmission, transmutation, and transmigration" instead of shared experiences (Burdett 332). It is this transmitted sympathy that makes it possible to welcome Mordecai's soul and ideal into Deronda. The occult resonance between them is intriguingly mysterious. And till now, sympathy in *Daniel Deronda* manifests itself as the most mysterious one.

Eliot had helped to craft had created the conditions for new versions of sympathy. The "natural" swelling of sympathetic feeling (its "direct promptings") could now readily be referred to an instinctual body system, working "automatically" in response to environmental stimuli. (Burdett **333**)

Sympathy, although works mysteriously and automatically, still serves as a way that men respond to the environment, and the corresponding way of self-regulation will invite the individual by relating him with the fibers of society. It embodies a possibility of reification for Deronda to return back to his national community.

It is well-known that Deronda is longing to know his birth information. While staying with Mirah and Mordecai, he gets to know what the national loyalty and religious duty means. He is shocked by their strong faith in national resurrection. Mordecai and Mila play an exemplary role to interpret the commanding principle of family and ethnic community concepts that Daniel Deronda cannot find in British society. "Community was felt before it was called good" (*DD* **561**). For any community contains essential emotional bonds and a sense of self-evident understanding. "Reciprocal binding sentiment as the peculiar will of a community is what we shall call mutual understanding or consensus. This is the special social force and fellow feeling that holds people together as members of a whole" (Tönnies **32**). ①Fellow feeling is so important for generating the consensus or mutual understanding of any community needs. Mutual understanding rests upon intimate knowledge of one another, reflecting the direct interest of one being in the life of another and willingness to share his or her joys and sorrows. The more likely this understanding is, "the greater the similarity of background and

---

① Ferdinand Tönnies in his *Gemeinschaft und Gesellschaft* (1887) use the word of "sympathie" to refer to fellow feeling, which is the main implication of sympathy in English emphasizing the conformity of feelings.

experience, or the more people's natural dispositions, characters, and ways of thinking resemble or complement each other" (Tönnies 33). Sympathy broadens the scope of common understanding with the similarity or similarity of life experiences, and transforms individuals in society into self in the community. That's why in a true community, "there is no motivation towards reflection, criticism or experimentation" (Bauman 12). For Daniel Deronda who is eager to find a national identity to explain himself, Mordecai's firm national beliefs and community consciousness is too passionate to ignore. He feels Mordecai's feelings and this weakens Deronda's habitual reflections. His consistent self-denial and the desire for others sublimate into a passion for public will and the establishment of national identity eases the neutrality and dissociation of Daniel encountered in British society. In short, the mysterious flow of sympathy actually derives from the conformity of feeling when an individual integrates himself into the national community. It is a process of mutual understanding that rejecting reflection or criticism. And this seemingly mysterious mental process offers Daniel an emotional preference and a direction for his action when he finds himself losing his social and political goals in British society.

  Sympathy should be understood as a mental aspiration when the inner world and the outer one collide with each other. And it needs to be understood as a fellow feeling causing mutual understanding in a community as well. It displays the infinite power to adjust the individual's mentality to submit to the reconstruction of a community. That is why despite the fact of projections or transfusions, sympathy after all saves Daniel from his reflective nature and propels him into new potential beyond the limits of his own, convincing him to serve a noble calling, since the story stops with an open ending, which means that Daniel's restoration of a country for the Jew will not be easy, and that will be another part of Eliot's realistic consideration in her last fiction.

5.4.2 Mysticism and the Myth-making in Realistic Art

When Eliot originally forms her artistic thought, she claims that "art is the nearest thing to life; it is a mode of amplifying experience and extending our contact with our fellow-men beyond the bounds of our personal lot" (*Essays*, 236). The artist seeks no doctrines but always to stimulate those sympathetic feelings for the carrying through of some "ennobling thought or purpose". When she mentiones sympathy, words like "extending", "elevating" or "ennobling" are habitually associated with it. In *Daniel Deronda*, verbs like "transform" and "enlarge" are stressed once again to form verb phrases with sympathy. In this way, Eliot once more restates her original intention of realistic writing. As usual, she expects that highly evolved nurture of sympathetic feelings might take new forms, so as to fully meet the needs associating the individual to a larger aim outside himself. She then claims that a critic should inquire whether a badly-flawed work contains "that salt of a noble enthusiasm which should rebuke our critical discrimination if its correctness is inspired with a less admirable habit of feeling" (qtd. in Preyer 40). That is to say, feeling and enthusiasm are two qualities to label a piece of good artistic work. During the long development of romanticism, feelings have also been highly valued for the making of good poetry, but feelings are also confined by strong sense of ego-oriented tendency, so the validity and efficacy of the feeling transmitting from the poet to the common people become limited for the Victorians who have been baptized by the analytical thinking. That is why the novel enjoys a privilege for its detailed delineation of the ordinaries. Feeling and sympathy with its incarnation carries more convincing power. In the Victorian age, the society is boring and full of dread, and lifeless, that is why something to satisfy the demands of the ardent natures that harbor a hope and admiration for the good, the beautiful and even the sublime is needed. George Eliot is aware of the plight of people and she uses the word "dread" to describe the mental and cultural crisis in *Daniel Deronda*. But rules and all doctrines of action, all rebellion or defiance calculated will diminish fellow feeling and sympathy. Hopes and enthusiasms need to be activated in art—the art of imagination. And these facts leave Eliot space for exploring romance, mystery, and even the gothic elements. "The ideal potencies, the spiritual intermediator between the Divine fullness of light & the dim world—the pre-existence of the soul—the transmigration of souls—the magical operation of human actions on the higher world" (Irwin 175). By adopting the mysterious elements like soul transmigration or divine inspiration in *Daniel Deronda*, Eliot tries the magic operation of human actions to an elevating level, so as to explore the realistic possibility that realism has assured her and other Victorians.

In *Daniel Deronda*, Mordecai insists that Deronda has a mission, and Deronda is to fulfill the dreams and aspirations of this mission. He sensibly considers the possibility that Mordecai's visionary excitement may have turned his wishes into an overmastering impression, causing him to read a series of accidental meetings as a divine fulfillment. However, Deronda takes more into account than logic for "a wise estimate of consequences is fused in the fires of that passionate belief which determines the consequences it believes in" (*DD* 625). Man if relates themselves to "motives and actions, passionate belief", their "enthusiasm may have the validity of proof, and, happening in one soul, give the type of what will one day be general" (*DD* 625). Under such circumstance, "an emotional intellect may have absorbed into its passionate vision of possibilities some truth of what will be", that is why "the more comprehensive massive life" feeds "theory with new material", and new materials will reinforce the understanding of man toward himself and the other (*DD* 625). And once again, the power of feeling and sympathy is reexamined by George Eliot.

> Brief meetings after studied absence are potent in disclosure: but more potent still is frequent companionship, with full sympathy in taste and admirable qualities on both sides; especially where the one is in the position of teacher and the other is delightedly conscious of receptive ability which also gives the teacher delight. (*DD* 289)

While applying sympathy, both sides will enjoy the delight of the growth of the mind and the self-knowledge. By following the vision of Mordecai, Daniel Deronda also sees "sculptured fragments certifying some beauty yearned after but not traceable by divination", and that is where Deronda connects duty and citizenship with beauty in a wide social domain. Hazlitt asserts, "Without romance, we should have no ideas of beauty, no hope, no belief in social progress" (Parrinder 12). That is why the romanticism and mysticism are so urgently needed. Through myth-making, man will elevate social reality. This probably matters to Eliot at its utmost level. "Mordecai's mind power, in this view, is the dream version of the novelist's own" (Pinch 146). Mordecai expects Deronda to devote to the restoration of a national community by constructing a foresight view and Eliot puts hope on her readers to revitalize the British culture with inspiring art.

From the above discussion, it can be figured out that the provoking of sympathy is still a principle of George Eliot's writing in *Daniel Deronda*. In this novel, "Eliot was already pushing to its limits sympathy and (and in) its relation to realist form" (Burdett 321). The previous chapters prove that Eliot has worked long to fuse together the ethical and aesthetic dimension in realism, which makes the common human experience as the essentiality for moral consciousness and intellectual development. In *Daniel Deronda*, sympathy is particularly discussed by facilitating long-term goals of social progress. Based on such consideration, realism in this novel carries the color of myth-making and all the miraculous work in art, which is precisely embodying aspiration for exploring the ennobling and elevating possibility in real life. With sympathetic involvement in the process of experience and acceptance of art, the artistic vision sets up imaginative construction activities, which internalize the ideals of the community in the art world into the experiences or intuitive feelings of the reader's mind. The phenomenological revivification of such perceptual experiences constitutes the subtle mixture between the spirit and the reality, the community and the society, which leads individuals to focus on the transformative power of spiritual initiative to respond to changes in a historical context by reshaping the spiritual world. This is the very unique political vision that sympathy may embody in art creation.

Conclusion

Sympathy with humane care serves as a constructive and transformative force to regulate social behavior by adjusting, sublimating, and even correcting the individual's psychological state or mentality with an aesthetic involvement. Sympathy embodies a power of entering into or sharing the minds of the other, although it doesn't mean a full knowledge of them, it still urges the individual to participate in others' ideas and sentiments to some extent, so as to offer a kind of understanding or communication, which is vital for any healthy society calling for conversations and interactions. To Eliot, also as has been showed in *The Lifted Veil*, anyone lacking sympathy, like "Latimer", will grow a sense of indifference or quick insight into others' feelings, but neither mentality will bring about sympathy or intimacy toward others. Based on dissuasions in the above five chapters, this project first and foremost admits that sympathy between minds, or the omniscience in the realistic narration based on sympathy, is far from being ideal to realize the moral, cognitive or aesthetic end respectively, which leaves sympathy always under attack for demonstrating a limit or relativity in accomplishing its moral, cognitive or aesthetic mission. The reason lies in the very fact that the implications of sympathy in morality, cognition, and aesthetics intertwine with each other, and each side is confined by the others, but at the same time each side is also highlighted in the same manner. Comparatively speaking, it seems to be securer to discuss the moral purpose and epistemological end in the aesthetical dimension of sympathy. Sympathy then becomes a mechanism or vehicle for figuring out men's complexed psychological or emotional state and restoring them into order. Therefore, sympathy depends very much on the social and cultural context in which the individual translates his inner world into proper language and the variation in man's intellectual or understanding will bring about much instability while sympathy is operated. So the expected identification or agreement caused by sympathy actually always reveals itself as a kind of diversity, difference and even contradiction between different minds, which in turn makes universal sympathy impracticable and the self-evident understanding hard to achieve. On the contrary, the sympathetic process involves control and selection. It demands the selfhood and requires an otherness at the same time, and it is a selective and sublimating process in which a good imagination and a healthy mind gets in and gets out of the other's life properly; Generally speaking, the sympathetic process passes through an assimilating procedure by exalting those states of minds that cannot be articulated, or can't be comprehended by a man's self.

The second issue discussed in this project is that although there involves an instability, complexity, and even impossibility in knowing the other through sympathy, sympathy plays an irreplaceable role for a man to know himself by the exaltation or expansion of their minds out of the inarticulate mental chaos, precisely the unspeakable suffering. To George Eliot, the mechanism of sympathy helps people search for the congenial ways of the incomprehensible other through the internalization of self and the conversion within. Therefore, Eliot adopts the word "transform", "transformation" or "transformative" to describe such a mental process in which people reconstruct the experience of others in their own minds and generate follow-up thoughts and actions. In short, this psychological process is to transform the primitive sensory experience into sympathy, the aesthetic pleasure of sympathy into self-knowledge, and self-knowledge to the dynamic reciprocity of social improvement. Such an inner transformative process is Eliot's unique contribution to explain the evolutionary causality from an aesthetical perspective with human care, yet demonstrates the infinite potentiality of sympathy to construct man's cognitive and moral experiences.

Based on such consideration, it seems to be safe to draw a conclusion that it is Eliot's understanding of sympathy that guides her realistic writing, for both depend on man's cognition of the other and the outside world. The relativity of knowing not only causes instability for extending sympathy among human beings but also forms an internal tension of realist writing. The conversion of other's experience through sympathy is performed in the exact same way with what realism aims to transform the reader's mentality; the instability of sympathy immediately interacts with the realistic writing and brings about many non-realistic phenomena. It means that George Eliot has to adopt more openness and tolerance to invite the elements of Gothic horror, romantic enthusiasm and epic magnificence into her realist writing. This fact constructs a sense of romance, mystery and uncertainty and it, in turn, will guide readers to form subjectivity through imaginative cognition and moral judgment, so as to demonstrate the infinite potential of art for the growth of the human mind. During this process, the epistemological function of sympathy is relative and the moral is limited, so the aesthetic identification is to be introduced for securing and supplementing. This combination may exhibit itself imperfectly, but Eliot's faithful record of the difficulty during this process is precisely the unique charm of her realist writing. In addition, sympathy makes it possible for Eliot to tolerate and respect the unknowable other. This is the very humanistic value of her realism, embodying a prosocial inclination that Eliot is always investigating and exploring in her art.

It is well known that realism as a literature style calls for an objective investigation of everyday life and artists are expected to pursue a scientifically-based fidelity to nature. In the Victorian age, advancement in science and technology increases the mobility of people and the subsequent new ideas and cultural norms appear, so the realistic art should faithfully describe the constant transforming process in both the social transition and in man's mental world. Specifically, realistic art is to offer a completed model for portraying psychological growth. Since any individual is a microcosm of the society and every society is a collective of group ideas or traditions, the complexity of society stresses particularism yet orients to socialism and collectivism. In these complicated relations, the individuality can only exist and express itself in social life. That is why only by understanding other people or entering into life around other people could one individual find the actual meaning of his own effective existence. Sympathy offers a possibility of making the individual into the social life and vice versa with a flow of sentiments and motives. In this process, men need to find ways to construct integration with others, and that is why sympathy is urgently needed. Every man is but a constituent in a human-environment whole. His understanding of this wholeness consequently is the outcome of a highly complicated interplay of factors inseparable from the contributions of human perceptions, conceptions, and actions. In particular, this fact urges every individual to join with his collective activities in the ceaseless transitions of the conditions, and the inner transformation accordingly through sympathy will meet the need of any man wanting to keep in accordance with the outside world. To find elucidation of different situations, men should make an aesthetic inquiry into sociability as an aesthetic quality joined with the primacy of the social good. When society enters into the one with "endless prison-walls of brick, beneath a lurid crushing sky of smoke and mist," as Charles Kingsley has observed, the only site of hope and renewal lies in the place "where man meets man, and spirit quickens spirit, and intercourse breeds knowledge, and knowledge sympathy, and sympathy enthusiasm, combination, power irresistible" (Kingsley chapter 32). So Eliot's effort of figuring out ways to nurture and nourish sympathy is especially highlighting.

George Eliot is undoubtedly a prominent artist who has successfully made sympathy the bedrock of her realist novel for moral education and aesthetical edification. She precisely aims to wake man's special instinct or motive by postulating the mentality that explains collective behavior. To Eliot, society is a living and organic whole, which requires stability and exchange, uniformity and differentiation. Sympathy enables man to partake the life of others and form connections with people around. The sympathetic process depicted in the novel is far from being solitary activities, for the reading process will play a vital role in training the readers' feelings and expanding their imaginations, which makes art the best tool to spread man's knowledge of the self and the human life. In this way, sympathy "asserted [in art] human values which a purely aesthetic view of art seemed to deny. [So] criticism could be aesthetic without rejecting a humanistic foundation, and humanistic without sacrificing aesthetic values" (Armstrong 59). As has been demonstrated in this project, George Eliot realizes the aesthetic value and humanistic foundation of sympathy and devotes to nurturing sympathy through the arts. She believes that "[man] can free himself from subservience to sensuous instinctive and, mediated by the aesthetics, reach a state of mental and moral self-determination" (Guth 146). Such an artistic ideal starts with an imaginative drive reaching out to the other by accepting the difference between the self and the other, although this process is variously defined. A crude juxtaposition of the imperfect self with a different image of the other may shed light on improving one's knowledge to know more about himself. Then with the affective similarities and the similar way to interpret emotions and feeling, the capability of sympathy is expected to create a community basing on common feeling and mutual understanding, collective action and public responsibility. That is why George Eliot's realistic novels are set in a wider and wider social, cultural and political context, so as to investigate and corroborate the social potential of sympathy to the utmost degree.

Generally speaking, Eliot mainly treats sympathy as a transformative force to train people's minds for achieving some epistemological, aesthetical or political aim. Her understanding of sympathy is basically an evolutionary process capturing the docking moment when the inside world meets with the outside one in a secularized context, so as to reveal the transformative process of the individual's psychological response upon the social transitions. Sympathy to Eliot is also an evolutionary spirituality, serving as the ethical resource pertaining to self-discovery, conscious will, and self-control. As a result, the willed individual may contribute to the improvement of the whole nation. In this sense, George Eliot's sympathy stresses emotions, thoughts, and principles, and more importantly, the level of imagination for the social and communal good. Under the appeal for the sublime, imagination often yearns for the infinite and the larger whole to give man opportunities to observe himself in relations and a self-annihilation will always be a preferred access to self-discovery. That is why Eliot records the mental truthfulness in her novel, so as to illustrate the hard inward reality but harbors intense interest of romance to encourage man to break away from the mundane trivial and aspire for the higher truth.

  Beryl Gray asserts that "the degree to which [George Eliot's] protagonists are endowed with the capacity for human sympathy is invariably the key to how the reader is meant to judge them" (Rignall 425). That is to say, the notion of sympathy and its demonstration is always unfixed and transformed. In short, the notion of sympathy ranges from the philosophical sources as a moral sentiment to its literary implication; from the accounts of aesthetic judgment to the rhetorical appeals to common sense, an elaboration of the trajectory of sympathy in this book has showed that "in many aspects the critique of sympathy is like the critique of the sublime, determined as much by how it is performed as by what it means" (Lamb 2), so, the transformative force of sympathy on man's mental world is always accompanied by the transformation of the implication of sympathy itself, and the combination of these two join with Eliot's efforts exerts much influence on Eliot's realistic writing and it turns to be the very thing Eliot aims to show in her works. As a result, realistic writing comes to present multiple interpretations to show the psychological truth in adjusting internal structures to external events. Thus the transformation of man's mental world in literature will adapt man's mental world to the social good in reality. This labyrinth-liked relationship makes Eliot's realistic writings display various levels of outlooks and refreshes our understanding of the implication of realism. Realism means "omniscient narration serving the ends of a totalizing ideology", and it is also an "empiricist philosophy demanding our attention to ordinary experience". (Levine, "Surprising Realism" 62) That is why "realism remains a mixed and elusive concept, better understood as a series of overlapping currents than as a coherent style or movement" (Levine, "Surprising Realism" 62). All in all, George Eliot, with her profound knowledge and deep observation of humanity, launches a survey of the human race in scientific analysis on the one hand and harbors an enthusiasm of romance with imaginary optionality on the other. In this way, George Eliot truthfully records the complicated transformative process of man's mentality in the Victorian age.

Therefore, any misreading of sympathy will reinforce the fact of the widespread absence of sympathy and the excessive privatization which characterizes contemporary life. Whether willing to admit it or not, sympathy till now has been fruitful access to the disadvantaged other, and it will generate a well-intentioned and humanistic care to others both in art and in reality. While more and more people are starting to question the vitality of sympathy in modern life, this project tends to agree with the indispensability of it. Sympathy "needs to be understood more generally in terms of dynamics, as a principle of mobility, communication, and exchange, of matter and spirit as well as of thought and feeling" (Lobis 4). No matter it is an intuitive force or an empirical experience, sympathy helps man accomplish some transcendence out of the limits of the self. To George Eliot and other Victorians, such a transcendental process is manifested both in a mysteriously romantic process and an evolutionary routine. It is sympathy that realizes the compatibility of these two seemingly contradicting trends of thoughts and fuses them at the point that highlights man to survive the nature for its indestructible inner power of self-regulation and self-adaptation. Just as what has been discussed in the opening section of this book, while facing a social circumstance in which feeble emotions, collapse of ethics and the aesthetic decline entangle with each other to oppress man's emotional vitality, men need to reflect on the functions of serious art, especially classic literature, to reaffirm that the natural, noble, genuine and irreplaceable emotions are of much more significance. In this sense, George Eliot's effort of making feeling the object of knowledge to improve the knowledge of a man's self through the extension of sympathy in her artistic realm is of special research value. Similarly, she in her art offers an amplified experimental process to help the individual generate goodwill toward the other, so as to strengthen the social bond and promote the community consensus. Ultimately, this is of great significance in both theory and practice for men to adapt to the social environment and to restore the inner order during the social transitional period.

Bibliography

Ablow, Rachel. *The Marriage of Minds: Reading Sympathy in the Victorian Marriage Plot*. Redwood: Stanford University Press, 2007.

Ablow, Rachel. "Tortured Sympathies: Victorian Literature and the Ticking Time-Bomb Scenario." *ELH* 80 (2013): 1145-1171.

Ablow, Rachel. "Victorian Feeling and the Victorian Novel." *Literature Compass* 4 (2007): 298-316.

Adams, James Eli. "Gyp's Tale: on Sympathy, Silence and Realism in *Adam Bede*." *Dickens Studies Annual: Essays on Victorian Fiction* 20 (1991): 227-242.

Althusser, Louis. *Lenin and Philosophy and Other Essays*. Trans. Ben Brewster. New York: Monthly Review Press, 1971.

Anderson, Amanda, and Harry E. Shaw, eds. *A Companion to George Eliot*. Chichester: John Wiley & Sons, 2013.

Anger, Suzy. "George Eliot and Philosophy." *The Cambridge Companion to George Eliot*. Ed. George Levine. New York: Cambridge University Press, 2001. 76-97.

Aouadi, Leila. "Transgression in *Daniel Deronda* (1876)." *The Victorian* 3(2015):1-29.

Arata, Stephen. "Realism." *The Cambridge Companion to the Fin de*

Siècle. Ed. Gail Marshall. Cambridge: Cambridge University Press, 2007. 169-187.

Argyros, Ellen. *"Without Any Check of Proud Reserve": Sympathy and Its Limits in George Eliot's Novels*. New York: Peter Lang, 1999.

Aristotle. *Rhetoric*. Trans. W. Rhys Roberts. New York: Dover Publications, 2004.

Aristotle. *Poetics*. Trans. Joe Sachs. Bemidji: Focus Publishing, 2011.

Aristotle. *The Nicomachean Ethics*. Ed. Roger Crisp. Cambridge: Cambridge University Press, 2014.

Armstrong, Isobel. *Victorian Scrutinies: Reviews of Poetry, 1830-1870*. London: Bloomsbury Publishing, 1972.

Armstrong, Paul B. "Form and History: Reading as an Aesthetic Experience and Historical Act." *MLQ: Modern Language Quarterly* 69 (2008): 195-219.

Arnold, Matthew. *Lectures and Essays in Criticism*. Ann Arbor: University of Michigan Press, 1962.

Bailin, Miriam, and Argyros, Ellen. "'Without any Check of Proud Reserve': Sympathy and its Limits in George Eliot's Novels (Book review)." *Victorian Studies* 44 (2002):323-326.

Bauman, Zygmunt. *Community: Seeking Safety in an Insecure World*. Cambridge: Polity Press, 2013.

Beer, Gillian. *Darwin's Plots: Evolutionary Narrative in Darwin, George Eliot, and Nineteenth-Century Fiction*. Cambridge: Cambridge University Press, 2000.

Beer, Gillian. "Music and the Visual Arts in the Novels of George Eliot." *The George Eliot Fellowship Review* 5 (1974): 17-20.

Burdett, Carolyn. "Sympathy." *The History of British Women's Writing, 1830-1880*. Eds. Lucy Hartley and Jennie Batchelor. London:

Palgrave Macmillan, 2018. 320-335.

Blair, Kirstie. "Contagious Sympathies: George Eliot and Rudolf Virchow." *Unmapped Countries: Biological Visions in Nineteenth Century Literature and Culture*. Ed. Anne-Julia Zwierlein. London: Anthem Press, 2005. 145-154.

Blake, Kathleen. "George Eliot: The Critical Heritage." *The Cambridge Companion to George Eliot*. Ed. George Levine. New York: Cambridge University Press, 2001: 202-225.

Bloom, Harold. *The Western Canon*. Boston: Houghton Mifflin Harcourt, 2014.

Bloom, Harold. *How to read and why*. New York: Simon and Schuster, 2001.

Blow, Rachel. *The Marriage of Minds: Reading Sympathy in the Victorian Marriage Plot*. Stanford: Stanford UP, 2007.

Bodenheimer, Rosemarie. *The Real Life of Mary Ann Evans: George Eliot, Her Letters and Fiction*. Ithaca, NY: Cornell University Press, 1996.

Booth, Wayne C. *The Rhetoric of Fiction*. Chicago: University of Chicago Press, 1983.

Brantlinger, Patrick, and William Thesing, eds. *A Companion to the Victorian Novel*. Chichester: John Wiley & Sons, 2008.

Brody, Jules. *Boileau and Longinus*. Genèva: Librairie E. Droz, 1958.

Burgess, Miranda. "On Being Moved: Sympathy, Mobility, and Narrative Form." *Poetics Today* 32 (2011): 289-321.

Burke, Edmund. *A Philosophical Enquiry into the Origin of Our Ideas of the Sublime and Beautiful* (1757). New York: P. F. Collier & Son Company, 1901.

Burke, Edmund, and James Thompson Boulton. *A Philosophical Enquiry into the Origin of our Ideas of the Sublime and Beautiful*. London:

Routledge & Kegan Paul, 1958.

Carroll, David. *George Eliot: The Critical Heritage*. London: Routledge, 2013.

Carroll, David. *George Eliot and the Conflict of Interpretations: A Reading of the Novels*. Cambridge: Cambridge University Press, 1992.

Chandler, James. *England in 1819: The Politics of Literary Culture and the Case of Romantic Historicism*. Chicago: University of Chicago Press, 1998.

Christ, Carol T., and John O. Jordan. *Victorian Literature and the Victorian Visual Imagination*. Berkeley: University of California Press, 1995.

Clark, Candace. *Misery and Company: Sympathy in Everyday Life*. Chicago: University of Chicago Press, 1997.

Cohn, Dorrit. *Transparent Minds: Narrative Modes for Presenting Consciousness in Fiction*. Princeton, NJ: Princeton University Press, 1978.

Collins, Kenneth K. *George Eliot: Interviews and Recollections*. London: Palgrave Macmillan, 2010.

Cooke, George Willis. *George Eliot, A Critical Study of Her Life, Writings and Philosophy*. Cambridge: Cambridge University Press, 2010.

Cooley, Charles Horton. *Human Nature and the Social Order*. London: Routledge, 2017.

Capuano, Peter J. "Handling George Eliot's Fiction." *George Eliot: Interdisciplinary Essays*. Eds. Jean Arnold and Lila Marz Harper. New York: Palgrave Macmillan, 2019. 165-193.

Costelloe, Timothy M. *The British Aesthetic Tradition: From Shaftesbury to Wittgenstein*. Cambridge: Cambridge University Press, 2013.

Creeger, George R. *George Eliot: A Collection of Critical Essays*. Vol. 90. Prentice Hall, 1970.

Csengei, Ildiko. *Sympathy, Sensibility and the Literature of Feeling in the Eighteenth Century*. London: Palgrave Macmillan, 2011.

Culler, Jonathon. "Omniscience." *Narrative* 12 (2004): 22-34.

Dalal, Dalip Singh. *George Eliot: Philosopher as Novelist*. New Delhi: Sarup & Sons, 2006.

Dallas, Eneas Sweetland. *The Gay Science*. Cambridge: Cambridge University Press, 2011.

Dames, Nicholas. *The Physiology of the Novel: Reading, Neural Science, and the Form of Victorian Fiction*. Oxford: Oxford Univ. Press, 2007.

Darwall, Stephen. "Sympathetic Liberalism: Recent Work on Adam Smith." *Philosophy & Public Affairs* 28 (1999): 139-164.

David, Deirdre. *The Cambridge Companion to the Victorian Novel*. Cambridge: Cambridge University Press, 2012.

Davis, Lennard. *Resisting Novels: Ideology and Fiction*. New York: Methuen, 1987.

Day, Gary. *Literary Criticism: A New History*. Edinburgh: Edinburgh University Press, 2008.

Dolin, Tim. *George Eliot (Authors in Context)*. Oxford: Oxford University Press, 2005.

Doyle, Mary Ellen. *The Sympathetic Response: George Eliot's Fictional Rhetoric*. New Jersey: Fairleigh Dickinson University Press, 1981.

Duncan, Ian. "Adam Smith, Samuel Johnson and the Institutions of English." *The Scottish Invention of English Literature*. Ed. Robert Crawford. Cambridge: Cambridge Univ. Press, 1998. 37-54.

Duncan, Ian. "George Eliot and the Science of the Human." *A Companion to George Eliot*. Eds. Amanda Anderson and Harry E. Shaw. London: John Wiley & Sons, 2013. 471-485.

Duncan, Ian. "Realism." *Victorian Literature and Culture* 46 (2018):

835-840.

During, Lisabeth. "The Concept of Dread: Sympathy and Ethics in *Daniel Deronda*." *Renegotiating Ethics in Literature, Philosophy, and Theory*. Eds. Jane Adamson, Richard Freadman, and David Parker. Cambridge: Cambridge University Press, 1998.

During, Simon. "George Eliot and Secularism." *A Companion to George Eliot*, Eds. Amanda Anderson and Harry E. Shaw. London: John Wiley & Sons, 2013. 428-441.

Dwyer, John. *The Age of the Passions: An Interpretation of Adam Smith and Scottish Enlightenment Culture*. East Linton, Scotland: Tuckwell Press, 1998.

Eagleton, Terry. "Power and Knowledge in *The Lifted Veil*". *Literature and History* 9 (1983): 52-61.

Eigner, Edwin M., and George J. Worth, eds. *Victorian Criticism of the Novel*. Cambridge: Cambridge University Press, 1985.

Eliot, George. *Adam Bede*. Ed. Carol A. Martin. Oxford: Clarendon Press, 2001.

Eliot, George. *Daniel Deronda*. Ed. Graham Handley. Oxford: Clarendon Press, 1980.

Eliot, George. *Essays of George Eliot*. Ed. Thomas Pinney. London: Routledge and Kegan Paul, 2009.

Eliot, George. *Felix Holt, the Radical*. Ed. Fred C. Thomson. Oxford: Clarendon Press, 1980.

Eliot, George. *Middlemarch*. Ed. Bert G. Hornback. New York: W. W. Norton & Company, Inc., 2000.

Eliot, George. *Selected Essays, Poems and Other Writings*. Eds. A. S. Byatt and Nicholas Warren. London: Penguin UK, 1990.

Eliot, George. *The Essays of "George Eliot" Complete*. Ed. Nathan Sheppard. New York: Funk & Agnalls Publishers, 2009. 144.

Eliot, George. *The George Eliot Letters*. Ed. Gordon S. Haight. 7 vols. New Haven and London: Yale University Press, 1954-1955.

Eliot, George. *Impressions of Theophrastus Such*. Ed. Nancy Henry. Iowa City: University of Iowa Press. 1994.

Eliot, George. *The Lifted Veil·Brother Jacob*. Oxford: Oxford University Press, 1999.

Eliot, George. *The Mill on the Floss*. ICON Group International, Inc., 2005.

Ellis, Markman. *The Politics of Sensibility: Race, Gender and Commerce in the Sentimental Novel*. Cambridge: Cambridge University Press, 2004.

Ellison, David. *Ethics and Aesthetics in European Modernist Literature: From the Sublime to the Uncanny*. Cambridge: Cambridge University Press, 2001.

Engell, James. *The Creative Imagination: Enlightenment to Romanticism*. Cambridge, MA: Harvard University Press, 1981.

Ermarth, Elizabeth Deeds. "George Eliot's Conception of Sympathy." *Nineteenth-Century Fiction* 40 (1985): 23-42.

Eskin, Michael. "Introduction: The Double Turn to Ethics and Literature?" *Poetics Today* 25 (2004): 557-572.

Faflak, Joel, and C. Sha Richard, eds. *Romanticism and the Emotions*. Cambridge: Cambridge University Press, 2014.

Farina, Jonathan. "*Middlemarch* and 'that Sort of Thing'." *Romanticism and Victorianism on the Net* 53 (2009): 50-61.

Ferguson, Frances. "Jane Austen, *Emma*, and the Impact of Form." *MLQ: Modern Language Quarterly* 61 (2000): 157-180.

Feuerbach, Ludwig. The Essence of Christianity. Trans. George Eliot. New York: Cossimo, 2008.

Fisher, Philip. *Making Up Society: The Novels of George Eliot*.

Pittsburgh: University of Pittsburgh Press, 1981.

Fleishman, Avrom. *George Eliot's Intellectual Life*. Cambridge: Cambridge University Press, 2010.

Flint, Kate. *The Victorians and the Visual Imagination*. New York: Cambridge University Press, 2000.

Fludernik, Monika. "Eliot and Narrative." *A Companion to George Eliot*. Eds. Amanda Anderson and Harry E. Shaw. Chichester: John Wiley & Sons, 2013. 21-34.

Frazer, Michael L. *The Enlightenment of Sympathy: Justice and the Moral Sentiments in the Eighteenth Century and Today*. Oxford: Oxford University Press, 2010.

Fulmer, Constance M., and Margaret E. Barfield, eds. *A Monument to the Memory of George Eliot: Edith J. Simcox's Autobiography of a Shirtmaker*. London: Routledge, 2013.

Gallagher, Catherine. "George Eliot: Immanent Victorian." *Representations* 90 (2005): 61-74.

Galvan, Jill. "The Narrator as Medium in George Eliot's *The Lifted Veil*." *Victorian Studies* 48 (2007): 240-248.

Garratt, Peter. *Victorian Empiricism: Self, Knowledge, and Reality in Ruskin, Bain, Lewes, Spencer, and George Eliot*. Vancouver: Fairleigh Dickinson University Press, 2010.

Gaston, Sean. "The Impossibility of Sympathy." *The Eighteenth Century* 51 (2010): 129-152.

Gatens, Moira. "The Art and Philosophy of George Eliot." *Philosophy and Literature* 33 (2009): 73-90.

Gatens, Moira. "Compelling Fictions: Spinoza and George Eliot on Imagination and Belief." *European Journal of Philosophy* 20 (2012): 74-90.

Gilbert, Sandra M., and Susan Gubar. *The Madwoman in the Attic:*

The Woman Writer and the Nineteenth-Century Literary Imagination. New Haven: Yale University Press, 1980.

Gindele, Karen C. "The Web of necessity: George Eliot's Theory of Ideology." Texas Studies in Literature and Language 42 (2000): 255-289.

Glendening, John. *The Evolutionary Imagination in Late-Victorian Novels: An Entangled Bank*. London: Routledge, 2016.

Gould, Rebecca. "Adam Bede's Dutch Realism and the Novelist's Point of View." *Philosophy and Literature* 36 (2012): 404-423.

Graver, Suzanne. *George Eliot and Community: A Study in Social Theory and Fictional Form*. Berkeley: University of California Press, 1984.

Greiner, Rae. *Sympathetic Realism in Nineteenth-Century British Fiction*. Baltimore, MD: The Johns Hopkins University Press, 2012.

Greiner, Rae. "Sympathy Time: Adam Smith, George Eliot, and the Realist Novel." *Narrative* 17 (2009): 291-311.

Greiner, Rae. "Thinking of Me Thinking of You: Sympathy Versus Empathy in the Realist Novel." *Victorian Studies* 53 (2011): 417-426.

Griffin, Cristina Richieri. "George Eliot's Feuerbach: Senses, Sympathy, Omniscience, And Secularism." *ELH* 84 (2017): 475-502.

Griffith, Jody. "Constructing Ordinary Time in Adam Bede: The Architectural Structure of Eliot's Realism." *Studies in the Novel* 48 (2016): 1-18.

Grube, George Maximilian Anthony, ed. *On Great Writing: (On the Sublime)*. Indianapolis: Bobbs-Merrill Company, 1957.

Gruber, Howard E., and Paul H. Barrett. *Darwin on Man: A Psychological Study of Scientific Creativity Together with Darwin's Early Unpublished Notebooks*. New York: Dutton. 1974.

Guth, Deborah. *George Eliot and Schiller: Intertextuality and Cross-cultural Discourse*. London: Routledge, 2016.

Guyer, Paul. "Feeling and Freedom: Kant on Aesthetics and

Morality." *The Journal of Aesthetics and Art Criticism* **48** (1990): 137-146.

Hadjiafxendi, Kyriaki. "'George Eliot', the Literary Market-Place, and Sympathy." *Authorship in Context: From the Theoretical to the Material*. Eds. Hadjiafxendi, Kyriaki, and Polina Mackay. New York: Springer, **2007**. 33-55.

Haight, Gordon S. *George Eliot: A Biography*. Oxford: Oxford University Press, **1968**.

Halliwell, Stephen. *The Aesthetics of Mimesis: Ancient Texts and Modern Problems*. Princeton: Princeton University Press, **2009**.

Hardy, Barbara. *Forms of Feeling in Victorian Fiction*. London: Methuen & Co. Ltd, **1985**.

Hardy, Barbara. "Introduction." *Daniel Deronda*. By George Eliot. Ed. Barbara Hardy. London: Penguin, **1967**.

Hardy, Barbara. *The Novels of George Eliot: A Study in Form*. London: The Athlone Press, **1959**.

Hardy, Zachary J. "'A Constant Unfolding of Far-Resonate Action': George Eliot's *Middlemarch*, Spinoza, and the Ethics of Power." Diss. **2015**.

Harkin, Maureen. "Adam Smith's Missing History: Primitives, Progress, and Problems of Genre." *ELH: English Literary History* **72** (2005): 429-451.

Harris, Margaret. *George Eliot in Context*. Cambridge: Cambridge University Press, **2013**.

Henberg, M. C. "George Eliot's Moral Realism." *Philosophy and Literature* **3** (1979): 20-38.

Henry, Nancy. *George Eliot and the British Empire*. Cambridge: Cambridge University Press, **2002**.

Henry, Nancy. *The Cambridge Introduction to George Eliot*. Cambridge: Cambridge University Press, **2008**.

Henry, Nancy. *The Life of George Eliot: A Critical Biography*. Chichester: John Wiley & Sons, 2014.

Henson, Miriam. "George Eliot's *Middlemarch* as a Translation of Spinoza's Ethics." *The George Eliot Review* 40 (2009): 18-26.

Herdt, Jennifer. *Religion and Faction in Hume's Moral Philosophy*. Cambridge: Cambridge University Press, 1997.

Hertz, Neil. *George Eliot's Pulse*. Stanford, CA: Stanford University Press, 2003.

Hinton, Laura. *The Perverse Gaze of Sympathy: Sadomasochistic Sentiments from Clarissa to Rescue* 911. Albany: SUNY Press, 1999.

Hipple, Walter John, Jr. *The Beautiful, The Sublime and the Picturesque in Eighteenth Century British Aesthetic Theory*. Carbondale: Southern Illinois University Press, 1957.

Hobbes, Thomas. *Leviathan*. Ed. Richard Tuck. Cambridge: Cambridge University Press, 1996.

Horace. "Art of Poetry." *Literary Criticism and Theory: The Greeks to the Present*. Eds. Robert Davis and Laurie Finke. New York & London: Longman Inc., 1989.

Hughes, Kathryn. *George Eliot: The Last Victorian*. London: Rowman & Littlefield, 2001.

Huhn, Tom. "Burke's Sympathy for Taste." *Eighteenth-century Studies* 35 (2002): 379-393.

Hume, David. *A Treatise of Human Nature*. Eds. David Fate Norton and Mary J. Norton. NY: Oxford: Oxford Univ. Press, 2000.

Hyslop-Margison, Emery J. "Smith, Hume and the Moral Imagination: Sympathy and Social Justice." *Pastoral Care in Education* 24 (2006): 26-30.

Irwin, Jane, ed. *George Eliot's Daniel Deronda Notebooks*. Cambridge: Cambridge University Press, 1996.

Irwin, T. H. "Sympathy and the Basis of Morality." *A Companion to George Eliot*. Eds. Amanda Anderson and Harry E. Shaw. Chichester: John Wiley & Sons, 2013. 279-293.

James, Henry. "Daniel Deronda: A Conversation." *George Eliot: The Critical Heritage*. Ed. David Carroll. London: Routledge & Kegan Paul, 1971.

Jaffe, Audrey. *Scenes of Sympathy: Identity and Representation in Victorian Fiction*. Ithaca, NY: Cornell University Press, 2000.

Jaffe, Audrey. *Vanishing Points: Dickens, Narrative, and the Subject of Omniscience*. Berkeley: University of California Press, 1991.

Jewusiak, Jacob. "Large-Scale Sympathy and Simultaneity in George Eliot's Romola." *SEL Studies in English Literature 1500-1900* 54 (2014): 853-874.

Kant, Immanuel. *Critique of Judgment*. Trans. Werner S. Pluhar. Indianapolis: Hackett Publishing Co., 1987.

Kant, Immanuel. *The Metaphysical Principles of Virtue*. Trans. James Ellington. Bobbs-Merrill, 1964.

Keats, John. "On Seeing the Elgin Marbles." *Poetry Foundation*. 1817.

Keats, John. *Selected Letters*. Ed. Robert Gittings. Oxford: Oxford University Press, 2002.

Keen, Suzanne. *Empathy and the Novel*. Oxford: Oxford University Press, 2007.

Keen, Suzanne. *Victorian Renovations of the Novel: Narrative Annexes and the Boundaries of Representation*. Vol. 15. Cambridge University Press, 2005.

Kennedy, Meegan. "'A True Prophet'? Speculation in Victorian Sensory Physiology and George Eliot's 'The Lifted Veil'." *NINETEEN CENT LIT* 71 (2016): 369-403.

Kingsley, Charles. *Alton Locke, Tailor and Poet: An Autobiography*. London: Macmillan, 1896.

Knight, Richard Payne. *An Analytical Inquiry into the Principles of Taste*. London: C. Mergier, 1805.

Knoepflmacher, Ulrich Camillus. *Religious Humanism and the Victorian Novel: George Eliot, Walter Pater and Samuel Butler*. Princeton: Princeton University Press, 2015.

Knoepflmacher, Ulrich Camillus. "George Eliot, Feuerbach, and the Question of Criticism." *Victorian Studies* 7(1964): 306-309.

Konstan, David. *Pity Transformed*. London: Bloomsbury Publishing, 2015.

Kornbluh, Anna. "The Economic Problem of Sympathy: Parabasis, Interest, and Realist Form in Middlemarch." *ELH* 77 (2010): 941-967.

Kreisel, Deanna K. "Incognito, Intervention, and Dismemberment in *Adam Bede*." *ELH* 70 (2003): 541-574.

Kucich, John. *Repression in Victorian Fiction: Charlotte Brontë, George Eliot, and Charles Dickens*. Berkeley: University of California Press, 1987.

Lamb, Jonathan. *The Evolution of Sympathy in the Long Eighteenth Century*. London: Routledge, 2015.

Laporte, Charles. "Victorian literature, religion, and secularization." *Literature Compass* 10 (2013): 277-287.

Laurand, Valéry. "Universal Sympathy: Union and Separation." *Revue De Métaphysique et de Morale* 4 (2005): 517-535.

Leavis, Frank Raymond. *The Great Tradition: George Eliot, Henry James, Joseph Conrad*. London: Faber & Faber, 2011.

Leavis, Frank Raymond. *The Great Tradition*. New York: Stewart, 1948.

Leitch, Vincent B., and William E. Cain, eds. *The Norton Anthology* of Theory and Criticism. London: WW Norton & Company, 2001.

Levine, Carraline. "Surprising Realism". *A Companion to George Eliot*. Eds. Amanda Anderson and Harry E. Shaw. Chichester: John Wiley & Sons, 2013.

Levine, George. Mary Ellen Doyle. "The Sympathetic Response: George Eliot's Fictional Rhetoric" (Book Review). *Nineteenth-Century Fiction* 38 (1983): 111-117.

Levine, George. *Realism, Ethics and Secularism: Essays on Victorian Literature and Science*. Cambridge: Cambridge University Press, 2008.

Levine, George. "Review." *George Eliot Review* 45 (2014): 83-85.

Levine, George. *The Cambridge Companion to George Eliot*. Cambridge: Cambridge University Press, 2001.

Lewes, George Henry. *Problems of Life and Mind*. Charleston: BiblioBazaar, LLC, 2009.

Lewes, George Henry. "The Women Novelists." *The Victorian Art of Fiction: Nineteenth-Century Essays on the Novel*. Ed. Rohan Maitzen. Peterborough: Broadview Press, 2009.

Lewes, George Henry. *A Biographical History of Philosophy*. Cambridge: Cambridge University Press, 2012.

Lewes, George Henry.. "The Condition of Authors in England, Germany and France." *Fraiser's Magzine* 35 (1847): 285-297.

Lloyd, Tom. *Crisis of Realism Representing Experience in the British Novel, 1816-1910*. Lewisburg: Bucknell University Press, 1997.

Lobis, Seth. *The Virtue of Sympathy: Magic, Philosophy, and Literature in Seventeenth-Century England*. New Haven: Yale University Press, 2015.

Logan, Peter Melville. *Nerves and Narratives: A Cultural History of Hysteria in 19th-Century British Prose*. Berkeley: University of California Press, 1997.

Longinus. "On Sublimity." *Classical Literary Criticism*. Eds. D. R. Russell and M. Winterbottom. Oxford University Press, 1989.

Lowe, Brigid. *Victorian Fiction and the Insights of Sympathy: An Alternative to the Hermeneutics of Suspicion*. London: Anthem Press, 2007.

Luckhurst, Roger. *The Invention of Telepathy 1870-1901*. Oxford: Oxford University Press, 2002.

Lutz, Catherine A. *Unnatural Emotions: Everyday Sentiments on a Micronesian Atoll: Their Challenges to Western Theory*. Chicago: University of Chicago Press, 1988.

Macarthur, John. "The Heartlessness of the Picturesque: Sympathy and Disgust in Ruskin's Aesthetics." *Assemblage* 32 (1997): 127-141.

McCormack, Kathleen. *George Eliot's English Travels: Composite Characters and Coded Communications*. London: Routledge, 2005.

Mackenzie, Hazel. "A Dialogue of Forms: The Display of Thinking in George Eliot's 'Poetry and Prose, From the Notebook of an Eccentric' and Impressions of Theophrastus Such." *Prose Studies* 36 (2014): 117-129.

Mahawatte, Royce. *George Eliot and the Gothic Novel: Genres, Gender, Feeling*. Cardiff, Wales: University of Wales Press, 2013.

Makkreel, Rudolf. "Imagination and Temporality in Kant's Theory of the Sublime." *The Journal of Aesthetics and Art Criticism* 42 (1984): 303-315.

Mansell, Darrel. "George Eliot's Conception of 'Form'." *Studies in English Literature, 1500-1900* 5 (1965): 651-662.

Marshall, David. *The Surprising Effects of Sympathy: Marivaux, Diderot, Rousseau, and Mary Shelley*. Chicago: University of Chicago Press, 1988.

Martindale, Charles, and Colin Martindale, eds. *Latin Poetry and the Judgement of Taste: An Essay in Aesthetics*. Oxford: Oxford University Press, 2005.

Marx, Karl. *Capital, Volume One. 1867*. Trans. Ben Fowkes. Harmondsworth: Penguin-New Left Books, 1976.

McGowan, John P. "The Turn of George Eliot's Realism." *Nineteenth-Century Fiction* 35 (1980): 171-192.

Menke, Richard. "Fiction as Vivisection: G. H. Lewes and George Eliot." *ELH* 67 (2000): 617-653.

McSweeney, Kerry. *Middlemarch: Study of Provincial Life*. London: Allen & Unwin, 1984.

Meredith, George. *The Letters of George Meredith* (Ⅱ). Ed. William Meredith. NewYork: C. Scribner's Sons, 1912.

Mestrovic, Stjepan. *Postemotional Society*. London: Sage Publications, 1996.

Mill, John Stuart. "Nature." *Collected Works of John Stuart Mill* (Vol. 10). Ed. F. E. L. Priestley. Toronto: University of Toronto Press, 1969.

Miller, Andrew H. *The Burdens of Perfection: On Ethics and Reading in Nineteenth-Century British Literature*. NY: Cornell University Press, 2006.

Miller, J. Hillis. *Reading for Our Time: Adam Bede and Middlemarch Revisited*. Edinburgh: Edinburgh University Press, 2012.

Mintz, Alan. *George Eliot and the Novel of Vocation*. Cambridge, MA: Harvard University Press: Cambridge, 1978.

Monk, Samuel H. *The Sublime: A Study of Critical Theories in XVIII-Century England*. Ann Arbor: University of Michigan Press, 1960.

Morton, Adam. *Emotion and Imagination*. Chichester: John Wiley & Sons, 2013.

Moyn, Samuel. *Origins of the Other: Emmanuel Lévinas between Revelation and Ethics*. Ithaca, NY: Cornell University Press, 2005.

Mukherjee, Tapan Kumar. "Sympathetic Vibrations: Fictional

Treatment of a Scientific Concept in the Novels of George Eliot Compared and Contrasted with Analogous Treatment by Contemporary Victorian Novelist Charles Dickens." *The Victorian* 3 (2015): 1-5.

Nazar, Hina. "Philosophy in the Bedroom: *Middlemarch* and the Scandal of Sympathy." *Yale Journal of Criticism* 15 (2002): 293-314.

Nehamas, Alexander. "Pity and Fear in the Rhetoric and the Poetics." Eds. David J. Furley and Alexander Nehamas. *Aristotle's "Rhetoric": Philosophical Essays*. Princeton: Princeton University Press, 2015.

Nestor, Pauline. *George Eliot: Critical Issues*. Palgrave: Hampshire, 2002.

Newman, Francis. *The Soul: Its Sorrows and Aspirations: An Essay towards the Natural History of the Soul, as the True Basis of Theology*. London: George Manwaring, 1849.

Newton, K. M. *George Eliot: Romantic Humanist: A Study of the Philosophical Structure of Her Novels*. London: Macmilla Totowa, NJ: Barnes & Noble, 1981.

Newton, Kenneth M. "George Eliot and Racism: How Should One Read 'The Modern Hep! Hep! hep!'?" *The Modern Language Review* 103 (2008): 654-665.

Nietzsche, Friedrich Wilhelm. *The Will to Power*. Trans. Walter Arnold Kaufmann and R. J. Hollingdale. New York: Random House, 1967.

Nunokawa, Jeff. "Eros and Isolation: The Antisocial George Eliot." *ELH* 69 (2002): 835-860.

Nussbaum, Martha. *The Fragility of Goodness: Luck and Ethics in Greek Tragedy and Philosophy*. Cambridge: Cambridge University Press, 1986.

Nussbaum, Martha. *Poetic Justice: The Literary Imagination and Public*

Life. Boston: Beacon Press, 1995.

Nussbaum, Martha. *Cultivating Humanity*. Cambridge, MA: Harvard University Press, 1997.

Nussbaum, Martha. "Exactly and Responsibly: A Defense of Ethical Criticism." *Philosophy and Literature* 22 (1998): 343-365.

Nussbaum, Martha. *Upheavals of Thought: The Intelligence of the Emotions*. Cambridge: Cambridge University Press, 2001.

Nünning, Ansgar. "'The Extension of our Sympathies': George Eliot's Aesthetic Theory and Narrative Technique as a Key to the Affective, Cognitive, and Social Value of Literature." *Values of Literature* 278 (2015): 117-136.

Orr, Marilyn. "Incarnation, Inwardness, and Imagination: George Eliot's Early Fiction." *Christianity and Literature* 58 (2009): 451-481.

Osterhammel, Jürgen. *The Transformation of the World: A Global History of the Nineteenth Century* (Vol 15). Princeton and Oxford: Princeton University Press, 2015.

Parrinder, Patrick. *Nation and Novel: The English Novel from its Origins to the Present Day*. Oxford: Oxford University Press, 2008.

Paris, Bernard J. *Rereading George Eliot: Changing Responses to Her Experiments in Life*. New York: State University of New York Press, 2003.

Pater, Walter. "Winckelmann." *The Renaissance: Studies in Art and Poetry*. Ed. Donald L. Hill. Berkeley: University of California Press, 1980.

Paxman, David. "Metaphor and Knowledge in George Eliot's *Middlemarch*." *Metaphor and Symbol* 18 (2003): 107-123.

Payne, David. *The Reenchantment of Nineteenth-Century Fiction: Dickens, Thackeray, George Eliot and Serialization*. New York: Springer, 2005.

Perlis, Alan. *A Return to the Primal Self: Identity in the Fiction of George Eliot*. New York: Peter Lang, 1989.

Peters, Laura. *Orphan Texts: Victorian Orphans, Culture and Empire*. Manchester: Manchester UP, 2013.

Pillow, Kirk. "Imagination." *The Oxford Handbook of Philosophy and Literature*. New York: Oxford University Press, 2009.

Pinch, Adela. *Strange Fits of Passion: Epistemologies of Emotion, Hume to Austen*. Redwood: Stanford University Press, 1996.

Pinion, Francis B. *A George Eliot Miscellany: A Supplement to Her Novels*. New York: Springer, 1982.

Pinion, Francis B. *A George Eliot Companion: Literary Achievement and Modern Significance*. New York: Springer, 1981.

Plotz, John. "Two Flowers: George Eliot's Diagrams and the Modern Novel." *A Companion to George Eliot*. Eds. Amanda Anderson and Harry E. Shaw. Chichester: John Wiley & Sons, 2013. 76-90.

Preyer, Robert. "Beyond the Liberal Imagination: Vision and Unreality in *Daniel Deronda*." *Victorian Studies* 4 (1960): 33-54.

Price, Leah. *The Anthology and the Rise of the Novel: From Richardson to George Eliot*. Cambridge: Cambridge University Press, 2003.

Pulham, Patricia. "The Arts." *A Companion to 19th-Century Britain*. Ed. Chris Williams. Chichester: John Wiley & Sons, 2006.

Pykett, Lyn. "*Sensation and the Fantastic in the Victorian Novel*." *The Cambridge Companion to the Victorian Novel*. Ed. Deirdre David. Cambridge: Cambridge University Press, 2012.

Pyle, Forest. "A Novel Sympathy: the Imagination of Community in George Eliot." *Novel: A Forum on Fiction* 27(1993) 5-27.

Pyle, Forest. *The Ideology of Imagination: Subject and Society in the Discourse of Romanticism*. Redwood: Stanford University Press, 1995.

Ramsden Balmforth. *The Ethical and Religious Values of the Novel*.

London: Allen, 1912.

Ratcliffe, Sophie. *On Sympathy*. Oxford: Oxford University Press, 2008.

Rectenwald, Michael. *Nineteenth-Century British Secularism: Science, Religion and Literature*. New York: Springer, 2016.

Redfield, Marc. "George Eliot's Telepathy machine." *Phantom Formations: Aesthetic Ideology and the Bildungsroman*. Ithaca, NY: Cornell University Press, 1996.

Reilly, Ariana. "Always Sympathize! Surface Reading, Affect, and George Eliot's Romola." *Victorian Studies* 55 (2013): 629-646.

Rignall, John, ed. *Oxford Reader's Companion to George Eliot*. Oxford: Oxford UP, 2000.

Roberts, Nancy. *Schools of Sympathy: Gender and Identification through the Novel*. Montreal: McGill-Queen's University Press, 1997.

Roberts, W. Rhys, ed. *Longinus on the Sublime: The Greek Text Edited After the Paris Manuscript*. Cambridge: Cambridge University Press, 2011.

Robbins, Bruce. "The Cosmopolitan Eliot." *A Companion to George Eliot*. Eds. Amanda Anderson and Harry E. Shaw. London: John Wiley & Sons, 2013. 400-412.

Röder-Bolton, Gerlinde. "'A Binding History, Tragic and yet Glorious'—George Eliot and the Jewish Element in Daniel Deronda." *English* 49 (2000): 205-227.

Rodgers, James. "Sensibility, Sympathy, Benevolence: Physiology and Moral Philosophy in Tristram Shandy." *Languages of Nature: Critical Essays on Science and Literature*. Ed. L. J. Jordanova. London: Free Association Books, 1986.

Royle, Nicholas. "The Telepathy Effect: Notes toward a Reconsideration of Narrative Fiction." *Acts of Narrative*. Eds. Carol Jacobs and

Henry Sussman. Stanford: Stanford University Press, 2003. 93-109.

Royle, Nicholas. *Telepathy and Literature: Essays on the Reading Mind*. Oxford: Blackwell Publishing, 1991.

Rudd, Andrew. *Sympathy and India in British Literature, 1770-1830*. New York: Springer, 2011.

Ruskin, John. *Lectures on Arts*. Wokingham: Dodo Press, 2007.

Said, Edward. *Culture and Imperialism*. London: Chatto and Windus, 1993.

Said, Edward. *Orientalism*. New York: Vintage, 1979.

Said, Edward. *The Question of Palestine*. New York: Vintage Books, 1992.

Saintsbury, George. "Daniel Deronda." *The Academy* 10 (1876): 253-254.

Schaper, Eva. "Aristotle's Catharsis and Aesthetic Pleasure." *The Philosophical Quarterly* 18 (1968): 131-143.

Schutjer, Karin. "The Persistence of Sympathy in Kant's Aesthetics." *Monatshefte* 91 (1999): 170-187.

Scudder, Vida D. "George Eliot and the Social Conscience." *Social Ideals in English Letters*. New York: Chautauqua, 1898.

Semmel, Bernard. *George Eliot and the Politics of National Inheritance*. Oxford: Oxford University Press, 1994.

Shaftesbury, Anthony Ashley Cooper. *Shaftesbury: Characteristics of Men, Manners, Opinions, Times* (Ⅰ-Ⅲ). Indianapolis: Liberty Fund, Inc., 2001.

Shaw, Harry E. *Narrating Reality: Austen, Scott, Eliot*. Ithaca, NY: Cornell Univ. Press, 1999.

Shelley, Percy Bysshe. *A Defence of Poetry*. Ed. Francis B. Pinion. Girard: Haldeman-Julius, 1969.

Showalter, Elaine. "The Greening of Sister George." *Nineteenth-

Century Fiction 35 (1980): 292-311.

Shuttleworth, Sally. *George Eliot and Nineteenth-Century Science: The Make-Believe of a Beginning*. Cambridge: Cambridge University Press, 1984.

Simcox, Edith. "George Eliot." *Nineteenth Century* 1881.

Sklar, Howard. *The Art of Sympathy in Fiction: Forms of Ethical and Emotional Persuasion*. John Benjamins Publishing, 2013.

Smith, Adam. *The Theory of Moral Sentiments*. Oxford: Oxford University Press, 1976.

Sober, Elliott, and David Sloan Wilson. *Unto Others: The Evolution and Psychology of Unselfish Behavior*. Cambridge & Harvard University Press, 1998.

Sperlinger, Tom. "'The Sensitive Author': George Eliot." *The Cambridge Quarterly* 36 (2007): 250-272.

Spillman, Deborah Shapple. "All That Is Solid Turns into Steam: Sublimation and Sympathy in George Eliot's The Mill on the Floss." *NINETEEN CENT LIT* 72 (2017): 338-373.

Stang, Richard. *The Theory of the Novel in England, 1850-1870*. New York: Columbia University Press, 1959.

Star, Christopher. *The Empire of the Self: Self-command and Political Speech in Seneca and Petronius*. Baltimore: Johns Hopkins University Press, 2012.

Strang, Richard. "The Literary Criticism of George Eliot." *PMLA* 72 (1957): 952-961.

Sugden, Robert. "Beyond Sympathy and Empathy: Adam Smith's Concept of Fellow-feeling." *Economics and Philosophy* 18 (2002): 63-87.

Tegan, Mary Beth. "Strange Sympathies: George Eliot and the Literary Science of Sensation." *Women's Writing* 20 (2013): 168-185.

Thomas A. Noble. "The Doctrine of Sympathy." *George Eliot's*

Scenes of Clerical Life. New Haven: Yale University Press, 1965.

Thomas, Esther Eleanor. *Ruskin's Theory of Truth in Art*. Iowa Research Online, 1913.

Toker, Leona. *Towards the Ethics of Form in Fiction: Narratives of Cultural Remission*. Columbus: Ohio State University Press, 2010.

Tondre, Michael. "George Eliot's 'Fine Excess': *Middlemarch*, Energy, and the Afterlife of Feeling." NINETEEN CENT LIT 67 (2012): 204-233.

Tönnies, Ferdinand. *Community and Civil Society*. Ed. Jose Harris. Cambridge: Cambridge University Press, 2001.

Tucker, Irene. *A Probable State: The Novel, the Contract and the Jews*. Chicago: University of Chicago, 2000.

Voskuil, Lynn. "George Eliot among Her Contemporaries: A Life Apart." *A Companion to George Eliot*. Eds. Amanda Anderson and Harry E. Shaw. Chichester: John Wiley & Sons, 2013. 233-246.

Ward, Bernadette Waterman. "Zion's Mimetic Angel: George Eliot's Daniel Deronda." *Shofar: An Interdisciplinary Journal of Jewish Studies* 22 (2004): 105-115.

Werses, Shmuel. "The Jewish Reception of Daniel Deronda." *Daniel Deronda: A Centenary Symposium*. Ed. Alice Shalvi. Jerusalem: Jerusalem Academic Press, 1976.

Wetmore, Alex. "Sympathy Machines: Men of Feeling and the Automaton." *Eighteenth-Century Studies* 43 (2009): 37-54.

Williams, Raymond. *Keywords: A Vocabulary of Culture and Society*. London: Fontana, 1988.

Williams, Raymond. *Marxism and Literature*. Oxford: Oxford UP, 1997.

Williams, Raymond. "The Knowable Community in George Eliot's Novels." *Novel: A Forum on Fiction* 2 (1969): 255-268.

Williams, Raymond. *Culture and Society*. London: Harmondsworth, 1958.

Wordsworth, William. "Essay on Morals." *The Prose Works of William Wordsworth* (I). Eds. W. J. B. Owen and Jane Worthington Smyser. Oxford: Oxford University Press, 1974.

Woolf, Virginia. "Professions for Women." *Virginia Woolf: Women and Writing*. Ed. Michèle Barrett. London: The Women's Press, 1979.

Wright, John P. *Hume's "A Treatise of Human Nature": An Introduction*. Cambridge: Cambridge University Press, 2009.

Yeazell, Ruth Bernard. *Art of the Everyday: Dutch Painting and the Realist Novel*. Princeton: Princeton University Press, 2008.

Young, Jock. *The Exclusive Society*. London: Sage, 1999.

Zenzinger, Ted. "Spinoza, Adam Bede, Knowledge, and Sympathy: A Reply to Atkins." *Philosophy and Literature* 36 (2012): 424-440.

程丽蓉."现实主义"的符号学阐释[J].浙江社会科学,2019(10):134-140,150.

高晓玲."感受就是一种知识!":乔治·艾略特作品中"感受"的认知作用[J].外国文学评论,2008(3):5-16.

高晓玲.乔治·爱略特的"同情"观及其哲学渊源[J].外国文学,2009(1):61-66.

高晓玲.诗性真理:转型焦虑在19世纪英国文学中的表征[J].外国文学研究,2018(4):47-57.

蒋承勇.19世纪现实主义文学经典的生成[J].浙江工商大学学报,2018(1):5-11.

金雯.启蒙时代的"同情"[J].兰州大学学报(社会科学版),2018(5):11-18.

李维屏,张定铨,等.英国文学思想史[M].上海:上海外语教育出版社,2012.

廖昌胤.悖论叙事:乔治·艾略特后期三部小说中的政治现代化悖论[D].杭州:浙江大学,2006.

林懿,王守仁.在悖论中坚守:现实主义文学的当代发展与理论争鸣[J].外国文学研究,2016(3):152-160.

王海萌.当代西方乔治·爱略特研究述评[J].国外文学,2010(1):35-42.

王守仁,胡宝平,等.英国文学批评史[M].南京:南京大学出版社,2012.

魏晓红.乔治·艾略特小说的心理描写艺术研究[D].上海:上海外国语大学,2010.

殷企平.从自我到非我:《丹尼尔·德隆达》中的心智培育之路[J].外国文学研究,2015(2):73-82.

殷企平.西方文论关键词:共同体[J].外国文学,2016(2):70-79.

殷企平.英国文学中的心智培育与文明进程[J].外国文学研究,2018(4):11-21.

殷企平."文化辩护书":19世纪英国文化批评[M].上海:上海外语教育出版社,2013.

殷企平.推敲"进步"话语:新型小说在19世纪的英国[M].北京:商务印书馆,2009.

赵婧.乔治·艾略特小说的史学意识与民族共同体建构[D].福州:福建师范大学,2016.

朱桃香.叙事理论视野中的迷宫文本研究:以乔治·艾略特与翁伯托·艾柯为例[D].广州:暨南大学,2009.

朱玉.自我与忘我:英国浪漫主义传统中的同情思想[J].外国文学评论,2013(2):48-62.

朱玉.作为听者的华兹华斯[M].北京:北京大学出版社,2018.